THE PROMISE

"You're scared, ain't you?"

"Of course I am. I haven't had people point knives at me before."

"That isn't the whole story," he said. "You like thrills. High-wire, loop-the-loop. You *like* them." He moved closer. "I won't hurt you. I promise I won't . . ."

THE INTRUDER
ANTON MYRER
author of
THE LAST CONVERTIBLE

"STRONG!"—*St. Louis Post Dispatch*

"EXCELLENT!"—*Boston Sunday Herald*

Berkley Books by Anton Myrer

THE INTRUDER
THE LAST CONVERTIBLE
ONCE AN EAGLE

THE INTRUDER

ANTON MYRER

BERKLEY BOOKS, NEW YORK

The author acknowledges with special thanks permission to reprint
several lines from the School Edition of Brian Hooker's translation of
Edmond Rostand's CYRANO DE BERGERAC, copyright 1923 by
Henry Holt and Company. Reprinted by special permission of Holt,
Rinehart and Winston, Inc.

This Berkley book contains the complete
text of the original hardcover edition.
It has been completely reset in a type face
designed for easy reading, and was printed
from new film.

THE INTRUDER

A Berkley Book / published by arrangement with
Little, Brown & Company

PRINTING HISTORY
Little, Brown edition published 1965
Dell edition / February 1966
Berkley edition / October 1980

ISBN: 0-425-04661-3

A BERKLEY BOOK® TM 757,375
Berkley Books are published by Berkley Publishing Corporation,
200 Madison Avenue, New York, New York 10016.
PRINTED IN THE UNITED STATES OF AMERICA

DEDICATION: for JUDITH

"... tu primus et ultimus illi ardor eris,
solique tibi devovet annos ..."

A man needs only to be turned around once with his eyes shut in this world to be lost.

HENRY DAVID THOREAU

Chapter One

It was a beautiful house. It rose at the end of a gentle slope of lawn in a pleasing balance of horizontals and fixed vertical panes of glass flanked by panels of Douglas fir, silvered now in this fifth summer. Four small floodlights fell on the lawn and on the clumps of laurel and yew, a soft yellow diffusion, and more light poured from the living room windows. Gardner Lawring stopped his car at the edge of the drive and got out and studied the place, felt the old quiet elation stir him. It *was* beautiful, if he did say so: exciting, but not flamboyant. There were some things he'd do differently if he had it to do over again, of course. That pergola between the garage and the service area wasn't practical, the snow blew through there like a wind tunnel all winter and choked the doors; it would have been better to have tied the garage right into the service wing much the way the old north-of-Boston farmers used to do, adding out and out until they reached the barn. The balustrade along the second story outside the master bedroom had been carried a little too far—it was a touch suggestive of a flying bridge, especially in winter when the big sugar maple near the south corner was stripped of leaves. Now however, with the dense green foliage lying close against the cornice, it looked all right. The breeze came up across the open field behind Franz Hoelder's and set the leaves to seething; viewed this way behind the sway of the big trees and with the lights on in half the rooms, the house looked like a handsome ship slipping along some channel through dense jungle: a bright, clean world of order and proportion. Every jot and iota of it he had designed himself, foundations and fenestration and wiring, and Carlsson had built it with slow, finicky Scandinavian competence. Five years and now it was done, even the cellar rooms and workshop—and he thought,

with a sudden little sense of loss in the middle of his elation:
Nothing will ever be as much fun to draw up and put together
again . . .

The breeze died, the leaves dropped limply, and he heard
voices coming from the living room and a bright yelp of laughter
from Brian. "Dulce domum," he murmured aloud, and yawned
in spite of himself. He had forgotten nearly all the Latin he'd
once known, but he loved that phrase: the reverberant thrum of
the last word had a quality that pleased him. *Dulce domum*.

He got back into his car and pulled up to the garage, pressed
the little red button on the dash and watched the door slide
gently out of sight like a vertebrate curtain. He drove in and
parked.

In the kitchen Mrs. Pruitt was bent over the sink, washing
something in a miasma of steam. She peered at him from over
her steel-rimmed spectacles, that look of implacable censure he
knew, and said:

"Well! The late Mr. Lawring."

"Everything all under control?" he asked.

"Now you've turned Boston upside down so's a body can't
find her way around in it any more, I expect you want some
supper."

"No, I ate in town."

Her thin lips compressed still further. She looked down,
turned on the hot water faucet full blast and said in a terse,
injured tone: "We had rack of spring lamb."

"Oh! I'm sorry I missed it."

"I shouldn't wonder. Mr. Hoolden came over and ate it
instead. Carved it very poorly too, if I do say."

Lawring suppressed a smile. Mrs. Pruitt always mispro-
nounced the names of people she disliked. "You mean Professor
Hoelder?" he inquired innocently.

She disdained any reply. "Your father didn't act like this,"
she declared. "Coming in at all hours. He was a busy man but he
wanted his supper. And he came in on the dot of six for it."

"My father had his own business," Lawring said. "I'm just a
poor hireling."

"Blamed if I can see what you do in there every evening. No
rackety old highway or housing development is all that
important."

"The world's work, ma'am," he said sententiously. "The world's work." He approached her in conspiratorial stealth, towered over her bony little frame and put the back of his hand to his mouth. "I'm keeping a blonde," he said in a heavy stage whisper, and dilated his eyes. "Little flat on the backside of the Hill. Joy Street."

She stared up at him with wintry tartness. "Yes. Well. First they joke about it, then they do it. You look out."

He laughed out loud and swung away and walked through the hall. In the living room a man's voice was saying hoarsely: "I have decreed it! It is done . . ." He paused at the threshold, gazed with a fond smile at the tableau. Janet, swaddled in one of the old blue brocade draperies from his mother's house, was kneeling in extravagant entreaty before Franz Hoelder, who was wearing a turban and a green velour cape and holding a poker in his right hand. Facing him was a very excited Brian, wielding a broadsword and a shield made from a sliding pan adorned with a gryphon Lawring had painted on its face that winter. The rim of the old-style coal bucket he was wearing for a helmet came down to the level of his eyes.

"Your Majesty," Brian cried, "she is innocent—don't you see? She couldn't know I was of base birth . . ."

"Utterly irrelevant," Franz retorted, quivering the end of the poker tautly, like an épée. His thin, lined face looked startlingly implacable and sinister. He glared out at Lawring, then winked—the dropping of one lid, so fast Lawring was scarcely sure he'd caught it. "She has flouted my royal will. What I have once decreed may never be undone." Oddly, his German accent always became more pronounced during these impromptu theatricals. "You must both go into exile. You, Sir Nigel, beyond the sandy mountain wastes of Bainonji Birkutsk. You, my errant daughter, to the fetid jungles of darkest Kamundu. There to live in sorrow and misery, never to lay eyes upon each other, until death . . ."

"—If you part us asunder," Brian shrilled, and flapped his shield up and down like a seal's flipper, "if you do this dastardly deed, I will be your implacable enemy forever and ever!"

"Ha!" Franz emitted a single bark of disdain. "I am King Tancred of Silistria. What have I to fear from you—a knave, the son of a peasant?"

"Oh, Sire," Janet pleaded. She clasped her hands in the best tradition of the silent films although her knees were hurting her, Lawring could tell from the way she kept hitching herself forward. "Your pride will be the ruin of us all. Do what you will with me, your foolish daughter—but spare, I beg of you, this young soldier, who is the most faithful subject in all your vast domains..."

King Tancred refused to relent. Lawring could see it was going to be quite a long drama. He caught Janet's eye and mouthed a kiss, slid into a chair at the darkened end of the long room and crossed his legs. The plot unwound fitfully, there were conferences and résumés. Sir Nigel escaped from exile by joining a band of desert marauders, became their chief and amassed a mighty fortune attacking camel trains, lost it all when his ship was sunk by Turkish pirates, and half-drowned and clinging to a chest was washed ashore on the coast of Kamundu where he was saved by the exiled Princess Celestina. The chest had nothing in it but one jewel, a sapphire worth all his former riches. Sir Nigel made a balsa raft and the two lovers sailed across the Sardonix Sea and returned to find their beloved Silistria menaced by a dragon and the old king in tears and anguish.

Lawring watched indolently, letting his hands lie nerveless in his lap, forcing himself to relax, to thrust out of his mind the tumult of projects, decisions, frustrations, the compromises and conflicts of will that had choked the day; dwelling on nothing now but tangible, concrete images—Brian's bare arms like smooth little golden cylinders; Franz's worn, expressive hands, Janet's face pale and lovely, her large violet eyes shining with that extravagant emotional fervor that always filled him with wonder. Loosening his collar he slumped down in the big leather sling chair, dazed from the long day's battles and now simply thankful, a weary bedouin at the promised oasis, sprawled under the cool fronds...

My home and my family and my friend, the thought stole upon him: God help me if I were to lose them. He dismissed the fear with a little tremor of irritation. Still, it was true: if he didn't have this—a beautiful home, a loving wife and son, a staunch old friend, if he didn't have these to return to each day there wouldn't be an awful lot of purpose in it. Work for work's sake—his father had lived that way. "The best cure for all diseases," Work as a drug, an unscalable mountain, work as a universal, omnivorous be-all and end-all.... and his father had died from a stroke at fifty-nine. Henchey worked like that now, driving himself nights and weekends, eating a box lunch in the office like a day laborer, seeing his family on snatches of Sundays and sometimes not then. It was no way to live. Work was good, work was necessary, we had obligations commensurate with our status, a kind of destiny to fulfill, he believed that all right; but to become a drafting machine like Henchey or a walking calculator like Morrison—no: it was the death of the spirit. He would never succumb to that, he would never let the firm swallow him up and turn him into a soulless piece of equipment. He was a fool to let this wretched row over Urban Renewal tie him up like this, it was absurd—what difference did it make, ultimately, whether that damned Expressway got finished this year or next? It was sapping his enthusiasm, involved as he'd become in all the administrative wrangling, the hearings and compromises and the interminable conferences with lawyers; he was losing his sense of excitement for building, for fleshing out his ideas in arresting patterns of concrete and wood and steel. He was sliding away from the real thing; wasn't he? The air-built castle and the golden dream...

He sighed, and shifted his feet. Yes, but it was more complicated than that, too; it was the principle of the thing. That pack of fools and hoodlums and malcontents, did they actually think they were going to block a desperately needed arterial expansion by protests and committees and litigation, by all kinds of cheap subterfuge and—

He rubbed his eyelids and yanked himself back to the play again. They were winding it up. Sir Nigel had apparently slain the dragon (played by Franz on all fours under a polar bear rug Lawring's Uncle Archie had given him twenty years ago for his room at college) and the grateful old King Tancred (played by Franz, again in turban and cape) tapped Brian's slender shoulders with the gold-headed poker and proclaimed: "Arise, Sir Nigel, Prince of Silistria. Know all nobles here assembled that this brave knight shall inherit my domains upon my death!" And Janet, curtseying low, cried, "Oh Sire, I knew it! I knew you would relent..."

Lawring applauded fiercely and got to his feet. Brian tugged off his helmet and came running up to him. "Dad! Wasn't it terrific?"

"It was tremendous."

"You missed the opening scenes—"

"I know. But I think I saw most of it."

"Oh, it's the best one we ever did!" Brian was shivering with delight, his eyes gleaming like onyx pebbles. He whirled around and said to Franz Hoelder: "Can we do another one?"

"*Another* one!" Janet exclaimed. "Certainly not, Boo. It's after ten."

"But they're so much fun . . . Franz, can't we?"

Franz Hoelder, minus turban and cape and looking very European with his face red with exertion and his silver hair mussed, picked the boy up in his arms and scowled at him with mock severity.

"Everything," he declared. "Everything comes to an end. And then begins again. *That—is—life,*" he chanted, exposing his long, yellowed teeth in a ferocious glare.

"Is that true?" Brian turned to his father. "Is that what life is?"

Lawring smiled. "That's part of it, all right."

"Come," Janet said briskly. "To bed, young fellow-melad. To bed."

"What—about a story?"

"No, no story—the play was in place of a story and you know it. You've done very well as it is."

Cornered, wound-up, apparently on the verge of tears, Brian all at once smiled—that swift flood of merriment that was just like his mother—and said: "Well—next week: what's the play for next week, Franz?"

"Next week." Franz's brow furrowed, his lips moved heavily, his eyes darted around the room. "Next week—next week we will enact the story of a man who lives for revenge—and who suddenly finds out that it is his own brother he is on the verge of destroying."

"Oooh, great!" Brian did a little swirling dance of ecstasy in the middle of the room, and brandished his sword. "Revenge, revenge—!"

Franz Hoelder rolled his tired eyes at Lawring. "What would we do without the Greek myths and Boccaccio? With a few omissions, of course."

"What's his name, Franz?" Brian persisted.

"That's enough, Boo," Janet ordered. "Come on, now: up you go."

There was the little ritual of hugs and promises and good nights; and the two men watched Janet and Brian march up the stairs, singing "The Two Grenadiers" in rhythm to their steps:

—*And as . . . they came-to-the-German-frontiers*
(Boom-boom-boom-boom!)
Their heads were bowed down with weep-ing . . .

They clumped along the hallway overhead, their voices reedy and defiant and far away. A door banged, and the singing stopped.

"He's a fine boy, Gardner," Franz said. "A wonderful imagination. He will do something tremendous, mark my words. Something memorable. He has the milk of paradise, the fine frenzy rolling . . ."

Lawring smiled awkwardly and shrugged. Like most big men he was rather reticent, and Franz's romantic turns of phrase often embarrassed him. "Fine frenzy rolling" sounded like Shakespeare, but he couldn't be sure.

"He's got good stuff in him," he answered a little gruffly, as though it were someone else's child. "He'll be all right, I guess."

Franz Hoelder threw up his arms. "You Boston Yankees! He's a marvelous boy—a perfect little Ganymede and you know it. Be absurd, be proud!" He waggled a finger at Lawring. "You don't know how abominably lucky you are . . ."

"No: I guess I don't." He did though, or believed he did, and this for some reason irritated him. "How about a drink?" he said, to change the subject.

"No—I have stayed long enough. I have final papers to read." Franz wagged his head—a fussy, professorial gesture—and passed his hand through his hair. "Poor darlings: they try so hard to grapple with the cruel world and they're so *bad* at it! Well, it's a miserable time of year to be serious. How can they concentrate on the deep-dyed plans of Bismarck when all their thoughts are on fire with sun-drenched beaches and the wide, tanned shoulders of some boy? Mr. Eliot was wrong—*June* is the cruelest season: the very air betrays all your resolves . . ."

Janet came into the room again and he turned to her; taking her hand with formal gallantry he smiled his charming smile. "My dear, you were scintillant. As always. Thank you for enlivening a cranky old man's evening."

"You're not cranky," she protested.

"Yes, I am. I know I am." He smiled at them lugubriously. "When you are twenty and dancing heedlessly under the lemon trees, you catch sight of some obsessive old fool and you laugh and say to yourself: 'Well, I'll never be like that, at least I'm safe from *that* fate!' And then lo and behold, forty-odd years later you find yourself walking toward that peculiar, particular mirror at the end of the longest hall of all, and the approaching figure grows more and more familiar—and all of a sudden there you are, face to face with the obsessive old fool . . . Life is a series of examinations for which we are never quite prepared. Right?" he asked Lawring.

"Right."

"I think you're the very nicest obsessive old fool I've ever met," Janet said, and kissed him on the cheek.

Franz, now at the door, laughed soundlessly and put his hand over his heart. "Ah, call back yesterday! . . ." Abruptly his manner changed. "Well: Pflicht und Treue, Pflicht und Treue."

"What does that mean?" Janet asked him.

"All work and no play."

"Horrible! Thanks so much for coming over. Brian loved it."

"My pleasure: really. Good night."

"Good night . . ."

Half an hour later in the master bedroom upstairs the Lawrings sipped at their highballs and undressed slowly while the eleven o'clock news unraveled on the television screen. There were troubles in Algeria and the Congo, there was a new Russian astronaut, the Macmillan government was in an uproar over the Profumo affair; Castro, looking startlingly old and fat and myopic in batwing glasses and beret, was again thundering threats and defiance; there was violence in Birmingham, in Jackson, Mississippi, in Maryland and Virginia. Locally, two men had been indicted for fraud in the Boston Common Garage scandal—and there now was Assemblyman DiCalco facing them behind his desk, shouting at them that the demolition work for the Boston Expressway and Urban Renewal projects in the

North End was absurd and unjustified, a willful violation of the rights of private citizens engineered by unscrupulous real estate interests; the North End Citizens' Committee would continue to fight it with every means at its command. His eyes were narrowed, his mouth opened and closed like a rectangular trap, one hand sawed pawlike at the air beside his head.

"Lousy demagogue," Lawring muttered.

"Is he?"

"Of course he is. It's all an act. He's using it as an excuse to draw votes, grab himself some limelight. Sir Angelo defending the bridge against the dragon."

Sipping her drink, Janet cocked her head judiciously. "Well, it must be hard for them to give up their homes. All those people." Lawring was sitting on the bed with his fists on his thighs, and she watched him a moment, gravely. "When they put in the underpass and widened the road in Somerville they just came through and took all our front lawns, the elms and maples and everything." Her eyes grew wide and dark and appealing, the way they did whenever she became emotionally involved, which was often. "It makes you feel terrible, there's nothing you can do about it..."

"You were paid, weren't you? your folks? The town paid you for the land—"

"Yes, a little money, but that wasn't the thing, Gard, it was the—the *invasion* of it. We got home from school one day and there were all the machines—the bulldozers and graders, you know, and all the beautiful trees down, even the one Pa put the swing in for us, and the front yards looking like horrible front-line trenches or something. Not our street at all... Imagine what it's like if the house you've been born and brought up in—"

"But they're *slums*, Janet, they're just old rat-traps. I know, I've been inside them—"

"Yes, but they're *their* rat-traps..."

"And so what's the answer?" he demanded with an exasperated laugh. "Never build any expressways or put up any high-rise structures at all? Should a million and a half people go without adequate highway facilities because of a bunch of immigrants in old buildings that are going to fall apart in another few years, anyway?" He scowled, and rubbed the side of his face; he could hear the tension in his voice but, still wound up from the day's pressures, he felt constrained to go on. "Look, they're all going to be relocated, we've told them so, real palaces compared to what they're living in now—a big new development with elevators and sun porches and service areas in the basement and playgrounds for the kids... My God, you'd think we were taking them out and shooting them by platoons to hear that damned committee..."

"I know. I'm sorry." Quickly contrite she came over to him. "You're so tired. Working late every night. It's not fair." She took his head in her small hands and bent over and he kissed her.

"I love you when you're a Dutiful Wife," he said softly, and smiled.

"I'm not. I mean it. I just get mad at this stupid highway, Urban Renewal, the whole hideous *row* of it. You look worn to a frazzle." She ran a finger down his cheek. "Dan'l Webster lines. I wish you were still designing fishbowls and cantilevered igloos and things. And home every night early..."

He watched her move away from him to her dressing table and sit down at it, her body fine and exciting under the white slip. He sighed, and massaged his face and eyes, feeling the weariness deep in his forehead and neck and shoulders; and a strange sensation—pride and fear commingled—stirred in him. Her figure was as slender and firm as the day he'd first laid eyes on her, ten years ago—as though her tremendous vitality, her impulsive, heedless generosity had rendered her invulnerable to the pressures of time... It had been at the Bigelow Foundation, a decrepit old pile out on Commonwealth Avenue he'd been called in to renovate, and they'd given him an office just off the library. Janet had been a sort of glorified research librarian and receptionist. He remembered the very moment he had become aware of her. He'd been discussing some possible changes with old Wayvell; in the scan of his vision Janet had been typing a letter, and doing a good deal more erasing than typing. All at once she reached around and picked up a dictionary, presumably to look up the spelling of some word—and then for the rest of the time he was talking with Wayvell she browsed about in it, her little fist at her cheek, her eyes pale and absorbed. She had forgotten completely about the letter. For the first time in weeks Lawring found himself thinking of Peg with a sudden, raw rush of grief—and then to his great surprise without any grief at all . . . Wayvell had been looking at him a bit curiously by then, and he'd given himself a little shake and settled down to the task at hand. It had been an effort to wrench his mind away from the girl.

The Foundation dealt with missionary work in faroff lands and it had been on Commonwealth for a long time. The building was baffling, with its enormous circular central staircase, a vast basement kitchen, labyrinthine halls and anterooms and alcoves cluttered with alabaster figurines. It had been built by one of the Witkins, a madcap clan who gambled or lost their heads over Egyptian belly dancers or designed insanely elaborate mechanical contrivances for putting postage stamps on letters, or went in for table-tapping séances. More like Philadelphians than Bostonians if the truth were known, Lawring's mother had often said. She had known one of them—a tall, fantastically thin, vacant-eyed man who wore a slouch hat with a trailing plume and jack boots and claimed to be the direct descendant of Bonnie Prince Charlie, and who had vanished one night without a trace. Lawring, smiling grimly, figured he must have got lost in the cavernous closets under the main staircase. There was no way to take hold of the place. He became fascinated, then alarmed, then—because he was a Yankee—obsessed. He attacked the problem for three weeks, night and day, and by the end of that time he was exhausted, but he'd beaten it. Janet came in to him late one afternoon during the third week with a cup of coffee and a Danish pastry. He gazed up at her in surprise.

"Office party?"

She laughed—a fine, clear, vibrant laugh that pleased him. "*Here?* Good God, no. No, you looked so completely baffled and worn out I couldn't resist bringing you this. You'll strain your eyes, you know."

"Will I?"

"Oh yes." She nodded emphatically; her own eyes, overlarge in her lovely little heart-shaped face, were serious. "On an empty stomach. It's the worst thing you can do."

They chatted for a while and joked about the place, and she asked him if he'd seen the ladies' room. "The pulls are of gold and porcelain. You feel as if you're handling an objet d'art every time you flush!"

He drank the coffee very slowly. He found he was charmed by her gaiety, her impulsive warmth: the room seemed brighter since she'd entered it. "How do you happen to be working here?" he asked her, mystified.

"I don't know. It was a job."

"No, but I mean a young, good-looking girl like you—you hardly fit in with Miss Tannersley or Miss Watts..."

"Yes, it's funny, isn't it?" Her eyes took on a rapt and dreamy look. "I guess I applied because of the travel."

"The travel!"

"Yes. I heard the Foundation sent people to all these exotic places—Bangkok and Zamboanga and everywhere—so I came in here all steamed up and ready to go. I didn't know they only sent *preachers!*..."

At the end of an hour Lawring was completely captivated. The numb hollowness that had pressed against his heart since Peg's death had vanished like morning fog; was it possible to be this fickle in your affections? Two nights later he drove Janet home from work, and a month after that they found themselves lying in his old bed in his mother's house in Brewster down on Cape Cod, caught up in a fever of desire, and he knew beyond a shadow of a doubt that he had never been in love before—not even with Peg: a heretical thought—but it was true, and he was too honest a person to deny it. Three months later, over his mother's most austere protestations, they were married—he at twenty-eight, she at nineteen—and she quit her job at the Foundation; which was a good thing because, as he often liked to tease her, she had very nearly wrecked the outfit while she'd been there...

"Franz is wonderful, isn't he?" she was saying now, brushing her hair with a long, proud movement of her whole arm.

Hands at his chin, Lawring watched her and thought, Women should always sit that way: very erectly, staring ahead into a mirror, the right arm sweeping down in that fine, rhythmic arabesque. If they're ever in danger of losing their husbands they should sit like that in a dim light in their slips, and brush, and ceaselessly brush, and their hair... Not that this girl was in any danger, or ever would be.

"He called himself my *cavaliere servente*. What does that mean?"

"Oh, a knight who waits upon a married lady, something like that." He grinned. "Or it could mean her lover."

She rolled an eye around at him. "Could it? That's exciting . . . He's such a darling," she went on. "You know what he said this evening? 'Most ladies' men have no sense of humor.' I wish I could think up epigrams like that. You know, I don't think I've ever made up an epigram in my whole life." She looked thoughtfully into the blued glass. "Why do you suppose he comes over here and spends so much time with Boo, these loony theatricals?"

Lawring bent over and drew off one of his shoes. "Well, he's lonely."

"I know. To lose his wife that way. The things he's suffered through!" Her eyes darkened, and Lawring could see her imagination soaring about in a riotous farrago of black-uniformed figures, doors shattered by hobnailed boots, flights along snow-swept timberlines, barbed wire enclosures where men in ragged overcoats shuffled hopelessly, day after leaden day . . .

"Well, he survived," he said simply, to bring her down to earth again. "He survived it all, and now he has a fine position in a very eminent college for young ladies."

"But how awful it must be. After going through all that—seeing your own country turn into a nightmare, and your wife killed, and then to be betrayed by your best friend and hunted down like a mad dog . . . How can you ever believe in people again? I don't think I could."

"Of course you could. You can get over anything."

"Do you think so?" Dubiously she considered this. "There are some things I don't think I could ever get over. If they tortured me and I gave away the rest of the underground people, or we got split up for years, you and I did, and didn't know where the other one was, or storm troopers came into the house"—her eyes dilated all at once—"and smashed everything and got drunk and took me and—"

"Well, it probably isn't going to happen next week," he said calmly. "At least the odds are heavily against it."

"I suppose so." She seemed almost disappointed. "I'd be good at disguises, anyway." She piled her hair high on her head, let it drop again and drew a violent orange scarf up to her eyes.

"Do you think I'd make a good siren?"

This reminded him of the play that evening, and he frowned. He drew off his socks and wriggled his toes back and forth, watching them. "All the same, do you think it's right?" he asked.

"Think what's right, darling?"

"Filling the boy with all these fairy tales? Buried treasure and dragons and being given the king's daughter and all that stuff?"

Her head snapped around, whipping her hair about her face. "Why—what's wrong with them?"

"Well, he'll get to feel things come without earning them, that you can just wish anything into existence. It isn't right..."

"But he's eight and a *half*, Gard," she protested. "He isn't entering law school. That's what fairy tales are for—children. Children and old people..."

"Sometimes I'm worried he'll go off into a dream world. He's got to learn to cope with life as it is."

"Oh, he'll have time enough for that. Besides, he's going away to camp in a few weeks. That's coping with the world, isn't it?" She eyed him a moment—a swift, sly smile—for this had been a bone of contention between them during the winter. Lawring had wanted Brian to go—after all, the boy *was* eight, he needed to play with other kids more, participate in group activities, break out of this private fantasy world of his; Janet had wanted to keep him home one more summer: he was so young, and he was away at country day school all winter anyway. But Lawring had finally prevailed.

Now Janet made a face at him and said: "You're just jealous. Because you can't handle all these demanding roles."

He shied a hand at her and grinned. It was true; secretly he *was* a little jealous. He had never been able to play any kind of part himself—his excursions into drama at school had been short-lived and ludicrous—and his few efforts in the improvised plays with Brian had been depressingly bad. He could not somehow imagine himself a bloodthirsty Norman baron or a crafty Turk. It was like slipping beneath the surface of the sea: how could you eat or talk or make love in that still, dreamy, greenhued world...?

"Isn't it funny?" he said aloud. "I try to think of being someone else and I can't. I'm just—"

"You're just Gardner Lawring," she finished. "And that's good enough for this spouse."

He sighed and pulled off his shirt. He didn't like to be taken off the hook this lightly. "Why do you suppose I can't?" he pursued. "Seriously."

"It's your dreadful Puritan ancestors," she declared. "They've spent so many centuries being Boston bluebloods they can't act any other way. It's like thoroughbred horses or something."

"I don't know about that. My Uncle Archie—"

"Oh, your Uncle Archie!" she cried, and her eyes began to shine. "He's a glorious anomaly. He'll never happen again. He must have been a by-blow."

"Stop it," he said, amused.

"I meant it. Uncle Archie is tremendous. Your mother hates him."

"She doesn't hate him. She feels he's—she feels he's evaded his responsibilities."

"She feels he's failed her. Along with everyone else."

"Oh, come on."

"It's true! You know what Franz said about life being an examination? Well, life is an oral exam everybody has to flunk except Marcia Lawring. And Archie doesn't care whether he flunks or not: that's what's great about him ... You know that crazy postcard of those nautch girls or Ouled Naïl or whatever they are, do you know where he sent it from? *Fitchburg!*" She burst into laughter, bent over, hands pressed between her knees. "Oh, he's wonderful. If I'd met him before I met you I'd have gone off with him. Florence, Taormina, Cairo—anywhere he said. At the drop of a hat."

He said soberly: "Would you?"

She caught his eye and laughed, a quick low chuckle, came over and flopped on the bed beside him. "Old Mr. Sobersides," she said, and placed a hand against his chest. It felt diminutive and very warm. "Even when you *know* somebody's kidding. It makes a girl feel positively wicked."

"Does it?"

"Yes. It does." She looked up at him from under her brows; her eyes moved over his face. Softly she said, "Could you fall for me, kind sir."

He smiled, loving her, loving everything about her even through his mountainous weariness—the fine, faintly aquiline nose, the large warm eyes, an inky purple now with love, the wide, full-lipped mouth whose lower lip was quivering ever so gently... Her hair, a silky little chestnut mantle, fell voluptuously against his hand.

He murmured: *"Perdition catch my soul, but I do love thee! And when I love thee not, chaos is come again..."* It was just about the only Shakespeare he remembered.

"Yes," she said.

Her eyes were closed now. He bent over her, took her in his arms. She was trembling minutely all over, her eyelids quivering at the corners the way they always did when she was aroused. She looked unutterably beautiful. Her ardor bore him along and he caressed her, feeling her impulsive, thrusting vitality under his hands, making love as they often liked to do, in a half light, so that now and then they could glance at each other with dreamy tenderness, catch the image of their love mirrored in each other's eyes. He remembered her running across a broad sweep of lawn, and another time, her face soaked with spray, crystal drops like diamonds on her face and hair, her lips parted in a shriek of laughter and the shoulder of Nount's Head slipping by in the flat, hard summer light...

Except that something was wrong. Very wrong.

It had never happened to him before. Not remotely. There he lay, loving her, his lips brushing her cheeks and eyelids, his hand stroking the undulant swell of her breast—and he felt nothing. Nothing at all. His loins were like a numbed limb that had been slept on for hours. In a gathering turmoil, frightened now, feeling his heart beat in ponderous quaking jolts he stopped fondling her and lay there stiffly, hollow as a gourd and as ludicrous, until his alarm communicated itself to her.

"What is it, darling?"

"I don't know," he said thickly. "I don't know. I—I can't do anything..."

"Do you feel ill?"

He shook his head. "I don't know what to make of it."

There was a little silence.

"It's nothing, sweet," she said

"I'm sorry..."

"It's nothing." Her voice held an airiness he knew she didn't feel. "You've been working too hard, you're all worn out and tense over this rotten Urban Renewal battle."

"Maybe so . . . I'm sorry," he repeated. "I got you all—stirred up . . ."

"It's my fault. It was selfish of me—I shouldn't have lured you on the way I did. It was selfish."

"Don't say that, sweet."

"It was. Sometimes I don't have the few brains I was born with." She passed a hand along the edge of his jaw. "It's nothing, Gard. Really."

"I hope so. I hope it's nothing."

"Why don't you go see Doc Bolton if you're worried it might be something else?"

"Yes. I guess I'd better."

"You're just tired, darling. Don't lie there worrying about it, now . . ."

They got ready for bed and he turned off the television set and the lights and got in beside her. But it wasn't nothing; he couldn't believe it was nothing. He lay on his back in the darkness with his hands folded on his chest, inert as a corpse laid out for interment, listened absently to the peepers chirruping down in the swamp, and tried to beat back the fear. Maybe it was true—maybe he was working too hard, had spread himself too thin. The interminable Board of Estimates meetings, the City Council hearings, wrangles with the citizens' committees all in addition to his own work, there was the Pan-Am building out at Logan Airport that was all fouled up, and the art museum for the new Civic Center—everyone in New England had a different idea about what *that* ought to look like, Townsend wanted a Renaissance palazzo and McNally wanted some sort of all-glorious Taj Mahal with elevators, and Mrs. Pinchon—dear, deadly Helena Pinchon—wanted a turreted German pillbox like Wright's Tomb on Fifth Avenue down in New York City—they all wanted *anything* but a place to display paintings to the best advantage; and Siegersen the importer had given him carte blanche on a new house near Newport, a wonderful chance for him to pull all the stops and show what he could do in the way of a bold, inventive waterside structure—if he could ever in God's name get his hands free enough to do it. He sighed. Maybe he *was* trying to do too much. But his father—lord, his father would have laughed at this as child's play. The corporation and the fund, the State Street Trust, chairs on five boards, the cordage factory in Kingston and real estate developments in Quincy and Pembroke. Yes, but his father had died at fifty-nine. And maybe something like this had happened to his father. How did you ever know about these things?

He unclasped his hands and began to wind his watch with slow care, counting to thirty. There was no sense getting panicky about this. He was only thirty-eight, only a year or so over the halfway mark; that's what they said, anyway. Grandpa Endicott hadn't even married until he was thirty-four...

It had never happened to him before. Except once, in France, long ago; and he'd been drunk then, very drunk, so it didn't count. A girl named Adrienne with thick dark hair and that wonderfully long, wonderfully straight Gallic nose who had a sad, slow smile and whose favorite reply to anything and everything was, "Sans blague, kid..." *Sans blague.* Lying under the stiff, freshly laundered sheet, sweating lightly in his pajamas he found himself thinking persistently of the girls he'd made love to—as though dwelling on those earlier embraces would rouse his ardor for the one girl he'd ever loved. Buff Haviland, with the chunky little body and bright flaxen hair, who could bend over and touch her knees with her forehead, and who loved to jitterbug, which he did not; in France Adrienne and later on convalescent leave in Nice a girl named Celeste whose ambition was to open a stylish sweater shop in Paris after the war; and in San Francisco a sexy little Wave officer with a snub nose and a clear, high little bell-like laugh—she had refused to use contraceptives and had scared him half to death. Then after the war the nervous, aggressive set designer Roberta Mountain, and later Jeanne Tucker, a lanky, handsome girl who had married and separated from a nationally prominent astrophysicist, who would curl up on the window seat of her apartment out in the Fenway and get slowly and portentously drunk and tell him about the moment when she realized that she was married, at eighteen, to a terrified homosexual...

Then he'd run into Peg again after an interval of six years, at Symphony, and, borne along on the weight of his mother's approval and Peg's quiet, forthright charm, the tremendous sense of familiarity she exuded, had found himself married to her. Before a year had passed she'd gone down to that stupid class reunion in New York City, had insisted on flying down in the teeth of the worst snowstorm December had seen in twenty years, and been killed in the crash just outside of Idlewild; and stunned, embittered, he'd thought his life was over. And it hadn't been at all.... Six girls, before Peg. Not very many, really, for a vigorous young American bachelor. Perhaps that was why they were all so vivid now. He thought of their different ways of making love, a divergence of stimulation and response whose very strangeness had often put him in a tumult of desire, his throat dry and his calves trembling—

He yawned and stretched carefully; thrust the images away. What the devil was the matter with him? He was acting like a schoolboy; next thing he would try the schoolboy's sorry stimulus...

There was a faint sound from down the hall, a smothered cry. He felt Janet stir and murmured, "Stay down, I'll go," eased himself out of bed and walked down the hall to Brian's room. The boy was lying on his back, his left arm above his head and his right leg doubled under the other so that he looked as though he were posing for some recumbent Highland fling. His head turned on the pillow, he muttered a word that sounded like "gold," or perhaps "hold," then relapsed into untroubled sleep again. Lawring drew the sheet up to his chin and Brian accepted it trustingly, even deep in sleep, nestling his cheek toward his father's hand. For several moments Lawring hung over the bed, watching the boy, remembering the afternoon they'd ridden in the sled down the old wood road behind Franz's house: the sting of cold air and the swoop and drop of the sled, the skate-slur of the runners, and the almost sensuously protective awareness of the vulnerable little body, his own flesh and blood, enfolded in his arms ... The worlds that lay ahead of him! The victories, the defeats, the friendships and sunderings and reconciliations; the countries he would travel through, the dangers and delights, the women he would sleep with—

The whippoorwill began, startlingly near and he shivered. One call, then a succession of cries with increasing rapidity and volume: whippoorwill, hipper-rill, dipper-twill, *hit-her-ill, bitter-pill* WHIP-HER-WILL *RIPPER-KILL*—broke off abruptly. Then it began all over again. Morbid, inane, rather menacing in its shrill reiteration. Idiot song. He hated them. He remembered a summer in Brewster when he was ten, when one of them used to call and he would wake in the dead of night with the sensation that some madman had him tied to a table and was boring into the center of his brain with a hideous mechanical contrivance. One night he had crept out of bed and got his rifle, a fine old Sharps .22 with an octagonal barrel his Grandfather Endicott had given him; with enormous care he had eased up the screen, put his pillow on the sill and rested the rifle on the pillow, finally had spotted the bird squatting on a window ledge of the garage, an indistinct big-headed blob in the gray-green light, had taken aim—and then had realized with a hot flash of fright that behind the ledge was a glass pane of window, and behind the glass pane was his father's Packard . . .

The air felt suddenly cool on his body, and he turned and moved soundlessly back through the long hall and got into bed again. Janet said, "Everything all right?" and he could tell by the timbre of her voice that she hadn't got to sleep either.

"Yes," he said. "Talking to himself. Dreams. Can I get you a glass of water or anything?"

"No. I'm fine."

She drew close to him, and he took her in his arms as gently as he knew how, knowing that she wanted to comfort him. But the whippoorwill began again, from the rock wall behind the garden; and stung by exasperation and anxiety he knew he was in for a long night of it.

Chapter Two

"Now remember, Boo," Gardner was saying. "Manners are the cornerstone of human relationships. People will judge you by them all your life. When Arthur's mother or father ask you if you'd like another helping you say, 'Yes, thank you,' or 'No, thank you.' And remember to fold your napkin after you've finished."

"Sure, Dad," Brian said easily, but this was his first overnight visit away from home and his eyes were grave with responsibility. "Will I get a napkin ring?" he asked.

"They may have one for you, the way we do for Franz when he comes to eat with us. But if they don't you fold your napkin up, follow along the creases, and lay it to the left of your plate. And remember to cut your food into little pieces and eat it one forkful at a time."

"—That isn't what Franz does," Brian broke in jubilantly. "Franz turns his fork over and piles the stuff up on it with his knife and goes *ulp!*—and that's all, brother!"

Janet saw his father suppress a smile. "Franz was brought up in Germany, where it's acceptable to eat that way. But in our country we cut our food up and transfer the fork to the right hand and take it up in small bites. Right?"

"He'll be all right, Gard," Janet said. "He'll do fine. Won't you, Boo?" and she crouched down and hugged him impulsively. "Just do what seems natural and right to do and you'll be fine..."

They were standing on the platform at Route 128 waiting for the New Haven train. A few years before they would have been waiting for the Boston local at the drab, brown little station at Holcomb Hill, but with the coming of Route 128 most of the inhabitants of the neighboring towns had deserted their old stations for this smart new one, with its express trains and billboards flamboyantly heralding the current Broadway musicals. In the morning it was a tumultuous affair, with husbands striding purposefully to the cars, briefcase and morning *Herald* in hand, while their wives smiled wanly at each other from behind the wheel. Now in the early evening it was fairly quiet; only a few little groups stood about here and there, talking with the desultory cheerfulness of people who have time they know they must kill. A row of cabs was drawn up in front of the station, and behind them was a parking lot crowded with cars, like some vast grazing land for giant turtles. Farther away to the east lay a spanking new shopping center of antiseptic rectangular buildings glowing unhealthily with fluorescent lights. Janet hated to shop there—the wash of colors and canned music jangled her so badly she couldn't remember half of what she'd come for, and the light hurt her eyes; she preferred to go over to Wellesley or wander around in Truscott's grocery store in Holcomb Hill, lulled by the odors of fruit and damp wood and coffee beans...

"I'll give you a ring tomorrow," Gardner was saying. "Or the day after. Have to draw him out, see what's in the back of his mind."

She nodded attentively, watching him. He seemed different at railway stations—he took on a kind of dry, false austerity, a hauteur she associated with his mother. Then she felt obscurely disloyal for having thought that, and she squeezed his arm and said: "That's all right: you stay as long as you feel you need to. Only don't let him get you upset. They're a pack of idiots, *I* think—they all want everything and the moon. You be ruthless."

"You bet. I'll be as insufferable as Frank Lloyd Wright. Maybe I ought to dye my hair white and wear a cape."

She smiled and hugged his arm again It was pleasant, standing here in the warm, sultry twilight, looking at her two men who were both leaving her. Brian had been invited to spend a few days with a school chum who lived near Rehoboth, and for the past week Siegersen had been pressing Gardner to come down to Newport and walk over the site with him. On the spur of the moment Gardner had decided to go; it would enable him to accompany Brian on his first train ride as far as Providence, and also he was afraid if he delayed any longer Siegersen might change his mind and get someone else.

"Thunderchiefs!" Brian shouted, pointing; and looking up Janet saw the two black darts shoot down the sky, giving off faint trails of exhaust, and plunge behind a bank of storm clouds looming up out of the southwest. "Hey Dad, look! Look at them go!..."

"Mmmm," Gardner said absently. His mind was full of the trip, she could tell; he was thinking about how he would present his ideas, maintain that odd little balance of deference and assertion that he'd told her was the most effective way of dealing with a client, especially a very rich one.

"You sound like a promising architect," she said, and he looked at her and grinned, his hands in his trouser pockets, his feet wide apart, solid as a rock. He was wearing his green Dacron suit, which she loved. Everything about him pleased her: the big, full jaw, the deep-set, steady gray eyes, the prominent nose that had been broken twice playing football in college and again during the war; the ruddy tinge to his skin—a faint coppery glow, as if he'd just been lightly sunburned—and the way he had of swinging his head around like some huge, friendly animal when you spoke to him. She loved the comforting massiveness of his body—he was six-three and weighed just under two hundred pounds—which was big without being gross. Moving beside her with his quiet, contained power, head and shoulders above her, watching the world from those steady, undaunted gray eyes he seemed to shield her from its pitfalls, and consequences of her own impulsive actions...

"You look lovely," she murmured. "You look—noble..."

He laughed at this, his eyes roved over the people on the platform, came back to her with a little flicker of uncertainty; and she knew he was thinking about that evening three nights ago. They had not tried to make love since then—she cared about him far too deeply to importune him, and she knew that if he himself had felt any prompting he would have approached her. He was tired, overtired, she'd told him next day, his reserves were low, all he needed was to get rid of some of these continual pressures and rest up a bit. It was silly to work up a mystique about something like this: why didn't he make an appointment with Doc Bolton, get a complete checkup, see if he could find anything? He'd agreed, had gone the day before yesterday and returned, somber and crestfallen: there was nothing wrong with him; organically he was as healthy as a horse. "Then it's just weariness," she'd concluded lightly. But she had been upset, all the same. She was usually the one to get things all out of proportion and fall a prey to brooding and morbid imaginings; she relied on Gardner's imperturbable self-possession to bail her out—and seeing him off-balance like this, harried by nameless worries, she didn't know how to deal with it. It was a disconcerting sensation.

Now, to thrust their thoughts away from the problem, she said: "We never decided about the Wellivers."

He frowned at this. He was immensely traditional in many ways: he felt that social engagements were the wife's responsibility—she could tell he was secretly annoyed with her for not foreseeing that he might be called away like this. "When was it for?"

"Tomorrow night."

"Can't you shift it? Next Friday, something like that?"

She bobbed her head. "I'll phone Lois. Friday's all right for you, then?"

"As far as I know."

"All right. We'll work out something."

The train was coming: two moans, a bass thrumming that sounded impersonal and grim in contrast to the sweet, wild whistle-wail of the trains of her childhood. Gardner had his and Brian's bags already in his hand.

"No," Brian cried, "I want to carry mine..."

"What? Okay, chief." He handed the little athletic bag to the boy, slipped his drawings case under his arm and winked at Janet. His face seemed brighter now, smooth with purpose; as though he were taking the world's measure. He must have looked like this coming up to the line of scrimmage or leading his platoon toward some hostile German town. The cars swept past them, a sharp hot smell of burnt air and cleaning fluid and grease. She knelt in front of Brian, whose eyes were shining with adventure.

"Be a good boy, Boo," she said. "If Arthur suggests something you agree to do it even if it shouldn't be just what you want. You might find out you like it, anyway."

"Right, Mom." He let her kiss him but he broke away quickly. He was in a man's world now, grabbing grips and boarding trains. No time for sentiment. She embraced Gardner who said, "Bye bye, sweet. Don't do anything foolish."

Their old ritual. "Not unless I can help it," she called. They mounted the iron steps, and she watched them move through the aquarium tunnel of the car. They vanished, reappeared at a window. Brian, all at once boyish and hilarious again, clasped his hands and shook them above his head like a triumphant prizefighter, and she waved back and blew him and Gardner a kiss.

The train was moving: one brisk jerk, then that dreamy sliding motion like the world easing away. She walked a few steps with it, waved again, they waved back and Brian shouted something she could not hear, could only see his lips moving, mouthing silence. I'll never see them again, the thought flashed like an arrow, never again like this—and walking faster she felt a pang of fear, she wanted to race down the new concrete platform and catch them, drag them back. They were gone, the train was gone, curving into cones of distance. My baby. Going away because of someone else, a boy named Arthur Gratiot, and then off to summer camp and he would come back with scars on his shins and his hair cropped short and stare at her like a cold-eyed little stranger...

Ridiculous. Half-smiling she turned and walked back to the car. Sitting behind the wheel she was filled with that curious little sense of release one always feels on the departure of friends or family, of being utterly on one's own, rid of that reflected image of the self that is the greatest burden of all.

The platform was deserted now. She put the car in gear and eased out of the lot slowly. She had felt like this when she'd first been working, after getting out of high school, running free to her own enthusiasms and needs; though her childhood had been happy enough. She had grown up in an old clapboard house in Somerville, in a large French-Irish family, three sisters and two brothers; a household of ebullient high spirits and chaotic plans. Her father was a plasterer by trade and an incurable optimist by profession. He was a little cricket of a man, blessed with phenomenal energy, and nothing on this earth had ever daunted him. On one vicious, snow-lashed February morning with the temperature fifteen below zero, when a hot water pipe had burst and even the Chevy pickup had refused to start, he had rubbed his hands together briskly and called: "Cheer up, Norma, only six weeks to bluebirds"—an observation that brought forth howls of dismay and became a family classic during moments of crisis, which were very frequent.

Harry Delannoy's great love was tinkering, remodeling, do-it-yourself projects: he would knock out a wall here, add a wing there, install a bulging bay window like a carbuncle in the dining room. He sometimes had two or three projects going at the same time, but he tried to do them all by himself and they were never completed. One season, Janet remembered vividly, there was only a huge piece of tarpaulin tacked over an aperture where the wall had been, and now and then rain drove in under the canvas, making long molasses stains on the bright pine floor. The garbage disposal problem was solved—at least temporarily—by a zinc chute which ran up from the cellar to a round hole sawed in the kitchen floor beside the sink: Harry Delannoy was a long time making a cover for this hole, which necessitated some fancy footwork when four women were clearing the table and washing dishes. And there was the summer her father decided it would be pleasant to have a live tree growing in the living room—a Japanese katsura that littered the floor with little dead scrolls of leaves until in October its crown began to droop toward the fireplace, curving over farther and farther, and at last it died.

Her mother had never complained; she adored her husband. "Harry's so energetic," she would say with a proud, placid smile. She was a large, big-breasted woman with a genial, unruffled expression and a lovely voice, and she ladled out lamb stew or Yankee pot roast to a table crammed with aunts and uncles, school chums of the children, friends down on their luck or neighbors who just happened to drop in. You passed with one hand and ate with the other, and the talk was general. It made for an atmosphere of turmoil and caprice, a lively, untidy arena where bold and implausible and immensely delightful things were happening—a half-finished hearth consecrated to the supreme importance of spontaneity and laughter and generosity of spirit.

Now that was all in the past. Four years ago her father, still spry as a cricket and now aflame with wanderlust, had sold the old house and bought a trailer, one of those swollen gondolas in pastel shades, and after a seven-thousand-mile trek (Harry

Dellanoy crossed the continent like a schooner beating against a contrary wind, and a succession of garish postcards depicting eagles' nests, gambling casinos, caverns and Indian dances informed Janet of their erratic progress) had landed up in a trailer park in Long Beach, California, where for all Janet knew he was still tearing out walls and adding cupolas and her mother was feeding the multitudes. The family was scattered. Wally had stayed in the air force, Frank was working in Chicago, all her sisters had married and the only one she saw much of was Edna, who lived out in Swampscott with a boisterous ménage of four children and three dogs and a thin, terrified cat. Jim worked at the General Electric plant in Lynn, they went out every Saturday night and worked on their tract house all day Sunday; and Janet, playing with the children or helping in the kitchen on the relatively few occasions they went over to visit them, would find herself thoroughly relaxed and happy, and touched by an unmistakable twinge of nostalgia . . .

She drove with care through the gathering dusk. The storm clouds had piled high overhead, the sun had slipped far behind them, and the evening light had a filmy, depthless quality, vaguely portentous and still. She was a very bad driver and so she drove slowly, wandering half out of her lane and back again, waiting for the other car at intersections and turns, trying to curb her natural impulse to shoot ahead. She had been involved in several accidents, all of them minor, and finally Gardner had rubbed his chin with his knuckles and said in a tone of weary resignation: "Well, you've *got* to drive, and neither I nor God nor the Commonwealth of Massachusetts can seem to make you any better as a driver—so your only hope is to drive so slowly you can't kill anybody or demolish the car. Ninety per cent of good driving is anticipation, and you won't anticipate: so you've got to creep. Now will you do that?" Solemnly she'd promised, and for the most part she'd adhered to it.

She had never been able to cope with mechanical things. She distrusted them: they had a life of their own, they bristled with inexplicable knobs and sparks and inner workings, they were merely waiting for the chance to control you, subject you to their insensate wills, even kill you if they could. She feared plane trips—the giddy elation of flying was canceled out in the awful soundlessness of the jets, the sense of being controlled—and the

Anton Myrer

flatulent snore of a chain saw she hated passionately. She had resolved to get through life with as little contact with machines as possible. She knew it was cowardly but she didn't care. Some people, like Gardner, could cope with them—could drive blithely off on a motorcycle for the first time or repair a well pump or a rotary mower, but she could not: she was content to stand on the sidelines and applaud—but at the same time keep clear of the sparks and wheels and blades.

The overhead stoplight at Dover Avenue was red and she slowed for it. It changed then, and across the intersection she saw a man standing in the dusk, thumbing a ride in the direction she was headed. She slowed again instinctively, then remembered what Gardner had told her about hitchhikers ("You have an accident and they get hurt and *you're* responsible, sugar, you and no one but you: they can sue you for every cent you've got. And anyway, it isn't the way it used to be, everybody's got money enough to travel nowadays . . .") and looked up to see the man crossing toward her: he intended to get in the car. She plunged ahead, he leaped back wildly—a tall rangy man in a crushed felt hat and blue jeans—and gaped at her, eyes and mouth wide with anger, shouted something at her as she moved by.

She stalled the engine. The car rolled on the slight downgrade for thirty or forty feet and stopped. In the rear-view mirror she saw the man pause, perplexed—start toward her again with a gangling, loose-jointed walk, his hands hanging at his sides like hooks. In a flash of panic she turned the key and stabbed at the accelerator several times, pumping it as Gardner had taught her; the motor fired all at once and she shot away just as the man came up to the rear fender. This time he let out a bellow of rage and struck the fender with the heel of his hand.

For an instant she was afraid she'd hit him, somehow; then she caught sight of him in the mirror. He was shaking his fist at her. He looked huge and menacing, with his battered face and wild eyes, standing in the middle of the deserted road with one black knob of a fist raised above his head. She swallowed nervously and frowned. What a ridiculous episode! Good thing she hadn't stalled a second time. For a while she sat very erect, forward of the cushions, concentrating on her driving, but she couldn't rid herself of the absurd encounter: it fused with the towering rain clouds, the lush green foliage lining the road, the etched white of the houses in a sensation of peril, oppressive and intoxicating at once. She felt as though she had gulped a lungful of pure oxygen and all her senses had come alive; her fingertips tingled, and the small of her back. With one hand she fumbled in her purse and found a handkerchief and wiped her forehead and throat; then lighted a cigarette. She felt a little ashamed of this tremor and yet she wanted to treasure it too, sustain it somehow, watching the barns and trunks of trees stand out against their background of green with an almost sacred vividness.

When she reached the house it was dark. She drove into the garage with caution—she had twice scraped the side of the car against the door frame—and went in through the kitchen. Mrs. Pruitt had finished up and gone home. She threw her raincoat in a chair, thought better of it and hung it up in the hall closet. For a time she wandered around in the living room, gazed vaguely at the book-shelves, most of whose contents she had never read, at the piano she couldn't play, the ashtrays they had bought in Vallauris and Santa Margherita three years ago. Thinking of Europe she sat down and picked up a magazine, let her eyes slide indifferently over the slim, hard models and travel ads and theater gossip; dropped it again on the end table.

The stillness was oppressive. There was the rumble and bump of thunder; a puff of breeze lifted the maple leaves once fitfully and died away. She turned on the radio, turned it off before the tubes had warmed up. She felt irritable, tensed-up, excitable—as though if she didn't force herself to sit with her hands folded in her lap she would leap up and skip whirling through the rooms, clipping over candlesticks and furniture and crockery as she went. Whirling dervish randy-ro, and at its center was the sullen grumble of thunder and the man at the Dover Avenue stoplight, black and massive and misshapen, cursing her. Was it a portent, some kind of portent? Her imagination conjured up scenes with reckless haste, derailments and telescoped cars, rescue crews working feverishly in the yellow glare of searchlights among mountains of scorched and shattered iron. Ridiculous. Nothing ever happened on the New Haven Railroad. The first night in years without Gardner or Brian in the house and she was acting like a hysterical female. Thank God I was too young to have known Gard during the war, she thought; I'd have gone crazy with worry...Prevision was absurd, we couldn't see one micromillimeter into the future and a good thing it was, too. Gardner saying that to her once, sitting at a table somewhere, dining out, his hands at his chin, his eyes creased with affection, faintly amused; he was often faintly amused at her. What had she said? She couldn't remember. Two years ago, the Crown & Anchor at Yarmouth, his mother had been in England, and afterward they had swum nude and lain on a blanket on Nount's Head and watched the moonlight running silver scrolls over the bay—

She got to her feet quickly and made herself a drink, scotch and water, took several methodical swallows and went slowly upstairs, her feet soundless on the carpeting; turned right along the hall and entering the bedroom walked up to the full-length mirror with a slow, resolute step and snapped on the light and paused. Her face looked back at her coolly, a shade defiantly, with the full lower lip thrust forward. Had she failed him in some way? lost her attractiveness, her excitement for him? It happened, apparently. Jean Furman's husband had left her after sixteen years; and only last month Sally Hammarth had told her about her friends Bill and Helen Peters. Bill taught at Harvard. He had confessed to Helen that he no longer felt any sexual drive—and then a few months later the Radcliffe girl had some kind of nervous breakdown and it had all come out: a horrid mess. They were divorced now—Helen back in Michigan with the kids, Bill God knew where. It happened.

She leaned forward; her eyes went over her face, a slow, searching look. She pressed one hand against her cheek and chin. She was not good-looking really, nothing remotely resembling that wonderful classic balance of feature such as Sally or Mary Allerton had. Her eyes and mouth were too large, her neck was too long and thin; she looked like one of those chickens hanging on a hook by its neck in DeLuca's market. She thought of Gardner's first wife, whom she knew only from a studio photo, prettied up no doubt, but she'd been a handsome girl; and there was such a calm assurance in those soft pale eyes, the faint forward tilt of the head. Old Boston...

I'm not like them, she thought heavily, Gard or any of them, the kind of thing he's been used to: that instinct for reacting correctly to anything, no matter what it is. She remembered a class reunion party in Cambridge after one of the Yale games, years ago, with the rooms swirling with cigarette smoke and phonograph music and a staccato radio voice off in a corner announcing some other game being played out on the Coast. Chuck and Mary Allerton she knew, but the others were mostly strange faces, and her heart caught at the ease with which they smiled and drank and talked of past days together: the self-assurance they had, the almost indolent way they moved, the insuperable steadiness in their gaze! They *knew* there was nothing which could disconcert them. She'd found herself talking with Mary Allerton, who looked lovely in a fawn-colored cashmere sweater with a curious amber pendant at her throat, and she'd thought, That's the kind of girl Gard ought to be married to, not me—why on earth did he marry me? and then remembered that of course he *had* been married to a girl like this, and she had died. Beyond the slender-mullioned windows the elms, stripped now of leaves, had inclined their branches toward the pale pewter face of the river; a delicate Oriental calligraphy. She felt vaguely excited by the game—unlike most women she knew a good deal about football, she'd played countless games of touch with her brothers and sisters; she had been briskly cold and now the heat of the fire swam against her face. She had a second drink and felt more at ease, gave free rein to her natural warmth and ebullience, wanting these old friends of Garner's to like her. They certainly seemed to: they smiled at her like indulgent older brothers—they were all nearly ten years older than she—saluted her with their highball glasses and laughed at things she said, and she left in a delightful sense of well-being, knowing in the depths of her ardent romantic heart that that afternoon would dance aloft in her mind, bright as the firelight itself, whenever she thought of cocktail parties...

Later she came to know better. They never really accepted her; they couldn't even if they wanted to: there were too many generations. There had been the afternoon, a month before they were married, she had driven over to meet Gardner at the Beacon Hill house. Mrs. Lawring was out, Gardner had been held up at the office apparently, and Janet hadn't liked the idea of hanging around in those stately, shadowed rooms under the proprietary eyes of cooks and maids. She went out and sat in the car for over an hour, quite still, watching all around her this tight little smooth brick country where silver-haired men in gray flannel suits flashed furled-up newspapers at each other in tart greeting and little old ladies met and chatted interminably, and even the deliveries were made with the gravity and decorum of some court function. An interloper: she was an interloper in this maroon-and-amethyst community of heritage and taste stretching back three Godforsaken centuries, a community upon which it would be the height of impudence to intrude. An interloper and a fool. She had no business here. Twice she was on the point of driving away. By the time Gardner came along she was chewing her lip in a storm of misgivings. He caught sight of her sitting behind the wheel and stopped in surprise.

"What on earth are you doing out in the car?" he queried.

"—What do you think I'm doing—sitting here waiting for *you!*" she lashed out at him—and then burst into tears.

He was all solicitude. "What's the matter, honey? What's happened? Here, you're all nervous and upset—come on in the house and we'll—"

"I don't *want* to go in that house!"

"All right. It's a free country. Move over, and I'll buy you a drink in a stygian bar. How's that? Cheer up now, or I'll go back down to the office and fight with Henchey. You don't want me to fight with Henchey, do you?"

She'd risen to it, with the easy movement of the years; had entertained Gardner's proper Bostonians—and others not so proper, too—and clients and business associates, and more recently a few of the political eminences of the Hub. Most of them found her charming, or professed to, and her dinners made up in conviviality and cuisine what they lacked in urbanity. She wanted with all her heart to be a good wife, and she forced herself to learn the ground rules—order of seating and the choice of wines and tapers and how to keep the conversation gliding like a beach ball on a smooth sea; she did reasonably well, but she was never happy at such functions. What she loved best was an informal evening with Franz or Lou and Polly Enright, or an impromptu party where six more people came than she remembered inviting, an evening bubbling with wild racontage and gales of laughter, while Pruitt muttered and fumed in the kitchen and hordes of kids raced up and down the stairs or thumped mercilessly on the piano ...

Turning from the mirror she went over to the windows and drew the blinds; slipped off her blouse and hung it on the back of a chair. Maybe Gardner was seeing another woman: some girl in the office, or a client, or that interior designer from New York with Indian cheek bones and wild red hair that looked as though she'd chopped at it with a meat axe. If he was, she deserved it. The fact was she didn't know how to hold a man, really. A better wife and lover would have known how to catch up his affection at a time like this, direct it toward her more intensely. In their love-making Gardner was the one who made most of the advances; there had been no need for it to be any other way. It had been a fortuitous mating—up till now Gard had been if anything too quick to respond; but her own great ardor, borne on her native impulsiveness and her unflagging love for him, had been more than equal to the challenge. Sitting down she drew off her stockings thoughtfully. Another girl might be slower-paced sexually—but another girl would probably know a good deal more about sex than she did. For all her gregariousness and vivacity, her swift generosity of spirit—she was a fine dancer and had been much sought after during high school days and later—she knew very little about the ways of sex: she lacked sophistication. There had been the disastrous affair with Jimmy—a period of raw, inflamed anguish as unrelenting as an abscessed tooth, which had finally, unbelievably, mercifully worn itself out; and then, less than a year later, she had met Gard...

The thunder bumped and rumbled away again. The peepers in the yard had fallen silent and she frowned, listening, imagining she heard the sound of something moving through the laurels near the house. Cloth brushing by foliage. Was it? For an instant she thought of calling up Franz; snorted at herself for such a notion. She hadn't been home an hour and already she was getting like her spinster Aunt Harriet, phoning the police or the fire department or anyone else who would listen about suspicious noises ("I tell you there's somebody out there, I'm *not* hearing things—I've lived in this house forty-three years and I know it as well as I know my own *body!*") and then, having pinned down her audience for that evening, talking on for hours, her voice querulous and shrill. "I think it's just disgusting the way we've let the Russians get ahead of us in space, they'll be on the moon before we know it and spying on us with instruments, watching every *single thing we do!*"

She rose and went into the little alcove in the upstairs hall where the extension phone sat on a table. Gardner wouldn't agree to its being beside the bed ("I was blasted awake for years with bugles and bullhorns and sirens and God knows what else, and I'm not going to have a phone going off in my ear at two in the morning just because Horace has some hot idea.") and so they'd had it installed just outside the door. She dialed slowly, listened to the burr of the ring, was on the point of dropping the speaker when it clacked and a voice said:

"—*told* you to put it down I won't tell you *again*— hello!"

Janet laughed and said: "The Enright residence, I presume..."

"Oh! Hi, Jan."

"Did I catch you at a bad time?"

"Hell, no. *Any* time's a bad time." Janet could hear the hiss of air as Polly Enright expelled her breath against the speaker. "En*wrong* residence, you mean. Lord, I've had it, I've really had it. They sell 'em in Arabia, I'm told."

"Sell what?"

"Kids, *kids*—what else? Negotiable cash assets. All boy children, too. And my God, think of the relief.—*Billy*—" her voice rose threateningly, returned to the phone again. "Spoiled rotten. Can you imagine what it's going to be like around here in ten years? Less. Five—J—D's," she enunciated, almost with awe. "Maybe they'll band together like the Dalton Brothers and we can retire. If they haven't been burned at the stake first."

"They're wonderful kids," Janet protested.

"They're monsters. Here, hold on a minute while I light a cigarette and soothe my shattered nerves, will you?" The phone clattered on something hard, and Janet could see Polly bent forward, cigarette clenched between her lips, her lids slitted against the flame, looking eerily tough; then relaxing with the first puff, her eyes round and eager. "There. *I* know what you're calling for, sweety, you're calling to say you've got three handsome, stimulating young Harvard professors all lined up for the remedial reading staff. Right?"

Janet laughed awkwardly. "No—I haven't even got started on that. Polly. I'm sorry..."

"I was afraid you'd hand me some hard-luck story. How's everything otherwise?"

"Empty and dull. My men have gone off and left me. Boo's visiting a school chum in Rehoboth and Gard's gone to Newport."

"Really? Wow. You ought to go out on the town. What wouldn't I give for a chance like that."

"I suppose so, I feel lonely, though."

"Lonely!"

"I know. Isn't that silly?"

"It certainly is. This is your chance, gal—fly out to Frisco. Or Paris. Lie on the sand at Siasconset and have an affaire de coeur with a successful playwright . . . Do you mean to tell me you're staying *home?"*

"I know it's goofy to feel this way."

"It certainly is—you're free!" The last word was like a wild cry, and Janet laughed and said:

"Say, let's have lunch together soon."

"Fine. We're on."

"How about tomorrow?"

"Tomorrow?"

"Yes. I—I want to talk to you about something—I think I'm in need of some sturdy female advice."

"What? Oh sure. Any time. Nothing dire, I hope?"

"No." She smiled gently. "It'll keep. I'll give you a ring around eleven-thirty. Bye bye."

"Bye bye."

She replaced the phone in its cradle and stared at it, her hands in her lap. No: Gard was too straight for affairs in town. Besides—if it were something like that she would know: she was sure of it. He was as bad at concealing things as she was herself. His Puritan background simply wouldn't let him hide a relationship like that for ten minutes. No, he was tired, that was all—weary and harassed and trying to do too much, spreading himself too thin, as he said. He had always done that, really, and the past winter had been a terrific drain on his energies. Still, it would be good to talk with Polly, feel her out a little, see what she had to say . . .

A peeper began, two full chirps, then stopped as if strangled. A car rumbled over the wooden bridge below Thayers' and was swallowed up in a steady mutter of thunder. She set down her empty glass and went over to the television set and turned it on; bumped the knob past news, a night baseball game, a western, stopped at a suspense drama and watched it haphazardly while she undressed. Oddly, the drink hadn't relaxed her: she felt dry-eyed and quivering, unnaturally alert. She picked up the empty glass again, looked at it; set it down. That was silly. She was just a little edgy, that was all. She would get into bed and watch TV for a while and then take a warm bath and go to sleep and tomorrow would be another day.

She got into her housecoat, snapped out the light and got into bed, propped three pillows behind her and watched the screen. The private eye—he acted like a private eye, anyway—had slipped into an empty theater, was moving now with tense stealth past curtains that swayed and billowed softly. He paused, uncertain, the shadow rose behind him, he turned, his face flat with terror, and the blow on his skull—a horrific crunching sound—coincided with his moan, drowned for some reason in a crescendo of crashing bells. Then it quickly faded and there was the hard, depthless light of California and a ranch house, green lawn and neat asphalt drive and a station wagon with children climbing in and out of the doors and a man loading suitcases and camping equipment into the back, the whole family off for a weekend in the Sierra, laughing and calling to each other and the confidential masculine voice was saying: "Can you afford *not* to buy a Rambler this year?"—and at that instant she glanced around and saw the figure in the doorway.

A man. Snap-brim straw hat, dark glasses, slender. Absolutely motionless in the doorway. She heard herself give a gasp; a quick, tight intake of breath. For a long instant they gazed at each other as if they were both carved out of stone, while the television voice chattered amiably and its light flared and darted in the gloom of the room.

"—What do you want?"

Her voice sounded unnatural to her, off-key, someone else's voice. Her heart had swollen hugely; thick, quaking beats which were quite painful. But the words had broken the frozen immobility of the moment. The figure stirred, and for a brief second she thought it was the hitchhiker in the road at Dover Avenue; then she realized he was too thin. He came toward her indolently; his hand came up and she saw the long dance of light on the blade. He was at the edge of the bed now. He reached out and put his free hand on her shoulder and pressed her back against the pillows—an oddly gentle gesture that filled her with fear more than the knife. His face was long and dark, indecipherable behind the glasses.

"Where's your money." Slow Negroid accents, rather nasal. Not a question: A flat, declarative statement, as though it had been rehearsed, or often said.

"Over—over there." She tried to point, could not. Nor could she take her eyes off his face. "On the dresser. My purse. Is there."

He nodded somberly; he hadn't moved. "And where's the rest."

She stared up at him. "There *isn't* any rest—that's all there is in the house . . ." When he continued to gaze at her in silence, his face veiled by the jittering TV light behind him, she repeated, "I mean it, that's all we have. We don't keep cash around. My husband—"

That released her. She could move now. She started to get up. The hand shot out and pushed her back, more brusquely this time.

"My husband," she said again. "He'll be back in ten minutes, he should be back by now . . ."

The man shook his head; she fancied she saw the trace of a smile.

"He is, you'll see—we have a gardener, stays on the place, in the—"

"Lies," he said in the flat, nasal drawl, cutting her off. "All lies." He sighed, paused, then made an airy gesture with the free hand, the one that was not holding the knife. "That's all right. You go right ahead make up all the stories you want." He moved back to the dresser—a deft, side-slipping sort of movement, like an actor who still wants to face his audience, and said: "You stay there now. Just like that. That's right." She saw him open her purse, extract the alligator skin wallet and flip it open, take out the money and flop it back and forth between two fingers. Then, his elbows resting on the dresser, he bent over and peered at the bills as though to examine their serial numbers. She started to reach out toward the table lamp.

"Don't do that!" a sharp, tremulous voice, unlike the other one. Like another man entirely. The knife swung toward her and she froze. He came up to her again and paused, said in the former tone: "I tell you to stay quiet that's what I *mean*: stay quiet. You got that?"

"—At least put on a light, can't you?" she pleaded.

"No. No lights. TV's good enough. TV's fine." He became aware of the set apparently for the first time. "See all the rich folks, all the stuff they can buy? Nice, isn't it? Isn't it nice?" He seemed to expect no answer to this and went on gazing at the set pensively, nodding, like a man at a bar. When he spun back to her all at once she started.

"You're scared, ain't you?" he inquired pleasantly. "Real scared. Ain't you?"

"—Sure I am," she blurted out, "I haven't had people point knives at me before..."

"That's true. But that isn't the whole story, is it?" He considered this thought amusing. "You like thrills," he declared, and the words came quicker. "You do. Highwire, loop-the-loop, you *like* them. Don't you? Just live for them..." And with stunning deftness he reached out and flicked the blanket from the foot of the bed and flipped it over her head. She gave a gasp of protest and heard him say, "That's all right. I won't hurt you. I promise I won't."

She sat immobile, quivering, with the hot itchy pressure of the blanket against her face and shoulders, her mind refusing to work, simply refusing, caught in a thousand deadly conjectures that streamed in a torrent of light against her eyelids. She heard a rustling then, a swift sibilance close beside her which at first she couldn't fathom. Then she did and cried out and flung at the blanket but he was too quick for her. She felt the weight of his body. He was in the bed with her, holding her firmly, not hard. He was naked, she knew. She could feel both his hands on her and thought, *The knife, he has put down the knife,* and she began to struggle with all her might, a silent confused hopeless struggle; he had her pinned with his weight and was opening her robe now, a soft deference that amazed her even while she raged and fought, breathing through her clenched teeth. He had one of her arms pinioned against her side, the other held with his hand behind her head. He wasn't tired at all, he wasn't even breathing heavily—and the realization drove her frantic. He was everywhere, it seemed—an oddly gentle, inexorable pressure she couldn't withstand, couldn't oppose. In a torment of frustration and fear she felt herself beginning to cry, choked it back and wrestled on, weaker now, much weaker, she could sense it, conscious of the crackle and boom of the television voices, the near rumble of thunder; then that too became too much for her and she found herself weeping, bitterly, steadily, without pride or self-pity.

He was astonished at this; she heard him murmuring in still another voice, "Don't cry, don't cry, please don't cry like that, I won't hurt you, I swear I won't—" an incoherent, fumbling solicitude that, even while he held her so implacably, plunged her into greater confusion and anguish.

"—You!" she sobbed. "You don't—"

But she couldn't finish the thought, she didn't know what she could have meant to say, went on heaving and writhing in this absurdly unequal contest until in a flood of exhaustion and turmoil she knew she had lost. There was nothing left to struggle against. She had lost...and panting, pinioned, sprawled swinging in this net of conflicting sensations she felt the first tremors of a response she knew; her body, like some heedless alien organism, had hurried away downstream beyond her and burst into a spasm of release, a pulsing tumultuous surge she could not prevent—swooping now to unsuspected heights, flooding, torrential, bright with streaks of golden light...and then at last fading, falling away in blued quiescence. Over. He had murmured something close against her ear but she did not hear it.

She was beyond amazement.

He drew away then, got up from the bed and she heard him dressing. She did not look at him. She lay there drained of all capacity for movement, filled with weariness and shame and boundless rage at this body of hers which had betrayed her so. Her forehead was wet, her breasts and belly were damp with perspiration, and her right arm throbbed where he'd held it pinned against her side. My God, she thought emptily; oh my God. Was this man really standing there beside her bed, modestly turned away from her as he dressed, had he actually *entered this house*—?

Slowly she turned her head. He was standing in the center of the room, fully dressed again—he seemed able to clothe and unclothe himself with the speed of lightning—hat and dark glasses once more covering his face. She heard the dry chafe of a match and peered upward quickly but he had swung his head away from her with the flare of the flame. Then he swung back again in that effortless, lithe way and extended his hand.

"Cigarette," he said.

She made no answer. He must have thought she had refused because he put the pack away in his shirt pocket. Like a sleepwalker or some diver deep beneath the sea she raised herself in the bed and put her head in her hands, gripping her forehead in her fingers. I've got to get hold of myself, she thought tightly, pull myself together, do something... But she could not, the whole fierce outlandish episode had undone her: there was nothing to be done. Was there?

He began to move around the room again and she heard him opening and closing drawers, rummaging through her clothes and Gardner's. Then he opened the closet door. He seemed to be going through the pockets, but when she looked more closely she saw he was only fingering, in that pensive, almost dreamy manner, the material of one of Gardner's suits. His head snapped around then—almost as though, animal-like, he had felt the weight of her gaze, and the dark orbs of his glasses flashed once in the cold blue light of the television set which was still horribly, maddeningly, running on: the comedian Freddie Trommer—she instantly recognized the flabby round face, the brush cut and horn-rimmed glasses—was frowning and leering at a décolleté girl in tights, making jokes against a background of shrieks and wails of laughter.

"Nice stuff," the man was saying in his indolent drawl. He flicked the sleeve of a tweed jacket. "All the good labels. Brooks Brothers, Chipp, Rogers Peet..." On an impulse he slipped it on over his sport shirt and buttoned it with care. He was slender and it hung on him like a zoot-suiter's jacket, the shoulders sloping off absurdly, the front full of creases and bulges.

"Good fit, uh?" He stared at her challengingly. She made no reply. He crossed the room, slid back the screen door and wandered out on the sun deck outside the bedroom. She could see his silhouette against the hollow slate shell of sky. There was

no sound anywhere except for the TV—no thunder, no cars, no
night insects. A painful void. He had his hands in his pockets,
was looking up at the sky through the tree tops. She gazed at him
as though he were the last man to be seen on earth.

He came back inside, closed the screen door with meticulous
care, went over and slumped down in the big leather Saarinen
chair of Gardner's, hands crossed on his chest, legs extended.
She found he was staring at her intensely, she could tell from the
set of his head.

"You're beautiful," he said in the third voice. "They can think
anything they want to." There was a little pause. She strained to
see what he looked like, still could not. He seemed like a man at
the end of some prodigious exertion, or perhaps in the last stages
of a colossal drunk; exhausted, almost stupefied by the effort.
But his manner was at the same time curiously alert, as though
his mind were running at top speed, too fast even to give
expression to his thoughts. "No durability," he murmured.
"Only moments." He nodded, puffed out his lips. "The *moments*
are sacred..."

She started to say something, checked herself with an
inarticulate little sound.

"What's that?" he inquired in the easy drawl, as though she
had said something he hadn't quite caught. He threw back his
head, a soundless laugh. "Just like an old married couple." He
struck the chair arm lightly with the palm of his hand. "Funny,
isn't it? Here you are afraid of me, and I'm the one ought to be
afraid of you. Everything's upside down. You know? Yep.
Everything's just up—side—down..."

He kept gazing reflectively at the television screen. Freddie
Trommer was at the piano now, leering out frog-faced and
suggestive while his white fingers flashed over the keys, he had
just whispered something obviously not in the script and the
guest star—a tall, hard-eyed blonde—was convulsed, laughing
uproariously with the studio audience. Janet stared at the bulb
flickering its discordant lights, and then at the figure slumped in
the big chair. Was all this happening? Was all this really going on
happening to her? here in this bedroom? I ought to do
something, she told herself desperately, divert his attention and
get to the telephone, frighten him into leaving somehow, Gard's
old war pistol is in the storage closet, it must be in there

somewhere—but these schemes remained only remote fantasies, frozen in the clouded amber of her mind. She had passed through too many emotions in too short a space of time. She felt stunned, lethargic; her head was like a bottomless gulf choked with whirling bits of debris. How could he sit there like that, as though it were all some crazy joke?

Freddie Trommer had just whistled—a street-corner drug-store whistle, strident and lewd—and a very fat man dressed up as a woman in a floppy garden hat and hiked-up skirt was wobbling toward them on spike heels. The apparition, the hysterical laughter from the audience turned her sick, and she closed her eyes and buried her head in her arms. It was all a dream, a very bad dream, she would wake in the washed orange light of morning and all this would be a chill memory . . . but she knew from the stilled clamor of her body, the heavy-limbed languor and the dazed turmoil in her head that it was no dream; there was going to be nothing to awaken from.

When she raised her head again and opened her eyes he was not in the chair. She gazed around her wildly, couldn't find him. She reached for the bedside light, thought better of it, slowly studied every corner of the room. He was gone. He couldn't be in the bathroom, he would have had to open the door and it always clicked sharply no matter how carefully you turned it; she would have heard the screen door slide in its track if he had gone out to the sun deck again. Think. She must think what to do. Sensation was returning now in quickly succeeding waves, and with it came fear. Her heart was pounding. She must do something, and quickly. She started to get out of bed—and there he was in the doorway.

"Fell out of the moon," he declared. "Right on out of the moon. You know?" He was grinning at her nastily. "Scared, baby?" He had a highball glass in his hand, one of those blue-tinted, heavy-bottomed crystal glasses from Shreve's that Gardner's Uncle Archie had given them for a wedding present. He sat down in the big chair again and sipped at it. "All the comforts," he muttered. "Chivas Regal, Benson and Hedges, Brooks Brothers, wall-to-wall carpeting . . . all the delicious comforts of home."

He shrugged, a mirthless snort of laughter that was not laughter at all, and drank. He seemed out of sorts now, sullen and dejected. His Adam's apple, a prominent one, rose and fell with each swallow. She had crept back into bed again and was watching him covertly from under her lids. His hand on the chair arm was thin and supple and dark, like polished wood: the hand of a pianist, or an actor. The knife was nowhere in evidence. If she could only see his face! She became aware that she was trembling, shaking minutely from her head to her toes. She gripped the back of her neck with one hand and pressed her knees together. This was not possible. Not possible. It couldn't go on like this, hour after dreadful hour—

"Please go—will you please go away," she said wildly. "Now you've—done what you came for, go away—!"

He made no reply, and this stung her into further talk. She could feel her voice getting away from her, shaking, nearly out of control, but she couldn't help it. "What more do you want? What more—do you want to burn the house down, steal the car, tear up my husband's drawings, is that what you want? to—"

"Shut up!" He was out of the chair; had darted toward her in quick menace.

". . . You don't know," he said in the second voice, a rather deep, rough voice that made her think of kids playing ball in the playground back in Somerville. "You don't know what I want. You or anybody else . . . It's my turn, see?" he said slowly, and tapped his thumb twice against his wishbone in a way that filled her with dread. "My turn, now."

He doesn't care, she thought, he doesn't care about anything at all. His right hand, very near her eyes, was opening and closing; a spastic contraction. He's on dope, she thought, marijuana or something, he's an addict—and this new conjecture chilled her utterly. On heroin and he needs more of it, they all do, he might do anything, anything at all . . . But he didn't act like a heroin addict. Standing there gazing at her now he seemed oddly uncertain, almost pleading.

". . . Roxane," he murmured. "We could—if we had a—" he stammered; put a hand to the side of his face, thin, trembling fingers. He seemed racked with grief, regret, something. She said nothing, watching him, trying to see his face under the green-tinted wrap-around glasses, catch some distinguishing feature. He whirled around then and stomped off across the room and turned down the volume on the television set so that it was like a silent film, and stood hunched over staring at it from less than a foot away.

"See?" he demanded. "Just as much sense this way. More." He gestured toward the giggling comedian as though he were with them in the room. "Filthy slob. Keep pigs in penthouses and go to dirty parties out in Topanga Canyon—but will you admit it? Oh Christ no. Pure as the driven snow. Phony, lying sons of bitches. Give them a presidential citation. Why not? It doesn't show..." All at once he caught himself up, slipped a handkerchief out of his hip pocket and moved around the room with that lithe dancer's stride, wiping carefully the TV knobs, the handle to the sliding door, the top of the dresser, the highball glass.

"Prints." He smiled at her harshly; his teeth were bright and very even. "That's what you learn on TV. Other places, too. You know? Biggest school of all. Oh, sure."

When he came toward the bed again she was prepared for anything and tried to set herself, but she was trembling so badly she could hardly keep her teeth from chattering. The oversize jacket of Gardner's was beginning to bother him now because he shrugged his shoulders uncomfortably, the way a man does when he's too hot or something is chafing his neck. He started to take it off, changed his mind, shook his head at her and muttered, "You rich bastards..."

"Rich!" she cried, "rich—I come from a—"

"Don't tell me," he shot back at her. "I know all about you, you understand? Everything and then some..."

"You're going to get caught, my husband is—"

"Don't threaten me!" he shouted, and for the first time his voice shook shrilly. He darted toward her, cuffed the lamp off the table beside the bed; it struck the carpeted floor without a sound. "Just don't threaten me, that's all! And don't lie to me—I know all about him too, and where he's gone. I'll go when I'm good and ready, see? And not before..."

Then he seemed to regret this outburst. He bent over and picked up the lamp and set it on the end table again and stood there looking down at her, his head cocked at a strange little angle. And to her utter terror he reached out and touched her cheek gently with the back of his fingers.

"I'm sorry," he murmured in the deep, husky voice. "I didn't want to hurt you. I promised myself I—" He stopped, and the lines around his mouth deepened. "Only moments, all there are..." He withdrew his hand and moved off across the room. She saw him grope about in her purse again, then gaze at something at the back of the dresser, perhaps the photo of Brian. Then he stepped over to the doorway. "I really didn't want that. I thought—"

He broke off again and there was a little silence while they gazed sightlessly at each other.

"Remember," he said softly, like a command, and pointed a finger toward her. And recalling the pressure of his body against hers, his entrance and the resurgent clamor of her blood, she knew that he knew. "Remember..."

He was gone again. Soundlessly. It might have been a minute and it might have been ten, while she stared at the doorway in a trance that was like agony. I'm on the edge of madness, she thought with the awful clarity one has just before an accident. This is what it's like when you're going mad. She leaned forward in the bed, straining every nerve; she could hear nothing at all over the humming of insects in the garden. The thunder had died away. Damn these carpets, she thought petulantly, back home in Somerville this couldn't happen, those stairs were so creaky and warped a *cat* couldn't get up them without your hearing— realized all at once the absurdity of this train of thought and stopped it. She cursed the phone for being in that alcove in the hall; clenched her hands together and took a deep breath. Suddenly she felt very calm, icy calm and collected, without fear, as if her blood had been chilled and jellied. She got quickly and noiselessly out of bed and started toward the door, checked herself and went over to the vanity and feeling about with care dressed herself hurriedly, bra and panties and blouse and skirt, her eyes riveted on the doorway. Dressed, she felt better. She started to put on her shoes, thought better of it, picked them up and carried them in her left hand. She wanted terribly to turn off the television set but she knew it would make a sharp click and decided not to risk it.

She moved into the hallway, put her hand on the smooth black yoke of the phone, decided against that too, and went along the hallway to the stairs. Walking past Brian's room and one of the guest rooms frightened her though (was he in one of them, hidden behind a door—was he waiting to leap at her from behind?) and by the time she reached the head of the stairs she was trembling again. There was a pressure at her back, centered perfectly between her shoulderblades, and streaks of yellowish light shot up and down before her eyes. On the second step her leg gave way under her and she sat down, her head and hand pressed drunkenly against the wall. This was terrible. Up. She had to get up, she couldn't stay here. Gripping the railing she pulled herself soundlessly to her feet and forced herself to walk the rest of the way down the stairs, hugging the wall close. At the foyer she paused and listened. It was perfectly still. The thunderheads had passed over without rain, and the garden was asleep again; on guard. There was the faraway sound of a car in second gear on the upgrade beyond Thayers', then silence again. Was he still in the house, waiting to pounce on her? was this some crude practical joke to lure her downstairs, or worse? Or had he left?

Out: she had to get outside. No matter what. She was shaking so violently she was afraid she would fall down again if she didn't move. Light, gray and fitful, sifted in through the long panes of glass in the living room. Not my house, she almost said aloud, this house is not my house any more.

He could be in the cellar. He could be getting himself another drink; but he had left the glass on her dresser upstairs. Remembering this gave her a surge of confidence. Before she had time to think any more she stepped across the cool tile floor in five strides and was at the door, flung it open and thrust against the screen door and pulled the front door tightly behind her, let the screen door slam and was running swiftly, still holding her shoes clamped to her breast, the grass shockingly cold against her feet, the blacktop soft and warm; across the lawn and the drive and along the path through the rhododendrons, their branches slapping at her like switches, running faster now, gasping at the pain of roots and stones and stubble, through the gap in the stone wall and down across the open field toward Franz's house, watching it draw nearer and nearer like some infinitely friendly shore with the light like a comforting beacon burning upstairs, his study in the northeast corner—he said he always liked to work in an upstairs room and he hated to have sunlight fall across his desk—running still faster right up to the old paneled door, the brass knocker in the shape of a unicorn's head sweeping into her vision like some beloved childhood face, and flung herself at the door, gasping, her mouth dry as a bag of chalk, pounded and pounded on the long panels in an agony of need before she remembered to try it—found it unlocked, yanked it open and burst into the room crying, "Franz, Franz, oh help me, help me!" Someone was running along the hallway above her head, the light flicked on, warm bathing light, and there he was hurrying down the stairs in his dressing gown, coming toward her, his face long and white with concern, and at the sight of him everything inside her let go and she began to sob wildly, clinging to him with all her might, crying, "Help me, oh help me, Franz, a terrible thing, the most terrible thing—"

"... There," he was saying, his arms around her, holding her, his voice slow and Germanic and reassuring, "there now, it's all right, you are all right now..."

Then everything swung in slow, eddying circles, blotched and deepened, and swooped off in darkness.

Chapter Three

The house was all ablaze with light: it rained out of upstairs windows, flooded gardens and lawn, and the night breeze sent shadows swaying like dancers in a dream. Coming up the road from Thayers' in the taxi Gardner Lawring could see figures roaming through the upstairs bedrooms, the living room, crouched in the foundation planting below the kitchen. Prowl cars were parked haphazardly on the driveway; the revolving beacon on the roof of one of them was flashing like a savage red eye. Lightheaded and sleepless after the flight from Newport and the long cab ride out from Logan Airport, his belly taut with worry, with nothing to go on but Franz's brief summons, he watched the stealthy activity around the place and told himself, Hang on tight, boy. A steadying admonition he had used during personal crises ever since the war. Just hang on tight and we'll see what's what soon enough. He watched the police with a kind of avid fascination—their swarming presence made the trouble real and proximate. He was conscious of a rising nervousness and muttered, "Lord, they've got every light on in the place . . ."

The taxi slowed, and the driver said: "This where you want?"

"No," Lawring answered. "Keep going."

"Jeez, will you look at the cruisers." He whistled once between his teeth and tongue. "What's going on?"

"Take your first right," Lawring said.

They rolled over the wooden bridge, a sudden hollow shudder, and swung around to the right through dense woods. "What's it all about?" the cabby persisted.

Lawring snapped at him: "That's my business, chum. You just keep driving."

"Say, now listen, Mac—" The driver looked around irately,

his mouth open; took in Lawring's size and the set of his face, and thought better of whatever it was he'd had in mind to say. In silence they broke out of the woods and approached Franz Hoelder's house, a gaunt white Federal style structure with a delicate fanlight over the front door and two massive chimneys. All the lights seemed to be on here, too; more cruisers were parked at the edge of the driveway under the elms and a policeman stood at the door watching them.

"Right here," Lawring said. "This is it."

"Hey, what's up, Mac?" the driver asked—a suppliant tone this time. "What's the story, no kidding?"

"Couldn't tell you," Lawring answered shortly. "Here you go." He paid him off and tipped him five dollars. "That was good driving." He grabbed his suitcase and drawings case and got out, saw the blue uniform detach itself from the door and come toward him: Charlie Albiston, his eyes snapping with nervous self-importance.

"Mr. Lawring. Go right on in. They're waiting for you."

"Thanks, Charlie."

Janet was sitting on the couch with a man's sweater draped over her shoulders, her hands gripping her elbows; she was listening to Franz, who had drawn up a chair and was talking to her quietly. Behind the couch Doc Bolton was standing, his bald head perfectly round and pink and smooth, in conversation with two strangers, probably detectives. Lawring set down his bags and they all turned and looked at him, their faces sharply etched and void of expression. Janet was the first to recognize him; when she did her features were convulsed briefly by an expression Lawring had never seen before: a look of fear and consternation and boundless grief. She got to her feet as though her life depended on reaching him. The moment she was in his arms he could feel her shoulders shaking.

"Oh Gard," she was murmuring, "thank God you're here. Oh thank God."

"It's all right, honey. It's all right, now."

"Don't ever leave me. Oh Gard, don't ever leave me again, ever..."

"I won't, honey, of course I won't."

She drew back then and smiled at him wanly, dabbing at her

nose and eyes with a big white handkerchief, obviously one of Franz's. "I'm sorry," she said. "I swore I wouldn't break down. I—can't seem to help myself. Everything keeps setting me off..."

"Are you all right?" he asked her softly. "Did he—did he hurt you?"

"No. No. It was—just the whole thing, Gard. Coming out of nothing, nothing at all. You can't imagine—! I'll be all right, I guess."

She seemed so tiny and helpless, standing there looking up at him. Her face was drawn and smudged with tears, there was a long looping scratch under one cheek. Her eyes kept racing about the room.

"Don't you want to lie down, sweet? rest a little?"

"No." She gave a little shiver and wiped her nose. "That's just what I don't want. I'll be all right. In a little while."

"She wants to be with people," Franz said gently. "Have people around her. It's natural enough."

"Of course." Lawring put his hand on the older man's shoulder. "Thanks, Franz."

Hoelder shrugged. "Nothing. Less than nothing. I wish I had heard something. I didn't hear a thing until she pounded on the door."

"It's so—so upsetting," Janet said, and laughed nervously. "Just like that—without any warning!..."

"That's how it usually happens," Franz answered. He smiled at her—a sad little encouraging smile that she accepted gratefully.

Thank God Franz lives right over here, Lawring thought; thank God for that, anyway. There was something about the way he sat there in his dressing gown and slippers and with his silvered hair rumpled where he'd run his fingers through it; something indomitable, at once gentle and proud and infinitely resilient—as though this slender, worn old man had beheld all the folly and savagery and terror this world could hold, had acknowledged it and faced it out, every gesture of brutality and betrayal, and gone forward undismayed... Lawring was all at once conscious of himself as a pretty callow and inexperienced young man. Franz was able to comfort Janet in ways he could not; he saw this now, watching them, and it shook him subtly. He still felt nervous, irritable, off-balance in the face of this catastrophe that had taken place in his absence... He gave himself a little shake.

"... tried to give her sedation," Dr. Bolton was saying to him now, bending toward him. "But she refused any, the little minx. Said she wanted to stay awake till you got here. Now *you* look as though you need something..."

He glanced at Bolton, saw the old man was grinning; absently he shook Bolton's hand, lulled in the easy wave of reassurance most people feel in the presence of a doctor they have confidence in. "Me? No, I'm all right. I'm fine." Putting his hand on the old GP's shoulder he moved off with him toward the far corner of the room. "Tell me: how is she? No frills and flounces. *Is* she all right?"

Bolton nodded, his rimless glasses winking light. "Oh yes. I'd say so. When Hoelder rang me up I came right over. I brought her down to the office and went over her with a fine-tooth comb." He paused, his big blue eyes watching Lawring impassively. "She says there's no pain, only a slight soreness. There's certainly no sign of injury."

"But she was—" Lawring hesitated.

"Assaulted? Yes." Dr. Bolton's voice was perfectly level. "That's beyond question. I gave her a prophylaxis."

"But the scratch on her face—"

"A briar or a branch or something. Running over here in the dark. She's all right. Surprisingly steady, all things considered." Some men entered the house and Dr. Bolton looked at them indifferently. "But she ought to be knocked out for a good twelve hours or so."

"I see."

A tall man with a big fleshy face and shrewd little pale brown eyes came up to where they were standing and said: "Mr. Lawring?"

"Yes."

"I'm Chief Inspector Reardon." His hand was big and moist. "We've been checking things out over at your house."

"I see. Have you found anything?"

"Not too much." Reardon rubbed the lobe of one of his long

ears. "The assailant apparently entered the house through the downstairs bedroom. The little one off the kitchen."

"Oh yes, that one," Lawring answered. He felt all at once sluggish and numb; all he could seem to think of were idiotic banalities. In moments of stress events always moved faster than your mind did; the thing was to force your mind to keep pace with the events.

"Was it unlocked?" Reardon was saying. "The window?"

"Yes. Probably. That's the room Mrs. Pruitt—she's our cook and cleaning woman—uses to change in, and she leaves it open in hot weather; the room's pretty airless. What about the screen, though? That's an Andersen casement..."

Reardon's eyes opened a little wider. "That's right, it is. He slit it with a knife or something and lifted it out." He watched Lawring for a moment with the faintest trace of amusement. "Don't you folks lock windows at night?"

"No—I don't think so. There's never been any need to. Nothing like this has ever happened out here that I know of..."

"Until now."

"Until now. That's true." Lawring said suddenly: "Did Mrs. Lawring give you a description of the man?"

"Not yet. She said she wanted to wait until you got back from Rhode Island. That's one of the things we'd like to get around to now." He turned to Janet, who was sitting on the couch again. "I wonder if we could ask you some questions, Mrs. Lawring."

"Yes, of course."

Lawring said to Janet: "Don't you want to wait until you've had some rest? Doc Bolton says you—"

She shook her head. "No, I'm all right. I want to help all I can."

"That's very good of you, Mrs. Lawring," Reardon said. "We appreciate it, I can tell you." He sat on the chair Franz had vacated, and several other detectives grouped themselves around the couch.

"Just tell us what happened tonight," Reardon went on gently. "As fully as you can. Everything you remember."

Janet locked her fingers in her lap. "Well. I got home from the station, I'd taken Gard and Brian to the station, to 128. And then I drove home and made myself a drink and phoned a friend of mine, Polly Enright. We didn't talk long. And then I got into bed to watch TV."

"Did you notice anyone following you from the station? Any car that seemed to be following you, any people on the road?"

"No . . . There weren't any cars because I would have seen the headlights or parkers. There was a man at the stop-light at Dover Avenue, a man hitchhiking, and I got into a silly misunderstanding with him, but that had nothing to do with this."

"What do you mean, a misunderstanding?"

She looked up at Reardon, then at Lawring. "Oh, it was nothing, it was perfectly silly. I stopped for the light and he thought I wanted to give him a ride and he started over to me and then I went ahead and he got angry and shouted at me . . ." She stopped herself, went on: "But I know he wasn't the person, he was a big man in an old felt hat. I'd have recognized him instantly if he'd been the one."

"I see." Reardon's face was completely expressionless. "You were in bed watching TV. You had undressed?"

"Yes. I just had a housecoat on, I was going to take a bath before I went to sleep. I was sitting up watching some suspense show, I forget which one, and I looked around . . ." Her hand tightened. "And there he was, in the bedroom doorway."

"You didn't hear anything?"

"No. Oh, once earlier I thought I heard sounds, something moving in the laurel but I thought I was just imagining things—you know, the way you do. I was feeling a little tired and nervous, I thought it was just imagination."

Reardon nodded. "Could you describe him to us?"

"Well, he was thin and dark. Very dark."

"A Negro."

"I—yes, I think so. He was wearing a straw hat and dark glasses with little gold rims, like the ones pilots wear."

"How was he dressed?"

"He was wearing a sport shirt with the tail out—you know, over his trousers: one of those knitted sport shirts, yellow, with a little crocodile over the breast pocket. The trousers were a dark red, rusty color, very tight."

"Uh-huh. How about his face?"

"It was thin and dark..." She stopped, bit her lip. "You see, he kept those glasses on all the time. They were like goggles, they covered up half of his face."

"Any scars or marks, anything unusual about him you can recall?"

She paused, struggling to remember. To Lawring, watching her, she looked actually smaller and thinner, as though the force of the incident had worn some of her away; her face was white as cuttlebone.

"He was graceful," she said. "Slim and graceful; he moved like a dancer, or an actor."

Reardon smiled at her sympathetically. "Can't give us anything more than that?"

She shook her head, her lips compressed. "I wish I could, terribly. His Adam's apple was very prominent, I remember that." She paused. "I just never got to *see* him..."

"Okay. What happened then?"

"He came toward me very slowly, it was almost as though he were asleep. And he had this knife."

"What kind of knife?"

"I—I don't know. Very long. Terribly long. He came up to the bed and put his hand on my shoulder—right here—and pushed me back against the pillows... I suppose I should have known right then, but I didn't. And then he asked me where my money was." She frowned. "It was odd—it was almost as though he'd just thought of the idea..."

"And you told him," Reardon prompted.

"Yes. I said in my purse. And he went over and opened my purse and wallet and took the money out. I remember how much there was because I'd just cashed a check for thirty-five dollars at Truscott's that afternoon while I was shopping, and I knew there were three tens. And some change. He took it, and then he asked me where the rest was. I told him there wasn't any more, we didn't keep much money lying around the house. And then—" she looked nervously at the circle of men around her, and licked her lips "—he came over to the edge of the bed and looked at me."

"Looked at you?"

"Yes. He said, 'You're scared, ain't you? Real scared.' Just like that. I said Yes, I was. And then"—and her voice became very pinched and dry—"then he threw the blanket over my head and told me not to move, he wasn't going to hurt me..."

Standing there listening to his wife, his own wife seated on that battered old Empire couch of Franz Hoelder's saying these outlandish, terrible things, Lawring gripped his hands in his pockets and swallowed. A little man with perfectly round ears and horn-rimmed glasses tiptoed across the room behind them as if the whole thing were a bad amateur theatrical and he needed to get out for a smoke. Reardon and one of the detectives were listening to Janet with an impersonal reserve so great it looked almost hostile. Another detective was taking notes rapidly on a pad with a defective ballpoint pen... There was something he ought to be doing, wasn't there? some vigorous, necessary action he could take? But he could think of nothing, merely remained there bound in the smoke-laden three A.M. unreality of the scene, hanging on her every word, almost afraid to stir, feeling the flesh move on his forehead and neck. He was conscious now of a rising sense of fear and shame, and something else—a breath-held fascination that was like nothing so much as anticipation. What in Christ's name was the matter with him? It's happened, he told himself harshly, setting his teeth, this thing has happened. For the love of God pull yourself together... He could feel the heat in his eyelids.

"How long would you say you were underneath the blanket?" Reardon had asked.

"Oh—not long. Not long at all." Janet's eyes were darting around the room as though it were painful to stay on any one object for more than a fraction of a second. "I thought—at first I thought he—just didn't want me to be able to see anything. I guess that's what I thought. And then I realized what he was doing, I heard his clothes, I knew he was getting out of his clothes even though I couldn't see him, and I started to throw the blanket off. But he—" She struggled, her eyes fastened on Reardon now, riveted on his long, bland face. "—He was already on the bed. He—he—" She broke off, held her quivering lips clenched together. She was wringing Franz's handkerchief into shreds.

"It's all right, Janet," Dr. Bolton intervened. "Maybe that ought to be it, for a time.—Isn't that enough for you gentlemen to go on?" he inquired of Reardon in his low, even voice. "She's been pretty badly shaken up by this whole business..."

"I know," Reardon answered genially, "I know she has, and I think she's being a real brick about it. We all do. The thing is, we're pretty eager to find this fellow and I know you all are, too..." He turned his easy, sympathetic grin to Janet. "I've only got a few more questions. Do you feel up to it?"

She straightened her spine and passed one hand back through her hair. "Yes, it's all right, I want to help. All I can. I'm sorry," she added, "I seem to be all to pieces..."

"Thanks, Mrs. Lawring. I know how hard it is for you right now." Reardon hitched himself forward in the chair, his big hands between his knees. "Tell me, did you smell anything on his breath? Something sweet, like sugared cornsilk, molasses, ether—anything like that?"

She shook her head.

"Or liquor?"

"No. I don't think so. I'd have been able to tell if there'd been any strong smell. He didn't seem drunk or—under the influence of anything. Well, I thought he was for a while—he acted so strangely..."

"How do you mean?"

"I mean his mood kept changing. For a time he'd be—well, gentle and subdued, rather considerate, actually. I know it sounds silly to say that but he was...And then all of a sudden he'd turn all nasty and full of rage against everything."

"But he didn't hit you or wield the knife threateningly at any time?"

"No. Half the time he acted as though I wasn't even there. He just didn't seem to care about anything."

Reardon sighed, a slow heave of his shoulders. "I see. And then what happened?"

Janet's eyes began to race again. "Well, then he—he—"

"No, I mean after he assaulted you," Reardon went on easily. "What happened after that?"

"Well, then he..." She put her hand to the side of her head, pressed it hard against her temple. She had obviously forgotten what he had done next. "He went over and turned down the TV set."

"Turned it off, you mean?"

"No, he turned it down. The volume." She shook her head

and looked up. "No, first he went through the closet. He got dressed again and went through the closet. And he took out one of Gard's jackets and put it on."

"—One of my jackets?" Lawring heard himself say in a thin voice.

She nodded. "The Harris tweed. It was too big for him, he looked ridiculous in it. He kept it on all the rest of the time he was there. I think he must have taken it with him when he left."

Reardon and two of the detectives conferred over this, while Janet watched them out of large, haunted eyes and kept rending the white handkerchief. Lawring felt immensely disquieted. Why should the man have gone into the closet and put on one of his jackets?

"Good," Reardon said aloud. "That'll give us something to work on, if he's kept it. What happened after that?"

"Then—yes, then he wandered around the room, and then he sat down and watched TV for a while. He hadn't turned it down yet, it was the Freddie Trommer show."

Lawring was astounded. "You mean he sat there in the bedroom and looked at television?"

"Yes." She nodded slowly. "Just as though it were his own home. As though he hadn't a care in the world. 'Everything's upside down,' he said. Something like that. Things that didn't make any sense. And then he went downstairs and got himself a drink."

Reardon glanced at her in surprise now. "A drink? of liquor?"

"Yes. Quite a lot. Several ounces. He made some remark about the Chivas Regal so I suppose it was scotch."

"A big drink." Reardon was watching her very attentively and tugging at the lobe of his ear. "How long would you say he was downstairs, Mrs. Lawring?"

"I—don't know. I had my eyes closed, my head in my arms, like this. I was sitting in the bed, he'd told me not to move. And then when I happened to look up he was gone. I didn't know where he was. I couldn't see *anything* with that damned television screen flickering away and I couldn't hear anything, either. It was terrible. I didn't know what to do..."

"You didn't think of using the telephone?"

"What? Yes, I did—but it's out in the alcove in the hall, we don't have one on the table beside the bed. It seemed so far away

and I didn't know where he'd gone . . . I was just afraid, I guess.
Anyway, I started to get out of bed—and there he was again, in
the doorway—"

All at once she broke down and began to cry quietly, rocking
her head from side to side.

"Honey—" Lawring said.

"No, no, it's all right . . . I'm sorry," she murmured, and blew
her nose. "It's just—I keep seeing him in the doorway . . ."

She pulled herself together and went on, her voice low and
monotonal. Watching her covertly, admiring her fragile
courage, Lawring recognized the symptoms. She was in the third
stage, which was usually the worst. During the moment of
danger you often weren't too scared, or if you were there were
ways of evading or alleviating the fear: there were things you had
to do, or that you did anyway. Afterward, if you had emerged
unscathed there came the reaction—a garrulous euphoria, even
hilarity: he remembered sitting around with other men from his
company after an assault, cracking jokes, exchanging parodies
of one another's antics under fire, pounding one another on the
back gleefully, like kids after some hare-brained prank . . . And
then soon after that came a period of profound depression, a
desolate sense of one's monstrous vulnerability, the cockleshell
of your own solitary self cast adrift on a sea of illimitable
menace . . . That was what she was feeling now, and she was
struggling against it heroically. He was astonished at her
fortitude; his heart was wrung with affection, he wanted to take
her in his arms and wipe this savage, incredible night away with a
word, a kiss . . . But he was pinned there, hands still clenched in
his pockets, helpless as a fly in a web, blinking against the sting
of cigarette smoke.

". . . He seemed very angry about something," she was saying.
"He finished his drink and that's when he turned down the
volume on the TV. He talked, sarcastic things. Just like home, he
said. 'All the comforts of home.' Something like that. He said I
didn't know anything about him or what he cared about, but he
knew all about us. Everything."

"He did? He said that?"

"Yes. 'I know all about you, more than you can ever guess.'
He just laughed at me when I—you know, tried to frighten him. I
tried to tell him Gard was coming back soon. He was angry at

everything now. That was when he wiped everything with a handkerchief."

"Wiped off the prints?"

"Yes. Prints. That's what he said. He said he'd learned about that on television. He did the TV knobs and the door handle to the sun deck and the glass, and several other things."

"Ummmh." Reardon grimaced and struck his palm with his knuckles lightly. "That's too bad. What did he do then?"

She glanced at him in surprise. "That's all. Then he went out the door again. He kept doing that. Appearing and disappearing. Only this time he didn't come back."

"What time was it by then?"

"I don't know. I never looked. I waited awhile, and then I got out of bed and dressed as fast as I could and went down the stairs and out the front door and ran over here to Franz's . . ."

"You still didn't use the phone?"

"I just wanted to get out of the house. I thought he might still be in the house and hear me, I was afraid of the noise it would make. I just wanted to get out, get out—!" Her voice shook but she held it steadier this time; she was very near tears again.

Lawring got up and went over and put his arm around her. "Sweet, you've done wonderfully. But I think you'd better get some rest." He turned to Reardon. "How about it, Inspector? Can't we let it go for now?"

"Sure." Reardon got slowly to his feet. "Thanks, Mrs. Lawring, I can't tell you how much we appreciate this kind of cooperation." A moment longer he hung there, gazing at her with his big, bland, kindly face, reluctant to relinquish the opportunity. "You can't remember anything more about him—no bits of physical description, mannerisms, anything of that kind?"

"His hands," she said after a pause. "His hands weren't the hands of a workman, I mean a ditchdigger or longshoreman or anything like that . . . Oh," she said, and her face brightened, "he called me Roxane. Whatever that means."

"I see."

"Do you suppose he thought I was somebody else all that time?" There was a little silence and then she said quietly: "That would mean he was insane, wouldn't it?"

No one made any reply to this. Dr. Bolton came up then and

said, "I'm going to stick your arm, young lady. You need to go to sleep."

"All right." She turned to Lawring. "Franz says I can use the bedroom in there." She tossed her head. "Is it all right? I don't want to go back over there. Just now," she added.

"Of course, I don't think you should."

"Won't you stay here, too?"

"Sure. If you'd like. Perhaps it's better."

She took him under the arms, and her eyes darkened with that shadow of immense sorrow, although she smiled. "I'm so sorry about this!" she exclaimed.

"Don't be silly, sweet."

"So stupid. I took so long to pull myself *together.*" She said anxiously, "Do you think I should have got to the phone somehow or other? If only he hadn't come *back* that way..." She frowned, and the corners of her mouth drew down. "There was probably a time when I could have done it. Done something. That's what I keep thinking, over and over. Isn't that ridiculous? Now that it's too late."

Softly he said: "I think you're very brave, and very good."

Her eyes glittered with tears. She started to say, "Thank you—" and her voice broke.

"It's all right, honey. Don't go around on it." He let her weep against his chest, and stroked her fine chestnut hair. Catching Bolton's eye he grinned sadly and nodded. "Let Doc Bolton put you to sleep now, sweet."

"All right...I feel as if I'm dissolving into salt water. Isn't that goofy?—Oh, I made a date with Polly for tomorrow. For lunch. I don't think I'll be able to make it."

"No, I don't think so. It'll keep."

"I wish Boo were here now. Here with us."

"Well, maybe it's just as well he isn't. For a while, anyway."

"Yes. I suppose so." She seemed full of confusion. "I remember I thought at one time how wonderful it was that he wasn't here. When it happened, you know. But then I thought, If he were here it wouldn't have happened somehow. I guess that's pretty silly. Unrealistic." She started toward the bedroom with Dr. Bolton, turned back again with that naked, anguished point of light in her eyes. "You won't—go away anywhere, will you, Gard?"

"No, honey. I'll be right here. And so will Franz."

Watching her walk into the bedroom, rather unsteady on her feet, a hand to her head, Lawring thought, At least she's all right; she's unhurt. Many far more terrible things could have happened . . . But he felt no relief at this, and it angered him that he didn't. Overriding the relief and a simple prayerful thankfulness was this burdensome sense of inadequacy, of feebleness, as though some noxious parasitic larvae had lodged in his muscles and nerves and were devouring them with great speed. He wasn't accustomed to standing by helplessly in a crisis like some octogenarian aunt, bewildered, ineffectual, letting things go forward . . . but there seemed to be nothing he could do. It had happened, this *incident* had taken place and now it was all in the hands of professionals whose trade was violence and pursuit. But what a wretched break! Why had he had to go away, tonight of all nights—what malicious celestial connivance had chosen this one particular evening when he couldn't be there to defend his hearth and home? A profitless course of conjecture: it had happened, and now there was simply nothing he could do . . .

When he heard Reardon's voice he turned toward him in a little spasm of relief.

"I wonder if you'd care to come over and show us a few things about your house, Mr. Lawring?"

"I'd be glad to." He said to Franz: "If she wakes up and wants me tell her I'll be right back. We're just going over to the house."

"All right, Gardner."

They walked out to one of the cars. The thunderheads had swept off toward Boston and the night was clear now, and cool; the stars looked impossibly far away. His watch said ten minutes to four.

"I'd like to set up a twenty-four-hour stake-out," Reardon was saying. "Round the clock. Two detectives, and a police-woman for the phone. We'll want to monitor and trace all incoming calls, if it's all right with you."

"Fine," Lawring answered vaguely. "Whatever you believe is necessary. I think Mrs. Lawring is going to want to feel she has some protection." But the thought left him curiously dissatisfied, ill at ease, he didn't know why. "You think the man will call the house?" he asked.

Reardon's little amber eyes glinted in the lights from the parked cars. "You'd be surprised how often an offender returns to the scene of the crime, one way or another. Seeks to reestablish contact. Nobody knows why this is, but it's fairly frequent. Go ahead, get in . . . Lawring place," he said to the cop at the wheel. They eased down the drive and recrossed the wooden bridge, a sound like tumbrils. "There are bound to be quite a few calls from cranks, anyway. Cranks and perverts. There always are, after something like this."

Lawring turned and faced Reardon. "You'll keep this out of the papers, won't you, Inspector?"

Reardon puffed deliberately at a cigar, the flame spurting from the match end. "Afraid it's a little late for that," he said after a pause. "Reporters were out here some time before you got back." He leaned back in the seat of the cruiser and the cigar end pulsed like a stove. "They've got their headline for the day."

"I'm sorry to hear that," Lawring said shortly.

Reardon thrust out his lips and brushed invisible ashes off his shirt front and tie. "I wouldn't worry about it if I were you. It'll blow over soon enough. Nothing as dead as day-before-yesterday's splash." He turned then and looked at the architect. "Count your blessings, Mr. Lawring. It could have been a lot worse. Believe me. A lot worse."

"I've been telling myself that."

"You go right on telling yourself that. Because it's the God's honest truth. When we get a call like this one tonight we usually figure assault is the least of it: the very least." They crept up the drive between some of the other patrol cars and Reardon got out quickly. "That's a plucky little wife you've got," he observed. "A real brick."

"Yes. She's pretty wonderful."

Two men were in the kitchen installing the monitoring and tracing devices. A little sandy-haired man with a handlebar mustache went by and Reardon stopped him and said: "You find anything, Blake?"

"Nothing we can use so far, Chief."

Reardon squinted at the floor and rubbed his ear. "I was hoping we'd get some prints."

Lawring stared at him. "You mean a man was in this house all that time, doing all those things, and didn't leave any fingerprints anywhere?"

"He left them." Reardon smiled at him faintly. "He left them. But it's not that simple. The question is whether he's left any that are clear enough to use." Abruptly he started off. "Let's look for that jacket."

They searched the living room, the basement and workshop, the dining room and kitchen, the closets. Upstairs the lights were still on everywhere. Lawring walked into the bedroom. The bed was rumpled violently; sheets and the blanket lay in a heap on the floor. He bent over and picked up the wad of bedding, all at once bent over and peered at it, hoping to see he knew not what—flung it on the bed in disgust. The television set had been turned off, probably by the fingerprint man. The highball glass was standing on the dresser, and Janet's leather purse. He thought he heard a sound, stepped over to the bathroom and opened the door quickly. A man was sitting on the toilet with his hat on, his trousers wadded over his knees, smoking a cigarette. He grinned and said: "Hi, there."

Lawring said, "Sorry," and shut the door. He stood in the center of the room in a little tremor of indecision, then crossed to the closet and slid back the door and peered in. It was gone all right: the Harris tweed. The brown worsted slacks he usually wore with it were still there on the hanger. Listening to the sound of voices and something clicking and buzzing away downstairs, he fingered the material absently. Somewhere in Greater Boston a man was wearing his jacket. A man who had raped his wife and drunk his liquor and then vanished into thin air; a man who could be walking calmly down State Street tomorrow morning, or sitting in Bates Hall in the Public Library or slumped on a bench in the Common feeding the pigeons and watching the kids shriek and caper under the mercury spatter of water in the Frog Pond...

Reardon called something to him from the foot of the stairs. He dropped the cuff of the trousers and slid the closet door shut, conscious of a slow, unpleasant creep to his skin.

Chapter Four

"A dreadful thing," Marcia Lawring declared. "Dreadful. To think that something like that could happen here." By "here" she meant Boston, which was where her home was, and the thought caused her to purse her fine thin lips as she studied her knitting. "Do they have any idea who might have done it?"

Lawring shook his head. "Not yet. They have a few leads. There have been some other episodes of the same kind recently. Two over in Back Bay, one in Arlington, another one out in Needham." He smiled wryly. "I'm getting up on this sort of thing. It's curious what goes on all the time that you're not aware of at all..."

"I daresay."

"They seem to be interviewing people mostly, running down possibilities. Delivery people, garage men, that sort of thing. They even questioned old Sam Rawlis for half an hour."

Marcia Lawring stared at him. "Your gardener."

"That's right." He snorted; he was sitting forward, elbows on his knees. "The idea is: Who would have known that I was going away for a few days. Everybody did, it seems: the butcher, the baker, the man in the moon. It's incredible how many people know all about your life."

"Of course. That's as it should be."

He glanced at his mother again. She was a handsome woman, even at sixty-three, with soft gray hair and fine shoulders; her eyes were steady and gray-blue, like an easterly sea, and they rested on Lawring with an affectionate assurance that was irresistible. He remembered an evening long ago when she'd had exactly the same expression on her face. "You shouldn't be satisfied with third place, Gardy. Lawrings have always been leaders in every field they entered." That had been because he'd come in third in a drawing competition at school. Gazing up at her then, dressed in shorts and blazer, his hair low on his forehead, he had nodded, and believed her implicitly. Lawrings were always leaders: Q.E.D. She herself was an Alcock (her grandfather Darius had not changed the surname to Alcott when even crusty, cantankerous old Bronson had deemed it expedient. They were Alcocks and they would remain Alcocks, and certain contemptible souls could make whatever vulgar plays on words they chose; so much the worse for *them*) and Alcocks had been leaders in whatever fields *they* entered, too...

"No, it happened, it *did*—I saw it, for heaven's sake!"

Brian's voice soared up to them from the kitchen downstairs, where he was talking to Eunice, telling her some outlandish whopper probably, dressing it up as sober fact; and as though the boy's shrill voice had released him Lawring got up and went over to the front window and looked out on Mount Vernon Street. The trees were in full leaf, and sunlight and shadows lay in soft dappled patterns on the brick sidewalks, which were worn smooth as old horn. On this same street William Ellery Channing had been born, a few doors down Charles Francis and Henry Adams, below them a branch of the frosty clan of Cabots; two blocks west and south—from the roof of this house he could see nearly all of the others—had lived the Lodges, and the Hornblowers, and Oliver Wendell Holmes, and the historian William Prescott, and Julia Ward Howe and John Singleton Copley the painter; and the haunted actor Edwin Booth, and Emily Marshall Otis, who was so stunningly beautiful that William Lloyd Garrison had gone and listened to a reactionary minister just to catch a glimpse of her; and King John Hancock, who once snubbed George Washington himself and nearly got away with it, and Dr. John Warren, the nephew of the hero of Bunker Hill...

Standing at this window he could feel all around him, as he had as a child, the glorious, awesome beat of history, paced by his mother's voice. "...taken prisoner at the battle of Brandywine Creek. He was sent to the Tory prison at Mandota, a dreadful place, an abandoned mine it was actually, and he suffered terribly from cold and hunger. Then one day he was sent to get water for the other prisoners and he made his escape, without shoes or a coat. He walked three hundred and fifty miles and rejoined Washington's army at Tappahanock. Without shoes..."

That had been his great-great-grandfather Eben Gardner, from the Nantucket branch of the family, for whom he'd been named. His grandfather George had fought at Bull Run and Antietam and had lost a hand at Cold Harbor, his great-granduncle James (on his mother's side) had commanded the frigate *Monadnock* under Farragut. His great-grandfather Joshua Lawring had set the record from the Pagoda Anchorage at Whampoa to Boston in the *Andromeda*, his grandfather Silas, an Alcock, had been the leading surgeon of his day at Peter Bent Brigham; his great-great-granduncle Phineas, who was an Endicott, had participated in the Boston Tea Party and had later fought at Saratoga, his great-great-granduncle Thomas had been part of the mission to Amiens, and had seen Napoleon crown himself emperor and watched the Sultan enter Constantinople in a golden palanquin. There was no end to all they had done. It was an august litany, long and thunderous, which had set his boy's mind dancing with nocturnal bonfires and sea-swept decks and the rattle of musketry—

"How is he taking it?"

He turned. His mother had nodded her head curtly in the direction of the kitchen downstairs, where Brian's voice could still be heard running on in a state of high excitement.

"Oh—all right, I guess. We didn't tell him any of the—the details."

"I should think not."

"He knows a man broke into the house and stole some money." He shifted his feet uncertainly. "To tell the truth I can't say exactly how much beyond that he *has* picked up." There was another bloodthirsty cry from the kitchen. "Not too much, I'd think. Most of it is fantasy. Cops and robbers."

"I'd imagine it hasn't been the most salutary influence for an inquisitive little boy. Men of that sort all over the house."

Lawring smiled. To his mother detectives occupied a twilit area on the outer peripheries of society; a pretty shady group, somewhere between dock workers and out-and-out thugs, men who wore their hats indoors and talked out of the side of their mouths and drank more than was good for them; an impression constructed largely from the Grade-B suspense films at rundown flea circuses like the Tremont and the Strand she was fond of going to at odd moments during her busy week. It was her one vice, she said, and she liked to indulge it.

"It's beyond me how you stand them," she said.

"Oh, they're all right. They're doing the best they can. It's a dreary life at best: a lot of boredom and some real danger and not much pay . . ." He turned and faced Mrs. Lawring directly. "I'm awfully grateful to you, Mother."

"My dear, it's nothing. Don't give it a moment's thought."

"I know it's a lot to ask of you. He *is* pretty lively."

"I'll keep up with him!" Her eyes glinted warmly. "I'll take him down to Brewster with me next week. He can play on the beach and go swimming, work off some of his energy."

"It'll just be for a short time. Just till camp opens. Janet's pretty worn down. She wanted to keep him but it didn't seem right, with the police and phone calls and God knows what else."

"Of course. It's high time the boy was out of that atmosphere. I wonder one of you didn't think of it sooner. He's so impressionable."

Lawring looked hard at his mother at this, but she was knitting along with placid persistence. By "impressionable" she meant weak, unstable—the implication here, reinforced by several years' allusions, was that Brian had taken after Janet, had inherited too much of his mother's volatile high spirits and not enough of his father's steady self-reliance. Janet's boy, not his. Lawring found himself frowning—his mother had a faculty for intimation that was as forbidding as any he knew—and wandered off aimlessly around the room. Bulfinch had built the house, and he'd built it the way he always did, lavishly and impeccably: front portal in the classic style, flanked by two graceful Ionic columns, the double keystone and recessed arches above the first floor windows; black marble fireplaces in all the rooms, fourteen-foot ceilings, and massive mahogany doors with silver butt hinges that still clicked shut with a soft snap of perfect finality after one hundred and sixty years. Shaded by the elms outside and the gate shutters within it was cool and so still you could hear the air hum about your ears . . . and the feeling descended gently around him as it had when he'd been a child: Nothing can harm you here. But that wasn't true, apparently;

not true at all. His mother could be sitting there, right where she was in the old rosewood rocker with its yellowed lace doilies, and some wild-eyed lunatic from Dorchester or the South End could slip in that door—

"You *are* careful, aren't you," he said suddenly. "Make sure all the doors and windows are locked, things like that."

"Ohhh..." She waved a hand at him. "There's nothing to worry about here, you know."

"There's something to worry about anywhere."

"Callahan wouldn't permit that sort of thing on the Hill."

He ran his hand along the fireplace mantel, reached down and picked up the fire tongs with their ugly little brass eagle and hefted them. She obviously believed that; that perhaps it was true—probably the very hoodlums and criminal psychopaths themselves *knew* Callahan wouldn't permit it. He himself had always believed the house was sacrosanct and perhaps he was the only dissident, even now...

"Just the same, you ought to be careful," he said.

His mother looked up at him—a glance of pure solicitude that moved him strangely, made the tears start to his eyes. He felt all of a sudden inundated by an immense billow of dejection and worry.

"I guess I better get on down to the office." But he did not move; remained standing there with the tongs hanging slack in his hand.

"My poor dear old fellow," Marcia Lawring said softly. "I'm so sorry. It's such a wretched nuisance..."

He laughed once and bobbed his head. "Yes. It's been all of that. All of that and then some."

"You look so tired, Gardy."

"I guess that's true."

It had been a long three days since Franz had reached him at Newport. The next morning early the press had camped in the driveway in force and assailed him with questions: Who did he think it was? What had his wife told him? Could they speak to her now? Did he know of anyone it might be—some discharged gardener or chauffeur, some neighbor with a grudge? Harassed and on edge from worry and lack of sleep he had answered them rather testily. Sam Rawlis was their gardener and had been with them for years; they'd never had a chauffeur, they drove their own cars—or tried to; their neighbors were responsible people; he didn't know anything more than they did, he was leaving the detection and apprehension of the culprit in the capable hands of the police—now was it all right if he went in town to do a day's work? Even then a nervous kid with a crew cut followed him to his car and leaned in the window.

"Mr. Lawring! Mr. Lawring, do you have a statement?"

"A *what?*"

"A statement—some general observation...?"

"Yes. When a dog is drowning, everybody on earth offers him a drink."

The kid ducked his head back, looking frightened; the laughter of the reporters floated after him down the drive.

But he hadn't been able to stand it at the office, either. He'd barely got his hat off when the parade of phone calls and personal condolences began to come in: interminable lamentations by the women, ill-advised attempts at levity by the comedians, philosophy by the thinkers, strained allusions and befuddled offers of assistance—nearly all of them marked by a fugitive pulse of excitement, fascination, something; an unmistakable magpie gleam. By two-thirty he couldn't endure any more of that and fled to Holcomb Hill, to find two detectives in gaudy shirts sitting in the living room reading magazines in the company of a bright, vigorous policewoman, whose duty it was to impersonate Janet on all incoming calls.

That had been how it had started. Janet continued to be wonderful about everything; she rode in to Boston to police headquarters in a squad car and went carefully through the files, and found no one who resembled the assailant. Reardon came out again and they discussed people she had seen over the previous several days, and who might have known Lawring had left. "But Gard just up and decided to go—he only made up his mind definitely that afternoon, didn't you, darling?" Janet protested. "There weren't any long-range plans about it at all..." Her face was pale and drawn, with deep blue crescents like smudges of coal dust under her eyes. Reardon kept pressing her. Had she remembered anything new about him, any physical characteristic, anything he had said? No, she couldn't recall anything...It was his *voice*, though—that was the thing she couldn't get out of her mind.

"His voice?"

"Yes. It—kept changing."

"Changing? How?"

"Well, it was soft and lazy and—you know, the way you hear Negroes talk . . . and then it wasn't. I mean it was *like* him but not exactly like him. More like a brother. When he was angry or—or excited it was different, then it was like a Negro kid I went to high school with in Somerville . . ."

They pricked up their ears at this. Could he resemble him, even faintly? Were there any Negro boys she remembered from school, or later? Think hard, now: this could be important.

On and on it went, hour after laborious hour. Harried and wan, Janet bore with it, and then threw herself into household chores with such vehemence that even Mrs. Pruitt would beg her to let up. At night she slept fitfully, even with sedation, and she jumped at the slightest sound. When she and Lawring were alone together she would invariably allude to her assailant's trip downstairs for the drink. "I had time to get to the phone, I can see now that I did—but it seemed so far away, Gard: so awfully far away . . ." And she would look at him with a fearful, importunate gaze. He would put his arm around her then, enfold her in his solid bulk as though to shield her from her own thoughts; but there was nothing he could say. She wanted him to give his approval to what she had done—or rather not done—and he gave it gladly, with all his heart . . . but it was an empty offering: she had been there and he had not.

What was disconcerting to him was an air of abstraction that would occasionally possess her. She would all at once stare into space, as though she had just been arrested by some entrancing, half-caught melody no one else could hear, or as though she had recalled something so compelling it had drawn her right out of herself. When he asked her if she had remembered something from that night she would start, and shake her head, and go on pressing the name tapes on Brian's camp clothes. No, she hadn't remembered anything . . .

"Do you know what you ought to do, Gardy?" his mother was saying to him now. "You ought to go upstairs to your old room and nap for about two hours. Go ahead." She tossed her head toward the staircase. "Go on up. I won't tell on you."

He smiled. "I couldn't sleep. Anyway, it's out of the question; I'm swamped with work."

"It'll keep."

"Mother! Are you trying to tempt me into malingering?"

She shied a hand at him. "Nonsense. If I thought you were malingering I'd tell you so quick enough. Don't you think I would?"

"I certainly do." They watched each other a moment in silence, smiling faintly, thinking their own thoughts. Then, to thrust his mind away from its own rather unpleasant course he said: "By the way. While Brian's with you I wonder if you'd mind keeping one ear cocked for anything he might let drop about his trip to the Gratiots'. Particularly before we left."

Marcia Lawring's face became blank with surprise. "Why? What on earth for?"

"Well, it would be whether he might have told anyone at school or in town about the trip. The police are convinced the offender must have known we would both be away."

His mother looked down at her work, crossly. "I see. So the answer is to try and pump *clues* out of a little boy. Those detectives." Her needles clashed like sabers. "Haven't the intelligence to do their own sleuthing, I suppose."

"Mother, they're doing all they can..."

"I'm sure they are. Sitting around with their hats on and their feet up on someone else's desk, hanging around in smelly bars till all hours." She fastened her eyes on her son and said, "Gardy, you're taking entirely too deferential an attitude about this business, entirely too passive."

He laughed uncomfortably. "What would you have me do—take down my trusty shooting iron and track the blackguard down through the wilds of Roxbury?"

"You can laugh if you like, but it's true. They have no intention of solving this case."

"And why is that?"

"They've had three days and they haven't found him or anyone who even looks like him."

"My God, three days—"

"Sitting around playing cards and betting on the horses with taxpayers' money. I'd like to give that Reardon a piece of my mind."

"You would."

"I certainly would. Blabbing to the newspapers every time you turn around. Why didn't he keep this whole affair confidential? Disgusting. They can do it if they want to, don't tell me they can't. I'm afraid he doesn't realize who he's dealing with, here."

"He's been more than considerate, he's been—"

"What does anybody care what *he* thinks? Telling the reporters all about that jacket of yours—how do they think they'll ever recover it if they tell all of Boston about it? Does he think criminals don't read the papers?"

"Maybe you ought to fire Reardon and conduct the investigation all by yourself," Lawring offered, but there was an edge in his voice and he knew his mother had caught it. She nodded her head curtly and said:

"Well. I'd give him a few things to ponder. If he thinks we're to be trifled with, he'll find he's very much mistaken."

She could do it too, he knew: she could frighten that tall, bland man with twenty well-chosen words. She was an Alcock, and when it came to the sticking place she possessed a will of iron. There had been the time, soon after the war, when someone in the city government had sought to take up the brick sidewalks on Beacon Hill and replace them with concrete slab. The Society for the Preservation of Beacon Hill met and drew up a measured protest; to no avail. The city said the brick sidewalks were obsolete and they were dangerous: they were slippery in wet weather, people fell because of them and broke their hips, ice collected in the low places and the roots of trees raised them in ridges people tripped on. They were menaces. Concrete was safer and more modern. But they did not *want* concrete, the Society replied; true, people did slip on them now and then but they were an integral part of the character of the Hill and it was the feeling of the Society that they should stay as they were.

The second letter was ignored. A date was set, and a schedule for the removal, and on a gray, bitter February morning the trucks came, led by a contractor, a huge, dough-faced man with the voice of a bull—to find Marcia Lawring and a score of other ladies sitting on those brick sidewalks, wrapped in blankets, knitting and chatting together. The contractor was amused, then perplexed. He tried to reason with them. Didn't they realize this was a civic ordinance? Yes, they knew all about that, Marcia Lawring assured him; but they were staying where they were: they had meant what they said. The contractor left and reported to City Hall. The author of this pattern of progress, snug in his heated office, glanced over his shoes at the gelid clouds beyond the window and laughed genially.

"Donnelly, it's seventeen degrees outside. Didn't you know that? Take the boys over to Morrissey's and have a beer. A few old ladies—let them have their fun. They won't be out there long..."

When Donnelly came back two hours later and found there were still more ladies perched on the bricks he got angry. He had his orders, he told them loudly, and he was a man who carried them out, come what may. Now they had better get out of the way and get along home or somebody might get hurt. Because those bricks were coming up and they were coming up now. And he shouted at his crew to get going. At that moment Marcia Lawring put down her knitting needles and fixed him with those cold, gray-blue clipper captain's eyes of hers and said: "Young man, I advise you most strongly not to lay a single finger on any one of us. My lawyer is Minot L. Hough of Truslow, Witt and Hough and he is sitting in his office right now, waiting for his telephone to ring. Do you know what constitutes a battery in the Commonwealth of Massachusetts? I'll explain it to you." And she did.

The gang went away, over toward Cambridge Street this time. The day turned colder still—skies of metallic gray and a wind like a voice from the tomb; the kind of day of which country people like to say knowingly that it's too cold to snow. Donnelly phoned City Hall again, encountered ridicule and facetious advice, had lunch, and came back around two to find still more ladies sitting on the bricks with their backs against the house fronts—on Mount Vernon, Chestnut, Pinckney, West Cedar. They were everywhere. They were sipping tea and hot chocolate from Thermos bottles and now and then calling back and forth to each other like celebrants at some bizarre class reunion.

At three-thirty Donnelly had given up and called off the operation. At four Gardner, coming back from Widener Library, gasping with cold and with the high collar of his service overcoat up around his ears, spotted his mother and gazed at her as if he'd never seen her before. He went into the house and conferred with Mrs. Pruitt, went back out again and said:

"Mother, have you any idea what the temperature is right now? It's fourteen degrees above zero."

"I'm perfectly comfortable. We all are." She had a scarf wound around her head and her face was pinched and white with cold, but her lips were a fine, firm line. "Gardy, you know how I feel about leaving a thing half-finished."

"But it's after four," he pleaded. He was pounding his gloved hands against his thighs to force feeling back into them. "You've made your point..."

"The point to be *made* is to make it clear to that thoroughly disagreeable person and those behind him that we are quite serious about this matter of our sidewalks."

Back in the house Lawring became alarmed and phoned Miss Hewes, his father's secretary, and finally induced her—much against her will—to call him out of a board meeting.

"She's what? you say she's doing what?" Thomas Lawring shouted.

"Sitting on the *sidewalk* in front of the house..."

"—Gardner, this is a poor time to try pulling my leg."

"I wish to hell I were. I've been out there talking to her—I can't do a thing with her."

There was a short pause. "God damn," his father said. "God damn!...All right. I'll be up there as soon as I can. You tell her to come in out of that unless she wants Frank Shippard to take off all her fingers and toes."

By the time Thomas Lawring had got up from State Street the protest had broken up into little knots of women, draped in shawls and car blankets and the barbaric, ancient pelts of sleigh robes, who shook hands and dispersed, calling cheery farewells. Tomorrow, then. Yes, tomorrow, same time. Good night. Good night...

That evening Marcia Lawring was jubilant. They had a rib roast and potatoes persillés and parsnips and afterward she sat down at the Chickering and played with all her old verve, heavy chords and flowery right-hand trills, her elbows turned out awkwardly in the style of the Polish pianist who had taught her thirty years before.

"We have fought the good fight," she proclaimed, and her eyes twinkled. "We have met the enemy and they are ours!"

"You're a born fool, Marcia," Thomas Lawring said.

"You could have caught your certain death out there. You realize that, don't you?"

"But lamb," she retorted gaily, "it's the principle of the thing!"

"You could have perished from frostbite. *Sidewalks!*" —and he snapped the evening *Traveler* open like a pistol shot; but his voice all the same was touched with awe...

Lawring gazed at the high-backed Hitchcock chair his father had always sat in. Nobody to Lawring's knowledge had ever sat in it since his death, which made it easy to imagine Thomas Endicott Lawring still there, legs crossed, reading the papers— he devoured the *Traveler*, the *Wall Street Journal* and the *New York Times* every day without fail—with predatory disapproval. What would he have thought of this choice piece of tabloid violence? Even to his son it was like an unpleasant dream—all the more disturbing because he had not been there when it had happened. Peering out at the strange cars perched in his driveway, the detective hunched over the tracing device on the telephone extension in the kitchen, he had found himself feeling that in some odd way it was *he* who had been assaulted, overpowered and degraded. That a man, a sex fiend or whatever he was, had calmly entered his house, had walked up those stairs and ravished his wife in his own bed—it was impossible, utterly and unthinkably impossible... It couldn't happen, he thought for the hundredth time in three days, it simply could not happen—and it would not have happened if we had lived here; the way Peg and I did...

"What are you thinking?"

He started to say something, stopped himself and let his fingers tick along the dentils on the mantel cornice.

"Well, it's true, Gardy. You know it is."

His mother's eyes were quite calm—one might have called them placid were it not for the hint of force in them, that unquestioning assertiveness. She believes that, he told himself angrily, she's so set in her ways she can actually believe something as ridiculous as that...and yet, scowling at the Hitchcock chair with its hard, thin back rungs and the worn gilt acanthus leaves on its arms, he knew that something in him believed it, too.

"That's ridiculous," he said aloud. "—it could happen

anywhere, absolutely anywhere at all . . ."

Marcia Lawring shook her head. "They say cities are so dangerous nowadays. I can tell you right now I feel a good deal safer here than in some wild country area like yours."

"Yes, well . . ." He didn't want to quarrel with her. He was tired, he felt troubled in a way he had never been in all his life, and he didn't want to be at loggerheads with her—he wanted to bask, even if only briefly, in the sense of impervious solidity this shadowy, high-vaulted room exuded. "Well, you know Janet didn't want to live here," he added as if in extenuation.

"Yes, I know."

"She's never felt at ease in this house."

"Of course she hasn't. How on earth could she?"

"Look, Mother . . ."

"It has nothing to do with hurt feelings," she broke in on him. "Or what I might want. It's a matter of values, of what's right for *you*."

"—But *she's* right for me!" he burst out. "That's all that really matters . . ." He snapped the tongs together irritably. Arguments with his mother had a habit of running away from him like this, almost without his noticing—he was like a powerful swimmer in the middle of a tidal run, struggling mightily, even skillfully at times, but nevertheless borne inexorably out to sea. "I know you've never liked Janet," he asserted. "But if you could have seen her these past few days—the sheer courage and—and sweetness—"

"On the contrary. I like Janet a very great deal, I've always thought she was a fine girl. I'm only sorry you married her."

He made a little sound of displeasure. "Well," he said grimly, "I married her."

"I'm aware of that, Gardy." She paused, and he knew pretty much what was coming next. "I think you bore up splendidly after Margaret's death." She wagged her head and gazed out of the window as though she'd lost the thread of what she wanted to say. "A terrible, terrible loss. That poor girl . . ." She went on knitting again. "It's only that I always felt when you *did* remarry it ought to be someone from your own class, our own background. I told you that at the time, you remember."

"Indeed I do."

"It's a question of rearing. Two people can't see an incident in the same light when their upbringing, their standards and attitudes, are too divergent."

"For God's sake, Jan's not a Cambodian!" He gave an exasperated laugh and stamped on the hearth. "Well, I married her," he repeated. "And we love each other. And she's been—well, more wonderful than I would have ever believed possible."

There was a little silence. Watching his mother's face Lawring felt a sharp twinge of despondency. Nobody influences anybody, he thought heavily; nobody convinces anyone of anything, we're all born thinking one certain set of things and we go through life without a change, come hell or high water. What a waste . . . He felt his mother's eyes upon him; they were wide and clear and very blue, the way they always were whenever she was about to say something she deemed important. How clear that gaze was!—as though she had never in all her life run upon the murk of doubt that turns the baffled eye in upon the nature seeking to guide it . . .

"I know, everyone thinks that's all a lot of musty old claptrap now, absurd aristocratic standards," Marcia Lawring said; she put the needles together and rolled her knitting up in a tight ball and set it beside her. "One standard is all the rage now. Togetherness. The only trouble is, one standard means no standard at all. *Snob*—it's become such a pejorative term. Why should it be? What's wrong with being a snob? We're all snobs about something or other—books, cars, moving pictures, horticulture. Discrimination, is all it means: having standards and holding to them, disliking what falls below them and causes us to become less than we are . . ." She ran the fingers of one hand over the back of the other slowly, finger over finger. "It's the same thing with human relationships. Your father and I didn't always see eye to eye on everything, we had our differences of course, that's natural enough—but we understood each other perfectly. We were trained to each other's responses. Each of us always knew where the other one stood."

The telephone rang in the downstairs hall and she got to her feet with alacrity. "That's important. It's what you had with Margaret. Traditions, background, unanimity of view—you can't violate things like these, Gardy. We weren't meant to. Eskimoes and Hottentots, Chinese and Australians—you don't mix them all up in a kettle, like some mulligatawny stew..."

"It doesn't seem to me to be a question of that," he said quietly.

Eunice called from the foot of the stairs: "Mrs. Lawring, it's Mrs. Ryder on the phone about the Garden Club luncheon..."

"All right. Tell her to hold on a minute, I'll be right down.—You're one thing, Gardy," she said, and pointed a finger at him as though to fix him in that spot before the mantel. "You're that one thing and you *know* that's what you are. You shouldn't try to be a dozen other things. Whenever a person cuts against his grain the result, you'll find, is inevitably trouble."

"Mrs. Lawring," Eunice called again, "she says it isn't absolutely necessary to talk with you, she just wants to know if the arrangements have been made for the caterer yet..."

"I'm coming, tell her I'm coming right down!" Marcia Lawring made a brusque little gesture with one hand—half irritation, half demurral, said: "This is silly and to no purpose. You know how terribly sorry I am about the whole business, Gardy... I've got to answer this." She went out of the room.

He stood there in the cool, blued light listening to the hiss of an occasional car, his mother's voice on the telephone, Brian chattering away in the kitchen. There were a thousand things he wanted to say to his mother—that her ideas of caste were outmoded and absurd in a world which was fragmenting before their very eyes, dispersed in fluid motion like the atoms in a glass of water. There were other standards, weren't there?— contributions which other races and traditions had to offer that weren't exactly despicable, below consideration—and what in hell did all that have to do with this present crisis, anyway? He and Janet had loved each other for ten years, had lived in a kind of harmony his mother couldn't in all probability have known anything about...

He had to get back to work. He thrust the tongs back into their rack; they fell on the black marble apron with a clatter and he bent over quickly, afraid he had chipped the stone. No: it was all right. He replaced them and went down the stairs and out through the gloomy hall to the kitchen where Brian was sitting at the round table eating a plateful of chocolate chip cookies and talking a blue streak to Eunice.

"—and then he jumped up on the sun deck railing and he

said, 'All right, you rats—come and get me!' So the detectives said, 'Okay buddy, you asked for it!' and they drew their revolvers and let him have it—pow! pow! bee-YOWWW— that's a ricochet—and the crook grabbed his stomach, just like this, and *eeeeooooo!* —off the sun deck railing right into the pool. Ker*plosh.* And it turned all red with blood . . ." He looked up brightly at Lawring. "Hi, Dad. And there he was bobbing up and down there in the pool and the cops kept pumping bullets into him . . ."

"That right," Eunice answered automatically, from the stove. She was a heavy woman with wildly disordered hair and great sad eyes, and she had had a hard life. Both her sons had been killed in the war and her husband was an alcoholic. "Fancy that, now."

"When did all that happen, Boo?"

"Just yesterday—yesterday morning. I was telling Eunice all about it. The crook they shot in the pool. Wait'll I see Callahan!"

"Well, he's got a lively imagination if nothing else," he said to Eunice.

"No, it happened, it really happened—I was *there*!"

Lawring picked up a cookie and ate it. "You know, Boo . . . there's a difference between what we *want* to have happen and what *really* happens." He eyed his son askance. "We've been over that a bit, haven't we?"

"Oh sure," Brian answered, but his voice was subdued.

"It's okay to tell stories—you know, the way you and Mummy and Franz do evenings—as long as we know they *are* stories and don't confuse them with what's actually going on. Right?" He felt suddenly foolish, remembering Hoffman and Murphy sitting there in the living room with their .38's on their belts, and the rather sinister flurry of activity every time the phone rang. Where did one leave off and the other begin? Lawring reached out and tousled the boy's hair, then all at once drew him close and hugged him.

"Be a good boy, now," he said. Brian nodded, his mouth full of cookies. "Remember, Grandma is older than Mummy and Dad and she's not quite so rambunctious."

"We're going down to Brewster tomorrow!"

"That's great. It'll be good swimming. I'll give you a ring in a day or so, see how you're making out."

"Sure, Dad." The boy looked up at him again—that quick, wide-eyed, utterly honest glance; just like Janet. "Is Mummy going to the hospital?"

"No, she's not going to the hospital. What gave you that idea?"

"I just thought she might be going to."

"No, she's just very tired and upset and she needs a rest. That's all." Eunice was watching him out of her sad, drooping eyes, her mouth turned down in measureless despondency, as though Janet were dying of cancer and he were lying outrageously to his son; and it irritated him. "Don't worry about things, now," he said to Brian. "Remember what I told you about turning into a worry-wart."

"Okay, Dad."

He patted the boy on the head again, nodded to Eunice and left. His mother was still on the telephone and he bent over and kissed her on the cheek and she nodded goodbye and gave him an apologetic smile. The front door closed after him firmly. He turned right and started up toward the State House, then for no reason at all went down Walnut Street and entered the Common through the Winthrop Gate, passed the tablet to the Oneida football team, whose goal was never crossed—and to his great surprise found himself walking more and more rapidly, despite the June heat, down the long slope, with the Soldiers' and Sailors' Monument high on his left, toward the Public Garden; away from the office, the drawings for Siegersen and the meeting with Cullen and Dyer, away from all the appointments and obligations that pressed against his mind. What the devil was the matter with him? Where was he bound? His legs had taken control of him, he had crossed Charles Street, was drifting past Edward Everett Hale standing in his little alcove with his slouch hat hanging at his side, looking hollow-eyed and disillusioned with the world; on over the bridge across the pond, where the swan boats made their stately processional, the little girls' dresses like a gaudy patchwork quilt against the blue water; on past banks of tulips cunningly portraying hearts, a minute man, Old Glory, and the bronze statue of George Washington on his horse looking very resolute and proud, the kind of commander you'd like to serve with if you had your choice, and beneath whose shadow pre-school children played tag or pushed little toy cars while their governesses sat and watched over them serenely.

Boston, where nothing changed. Across Arlington and on out the Commonwealth Avenue mall, perspiring lightly now in the hot, damp southwest breeze, past Alexander Hamilton gazing ahead implacably, straight as steel, in breeches and hose; past Colonel John Glover, his employer's forebear and the hero of the Delaware crossing, his foot on a cannon and his sword drawn, his cloak hanging off one shoulder, his expression parrot-like and audacious, the kind of man who loved a fight; on toward William Lloyd Garrison, looking shabby and dome-headed, his nose like the prow of a ship, sitting in his leather-upholstered chair amid law tomes and a welter of spilled papers. *I am in earnest; I will not equivocate; I will not excuse; I will not retreat a single inch and I will be heard.* He knew it by heart, he had committed it to memory when he was ten, or eleven, and there it lay now, facing him in its thunderous defiance.

He had started to walk on again when he saw the man. Thin and dark, moving with that indolent, springy Negro's walk, snap-brim hat with a wide orange band, his lips moving very slowly, as if he were reciting poetry; coming straight toward him down the mall. Lawring stopped and let him come to him. He stared hard at the slender figure, whose eyes rolled out at him in sudden alarm. At that moment Lawring saw the carefully trimmed mustache, thin as a crayon line, and a broken front tooth. The Negro was singing "Blue Moon," almost inaudibly. He moved on by. A furled-up newspaper stuck out of his hip pocket. At the back of his shirt collar was a button, blue as a pearl, that glinted in the sunlight.

Lawring cleared his throat. He was sweating heavily now, and his neck felt sticky under his collar. This was ridiculous. What was he to do—run up to every thin Negro in a straw hat he saw in the city of Boston and slap a citizen's arrest on him? He was acting like a paranoid. At the foot of Garrison's statue some English sparrows shrilled and scuffled in the dirt. Rooted in confusion he stood there and looked around him slowly. Old men sat on the benches here, hands cupped over malacca canes, nurses off duty giggled and chatted amiably and a dog, a scruffy little black brute of a dog, sniffled at the base of an elm, hiked up

a hind leg awkwardly and squirted the rough gray bark. Life
went on, went on all around him: children played tag or
hopscotch on the smooth earth surface of the mall, his mother
laid plans for the Beacon Hill Garden Club luncheon, dogs peed
against tree trunks and nursemaids gossiped about their love
affairs and dreamed of making a good marriage or a guided tour
to Paris. Life went on, as though no filthy pervert in a snap-brim
straw hat and dark glasses had ever cut the screen in the
Andersen casement to Mrs. Pruitt's room and walked stealthily
up the stairs to the bedroom where his wife—

He drew his grandfather's bone-handled jackknife out of his
pocket and held it in his hand, tightly, chafing the bone ridges
with his thumbnail. Well: it happened, of course. It happened all
around you; radios shouted it, the tabloids shrieked it in block
letters from all the paper stalls downtown. ROXBURY WOMAN
RAPED. DEDHAM MATRON FOUND ON DUNES. SEEK MELROSE
SLAYER. Complete with illustrations. It went on, the assaults and
thefts and murders and we simply paid no attention to them,
that was all. It was a fact of life but it didn't concern *us*—it
always happened to other people, the lower orders, fools and
drunks and the hapless; this nasty, unclean sort of thing...

He turned back at Garrison's statue, walked north along
Dartmouth until he reached Storrow Drive; climbed the ramp
and leaning on the concrete balustrade of the overpass peered
down at the hurrying wolf packs of cars. They seemed very near,
hurtling along, creating their own world of motion; for an
instant Lawring had the unpleasant sensation that he was
rushing forward, diving down into them, about to crash against
their oncoming steel bodies. He turned away, watched two
workmen sitting in an unframed window aperture at the back of
a building on Beacon Street, talking. One of them dropped a
candy wrapper; it went swirling and fluttering down through the
warm air, dipped out of sight behind a board fence.

If only I'd been home, he thought; if only I'd been there ... Of
course anyone would have said—in fact several of them, friends
and associates, *had* said it to him: It could have happened to
anybody, a thing like that. To which he could only answer, or
want to answer: Yes—but it happened to us, to my wife and to
me. It had happened to him, that was the rock he could not get
around, and it lay like a poisonous blight on his spirit, sickened

and baffled and depressed him. If only, my God, if only he'd been home—even if he'd been killed he would at least have been there to defend his wife and hearth; and not have to hear the wretched tale from over the telephone, eighty-odd miles away ...

"I wasn't ready," he said aloud, watching again the mesmeric pour of cars. "I wasn't ready for something like this."

He crossed the overpass and strolled out along the Esplanade past the lagoon, sat down finally in one of the settees and stared vacantly at the sails dipping and slanting and cutting across each other like gay little paper cutouts in the Paris blue of the Basin. The conversation back at Mount Vernon Street was still troubling him and he chafed at it, as one morbidly picks at a blister. What had she been trying to say? that he and Janet were incompatible, that something like this was inevitable because Janet came from a shabby frame house in Somerville? Nonsense ... He thought of Peg—the grave, dutiful, determined face, the young boy's eyes, that funny little way she had of ducking her head when she walked. Traditions, unanimity of view, sure—but there had been none of the magic he'd known with Janet, nothing remotely like that swift little catch in the throat, a constriction that was almost like pain, that he could feel coming upon Janet unexpectedly, shopping or in the street ... He clamped his arms together and stared at his shoes. He felt stunned, profoundly dislocated—as though he had fallen asleep and awakened in another century, another hemisphere. All the events of the past hundred hours had about them nothing he could take hold of; they had nothing to do with what he had been taught happened to you in your life ...

He had been very fortunate, and he'd been taught some valuable things. He had been born to wealthy parents, of an illustrious ancestry, endowed with a powerful physique and a steady, cheerful nature. He had been taught early that success is the fruit of unremitting effort, that rewards are earned in this world as well as in the other, that one had a moral obligation to the work one elected; that in this world there are those who lead and those who follow, and that he was one of the class that was ordained to lead, to be the movers and shakers. Beyond that too, there was a causality to our existence: for those who lived soberly and wisely, good came; on those who passed their days in sloth or debauchery, ruin was visited. His father—lean, spare, erect as a ramrod, whose eyes under his thick, dark brows flashed like uncompromising beacons; who rose at six o'clock, even on Sunday, took a cold shower and walked up this same Esplanade to the Massachusetts Avenue Bridge and back before breakfast—his father, with his many positions of trust and authority in business, their church, civic committees, had exemplified these doctrines; but it was his mother who, in her quiet, persistent way, had articulated them. They were of the class that was to lead: that was how it had always been and would undoubtedly, God willing, continue to be—but there were obligations inherent in leadership, demands which were not to be shirked or evaded or ignored. They were the rules, the codes his kind of man always lived by. It was the Yankee tradition, and he was a Yankee.

He was sent to St. Mark's, where he was a good athlete and a better than average student, and then to Harvard, where he did even better; he made the Dean's List his sophomore year, became a varsity letterman in football and hockey, and began to give scope to that early passion for architecture which had so greatly pleased his mother—her Granduncle Rodney had littered half the towns of northern New England with Greek temples and Gothic spires nearly a century before. The Second World War came along in his junior year and gave him a good shock. He was lolling around with several thousand other college undergraduates in an army specialist training program in Iowa, marching to classes and drinking beer and swapping collegiate names and reminiscences, when all at once they were whisked out and away with dizzying speed to Norfolk, to Cherbourg, to a dismal, rain-soaked replacement depot east of Paris, and one chilly night found themselves in full combat gear, walking in column down a road powdered with light snow. The sound of artillery fire was disquietingly near. At the edge of a wood they were told to take off their packs and overcoats. They obeyed. They were then ordered to advance and engage the enemy and they began to walk forward slowly, ducking the branches, glancing at each other out of the corners of their eyes.

They had no idea at all where they were. The last road marker anyone had seen had said *Pessoux—12 km* and their sergeant, a dour, forbidding veteran of the Normandy landing named

Holzapfel, had glared at their incessant questions and said: "You're in Belgium. That's where all European wars are decided. Now shut up." They walked on through the woods, their teeth chattering, shouting and firing their rifles until they were nearly hysterical, giggling and cursing at each other, blundering about in thickets and stepping on one another's heels. There was a clearing then, gray under the starless December sky, and they began to move out across it—and without warning there was a curtain of violent orange fire from the far edge of the wood, flares began to float down like fireworks in a nightmare, and gripping the cold hard earth with all his might Lawring could hear the bark and clatter of tank engines warming up. A boy named Martin was hit and began to scream incoherently, flailing about on the stubble, and several others around Lawring jumped to their feet and left their rifles and ran. Were they pulling out? Was he all alone? There were confused, discordant cries and wails of anguish, the world was screwed tight with flame and shock and the brimstone stink of cordite, and in one terrible lull in the firing he heard someone shouting in German: a clear, steady voice that filled him with dread.

His training held, though; his training and his upbringing. He kept his head and hung on; he maintained a steady stream of fire on the dancing hobgoblin shapes at the wood's edge, he got help for Martin and steadied some of the other replacements near him. He was emptied of his initial fear as completely as an overturned pail; he felt calm and strong and indomitable. He could hardly believe his good fortune. A tank left the safety of the woods and he and Holzapfel hit it with two rounds from a bazooka and disabled it. Finally the German fire slacked off and they were pulled back; he gave someone else his rifle and dragged Martin back with them. When they attacked next day they carried the little rise and the wood; and later they learned that this was the deepest penetration the Germans had made in the Battle of the Bulge, this open slope near Havelange, four miles from the Meuse.

They went into Germany that winter. He was offered a field commission after Hexenbach and accepted it. He had never been in doubt about the outcome of the war: they, the Allies, were morally in the right, and therefore they would prevail. In Germany he was occasionally disturbed by some of the people who were reinstated in municipal authority, but how could you tell who had been a Nazi and who hadn't? and besides, it was none of his affair, he was not in Military Government. Many of his comrades-in-arms trafficked in government property and otherwise behaved in ways he did not always approve, but he was no prude, he was ready enough to indulge them. There were more than enough equipment and supplies to go around—and they would be consigned to rust soon enough, he knew. His men had suffered a great deal in the Siegfried Line battles, and if this was how they chose to reap their rewards he had no strenuous objection.

What did undergo a sea change was his attitude toward what Kipling had called "the lesser breeds," what his mother referred to as "other people," and what he had once heard his father, in a moment of choler, designate as "the great unwashed." His closest friend and fellow officer was an Oklahoma farmer, his platoon sergeant (who had saved his life during the Rhine crossing) a West Virginia coal miner, and he knew they were both better infantry leaders than he was: more resourceful, as competent, and with a far better sense of terrain. Maybe they hadn't been born to lead, as his mother implied he had been, but they had nonetheless acquired the faculty readily enough. Heroes—if there really were heroes—were made not born, it seemed. And Mac and Andy were a lot livelier company than most of the favored few he had known at home and at school; he came to feel deeply at ease with them, more than he would have believed possible.

Meanwhile the Pacific drama of this great moral struggle was still dragging on. He put in for redeployment, got it, and was at embarkation point in San Francisco when the Japanese surrendered. He went out and got mildly drunk—he felt he deserved at least that, amid so much wild rejoicing—met a charming little Wave officer at a party on Telegraph Hill and had a swift, lively affair with her that was more release than passion; and a month later he requested discharge. It had been a short and violent war for him, with a minimum of waiting and lots of excitement and new vistas. He had strolled beneath the plane trees on the Champs Elysées and stood in the great cathedral at Aachen; a German field marshal had surrendered to him personally; he had helped stem the last Wehrmacht offensive at the Meuse and he had shaken the hand of a Russian sergeant on the bank of the Elbe—so he could in a sense say he had taken part in the great ebb and flow of history for his time. The Forces for Good were victorious, the Four Freedoms were still intact.

He returned wildly eager to get back to work, press on to the fulfillment of those dreams that had haunted his imagination ever since childhood—that vision of soaring white towers, the stark miracle of mass thrust upon space and wedded to it: a desire vainglorious and humble, a simple urgency which flowed back to that antediluvian day the first human creature had falteringly placed one stone upon another. The sudden glimpse of a graceful spire or a perfectly proportioned building could make his heart leap in wonder. He wanted to throw up whole monuments of light, structures invested with a dramatic simplicity and a dedicated craftsmanship that would proclaim their own order and majesty for a score of lifetimes. In Europe this had become an obsession. Plodding through the icy wreckage of the Ruhr he was appalled at the devastation, the shattering of beautifully ordered space. It sickened him. He had helped call down destruction on these towns, reduced them to hideous filigrees of blackened iron and gray rubble. Now that was at an end; now he would build, and with a vengeance.

He re-enrolled in college in the February semester in 1946, graduated magna cum laude and went on to the Graduate School of Design, where Gropius praised his work for combining a remarkable lyric inventiveness with commendable adherence to classic structural principles. After a year of study with Mies van der Rohe in Chicago he joined the Boston firm of Glover, Sherriffe and Ball. His rise was very rapid. He possessed that immensely rare union of honesty and a charming disposition, he was as good as his word (or tried to be, which in this age is often just as good—and in architectural circles even better); and even in Boston he was known as a bear for hard work. When he was thirty he won the hard-fought competition for the Boston University Administration Building, three years later old Glover gave him the new court house, and the year after that he was invited to sit on the Urban Renewal and Expressway Commissions. He had fulfilled much of that destiny he could read in mother's calm gray eyes—but in the process he had been thrust away from a really creative use of space. The firm was too big, the stakes had become too high; the compromises and deals had crept in relentlessly, more than he could ever have imagined. Here he was now, saddled with a public relations job with architectural trimmings, he wasn't *building* any more—was that why he was having so much trouble with the Siegersen house? He was forgetting how to build...

Conscious now of laughter he looked up. Two boys of fourteen or so in jeans and T-shirts were throwing stones out into the Basin and laughing; and following the trajectory of the stones Lawring saw the mallard duck. One wing dragging in the water, it paddled furiously about, its neck outstretched, only to be brought up short by the water geyser of a stone; turning then in consternation, its little body rocking with its desperate exertions. One stone struck right beside the bird, a splash bright as quicksilver, the duck squawked in alarm, and Lawring rose up from the bench and advanced on the boys in a fury, shouting:

"Cut that out now, do you hear? Lay off that bird—can't you see it's hurt?"

They turned and gaped at him in surprise. Thin and wiry, overlong shocks of wild black hair—Italian; North End kids. One of them was grinning at him.

"Go on, God damn it, clear out of there!" Lawring roared; he walked toward them, scowling, waving one arm. "Come on—now beat it!"

The boys fled, off down the mall; their eyes slanted toward him blackly, full of hate. Watching their flight Lawring took out his handkerchief and mopped his face. An old gentleman in white trousers was gazing at him in astonishment from the little bridge at the end of the lagoon. Jesus, he thought, I'm getting loony, I'm beginning to act like Grandpa Endicott, shouting at people, waving my arms; taking the world by the ear and setting it straight... Beyond the stone embankment the wounded mallard was still swimming in nervous little circles.

I've got to go back to work.

He jammed the handkerchief in his hip pocket, turned and started back down the Esplanade toward Arlington Street with a slow, resolute stride.

Chapter Five

The man was standing with his back to Janet Lawring. He was tall and very thin, and wearing a snap-brim straw hat and a light tan waist-length jacket which was badly stained with sweat around the collar. A detective named Harry Esselyn was talking to him with quiet persistence and the man seemed to sway away from the detective when he spoke, as though his voice held an actual physical force.

"How about it?" Esselyn was saying. "Holcomb Hill, Wellesley, Needham—you know those places, don't you, you been out there a lot, haven't you?"

"No, sir," the suspect answered, and the straw hat swung slowly as he shook his head. "No, I never been out there, I wouldn't even know how to *get* out there, I swear I wouldn't . . ." A fearful, wary denial. Then Esselyn moved toward her, still talking, and the man turned so that he was in full profile: sallow, dusty face, faintly hooked nose a little like an Arab's, cheekbones knotted high under the eyes as though they were bruised and swollen, a Negro—and the little hot wire dancing up and down inside Janet's belly and breast stopped all at once. A sudden, inexplicable wave of relief swept over her. She stepped back from the one-way glass aperture and said:

"That's not the man. "

"You're sure, now," Reardon answered. His smoky amber eyes were watching her intently; he looked a little like a boy in a parlor game who knows where the object is hidden and is trying hard not to give it away.

"Yes. I'm very sure."

"Take your time, Mrs. Lawring. He's tall, he's thin . . ."

"He's too tall," she said. "I'd remember him if he were that tall."

"He's wearing one of those straw hats."

"Yes, and it's just like the one *he* was wearing." She gave the trace of a smile. "But he isn't the one."

"You're quite sure, now. He fits your description..."

"A little, yes."

"You never really got a good look at him, you admit that."

"I know..." She felt awkward standing here rejecting all of Reardon's arguments, like an obstinate child; but it was clearly not her assailant. She felt perfectly calm again, and tired; her heart wasn't even pounding. "I'm sorry, Inspector. But I know it's not the man."

"Is this Mr. Lawring's coat, would you say?"

Astonished she stared at the jacket Reardon had in one of his big hands now, was offering her. It was unbelievably dirty, as though it had been dragged along the floor of an empty coal bin and then left to soak for days in a swamp. One sleeve looked as if something heavy had run over it, like a truck tire, and the buttons were all gone from the breast and cuffs. She folded it so that the inside breast pocket was exposed, and turned it back. The patch of cloth with the wearer's name and address the firm of Brooks Brothers always put on their custom suits had been cut away; there was only the thread and a strip of cloth. She glanced at Reardon and then through the glass at the suspect, who was gesturing now with both hands and still talking to Esselyn; then she remembered and turned back the tail pleat and examined it closely.

"Yes, it's his," she said. "There's the patch. A cigarette burn. I did it, Gard hasn't smoked in years. He was awfully fond of it, so I took it to the Invisible Weavers, they do a terrific job. See? You can spot it on the reverse side easily."

Reardon smiled. "We know it's your husband's coat, Mrs. Lawring. We checked with Brooks Brothers. They keep a record of these things. I just wanted to see if you could identify it on your own."

"I see." Janet peered at the suspect again. "How did he get it?"

"He *says* he found it in a gutter on Columbus Avenue several nights ago. He pawned it in a hock shop out there. That's where we got the tip."

"But why are the buttons gone?"

Reardon shrugged. "Further effort to avoid identification.

See," he bent over and ran his thumb down the cloth, "he left part of the loop when he cut this one off. What were they, leather buttons?"

"Yes. A dark brown leather. Well, they darkened with time..."

There was a little pause while Reardon laid the coat over the back of a chair. His face was long with disappointment. He watched the suspect for a few moments absently, fingering the lobe of his ear. "I'd hate to give up on this too hastily, Mrs. Lawring. He still had the pawn ticket on him when we picked him up. And he fits your description so well."

"I know."

"He's got a record. Not a long one... Would you mind giving it just one more try? I hate to pass this up if there's any chance he might be the boy."

"All right—I'll look at him again..."

"Take your time. There's no hurry."

Troubled, harassed, she looked through the one-way mirror again. Esselyn had moved around so that it was his back now that was toward her and the suspect was at three-quarters. Esselyn was saying, a touch more sharply, "Come on now, don't be difficult, you might as well tell us the truth now as later," and the Negro was shaking his head and making low, inarticulate sounds of protest. Sweat was running down the sides of his face and his beard, though freshly shaved, glowed like a slick blue-black stain. He looked almost incoherent with fear. She started to step back and at that moment he burst out, "That *is* the truth, I don't know anybody in Holcomb Hill, I don't even know where it *is*, I found that coat on Columbus, I can show you the place, I never been in Holcomb Hill, I *swear*—" his voice high and thin, on the point of cracking, and he raised his right hand, palm out, beside his head, like a witness taking the oath—and at that instant she knew her assailant had not been a Negro: she knew it beyond question.

She stepped back from the window and turned to Reardon and said, tense with the discovery: "It wasn't a Negro at all. I know it."

Reardon blinked at her—a slow, massive dropping and raising of his lids, as though he'd been slapped. Then his head went back.

"It wasn't."

"No—I'm sure of it, now. There's no doubt in my mind."

"What—" He paused a moment and his eyes moved around the big room. Hoffman and Belanger came up to them then and glanced at Reardon. He looked back at them with an expression of acute distaste. "What makes you say that, Mrs. Lawring?"

"I don't know, exactly. But I'm sure. His hands," she went on rapidly, "they weren't a colored person's hands. His doing that just now, that gesture, reminded me."

"But you said he was dark . . ."

"He was."

"Well, then—"

"But not *that* dark . . ."

"Then he could have been a *light* Negro, light-complexioned, right?"

She shook her head vehemently. "No. It couldn't have been."

"I see." Reardon turned and called, "All right, Harry," and peered down at his hands, his big lips pursed. The other two detectives were looking at her strangely, their faces flat with surprise. They didn't believe her, it was obvious: none of them did. Oh, she *knew* it—they must believe her!

"I can't tell you how I know," she said, "but I do, I just do, I'm sure of it, there's no sense in looking at any more Negroes . . ."

She realized all this wasn't making too much sense and broke off in some confusion. There was a strained silence among the four of them. It was a long room, bleak and brown, with its floorboards scuffed bare and huge discolorations all over the walls, as though the misery and violence of fifty years had oozed, like sweat, from its pores. There were two long benches on opposing walls, and several desks and a couple of green metal lockers and that was all. A girl sat at the far end of one of the benches with her hands clenched on a shiny black purse, her face and body rigid with dread. Two detectives Janet did not know were standing beside one of the desks, matching coins. She felt vaguely sick. The sad, mean squalor of the place, its almost palpable atmosphere of callousness and despair, and now this Negro on the other side of the glass who was being held there and purposely baited so that she could observe him in his mounting fear, turned her stomach. She could feel perspiration break out on her forehead and neck, and she put her hand to her mouth.

"You feel all right, Mrs. Lawring?" Hoffman asked her.

"Oh, yes," she managed.

"You look sick. You sure you're all right?"

She nodded. Reardon was watching her the way a parent watches a willful child at a large social function, and she gritted her teeth and smiled at the three of them and said, "No, it's nothing. I feel fine."

Reardon said: "But his voice, Mrs. Lawring. You said his voice—"

"I know, but it kept changing and I couldn't tell you why, but now I can see why it was. He was trying to disguise it, he was trying to talk like a Negro to confuse me..."

"Or maybe he was a Negro trying to talk like a white man."

"No, it couldn't be. Besides, when he became upset and angry, his voice changed that way. I just know that's it..."

Esselyn came up to them. There was another little pause and Reardon said, "You boys want to talk to the suspect for a few minutes? I'll be right with you." He watched them move off toward the door, took off his hat and began running his thumb and first two fingers over the creases in the crown. When he looked at Janet again his eyes were very small and bright, almost lost in the long dun expanse of his face.

"Mrs. Lawring, is there something you haven't told us?"

She started. "No—I've told you everything I—everything I could remember..." She went on swiftly: "I know this seems silly but I'm really very sure, it was his voice going up like that and his hand that did it for me. I'm awfully sorry about this."

Reardon looked at her a second longer—a shrewd, hard gaze. Then he smiled and nodded his head once; a gold eyetooth glinted. "Well, if you're sure, you're sure. That's it, then. I had high hopes with this boy. It sounded so right." He clapped his hat back on his head and shoved his hands in his pockets. "Let's see. Where does this leave us?" His eyes slid along the ceiling slowly. "A man in his late twenties, slender built, white, but dark complexion..."

"And graceful," Janet said, "I mean he might be an ex-dancer or even a violinist. His hands were very supple and delicate—almost beautiful, actually..."

"I see." A uniformed policeman came up to Reardon and handed him a slip of paper which he read quickly and jammed into a pocket of his jacket. "Well, I've got to see someone . . . I guess we'd better forget about this colored fellow, then."

"I'm awfully sorry to let you down, Inspector."

"That's all right. Thanks for coming in, anyway. It's very good of you to be so cooperative. Just take a seat here, will you? I'll send Harry out to you."

She walked back and sat on the same bench as the girl with the shiny black purse, who was clearly in some kind of trouble. A detective was bending over her and asking her for her age and address. After a few minutes another detective came in, prodding ahead of him a boy in a black leather jacket and boots who was walking with a curious stilt-like, slouching gait and grinning a tasteless grin, a cigarette held between his teeth. He sat down on the bench facing Janet and his eyes flickered over her—face, breasts, thighs, legs, and back again. Street gang tough; she remembered them from high school. The ones that hung out in the back of the coat room, sneaking drags at cigarettes under cupped hands, or huddled in the back booth at Slater's Drugstore plotting something, and now and then erupting in harsh laughter. Watching them she used to shiver inside. Their hands were always dirty, and they looked at her with eyes overwise from all the wrong kinds of knowledge . . .

She forced herself to stare back stonily at the boy. He tried the hard, threatful smirk of the actor Robert Mitchum, whom he did vaguely resemble—then gave it up and slumped down on the dirty wooden bench, pelvis thrust out and black-booted feet extended, and picked at one thumbnail with the other, now and then shooting hate-laden glances at Janet and the sallow-faced girl at the other end of the bench. He thinks I'm in trouble, Janet decided, arrested for some crime or other; and the thought upset her. There they sat facing each other, victim and villain, bound in the same slow torrent of violence—and she wasn't sure, in this worn, dirty room, that there was so much difference: the place made them all alike.

She glanced at the girl and ventured a smile of friendship, commiseration, sympathy, something—but the girl was in too desperate straits to respond; her lip quivered and she looked away and clutched the shiny black purse still tighter. For the first time Janet was struck with the possibility that the police might not catch the man—that the weeks would drag on into months and then years and he would still be at large, prowling about, watching, waiting again for the chance to come noiselessly up those stairs... How could they ever find him, in this vast, uncaring tide of brutality and stealth? The thought chilled her and she sought to beat it back: This was ridiculous, it had only been eight days, they'd already found the jacket, and she herself had led Inspector Reardon astray with her description. How could she have been so confused as to think he was a Negro? It was incredible! What must they think of her? To be so absurdly, unforgivably wrong...

The boy in the black leather jacket was staring at her again with that mirthless, mouth-depressed smile, and she avoided his eyes. When she saw Esselyn coming toward her from the other room she got to her feet in a little tremor of relief.

"Polly?" she called. She rang the bell again, listened to the four-note chimes reverberating inside the house like some weird falsetto cathedral. Dang-dong-ding-*dang*. From a window upstairs she could hear the Red Sox baseball game Esselyn had been listening to on the way out from town. She stood there a moment longer, uncertainly, glanced back at the car where Esselyn sat watching her, the engine idling. "It's all right," she said, "she's probably around in back and can't hear—would you wait just a minute?—and I'll look and see..."

Esselyn nodded. She started along the flagstone path that led around the house. A little red dog came bounding up to her, wagging his tail wildly and barking. "Gypsy!" she said, bending over and patting the animal, feeling his tongue hot and moist against her knuckles and thinking: If we'd had a dog maybe it wouldn't have happened. A devoted dog with a good, deep, gruff bark, one that would stay around the place. Straightening again, holding her head up, forcing herself to breathe calmly on this first solitary venture outside her house since the incident, she walked between the dense green masses of lilac and saw at the edge of the brick terrace Polly Enright kneeling before a large shrub, pounding dirt around its base with her gloved fists.

"Sweety!" Polly scrambled to her feet. "Is it that late?" And Janet, moving toward her, could feel herself relax again and thought: There she is. Dear Polly. Dear steady, angular, wonderful old Polly. The two women embraced and Janet was surprised to feel tears in her eyes.

"How are you, Jan?"

"Fine. Just a minute, I want to tell Harry . . ." She went to the edge of the house and called to Esselyn, "It's all right, she's here! Thanks for bringing me over . . ." He nodded, this time with a faint smile, and slid away down the road.

"He offered to drive me over," Janet said in explanation. "I didn't feel too much like doing it alone."

"Of course not. You poor baby. I could have picked you up, I should have thought of it. I'm trying to do fifty things at once and I'm busier than a one-armed paperhanger with scabies." She gestured toward the shrub. "I've been trans-*planting*. What an ordeal." They walked over to the bush and Polly fingered a few of its leaves dubiously. "Look at it droop."

"It'll come back," Janet said. "They always do. Give it a few hours. Where'd you get it?"

"Melchman's. Four-fifty. It looked so noble standing there in its little tub I couldn't resist. Now look at it. Mean old thing."

"Did you give it plenty of water before you put it in?"

"God, yes—humus and peat moss and loam and God knows what else. It'll probably break out with the hives."

"It'll look lovely there. *Euonymus patens.*"

Polly smote her forehead with a groan. "I don't know *anything* about plants. I wish I'd listened to my mother once in a while instead of *combating* her; I might know something." She pulled off her gloves and slapped them against her blue jeans. "Darn thing weighed a ton."

"Where are the boys?"

"Off on a hiking trip. La Strada. Except for Douggy who's upstairs in bed with his foot bandaged, stuffing himself. Let's each lunch out here. I've got it all ready."

"Fine."

They brought food out in two trays to the trestle table. Polly sprawled back in one of the canvas chairs with her mouth full of salad and said: "What a week this has been. I'm a wreck. Honestly, it's enough to send a girl to the loony bin. My five monsters and my brother Ernie's two. Boy—I'm all for planned parenthood. Now that it's too late, that is."

"His children are here?"

"Yes. Ernie's deathly ill. Didn't I tell you? No, of course not. Hasn't been time."

"What happened?"

"He almost killed everyone in Selkirk, Vermont, in one fell swoop, including himself. The idiot. They had this big party a week ago Saturday and Ernie got the idea of serving *bear* meat. And everyone ate great quantities and Ernie ate more than anyone else, of course. And the bear had eaten garbage, all the bears eat garbage nowadays it seems, and they all got trichinosis. Ernie ate his steak almost raw, and the trichinosis bugs got into his nervous system and now they're attacking his *brain*." She rolled her eyes. "They say he's going to be all right eventually, but he's in terrible shape right now. He can't get any sleep because his nerves are affected, and sedatives don't seem to have any effect on him at all."

"That's terrible. He always seemed so big and healthy."

"Not when those bugs get at you. He looks like a skeleton."

"Good heavens. How about the children?"

"Oh, they're all right. You know kids. They didn't eat very much of it, and they woopsed it up and got rid of it. And Marion didn't eat very much of it either and she's all right except that she *looks* like God's wrath in the morning. Your eyes swell up and your neck and everything. And some of the guests are going to sue Ernie. He practically flattened the town. Oh, it's a mess, a perfect mess, and just what my big-dealing brother would get himself into." There was a burst of music, a thunderous jangle of brass and guitars, from upstairs. "Douggy! Turn—that— *down!*" Polly shouted like a cavalry commander, and the uproar died away.

"What's the matter with *him?*" Janet asked.

"Oh, they were building a hut out in the woods and of course he had to jump on a plank with a nail in it, and of course the nail had to be *rusty*. Why can't they step on clean, shiny nails once in a while? There must be a few clean, shiny ones kicking around." She clawed at her hair with one hand. "And he couldn't get his foot off the plank and Billy, he's the Pheidippides of the gang, came tearing down to the house with his shirt tail streaming out behind him howling forth the horrendous news, and I went up there and they were all milling around Douggy like an African tribe begging the heavens for rain. Sometimes I think we're a lot closer to Lou's primitive societies than we have any idea."

"—But what did you do?"

"With Douggy? Made him lie down and put my foot on his

chest and took hold of the board and pulled it off his sneaker."

"How'd you ever think of that?"

Polly blinked at her. "Good God, I don't know. I don't think I *did* think. I just did it. I *had* to make them stop bellowing."

Janet shook her head in admiration. "You're marvelous, Polly."

"Don't be silly. I'm desperate."

"No, you're not, you're wonderful—you know just what to do in any emergency. If you—"

She stopped and took a sip of iced coffee. Polly's expression was all at once affectionate and grave.

"Oh, no," she said quietly. "Don't you think that for a minute. It isn't so. You did just fine." Janet bit her lip and shook her head. "Of course you did. You're here, you're alive, and the creep is gone ... All right, so he raped you," she declared, but not harshly. "So what? It's nothing, basically."

"I wish I could believe that."

"You've got to, Jan." She paused. "Gard's all right about it, isn't he? I mean, he hasn't got any of those idiotic medieval notions about your being damaged goods, has he?"

"Oh no," Janet said quickly, "he's been wonderful."

"Good. That's all you need, then. I think you did just what you should have; and did it splendidly." She leaned forward, her sharp little chin in one hand. "God. If a man came upstairs with a knife and clambered into bed with me I'd go off my little wooden rocker. Even with Lou, it was years before I got to like being handled. You know what I mean. Oh, I went along with the gag at first, I knew that's what everybody did, but I didn't really like a man's hands on my private parts: it gave me the royal squeegees. I was pretty naïve about sex when I got married, and having kids didn't make all the roaring difference you'd think it would, either. Well, live and learn: die and start all over."

Janet laughed, watching Polly, liking her, wondering gratefully what indulgent good fortune had decided to throw them together. Polly Enright was all angles: her chin, her nose and elbows and knees and shoulders all gave her the appearance of being in violent motion even when she wasn't. The original analytical cubist's model, Gardner had once described her to Janet—though not maliciously, for he was fond of her, and the Lawrings and Enrights had had some good times together. For

Polly, mother of five turbulent boys, life was a grim, no-quarter contest against poison ivy, broken bones and contagious diseases, and she went forth each morning like a missionary in deep and dangerous jungle, or a surgeon in a field hospital right behind the lines; lantern jaw set, blue eyes glinting behind the heavy horn-rimmed glasses, hair bound back severely with a broad elastic ribbon. All the same, she could look quite pretty if she took the trouble to get herself up, which she did occasionally. She came from the Midwest, a minister's family, and she was several years older than Janet. Lou had been a year ahead of Gardner at St. Mark's and although they hadn't known each other very well there, it had given them something to start on when Lou had come straight from Ponapei to teach cultural anthropology at the college, four years before. Lou was balding, with a button nose and dry wit; he came from Philadelphia, and now and then the two girls had vividly dissected and compared the Boston and the Philadelphia manner, not without some hilarity... It's terribly important to have friends, Janet thought, close friends: they're the only solid bulwark against—well, the kind of thing that just hit me.

As if Polly had read her thoughts she said: "How's it been over there Jan? Pretty hectic?"

"All right," she answered. "I mean, not so good. I guess that's what I mean. I've just come from town again. They found the jacket and they were holding a man they thought had—been the person. But he wasn't. Not even close." She sighed. "Ive been all mixed up about what he looked like, apparently. The description and everything. I just realized it today." She frowned and said, "The hell with it. Let's not talk about it."

"Don't blame you a bit. Say, have you any idea about how to make shrimp mousseline? really make one that'll stand up on the plate?"

"No—I've let Pruitt carry the ball for so long I've forgotten almost everything I knew..."

They talked indolently, carelessly, in the manner of good friends, while the sun spattered down through the leaves and Gypsy rolled in the grass with his paws in the air and made unexpectedly deep growling sounds. Someone's power mower nearby droned along, coughed, stuttered and droned on again, and a phoebe rocked on the electric wire to the garage, looking about pugnaciously and giving its harsh warning call. This house is unchanged, Janet thought; Polly and Lou and the boys and the house are just the way they were two weeks ago; how curious that is...

"They were asking for you yesterday," Polly was saying from behind a boiling cloud of cigarette smoke. "Harriet and Sally and the others. Wanted to know if there was anything they could do—Harriet especially." She fixed Janet with a sardonic expression and dropped one eyelid. "I told them you wanted to be left strictly alone till you could get your feet under you. I said you'd be at the next omnium gatherum, maybe. That what you wanted?"

"Yes, it is. Thanks, Polly."

"De nada. Oh say, how'd you like to fling your hundred and sixteen pounds into this remedial reading project this summer, help corral some teachers? I mean if you feel like it."

"Sure—I'd like to."

"You're on. We ought to get a good competent staff, support the thing, pull all the stops. Harriet, bless her enterprising soul, says that's what they did over in Belmont. What do you think?"

"It—it sounds fine, Polly."

"I mean you'll have time on your hands now, with Brian away at camp. The main thing is to get rolling on it before fall rears up with the Big Ratrace. Nobody ever gets anything done after September first. And the college is closed now, Lou and the other men who teach will have more time—that's the theory, anyway..."

There was a face. Beyond Polly's shoulder, at the edge of the house, just above the hedge—a thin, young face dark with menace, blue visored baseball cap: it had ducked out of sight again. Glass smashed on the brick. Her glass. She had gasped, she heard herself, she was standing up rigidly—she was running for the house.

"Jan," Polly was saying, "Jan—"

The hedge shook and the visored face rose up again, one arm in a blue work shirt gesturing. She was inside the door muttering, "Oh Jesus, oh Jesus..." She put her hands against the screen door. The man was trying to get through the hedge now, thrusting, and Polly was shouting:

"Frank! Frank! What in heaven's name are you *doing—!*"

He stopped pushing against the hedge; his face became round and apologetic. "Miz Enrigh', I coon't fin' you I din' know where to pu' the grossries..."

"In the kitchen, take them into the kitchen!"

"Nobody in there..."

"It doesn't matter whether anybody's there—*take them into the kitchen!*"

Polly was coming toward her, had opened the screen door. "It's only Frank Rossini from Pierce's," Polly was saying to her, but she couldn't help herself now, she was trembling uncontrollably, shivering from head to foot; her teeth were actually chattering, clicking and clattering, she couldn't stop them from chattering no matter what she did. Polly had an arm around her, was saying, "Oh my poor sweety, I'm so sorry, oh I *am* so sorry, it's so stupid, that young idiot *knows* he's supposed to leave the junk on the kitchen counter—he's got some votive obsession about having to hand it to me personally. Oh I'm so sorry, Jan—I wouldn't have had this happen for the world..."

"It's all right," she heard herself say. "It just—took me by surprise, that's all. His head leaning over the hedge..." The hobgoblin shapes danced in front of her eyes, the hot dart ran up and down inside her body, filling her veins with water, a soft substanceless jelly that made her sick. She was afraid she was going to fall down in a heap on the dining room floor. And all the time she was thinking, This is terrible, I'm all in pieces, Polly would never act like this no matter what happened, and especially not something idiotic like this, oh I'm weak and cowardly and a fool—

"I'm all right," she said again. "Just let me sit down for a minute..."

In the living room, dark with stained paneling and heavy curtains and comfortably dilapidated furniture, the towering bookcases and Micronesian shields and figurines and the great deep blue map of the heavens Lou had hung up for the boys, these exotic and familiar objects, she got a grip on herself.

"—stupid of me," Polly was saying, "making you sit out there in the open, sometimes I don't use any sense at all..."

"It's not that. It was just his face. It caught me off-balance."

Polly stared at her. "It couldn't *be* Frank, by any chance—?"

"No. Oh, no. It's just a conditioned reflex, I guess. Any male

coming up on me suddenly obviously wants to ravish me." She
made a feeble attempt at laughter.

"Mother ..." Douglas's voice from upstairs, thin and eager.

"What?" Polly called back.

"What happened?"

"Nothing. Frank Rossini lugged in the grub for the next
forty-eight hours."

"Mother ... Can I have a glass of Bosco?"

"Not right now."

"I'm thirsty ..."

"I'm sure you are. You've only had birch beer, Seven-Up,
orange pop and two Cokes since twelve. You keep your shirt
on." She said to Janet: "That reminds me, though. What *you*
need is a good stiff hooker. You look as if you've been dunked in
a bucket of whitewash." She yanked open the doors to a large,
ugly brown cabinet and pawed around among bottles of various
shapes and hues, drew out a fat amber one and poured several
ounces into a highball glass. "Here you go. Slug it down. Go
ahead. It's Lou's private bottle. Martin's. Twelve years old."

"Oh no—" Janet protested.

"Don't be a lunatic. It never went to a better cause. Buvez."

Janet drank, gasped at the smoky dry burn of the liquor, her
eyes watering; drank some more of it dutifully, set the glass
down.

"Good," Polly said, standing over her and nodding, like a
nurse "Feel better?"

"I think I do. I don't know."

"You will."

"It's funny how your—your whole frame of reference shifts.
You know?" She now felt a great need to hold Polly there in the
room with her, close beside her—she felt she could if she only
talked rapidly enough. "I mean, in spite of every conscious effort
you make, your mind, or some part of it anyway, keeps racing
along some track of its own, ticking off every man you see—on
the street, in cars, especially driving delivery trucks, I don't
know why that is—hoping to spot him. God knows what would
happen if I did ..."

Polly frowned. "Will you know him? if you see him?"

"Yes. I know I will. Even after this afternoon. I know I will.
Absolutely. And I'm half afraid to." She laughed faintly. "That's

what's so weird. I want to find him and yet I'm scared to death. I can't think of anything else. Anything else at all. Isn't that silly? It seems to be the only *necessary* thing in my life—you know, the way you felt the moment you first started to menstruate? Like that—the only vivid, real thing in all the world, this desire to catch him, lay eyes on him again—and at the same time avoid him like the plague ... I'm talking nonsense."

"No, you're not."

"Yes, I am. I don't care, though."

"You look awfully tired, Jan. Can't you sleep?"

"Not very well. No. Doc Bolton's got me on some blue pills, I don't know what they are, but they don't work half the time. I feel if I could just sleep through *this* day and get to the next one somehow, the next one without living through this one, I'd get caught up—whatever *that* means. And then I'd be all right, I'd be able to cope with things. More or less. I know it sounds crazy but that's how I feel."

"Mother ..." Douglas called again.

"What now?"

"Couldn't I have a glass of Bosco soon?"

Polly clawed at her hair with her hand. "All right, you pitiful, undernourished, malnutrited soul, I'll get you one." She patted Janet's shoulder. "Don't go away. I'll be back in a jiffy."

Janet took another long swallow from the glass, listened absently to the sonorous bark of the baseball game upstairs, Polly rattling and banging around in the kitchen. Her best friend. Polly was her best friend—and now they were a million light years apart: as though a lead curtain had been lowered between them. She felt badly, sitting there. She admired Polly tremendously—not of course anything of the soft, wild worship she reserved for Gardner, but admiration nonetheless: for her competence, the firm, exact grip she had on the world, her refusal ever to let situations become complicated by mystical overtones; her steady, everyday effectiveness. She was depressed that Polly had seen her go to pieces like this. Getting to her feet, she wandered over to the great blue chart of the universe, gazed with a fond wistfulness at Boötes the Herdsman, and Arcturus, and Vega of the Lyre. *It is the stars, the stars above us, govern our conditions* ... Who had said that, and why? No one believed that, neither Polly nor Gard nor Franz nor even wildly visionary, superstitious old Harry Delannoy... But she did, a little: something inside her felt it, obscurely, as one thinks to discover immense, fantastic monsters slipping by beneath the surface of the sea...

Polly came back into the living room wiping her hands on her jeans. "Isn't this place a holy terror? I keep promising myself I'll pull myself together some morning and hoe it out or dynamite it or divert the River Alpheus through it or something. And every once in a while I do. But there's six of them and only one of me. So I can't win."

"No, it's fine," Janet answered. "It's all yours. No strangers... It's so odd now, with the detectives around all the time. The house seems actually colored by them: a different texture entirely. Cups of coffee and cigarette butts in all the ashtrays. One of them, a redheaded man named Hoffman, hawks up phlegm into his handkerchief every few minutes. You keep expecting them to *go*—like movers or repairmen—and of course they don't, they just keep staying on, replacing each other every eight hours. It must be what married life was like in the Middle Ages—the continual semi-intimate presence of a person you didn't know very well and weren't particularly drawn to but you couldn't get away from. You feel—*sealed off,* sort of..."

"Jan, why don't you go away for a while? Take yourself a holiday?"

She looked up and smiled. "Has Gard been after you, by any chance?"

Polly Enright blinked, then waggled her pointed jaw back and forth in the curious grimace she adopted when she'd been caught off. "Oh hell, I can't be artful. Yes he did, Jan, I'm not going to lie to you. He wants me to use my persuasive wiles—I, who can hardly pry Lou away for two weeks at White Horse Beach... But why not, Jan? Just a week, or even a few days. A completely different atmosphere. You *are* pretty tense, you know."

"I know."

"Gard is willing to take some time off, he told me he was. You could have a good, quiet holiday, just rest up and—"

Janet shook her head. "No good. I can't."

"Why not?"

"I just can't, that's all." She felt the rasp of irritation in her voice, the pressure in her sinuses. "I've got to stay, Polly. Till they find him. No matter how long it takes."

"But sweety, you know, maybe it'll be quite a—"

"I know. I can't help that. I've just got to stay anyway."

There was a silence. Polly was looking at her, her eyes bright and troubled. She shifted her position on the couch and swallowed. She wished she hadn't come over. Like all generous natures she exaggerated the intensity of other people's reactions, particularly toward herself: she mistook Polly's solicitude for disapproval. Polly didn't understand what she was going through—how could she? How could anyone who hadn't ridden that very hurricane? I ought to go back, she thought; right now. She took another small sip of the scotch and smiled at Polly to obscure her decision; and then, because she was impulsive and affectionate she was ashamed of her mood. But she could think of nothing to say, and dropped her eyes.

"Jan," Polly said quietly, "you mentioned something you wanted to talk to me about..."

She looked up in surprise. "I did?"

"Yes. Over the phone. The night it happened."

Janet folded her hands in her lap and stared at the chart of the heavens. Yes: the phone call. Long, long ago. All those light years of days ago. She felt like a spacemen who has just returned to earth after having experienced seven years of flight while the earth has known only seven minutes. Or perhaps it was the other way around . . . She had genuinely forgotten about it; now she remembered. She thought of Gardner standing in his pajama bottoms in the doorway, his face bronzed and fearful in the lamp glow. No, no matter how sympathetic and sensible Polly was, no matter how close a friend—and she *was* those things—she couldn't talk about that now; that conversation was over before it had ever begun. She knew if she brought that up now she *would* break down. It was too fraught with other things, too inextricably bound up with Thursday night. Now it would be a betrayal of Gard. Why now and not before she couldn't say: but it would. This was something she would have to cope with on her own.

She shook her head, feigning ignorance and confusion. "I can't remember. Sorry. God knows what it was . . . Thursday night has driven everything else out of my head."

"Sure." Polly nodded briskly. "I can well believe it. I just thought I'd bring it up in case it was on your mind."

They chatted of other things then, and did the dishes together. Polly had a library fund meeting at four and offered to drop Janet off on her way. As they pulled out of the driveway Polly said:

"Oh, I almost forgot. You know, I'd be glad to take Brian till camp opens."

"But you've got seven—! You're a glutton."

"One more would be as nothing. It's true he and Tommy aren't the closest friends in the world, but I could scrape up some things for them to do. The Junior Astronauts are going to be in session here all of Friday anyway, so the joint will be jumping. And Saturday, Lou is going to take the whole mob over to the observatory at Blue Hill. I thought maybe if you feel it's a bit too much to have him there along with everything else, you might be glad to unload him for a while."

"Thanks, Polly. You're a saint in martyr's clothing. I'd love to take you up on it. The fact is Gard's mother has taken him down to Brewster."

"Oh, sure. That's probably a lot better."

"No, I wish we could have left him with you. I must confess I wasn't wild with delight when Gard took him in to Boston. Polly . . ."

"Uh-huh?"

"Do Lou's parents seem particularly difficult at times of crises?"

"Ha! Absolutely. And then afterwards they're just as bad. To make up for it."

"What do you do about it?"

Polly chortled, and swung the car smartly around a curve. "See them as bleeding little as possible! No—well, Lou's pretty good about it. We had a couple of gymkhanas when we were first married, one was a real hassle, and I had to tell him I couldn't see myself passing every legal and illegal holiday impaled in the Metropolis of Brotherly Love. Besides, the water's utterly undrinkable."

"Do you feel they're judging you all the time? no matter what you do?"

"Oh sure. I know I'm not good enough. My God—Keokuk,

Iowa: how could I ever hope to meet Main Line Standards of Conduct? Answer: I don't. Never have, never will. Hell, that's what Lou fell in love with me for, partly. When Lou was at Columbia his mother was over every five minutes, raising a fuss about the way I ran a house and reared the monsters. I took that for a while and then I said to Lou: 'Look, this has got to cease. I may not be any model hausfrau but it's *my* household, to wreck as I please.'" She wrinkled her nose and pushed up her glasses with her little finger. "So now we see them two, three times a year, the grand levees, and that's that. Lou gets a little grumpy about it now and then, but he knows I'm right basically. You have one life as a child and daughter, and another one as wife and parent, and you can't be expected to keep sliding constantly from one into the other like Jekyll and Hyde. It's as simple as that."

"I suppose so." Janet stared disconsolately at the road. "Only I can't fight back now if I wanted to. Gard's mother always knew I was inferior—and now this business comes along to prove it."

"What do you mean?"

"The fact that it happened to me: it wouldn't happen to *her*."

"Road apples. It happens to anybody the creep happens to pick."

"That's what she thinks, though. She called the other day. I was still pretty wrought up, I'd just been in to town to identify a suspect, a terrible gargoyle of a drug addict with crazy bulging eyes and sores on his hands, and I could feel all this behind everything she said, and I broke down on the phone . . . Why can't I be like them?" she cried hotly. "Why can't I be hard and proud and *certain* of everything?"

Polly grinned at her, reached out and clapped a hand on her knee. "They're not, sweety. They just look good on stage. They've got all the props of money and snooty schools and clubs and things, and above all they've been taught *how* to act." She thumped the wheel with the flat of her hand. "Don't forget that: they've been taught how to react to most situations—and it makes them look wonderfully poised and steady and noble and all that candelabra. But when a situation comes up that they're not prepared for, they're just like you and me, honey. Maybe worse."

"I wish I could believe that."

"It's true. When we were on Ponapei a man was sent into exile for having spoken to his mother-in-law. It was largely an accident but he *did* speak to her, and they have very strong taboos about that. I've often thought—well, that's another story. Anyway, the man accepted it calmly enough, packed up his duds and got his outrigger ready to go. And Lou went half crazy. He knew Micronesian observances and taboos perfectly well but the man was a friend of ours and Lou simply wouldn't accept it. He went into a royal wing-ding. I had to practically clout him over the head to keep him from organizing an insurrection. And that's temperate, impassive Main Line Lou... You've got to roll with the punch, Jan. The old gal doesn't know what you've been through, she can't begin to comprehend it; and a good thing, too—she'd probably sail right on into the laughing academy if she did. Just get your own feet under you and to hell with her. That's all you have to do."

They drummed across the wooden bridge and up the grade past the stand of cedars and the house rose up to face her—a gray-white bastion flanked by the detectives' cars. That's all you have to do, she reflected, and smiled a short, bitter, wistful smile. If all this could only be by-passed somehow, and she could get rested up and think it all through in the slow, crystalline goblet of her rejuvenated mind, and make some sense out of what had happened to her. If only Boo were home, she thought with a sudden pang of longing; home here with me, where he belongs... Why had she agreed so easily to his going away to camp? Ridiculous. If Brian could be home and she and Gardner go back to their old ways everything would be righted almost automatically, wouldn't it? After all, there was no *reason* why this gratuitous incident should rend their lives. Anybody the creep happened to pick, as Polly said. The random plummeting of a meteor. That was what Polly would do—consider it simply a bizarre interruption, one of those stupid, isolate episodes that occasionally mar the bright, even tenor of people's lives; quite simply brush it aside, and go on.

She turned and looked with fond despair at Polly's vigorous, angular face. Only how in the name of all that was holy and good did you do that?

Chapter Six

The days dragged along. Lawring made an effort to get home early every night, and Franz Hoelder came over evenings and afternoons and tried to amuse Janet, swapped stories with the detectives or played a distracted game of chess with Lawring. There were five telephone calls, all from sexual perverts, each of them a series of feline insinuations and viciously indecent proposals. All of them hung up before the calls could be traced. Janet said she was willing to take the calls herself in the hope that she would recognize her assailant, but the second conversation physically sickened her, and the policewoman took the others. Occasionally Inspector Reardon came by with news of some new suspect for identification and Janet dutifully got dressed and went in to Boston, examined the man through the one-way mirror and then shook her head. No, he was definitely not the person. Yes, she was certain: she knew she would remember him when she did see him.

It was a hard time. After the initial flurry of publicity the press had pretty much lost interest in them, and Reardon gave them assurances that from now on their privacy would be respected as fully as the prosecution of the case allowed; but Lawring found the presence of the detectives a constant irritation, like a splinter in the ball of one's thumb. They were decent enough, they effaced themselves as much as two husky men in orange or yellow sport shirts with .38's on their hips can efface themselves in someone else's home. One of them particularly Lawring liked, a soft-spoken South Boston Irishman named Danny Shea with a deceptively soft round face and a warm smile; he had been with the army of occupation in Germany, and he and Lawring talked desultorily of Stuttgart and the Schwarzwald and the Schloss Grafenstein—forests and castles that seemed as remote to Lawring as the images left from childhood dreams...

But none of it had any reality: the automatic warning system that went off like a mechanical death rattle whenever anyone made contact with the doors or windows, the strange device like an obsolete gramophone that was used for monitoring incoming calls, these strangers with guns reading magazines or gazing patiently out through the glass door on the little pool behind the house surrounded by its rock garden... It gave off, all of it, an atmosphere of siege, of imminent assault and violence, and Lawring caught himself thinking increasingly of the war, of moments in bombed-out farmhouses or gloomy Gasthöfe, sitting around waiting for the harsh release of artillery fire, the whistle, the word—whatever would, terribly, mercifully, set things in motion again... But here there was no H-hour, no zero. Nothing happened. The June days followed one upon another in lush, unbroken regularity; Janet continued to examine suspects without success, the nights were long and full of wakeful starts, the brisk scream of the telephone would start a silent flurry in the big bright rooms downstairs.

Janet worried him. The dreamy, almost hypnotic trance that held her would be interrupted every now and then by periods of taut nervousness and exasperation, and these wild disparities of mood exhausted her; she began to look drawn and harried, her clear violet eyes unnaturally large in her pale face. She seemed shaken in some irreparable way—as though her inner ear had been deranged or the minuscule gyroscope that guides us through moments of crisis and confusion had come all apart, shattered beyond repair.

"I feel sometimes as though I'm dreaming the whole thing," she said to him once late in the second week. "Pure dream—the whole thing. Like being inside one of those transparent plastic bags they cover cars with. I can't tell whether I'm inside the bag or everything else is. It must be the way insane people feel all the time..." And she smiled a dull, hollow smile that alarmed him as much as what she'd said.

Her confusion over the color of her assailant astonished him. How in God's name could she have been unsure whether or not the fellow was a Negro? Reardon's attitude, too, seemed altered; in subsequent discussions with Janet his little amber eyes would rest on her with a curious impassivity. His voice was very measured. Could she perhaps have seen her assailant in profile against the glow of light from the television screen? Did she remember his using his handkerchief while he was in the room? Had he taken off the glasses when he'd got into bed with her? Her answers remained vague and confused. He'd only used his handkerchief to wipe off the handles and knobs—except once when he wiped his mouth and cheeks. She couldn't remember seeing his profile—though she did remember his nose at some point: it had been a long, rather prominent nose, but she couldn't be sure. Yes, he had taken off both his hat and glasses when he got into bed with her, but he'd put them both on even before he'd got dressed at all... Reardon and the detectives present had glanced at each other and drawn on their cigarettes in a ponderous silence.

Lawring, listening to her struggling with her memory, contradicting herself, catching herself up—and watching, too, Reardon's careful reticence—remembered how pitifully inadequate or deceptive one's memory could be after a moment of desperate exigency. He knew how implausible the truth invariably sounded. He had seen examples of this in business. You might be sitting in someone's office or the Union Club and say, "Micawber? Oh, he's all right, he's a good enough draftsman—the only trouble with him is he's such an incurable egocentric he's utterly unreliable in any social situation"—you said something like that and your listeners nodded and tapped their cigarette ends and believed you implicitly. But when you went on to buttress this monstrous generality with some substantiating fact—when you told them how Micawber had impulsively invited himself out to your place while you had these important clients the Nicklebys there for the weekend; how he helped himself to five martinis and socked a croquet ball through the picture window, put his arm around Mrs. Nickleby's waist, enraged old Nickleby through an impassioned eulogy of John F. Kennedy, and later broke one of your Eames chairs by falling into it like an expiring corpse—when you related this documentary chain of disaster which had led you to your evaluation, you could see their eyes glaze over with disbelief: No, this was too incredible, you must be exaggerating, old Micawber couldn't have done all *that*—he drank a little too much now and then, it was true, but there were two sides to every situation, this just didn't meet the eye ... Lawring could see a flicker of it now in the faces of the police. They lighted fresh cigarettes and grunted sympathetically, they were attentive enough—but there was something about it that made them uneasy. It troubled him and one evening he murmured, "Can't you really think of anything *specific* about him, honey?"

She glanced at him as though he'd threatened to strike her. "I've tried, my God I've tried to remember—don't you think I've *tried*—?" and her eyes filled.

She wouldn't sleep in the double bed any more. As soon as they moved back from Franz's house she had displayed a marked aversion to it—she wouldn't even sit on it to change her clothes—and chose to sleep in one of the twin beds in the main guest room at the other end of the hall. Lawring had been glad of this, in a rather inchoate way; he had the big bed taken out and another brought in, a box spring with a headboard and a coverlet of dull gold so that it would resemble the old one as little as possible. But still she continued to sleep in the guest bedroom, and so he moved in there, too.

He tried to comfort her. He sat by the side of her bed and read to her evenings, some newspaper item or magazine article he thought might divert her; he even tried to take an interest in the interminable television dramas. He wanted with all his heart to sponge the slate of that savage evening, blot out the shock of it in the vivid, pulsing warmth of their love—but his own affliction, illness, inadequacy, whatever it was, held him powerless.

Apparently he was no better off. He had gone in to Boston the following week to see Dr. Shippard, his family's physician, and passed a dully hopeful half hour while the old man prodded and tapped him and attached things to his arms and legs and took the prescribed tests, and finally sighed and told him there was nothing wrong with him physically, nothing that he at any rate could uncover. Had he been working a lot harder than usual, was he—and here Shippard paused a little wearily, as though constrained to ask a question whose merits or applicability he himself, a rock-ribbed old New Englander, didn't for one single minute believe in—had this recent trouble disturbed him emotionally, perhaps? Which left Lawring about where he'd been before he'd called. He thought about seeing a specialist, a man he'd heard of out on Bay State Road with very up-to-date apparatus and a brusque New York manner, but the pressures of work intervened and he put it off. In any event he had the feeling that the idea of sex was repugnant to Janet, as well it might be; she had developed a tremendous sense of privacy about her body, and she was immensely tired. And so he made no advances, forced himself to be content to lie beside her in the dusty light of late evening, surrounded by the soft roar of peepers and the thump and sizzle of June bugs against the screens, holding her head cradled in his arm, reading on and on softly, steadily, not sure at times whether she was awake or asleep . . .

When the tense, exasperated mood seized her he bore with it, tried to reason with her fears and tempers, the caged sensation she complained about. Life had to go on, even in such abnormal circumstances as these. Why didn't she go over to the club and take a swim, see Polly or Ellen Macomber, some of the girls she went around with, go on a shopping trip to Boston with them? It wasn't good to sit around out here, shut up all the time with her garden or TV; it would make anyone morbid and nervous. Why didn't they go away somewhere, to the shore or up into the Whites? He'd take the week off and they could drive anywhere they chose, find a secluded spot and swim or go fishing or just lie around in the sun. Why not?

She would shake her head quickly: she lacked the energy for travel, it wouldn't be any rest for her and anyway she wanted to stay here until they had found the person, cleared up who it was. She *had* to know who it was, couldn't he understand that? Feebly he remonstrated—the cops would wait, things would keep till they got back—but secretly he was glad. He, too, longed to have it wound up, the assailant behind bars—one less marauder, moral degenerate, sex maniac, whatever the hell he was—one less, anyway—at large. Then it would be over and they could take up their old lives again.

But at times he would even have his doubts about this. Watching Janet covertly, trying to minister to her, anticipate her reactions, head off her wild oscillations of mood, he had nevertheless begun to feel unsure of himself. He couldn't seem to come to grips with things, brush them aside or resolve them smartly. His work had suffered. McGrath hadn't liked his plans for the Pan-Am Building, and neither had Henchey; it was a clean design, glass and brushed aluminum in good Miesian sharp order, but it lacked excitement, it lacked the soaring dramatic *rightness* of a first-rate structure, and he knew it. McGrath had been particularly eager to get him for this job, and Lawring could see the little commissioner was genuinely disappointed. He said he wanted to take another shot at it, and McGrath had agreed, though with reluctance: he had his own pressures to contend with.

Maltisiak's people were inclining toward his and Henchey's submissions for the North End redevelopment area, but it was a hollow satisfaction; the Urban Renewal and Expressway controversies ground on and on, with threats and delays and endless litigation. The North End Citizens' Committee had grown by leaps and bounds, opposition had hardened further after the Chinatown and West End demolition work, and suits and countersuits abounded. Assemblyman DiCalco kept pouring fuel on the blaze at every meeting, every newspaper and radio interview. Lawring began to wish he had never got embroiled in the whole wretched mess: he had troubles of his own, God knew—and so did everyone else know it as well. And it was this that wore him down. Talking with Henchey or fellow commuters at Route 128 now he felt he could detect the subdued, faintly arch tones of pity, and it angered him. His wife had been despoiled, for all the world to see—and for all his background and position he had been able to do nothing about it. Conversations stopped when he entered offices or club rooms, people came toward him with the gauche deference shown to the bereaved or the incurably ill; and watching their apologetic manner, their half-averted eyes, he set his teeth and clenched his fists in his pockets. Was he going to be known from now till doomsday as the man whose wife got raped?

... What the hell, he kept telling himself doggedly, it could have happened to anybody in America—it could happen to the President, given the right—or the wrong— circumstances. And when the inevitable, inarguable answer came, as it always did, he scowled and told himself, It will pass: everything passes if you wait it out long enough. But it didn't pass. Everything seemed destined to drag on this hot. humid summer. Perhaps there were seasons when the very chemistry in the air was such that *nothing* could be resolved, for better or worse. Overtaxed, irascible, completely on edge, Lawring fancied he saw indefinable expressions of pity and contempt on the faces of secretaries, waitresses, salesgirls. After a violent outburst at the accessories counter at Jordan's, where he'd gone to buy something for Janet and wound up in a shouting match with an almost hysterical spinster brunette and her two assistants, he drifted into the men's bar below the lobby of the Touraine, where he was reasonably sure of meeting no one he knew, and sat in a corner with a scotch and water and brooded over it. Never before three o'clock or east of Park Street. What the devil was the matter with him? He was getting to be like some oversensitive poet, full of paranoid imaginings and self-pity. Where was his old vaunted steadiness, the imperturbable Saxon self-possession that had carried him through one snarled-up situation after another when everyone else was blowing up? This was ridiculous: he'd better get himself in hand ...

But now, fluttering always at the under edge of his composure like a horde of bats was the thought: If a thing like this could happen to them, right out of the blue, what else could fall upon them without warning? What couldn't happen to anyone at all?

And for this he had no answer.

"Feel that," Stan Brown said. He stamped his sneakered feet: a loose-jointed, shuffling stamp, almost a dance. "Four-inch clay base, packed solid. Makes you glad just to be alive. Only counselor and tournament finals on these two. The other four are for the kids, they can hack 'em out all they want."

"It's very nice," Lawring observed.

"Nice! It's a dream on Cloud X. Took me three years to get 'em like this." He swung an imaginary racket, an easy gliding motion, and laughed at himself soundlessly. "You play?"

"Now and then."

"How about a fast set?"

"Oh, I couldn't even give you a decent game ..." Lawring had owned a respectable game of tennis both during and after college, but he had played very little in the past five years. "I'm over the hill."

"Just as you like, dad. You look in pretty good shape to me."

Stan Brown was a Californian, a tall, rangy redhead with a prominent, high-ridged nose and a small mouth and very intense ultramarine eyes. He had been an amateur tennis champion several years before, Ray Lynes the camp director had told Lawring that spring, and for a time had been the pro at a club in New Jersey, Lawring couldn't now remember which one. He was in charge of Brian's hut.

"Better sharpen up, Gardner," Brown was saying; he kept drawing his tanned arm through a series of smooth backhands. "Better sharpen up or Brian will take the old man over the hurdles when he goes home. Spot you two games and knock you off in straight sets."

"Well, I'll be satisfied if he gets the ground strokes," Lawring replied, and added: "Actually his main interest is baseball."

"Uh-huh. Wants to be a *slugger,* eh?" Lawring glanced at him; Brown's thin lips were drawn down in a sardonic smile. "Well, we'll give him that, too." He moved toward the net in a graceful, gliding pirouette, still belting the imaginary ball. "Boom! Pow! Swooooosh! Point to Mr. Aloysius P. Mc-Shaughnessy..."

Lawring watched him, feeling ill at ease. This kind of sophisticated exhibitionism he always found embarrassing; and he didn't like it when people called him by his first name on fresh acquaintance. Brown had a casual, open-handed manner, but there was something about him that rubbed Lawring's fur the wrong way. Perhaps it was the dirty, floppy hat with its brim turned down all the way around in the style many tennis pros affected, or maybe it was the mixture of bravura and indifference, or the faintly sardonic ring to nearly everything he said—as though he had decided not to permit himself to laugh at things he considered ridiculous...

Brown was coming toward him now, grinning, moving, in that slinky, loose-hipped glide. To cover his thoughts he said, "Where's the ball field?"

"Which one do you want to see? We've got two. Come on: I'll show you around the plant."

They walked quickly over the grounds. Camp Mohican was the best equipped camp Lawring had been able to find in northern New England, and he had researched the matter with care. It was situated on the south shore of Lake Ossipee, and it boasted the six tennis courts he had just seen, two baseball diamonds, a basketball court, a general games field, a rifle range, and a superb lakefront swimming area with two floats and a diving tower. The huts were well screened, and there was a mess hall and a huge council house for sings and entertainments, whose front porch afforded a faultless view of Mount Chocorua. It wasn't the camp Lawring himself had gone to—Camp Standish had been ruined when the 1938 hurricane had blown down nearly every pine in the area—but it was a very good one; he could feel it.

"Ray handles most of the group athletics," Brown was saying. "There's an intracamp league of six teams named for the Giants and Dodgers and Braves, Ray's probably told you about them. They play each other twice each half-season, and everyone gets a chance to play, even the little fellows." They had passed the council house and were at the lake front, where several counselors were anchoring one of the dock sections. In the shallow water near shore ten or a dozen early arrivals, among them Brian, were hooting and splashing around under the eye of Stubby Overmeer, the swimming instructor.

"There he is now!" Stan Brown called, pointing toward Brian. "In six weeks he'll be clocking it off like an old pro. Looks good, doesn't it? How about a swim, Gardner?"

The still blue water was irresistible. "I'd love one. But I didn't bring a suit along."

"A nothing. I'll dig one up for you."

The water was fine, not too cool. He entered on the dead run, plunged until his momentum was lost, then stroked along with his choppy crawl until he reached the outer float, pulled himself up on it with one good thrust of his arms and sat there and watched the clouds roll overhead like puffy little parodies of clouds, behind Chocorua. There was something about the opening of summer camp that had always excited him—the vaguely frontier atmosphere with men stripped to the waist struggling with the section of dock, pickup trucks scurrying here and there with bedding or barrels or clumps of shrieking children, the proud fragility of the Old Town canoes drawn up along the shore in front of the boat house; the sweaty, intoxicating promise of it. Stubby Overmeer was teaching Brian and two other kids how to do a dead man's float. In a few moments Stan Brown swam out toward him with a smooth, effortless freestyle, climbed the ladder, knocked water out of one ear, and squinted up at the tower.

"Well, let's see how she feels." He climbed the tower, stood poised for an instant against the light, then leaped out and down with his arms extended, a falling man crucified, an imminent disaster—then at the last second his arms came together and he made a startlingly neat entry into the water, reappeared at the base of the float, pulled himself out again and sat down beside Lawring. There was something almost insultingly offhand about the way he did everything.

"Where'd you learn to dive like that?" Lawring asked him.

"College. Tennis and the dive were my sports. How about you?"

"Football, hockey, baseball."

"Physical contact stuff. You're the type. I was a maverick. Liked to do things all by myself."

They sat on the edge of the float and talked idly of long-ago days, contests and events neither of them remembered too clearly any more, nor cared very much about. Lawring, watching the thrust of pines low against the water's edge, a thin white strip of sandspit, the blue shoulder of Chocorua—he could just make out the wabbly *US* the granite outcroppings traced below the summit—felt at peace, relaxed, dissolving into the mood of the perfect New Hampshire summer afternoon...Then a cloud passed over the sun, a breeze ran cat's-paws in quick fingers over the lake, and he shivered—and thought of Holcomb Hill and the detectives and reporters and the monitored phone calls.

"Where's Ray Lynes, do you know?" he asked Brown.

"Gone over to North Conway. He had some errand over there, I've forgotten just what."

"When'll he be back?"

"Not for some hours, I guess. I know he said not to wait supper for him, he'd get something over there."

Lawring frowned. He realized now he should have taken Ray aside right after they'd arrived; he'd simply assumed the director would be around and he could talk to him before he left. Now he'd have to go back to Boston before he could see him. He glanced at Brown, who was whistling absently and kneading his thigh muscles. Well, Brown would have to do. After all, he was in charge of Brian's hut; perhaps it was even better this way.

"There's something I'd like to speak to you about," he began.

Brown's eyes snapped around to him. "Sure. Shoot, dad."

"It's about Brian. He's had a pretty difficult couple of weeks." He paused. "We've had some trouble at home recently. Do you know about it?"

"I don't think so." Brown's tanned face held a hint of amusement. "Should I?"

"I thought you might have seen the papers or something like that." He took a deep breath. For some reason he resented going into it all over again, up here in the high, clear air, amid the raucous noises of camp's opening. But Ray Lynes would have told Brown anyway. What was the matter with him? He said flatly: "A man entered our house a few weeks ago and assaulted my wife."

"Wow." Brown's face was smooth with surprise. "What—do—you—know," he exclaimed.

"And the boy—he wasn't there when it happened, but it's excited him unduly. You know, the whole cops-and-robbers business. He wants to know all the details and we feel it's better for him not to know them. All he knows is that a man broke in and took some money. Which he did. At least we think that's all he knows about it."

"I get you."

"The atmosphere has been bad for him—the place is crawling with detectives and gadgets and there's been a lot of coming and going . . . The point is, I feel the best thing, if he starts asking any questions about it, is to play it down, turn it aside, make as little of it as possible. Do you follow me?"

"Absolutely, Gardner. Don't you worry about a thing."

"There's also the possibility—I think it's pretty unlikely with kids his own age, but it's possible—that some other boy has read about it or heard about it from his parents. I'd appreciate it if you could keep your ears open, and stop any talk before it gets going."

"Right you are. Anyone brings it up I'll cool it right away . . . Did they get him?"

"No. Not yet."

Brown shook his head, a mystified head-wagging, and puffed

out his lips. "Just came into your house. Just walked in."

"Well, in a manner of speaking. He let himself in through a downstairs window."

"You didn't hear him?"

Lawring looked at Brown for a moment. "I wasn't there."

"Oh—you were away. Waited till you were out, then." He was slapping his thighs with his open hands, lightly. "Gee, that's bleak enough. It must have been a weird experience all around."

"Yes, it was."

"She all right? Your wife?"

"Yes, she's all right. Naturally, she was upset. Shaken."

"I should think *so* . . ." Brown shook his head in wonder, went on slapping his legs, a light pattering tattoo. "Man, that's tough. Not being there and everything. I mean, it must make you feel pretty helpless, a deal like that."

"Yes. It does."

"Just came in the house. Out of the blue. Like that . . . What did you do?"

Lawring glanced at him sharply, but the dark ultramarine eyes still held that serene, genial interest. Maybe it's me, he thought irritably, and locked his hands together. I'm beginning to see attitudes and inferences where none probably exist.

"I didn't do *anything,*" he said with a touch of impatience. "There wasn't anything *to* do . . ."

"I guess not. God, a thing like that would make anybody feel like two cents." Brown hummed tunelessly, picking at a toenail. "Yup, there's things in this world you just can't ever know about. You go sashaying along, trying to be a good Joe and minding your business, and the moment you step out of the house— boom! a thing like that racks you up. Makes you ponder, doesn't it?"

Lawring turned his head and stared hard at Brown, but the tennis instructor was gazing off toward the point, where a tiny red buoy bobbed on the light chop like a brand new toy. He decided he didn't like Brown an awful lot. There was something wrong with him: behind the genial, offhand facade lay an interest far too intense, and something else, too—something he couldn't fathom . . .

"You married?" he inquired all at once.

Brown bent away and gave a soundless laugh. "Me? No.

Curious your asking me that, though—I was just ruminating about her: little gal I *was* married to a while back. Cute little chick from Lancaster, P-A." He said the words like a circus barker. "It didn't take, as they say. Not half." He raised one arm and kneaded its shoulder muscles gently with the other hand. "I'll tell you one thing, dad—little caper like that happened to *me* I'd know it was no rape job. Not one time." His eyes glinted with amusement. "Who comes in when I go out, you know?"

"If you," Lawring started, and stopped himself. Brown, splashing his feet up and down in the water at the edge of the float, hadn't heard him.

"No, little miss Nancy-pants wouldn't have struggled very hard, I can cut you in on that for sure..." Sorrowfully he snorted, and grinned down at the foam around his feet. "You just never know, do you? What a wacky labyrinth..."

Lawring got to his feet. He was amazed to find that his belly was tight with exasperation. He swallowed and said evenly: "Well, it's Brian I'm concerned about here." He paused. "I'm counting on you to curb him if he starts talking about it or asking questions. He's got a very volatile imagination."

"Will do," Brown replied; his eyes still rested on Lawring with that amused intensity, deep blue with a glint of yellow at the centers. "No strain, no pain."

He shook hands quickly with Brown and swam back and said goodbye to a so-far-totally-unhomesick Brian, showered and dressed and set off for Boston. But the heat on the highway had him sweating again, and the conversation with Brown kept nagging at him, rasping at the underside of his mind. What the hell had the man been driving at? All right, it was a bad thing, bad and unfortunate, but it had happened, and that was all there was to it... And yet there was that stupid tennis bum sitting on the float with a moronic grin on his face, watching him with that funny expression: as if he were accusing him—as if, for Christ sake, it had been *his* fault that his wife had been attacked and violated—and worse than that, a sort of jocose suggestion that perhaps she hadn't needed to be raped after all...

He pulled out of line, overhauled two cars and a semi-trailer and shot in again just before the crest of the hill, his hands clamped hard on the wheel, his back stiff. Brown's bland and genial inquiries had pried open that corner of his mind he despised for existing but which existed nonetheless; and the doubts and conjectures that had been borne in on him over the past two weeks came pouring in on him again. Did Janet *have* to give in to the man? Wasn't it true that if women hated violation—really hated the very idea of it—they could defeat or frustrate their attackers? Bizarre tales swept through his mind, tabloid screamers of girls waylaid in cars, in parks, on deserted subway platforms in Ashmont or Sullivan Square, who had fought off their assailants by force or stratagem. Granted, she had been in a terribly vulnerable position: in bed, her clothing removed, no one else in the house; and there had been the normal fear of cold steel, and beyond that the heightened terror of the insane mind—and still beyond that perhaps some primordial voice that at the crucial instant had whispered, *Don't resist—or he will kill you: live* . . .

But wasn't there another voice which might have said: *Resist, no matter what; resist—?* And even leaving all that aside, couldn't she have frightened him off, a simple uneducated vagrant, with some threat of a husband or servant returning? When he went downstairs to get himself that drink, why hadn't she taken a gamble on getting to the phone? Risky, sure—but she could have chanced it, she could have said in a low, rapid voice: "Muriel—police, Lawring, *Lawring!*" and hung up. That would probably have done it. And if Muriel Talbott had called back to check and the man had let Janet answer—as he undoubtedly would have decided to do—she could have handled that deftly, too—let Muriel know by her tone that something was deeply wrong there . . . How could she have been in such confusion over whether he was white or Negro? And why had he hung around so long—why had he felt so infernally *secure* all that time? How could he have known that Lawring wasn't coming back that night? How could he have known?

He checked the headlong rush of his thoughts then, forced Stan Brown's genial southern California face out of sight and in his raw disquietude dwelt on his early years with Janet; their meeting, and the intoxicated vibrance of those first soaring months. He remembered her sitting in old Wayvell's office and the expression she wore at the typewriter—as though she were confronting some Martian contrivance placed there for her personal obfuscation; the way her hair would flail around her lovely face when she turned. She had been a marvelously terrible secretary: she lost correspondence, misfiled records according to some capricious, whimsical code of her own (the reports of the Delhi mission she had filed under K because, as she explained to an astounded Wayvell and Miss Tannersley, she'd read a lot of Kipling as a young girl and Kipling really *stood* for India to her). She made errors of horrendous scope; as a typist she was so bad it was a source of hilarity at the Foundation—the other girls had once presented her with a mammoth cardboard mock-up of one of those wheel erasers with a brush at one end—the brush in this case being a straw broom with the handle sawed off. And yet Wayvell indulged her; angry with her as he got, sputtering and hoarse, his eyes rheumy with exasperation, he couldn't bear to let her go—she had such a sense of *enthusiasm* about her, he once told Lawring, it was wonderful to see such enthusiasm!

Lawring had agreed with him. It was as simple as that, and as miraculous. Life was amazing, she seemed to say by the very way she laughed, or shrugged her shoulders, or rolled her eyes to the ceiling. For her every day was like the beginning of some gloriously endless childhood vacation, an adventure bubbling with all sorts of vivid, unforeseen moments; anything could happen and probably would, approached in this spirit of joyful acceptance. He had never met anyone remotely like her and she had charmed him right out of his skin. Even his mother's consternation and disapproval, her terse invocation of the shades of ten generations of Lawrings and Alcocks who had, it was true, now and then married "outside"—but never *below their station* (a phrase that had set off the only real quarrel they had ever had, a series of increasingly icy retorts that, with any other mother and any other son, would have ended in tears)—even his mother's bitterest disapproval had for once no effect on him at all. He was in love, and he was sure of his love. He had never looked back, never once regretted his decision; and when the baby was born, and Janet had smiled up at him weakly, her face shining with triumph, and whispered, "I'm going to name him Brian," he had grinned and bent over and kissed her damp little forehead and agreed, even though no Lawring had ever borne that name or one even remotely like it.

They had their quarrels, but they were minor and they never lasted. You could forgive her anything—you had to: she carried such a sense of exuberance about her, even in her very irresponsibility. She forgot things. She left the caps loose on bottles and jars, so that if you picked one of them up it would smash to pieces and its contents would run all over the tiles. She would park the car on Newbury Street and leave it for half a day with the key in the ignition; she got the linens mixed up and ran out of double-width sheets, she confused Lawring's socks with Brian's, once she ran the car completely out of oil—and yet these lapses never upset her at all. On their third date, driving back to her home from dinner and theater, her face had all at once been flooded with a startled, preoccupied look and she had said, "Oh, my goodness—we're going to have to find a drugstore. Do you mind?" He found one, and then pulled in to a gas station and bought three gallons—it was all that was needed to fill the tank—while she hurried into the ladies' room. Sitting behind the wheel watching the attendant's arm sweep over the windshield, he had been mildly astonished. Women were supposed to keep count of the days, weren't they? be prepared for these times . . .

"Wasn't that silly," she declared, as they ran out along the river with the lights from the Boston shore like bobbing night flowers. "Thank the lord it didn't happen during the play: golly! The trouble our old machinery causes us. Well," and she tossed her head airily, "can't be helped!" He found himself laughing with her, thinking of Peg, his sisters, other girls he'd known; her utter lack of embarrassment intrigued him—it was all as natural to her as a broken shoelace or a loose filling.

He'd been more surprised than that, however, when he'd discovered she was not a virgin. "But what's so amazing about that, darling?" she'd asked him with soft candor; they were in his old bedroom in the house at Nount's Head, and her eyes were wide and lovely, a deep amethyst in the evening light. It was nothing very catastrophic, she said; there had been a boy named Jimmy and she had thought she was in love with him and he with her, and then when he'd got out of the army his ideas had changed, he'd met someone else, he wanted a career in the state department and he went off to Trieste; he was in Beirut now, she thought. "I know it sounds silly, saying it like this; but I think I was in love with him."

"And so you went to bed with him," Lawring said: a musing voice, not censorious.

She smiled and flicked the edge of her teeth with her tongue. "Well: that's the kind of girl I am!" Then more gravely she added: "I know *now* I didn't love him, but I thought I did then. Really and truly." She watched him a moment. "Should you go through life waiting for some mythical Prince Charming to come tripping along? I might be sixty or something, all my juices withered up. I could never live that way..."

"Yes, but you're—everything's different after that," he protested.

"Was it for you?"

He stared at her impish merry little smile, so close to his own lips, and laughed. Sometimes it was fun being caught out. "Yes, in a way it was," he admitted, thinking of that afternoon with Buff Haviland in the hotel room in Des Moines—the absurdly transparent fiction of the nearly empty suitcase, the unbearable tension and prickly fear, and then the almost stupefying delight, beyond all his erotic conjecture...

"Do you wish you hadn't, then?"

"...No," he answered slowly, "no, I can't say that."

"Well, I feel the same way, I don't regret it. I think it's better to do what you feel in your heart than hold back because some day in the gray, grim old future you might regret it." The south wind whistled at the screen and poured cool as silk across their bodies; her skin chafed his in the most delicate tactile caress when she stirred. "The poor old body isn't anything, really," she went on. "What happens to it, I mean. It goes along like an engine, it's all nicely oiled and it gets lots of good fuel and things and it runs fine; or it breaks down and has to be repaired and patched up so it can run along again. I had my tonsils out when I was ten. Two years ago I had these pains in my womb and a doctor examined me there, they thought I had a tipped uterus or something. And what difference did that make? It's the same poor old body the doctor put all those instruments in that's lying here with you...

"I think it's the heart," she declared with light fervor; her eyes were moist and wide and full of little stars. "The heart is everything. That's what can't be patched up and repaired all the time. That's where things are different... My father saved a man's life once," she went on. "They were setting up this staging and Culetty, this man that worked for him, started to fall and

Pop caught him just in time. And then they went into partnership later and one day Culetty took all the money and disappeared. Just like that. And never showed up again. Pop never talks about it, you'd never know it because he's so lively, so—you know, full of beans and projects; but it cut him right to the heart. You're never the same after something like that. There's no way to patch that up, ever..."

Lawring had liked her father; but the atmosphere of the Delannoy home had dismayed him. This crazy ark in mustard with pale blue trim, littered with oversize fenestration and bulging bay windows and wrought-iron staircases, half of it surplus from a Charlestown shipyard, the I-beams and pillars planted at random in the middle of rooms through which strangers wandered casually, calling Hello, and kids played marbles or shot homemade balsa gliders—this whole noisy, wacky ménage redolent of cigar smoke and boiled cabbage and ammonia and the parched odor of ironing distressed him. What kind of way to live was this? But he noticed that Janet wasn't at all apprehensive about his reaction to it, and this for some reason pleased him. He drank a can of beer, went down into the cellar to inspect the new heating system Harry Delannoy had installed himself—a surrealist nightmare with forests of ducts swathed in white insulation, like shattered limbs, crossing and recrossing each other in tentacular confusion; he helped jack up a corner of the garage, played a raucous, sweaty game of volleyball with Janet's brothers and some neighbors from over the backyard fence—and after dinner, sitting on the front porch in a green wicker rocker while they all sang "Sleep, Kentucky Babe" and "On Moonlight Bay" and Mrs. Delannoy accompanied them on the piano from inside the house, he felt curiously at ease, and decided he liked them all very much. It was no way to *live,* of course—it was a sort of free-for-all headlong vacation and barnraising—but he could enjoy it as such.

The Delannoys were forever playing games: volleyball, horseshoes, badminton in a dusty little plot whose base lines were totally erased, occasionally even a bizarre variation of three-o'-cat played with a plastic bat and a whiffle ball you couldn't hit farther than thirty feet no matter how hard you swung; and there were darts and Ping-Pong in the cellar if it rained. He did well at all of these, he was a natural athlete and a good competitor, and he even got used to the confused, multitudinous dinners where he might be seated next to Mrs. Delannoy or Janet's happy-go-lucky brother Wally or some complete stranger, an ex-fireman or registered nurse from down the street. He laughed and joked with the others and reached for the bread and passed the heavy platters, but he couldn't take it seriously. Janet was what he wanted: they were going to get married, and soon; and after that things would be a bit different. "You mean you're going to take me away from all that?" she'd teased him once when he'd made some rather guarded reference to the Delannoy household, and he'd laughed with her, but it was true: that was pretty much how he looked at it. After their marriage they went out to Somerville less and less, and when he'd got the new courthouse commission and started building their own home in Holcomb Hill they hardly went there at all.

"She's like all of us, only more so," her mother had said to him one evening at dinner before they were married, apropos of what he couldn't remember. "She wears her heart on her sleeve." He had agreed, smiling, had glanced across the welter of ketchup and A-1 Sauce bottles and vinegar cruets and barbaric green fountains of celery to see Janet watching him with love in her eyes like the flash from Minot's Light. She did wear her heart on her sleeve—and it was one of the things he loved about her; if he'd been a different kind of man he would have leaped to his feet and run around the table and picked her up in his arms and kissed her right in front of the whole gabbling, gobbling crowd . . .

Now, remembering that brief, jubilant moment, he sighed and compressed his lips. Wasn't this, for God's sake, the very core of what he most loved in her—her warm, heedless irresponsibility? Why should he expect her to act with the swift self-possession of a counterspy? It was the very thing that had rendered her vulnerable—that glow of generosity and trust anyone could read at half a glance. He could reconstruct the scene perfectly: the shadow in the doorway, the knife, her voiceless terror; then the purse, the quick, terrible exchanges, and then he had come up to the bed and—

He groaned, watching the parched, barren land of the border country drift by him in the dusty heat. And he had not been there. Stan Brown's bland, tanned face came back then, too, the easy affability which the sharp inquisitiveness of the ultramarine eyes belied. *It must make you feel pretty helpless, a deal like that. I'll tell you one thing, dad—little caper like that happened to me ... You just never know, do you?* The son of a bitch ... It was ridiculous, he must not think this way. He must not think this way. Stalled at a construction tie-up near Chelmsford he ran the heel of his hand over his forehead and muttered aloud: "I want it to be over. Over ..." The talk with Brown inflamed his thoughts and he went over it again and again, worrying it like a dog with an old sock, chewing and rending it without satisfaction ... And there was Brian; was he leaving the boy in the hands of some kind of nut, some genial sadist? Still, he knew Ray Lynes well enough to know the director would surround himself with responsible counselors. He made a mental note to phone Lynes in the morning, explain the situation to him and ask him to keep an eye on it; maybe he could even feel him out a bit about Brown ...

There was more construction all along Route 128, the heat had gathered around Boston like a vise, and he arrived at the house in the early dark tense and overtired and troubled. Danny Shea's gray '55 Chevy was parked at the far edge of the drive. He mopped his face and neck with his handkerchief and came in through the kitchen.

Mrs. Pruitt yanked her head out of the oven door and said: "Mercy! Scare a person half to death, coming in like that." You could find her kneeling like this in front of the oven half an hour at a time, grinding off the measle-rash of grease stains with steel wool like a fanatic, even removing the bulb at the back.

"I'm sorry," Lawring answered.

"I suppose *now* you're hungry enough to eat a boiled owl."

"I ate on the way down."

She stroked her hands on the skirt of her apron. "Well. *You're* blue as a whetstone. What'd you do—get a ticket for speeding in Nashua?"

"Don't go through Nashua any more."

"That's a pity." She glanced at the stove clock and clucked once. "Eight-fifteen. Any rubber left on the tires at all?"

"Just poked along," he said, pouring himself a glass of water. He heard a burst of laughter in the living room, Janet and Franz Hoelder an octave apart, and for some reason this depressed him.

"I'll bet," Mrs. Pruitt was saying in her tartest tone.

"Well, I'm pleased to see you avoided being part of the day's death toll, at any rate."

He set the glass down, tried to think of some provocative rejoinder and couldn't; shook his head at her and swung into the living room. Reardon had cut the detectives down to one the day before—there had been no anonymous calls for over a week now—and only Danny Shea and a policewoman named Eileen Hanlon were sitting there, with Janet and Franz. He went up to Janet and kissed her on the cheek.

"How did it go, darling?" she asked him.

"Fine."

"Is my baby homesick?"

"Not a bit," he said with forced heartiness. "When I left him he was doing the dead man's float like Johnny Weissmuller. He says he's going to be the first to pass his canoe test, climb Chocorua, and win the gold cup."

"Do they give out gold cups at summer camp?" Franz asked.

"They used to. For best all-around camper. Gard won it twice. Didn't you, darling?"

He nodded glumly. They had all been laughing together before he had come in: now there was an atmosphere of constraint in the room, of false attentiveness, and Lawring felt irritated and unhappy. He went over to the side table and made himself a large gin and tonic.

"Boy, I'm weary. That's a long, dull drive. Anyone else?"

Franz raised his own glass lightly and Shea and the girls shook their heads.

"Danny's been telling us about a fantastic couple in Dorchester," Janet explained. "They used to get in fights with knives. It seems incredible that people could live that way . . ."

"If you can call it living," Shea said. His voice was soft and mild, with a ring of sadness. Lawring could imagine him as an altar boy at St. Matthew's, looking serious and dutiful, and with the same round, cherubic face. "They were the worst I ever had to deal with. Jerry was little, Doris weighed over two hundred pounds and big, enormous arms and shoulders—and fight! My God how they would fight, cut each other up and blood all over the floor and the sofa and everything else. One time she cut him all around the face and neck, and another time he stabbed her in the side and she walked all the way to City Hospital, twenty,

twenty-five blocks, and keeled over in the lobby. And then a month later they'd be at it again."

"Goodness. Why didn't they separate?" Janet exclaimed. To Lawring she seemed unnaturally vivacious; there was a spot of scarlet on each cheek. "They don't sound very compatible..."

"How is it you didn't arrest them?" Franz asked.

Shea smiled. "Neither one would prefer charges against the other, so there was no case. That's the way it works here. They both liked me a lot, they'd come to me and confide, each one would tell me about the other one and what he was going to do. 'Shea, she's getting awful mean again,' 'Shea, he's working up to something, he's spoiling for trouble, what am I going to do?' It kept on like that, and I tried to get them to break up. 'One of these days one of you is going to get *too* mad and then there'll be real trouble,' I told them, and they made me all kinds of promises but it didn't last. Finally one night they got into a real donnybrook, a really bad one. The street was in an uproar, all the neighbors screaming bloody murder, and I broke open the door and Doris had him pinned in one corner of the kitchen and was on the point of carving him up with a knife as long as your arm. Well, I got the knife away from her and after half an hour or so I got her to agree to talking the matter over, and that they'd better bust up before they killed each other. She agreed with me, she seemed to be really calm and subdued by then and I left—and I hadn't hardly got out of the building when I heard yelling again. So I ran back up the three flights, I didn't have to break the door down again, I'd already snapped the lock off once that evening, and so help me she had *another* knife and was chasing him all over the place. God, what a racket. Everything smashed to pieces. Jerry was holding her off with what was left of a kitchen chair and blood was running down his neck into his shirt collar. Well, this time I got angry, it was two-thirty in the morning and I'd had all I could take of those two for a while and I said: 'Doris, you people have given me a lot of trouble and if you don't put down that knife I'm going to have to shoot you. I don't want to but I will. I've taken all I'm going to and that's all.' And Doris looked at me and said, 'Well I don't want to involve you...'"

"Oh, that's priceless," Janet cried, "that's perfectly priceless!—"

"And I said, 'Well, you're going to if you don't put down that knife.' So she finally did. This time I took Jerry away with me. And later I got them to agree to split up."

"And did they?"

"Nope. He went back to her. It's funny—before, it was Doris who wanted to stick, but after they split up it was Jerry who wanted to go back and patch it up. And after a month or so he did."

"And that is how it all ended?" Franz asked him.

Shea threw open his hands. "Beats me. By then I was transferred to the detective squad. It's someone else's problem now." His mild blue eyes moved coolly around the room. "But those things usually end badly . . ."

Lawring sipped his drink, holding it on his tongue: the bitter bite of quinine, the sting of gin. His head ached and his blood felt as if it were boiling in his veins after the long, hard drive. Fitfully he listened to Danny Shea and these glimpses of the sea-surge of ignorance and squalor and violence that lay on the edges of life like the night marshes down in Brewster, waiting to fill in the dark; a seeping black invasion. He remembered all at once an incident on Washington Street when he'd been nine or ten. They had been shopping, a Saturday in the early fall. There was a commotion ahead of them and a young man in a white shirt was dancing through the crowds, and now in the street, dodging and swerving, a wild shock of black hair; and then the hue and cry, a policeman had jumped on to the running board of a passing car, commandeering it, was pointing ahead intently, then a further commotion at Winter Street, and then he hadn't been able to see anything more. What was it, what had happened?

"A thief," his father had answered. "That young man just snatched some woman's purse."

"Did they catch him?"

"Of course they caught him." A curt, almost severe tone, the tone that meant, All right now, that's enough, we don't talk about those things. And now the policeman was coming toward them along the sidewalk and the thin young man in the white shirt was walking close beside him; his face looked hollow and immensely tired, his eyes passed over Lawring's like the eyes of a man in a bad dream. Lawring turned around, but the crowd had closed over them again.

"But—" he stammered "—why did he do it, Dad?"

"I'm sure I don't know," Thomas Lawring said. "Too shiftless to work for a living, I suppose." His father's face moving high above him, looked hard and remote. The big hand took his own, firmly. "Come along, now. We're crossing."

There were a thousand questions he wanted to ask, hurrying along to keep up with his father. Was that agony—the fear and the hue and cry, the enormous wrong of stealing and the shame of being caught, with all the world to know of it—was all that preferable to working for a living? Had the man thought he could get away with it, among all these people? How did he know the purse contained any money—or enough to make it worth such a risk? Or was the man crazy, and couldn't judge what he was doing? He hadn't asked any of these questions, however. The subject was bad, shameful, something we didn't talk about...

"Disgraceful!" That had been another time, a year or so earlier, at South Station: his mother's voice, one winter night. A big man in an open mackinaw was haranguing them in the Summer Street entrance. Schofield was supposed to pick them up in the Buick but he'd been held up for some reason and they were waiting there in the cold, raw night air along with cab drivers, a porter or two and some hangers-on, part of the audience for the man in the mackinaw, who had a red, very happy face and eyes as blue as Easter eggs.

"And *that's* how it is!" he sang out pleasantly, swaying in the snow and shifting his feet, which were encased in a flimsy kind of moccasin and soaked through. He seemed to be oblivious of the condition of his feet. "And we're gonna start all *over* again!" He held up one huge red finger like a beacon. "Every man will get one axe, one rifle, and *one* bottle of Burke's Irish. That's *it*. No gilt-edge stock, no real estate out in Back Bay, no bank accounts—"

"That's telling 'em, Kerrigan," one of the cabbies called.

"Right! Gonna wipe the slate smooth as a baby's buttocks." His blue eyes shot around brightly, caught on Lawring's. "Hello there, sonny!" He waved genially: his hands were like huge red paws. "You gonna join? Grand new shuffle. And *then* we'll separate the men from the boys..."

"Disgraceful!" Lawring's mother was saying. "A grown man standing there like that..."

"And the *women* are all gonna be put in a big pen spang in the middle of Boston Common, in nothing but their little old birthday suits!" Kerrigan proclaimed jovially. "No Hattie Carnegie, no Ska-pa-relli, no Tiffany ti-aras, none of *that* skinnay..."

"Sing 'em, Kerry!" one of the cab drivers, a slender Negro standing near Lawring, called out.

"Right!" The word cracked like a whip and Kerrigan drove an enormous fist into his open palm. "All of 'em just milling around in there. Just the elementals. What we were all born with, no *more* and no *less*. You got me?"

"Sing 'em, boy!..."

Marcia Lawring turned to the Negro cabby and said: "Stop that. You stop that, now."

The man's face went sober in an instant, his Adam's apple bobbed. "Ma'am?" he said.

"I said to stop it. You go over and tell that man to stop mouthing that obnoxious rubbish."

The Negro stared back at her in alarm. "No, ma'am—not me. Don't *nobody* want to mess with Kerrigan when he giving the royal word."

"Well, don't you encourage him! You ought to be ashamed of yourselves. Egging on a drunken lout like that..."

"Yes'm," the cabby said.

"—And then they're gonna open up the pen and the best man goes in *first!* Get me? And that's gonna be the *real* New Deal..."

"Pour it on, Kerrigan!"

"Happy day..."

"Disgraceful," Marcia Lawring repeated. Her mouth was clamped shut and there was a thin vertical line through each of her cheeks. "Come along, Gardy."

"No, I want to hear," Lawring protested all at once, "I want to hear him..."

"You're coming back in the station with me," his mother enunciated with deadly calm. "And right now. Now come."

A second longer he hung back, pulling at his mother's arm, fascinated at this thunderous, breezy new gospel and its fearless promulgator—then dutifully followed her back into the raw white light of the station and up to the information desk.

"Who is in charge here?" his mother was demanding, in the voice that always made everyone apologetic and eager. "I want to see the stationmaster." He wasn't there apparently, he was only on duty until eight; he'd gone home. "Where, then, is the constable on duty?" They hadn't known that either, but she'd found him anyway—a dour, ponderous man with a scar over one eyebrow, sipping gingerly at a cup of coffee at a counter over on the Atlantic Avenue side. Marcia Lawring placed herself in front of him.

"Officer, there is a man in a woodsman's jacket just outside the Summer Street entrance. He is intoxicated and extremely abusive and I think you should take him in hand."

The policeman came off his stool with alacrity. "Yes, ma'am." He moved off through the grimy long hall of the station like a blue, uniformed bear; an easy, unhurried stride that was a good deal faster than it looked. When Lawring and his mother went out again Kerrigan and the officer had vanished and Schofield was there with the car, looking mournful. There had been a leak in the left front tire and he'd had to have it repaired, he was very sorry indeed. Marcia Lawring nodded and climbed into the deep seat and sat back, her face steady and serene, her duty done, the incident already behind her. That was life: you encountered—now and then, unfortunately—disorganization or divergence or even (implausibly) vulgarity in public places, and you checked it, corrected it. That was what you were trained to do. Wasn't it?

"Oh sure, plenty of time," Danny Shea was saying now in answer to some question Lawring hadn't caught. "There's no help for it. One night there was a mugging on my post and I thought I saw the assailant duck into a bar. One of the toughest bars in all of Boston. The victim wasn't very eager but I finally got him to go in with me and make the identification. I had a hunch where the joker would be, so we went straight through to the washroom and there he was all right, on the stool. I asked the victim, 'Is this your assailant?' He shook his head and said, 'No,' and I could see his face go all pale. Well, we couldn't stay in there, I'd been worried about taking him out of that joint as it was, so we left. And then later down at the station house the fellow admitted the joker in the washroom was the man. I asked him why he hadn't made the identification and he said he had to live in the area, that the guy's friends would—you know, take vengeance on him if he opened his mouth."

"Disgusting," Lawring heard himself say suddenly.

"Do you think so?" Franz queried.

"I certainly do. What happens to justice if everyone does that kind of thing?" He felt the edge in his voice and his hand tightened on his glass. Danny Shea was watching him curiously. "Don't you agree?" he asked him.

Shea folded his arms. "Well, it's too bad. When it happens. I don't blame him, actually—in one way."

"Well, I do. There is right and there is wrong, and you have to act on that. What becomes of our concept of truth and justice if everyone is afraid for his own skin?"

"... Truth and justice," Franz echoed softly, after a short pause. "A man I knew in France, during the Occupation, realized one afternoon that a friend of his, a prominent member of the Resistance, was under surveillance by the Gestapo—and was on the point of being apprehended. He knew that he could warn him and probably save him by deflecting attention on to himself... but to do so would have meant risking his own wife and child, who were Jews. He thought it over quickly—and did nothing. And his friend was apprehended, sent to a German concentration camp, and died there." Franz examined the fingers of his left hand. "What should he have done?"

"What his conscience dictated," Lawring said.

"But there were *two* consciences here—several, in fact: the cause, his loved ones—"

"You're wrong. There is only one." Janet was frowning at him unhappily and Shea was studying the rug, and it made Lawring cross all at once. This seemed like a very important point to make and it vexed him that none of them saw the importance it had. "Don't you see?—we have to make choices all the time," he said to Franz, leaning forward, "but one of them is always the right one—the choice of principle."

Hoelder smiled gently. "Only sometimes the choices of principle are so difficult..."

"He should have warned the Resistance leader," Lawring said stubbornly.

"And sacrifice his wife and son—let them be caught and tortured and put to death? And to what end—so that France might wobble along through her several governments and colonial wars and bomb brandishing?"

"You're arguing after the fact..."

"Perhaps I am. Perhaps, though, his allegiance to his wife and child was more important than his allegiance to his country."

"There is nothing more important than allegiance to principle."

"I don't think this argument is getting anywhere," Janet broke in, and got to her feet. "Is it? Let's play some cards."

"That's a good idea," Shea said pleasantly. "What'll it be?"

"Well, you know I'm partial to hearts—I go wild wondering who's got the deadly queen of spades? But I'll play bridge or even pinochle if everyone wants."

Lawring glared at her and finished his drink. Far from relaxing him the gin had heightened his tension and fatigue, as though it had turned a wrench on several already overstrained bolts in his brain. The sense that the others disagreed with his position, even disapproved of it, exasperated him. Of course: he was the only one to take a stand, care about principles and so they wanted to shut him up, pretend he wasn't there. Bad-mannered little boy, go stand in the corner. Well, the hell with that.

"Your friend should have warned the Resistance man and let the chips fall where they may," he declared.

"Gard, can't we let it go?" Janet pleaded in a quavering voice, and at the same moment Franz laughed and said:

"You fire-and-brimstone Yankees! You see everything so black-and-white. No shades of gray at all..."

"That's how life is."

Franz shook his head—an old man's gesture which infuriated Lawring. "Your solutions are too absolute for my taste, Gardner."

"And yours are too cynical for mine."

Franz's eyes flashed up at him, wide with surprise, a faded blue, and Shea's face had swung toward him with a sudden sharpness, like an animal alerted to a strange scent; but the anger was riding him now, borne on resentment at their opposition, their almost patronizing disapproval, it was goading him along and he said, "That's what's wrong with the world right now, if you want my opinion—sentiments like yours that blur away all issues into a—into a complete fog of cynicism and indifference. I know, that's all the fashion now—you blame your transgressions on childhood traumas or prenatal experiences or the pressures of a career or...or ignorance of the circumstances involved, or some damn thing. When all the time it's personal failure, pure and simple—failure to hold to one's deepest convictions, act on them in the face of all the other pressures..."

He ran down and stopped, scraped at his neck with his fingernails. Janet was standing with her back to him, peering out at the splashes of light and shadow the floodlights cast on the garden; he could tell by the hunch to her shoulders that she was angry. There was an awkward silence in the room. Lawring knew he probably sounded pompous and priggish and absurd, but he didn't care. The events of the day—his negligence over talking to Ray Lynes about Brian, Brown's bland insinuations on the float and the dusty drive back to Boston surged over him and left him slumped there feeling morose and defiant. And it *was* a point worth making all the same, they could think whatever they liked...He longed for another drink but he was damned if he was going to walk over and help himself to one in front of the four of them.

There was some fragmentary small talk, and finally Franz Hoelder got slowly to his feet and said, "Well, I must go. Tomorrow, whether it likes the idea or not, is another day."

"Please don't rush off, Franz," Janet pleaded. "It isn't even ten yet..."

"No. I must go. I have put myself on a ferocious schedule: up at five-thirty, to to work at six. Breakfast at eleven. That was my regimen at Göttingen. Long, long ago."

"How's the book going?"

"Torrentially. I am going to write it without footnotes. Can you imagine?—a book by a German historian without footnotes? It will be a sensation. Or I will lose all status immediately, they will fire me and I won't be able to reminisce about my student days, with all those lovely young girls hanging on my every word." He rubbed his eyes as though he'd been staring at manuscripts for hours. "It's curious. I was working on the same subject at Göttengen—Voltaire and Frederick the Great. But now it's like another subject altogether. Before, it was just a—an exercise in two personalities. Characters, you call them. Two eccentric characters..." He raised one hand to the level of his shoulder—a hieratic gesture, two fingers extended. "All our troubles begin there, do you know that?"

"How do you mean?" Shea said.

"All of them. Political power and the needs of the intellect. Individual dignity versus the authority of the state. Our poor old tortured modern world started with those two." His eyes narrowed. "Interesting: Old Fritz thought he had the last word in the quarrel. But he did not."

"Tell us about it," Janet coaxed him.

"Too complicated. Besides, I don't want to talk it out—isn't that what they say out in Hollywood?" He made his courtly little bow to Janet and kissed her solemnly on the cheek. "Thank you for the charming repast, as always."

"That wasn't me, that was Pruitt."

"Do you think if I ate a third helping she might become more fond of me?"

"I doubt it. She's awfully set in her ways. She's a dyed-in-the-wool Yankee, like Gard."

"Perhaps I should go to carving school." He nodded to Shea and the Hanlon girl, turned to Lawring then and smiled gently. "Goodnight, Gardner."

"Goodnight," Lawring answered; his throat was dry.

Twenty minutes later, upstairs, undressing to the click and shimmer of the television set Janet said: "There was no real need to do that, was there?"

"Do what?"

"Pick a quarrel with Franz."

"I *didn't* pick a quarrel with Franz . . ."

"You certainly did."

"Look, can't there be a difference of opinion between two people?"

"It was a lot more than that and you know it. He's been a good friend, a warm, affectionate person . . ."

He was still on edge, weary, resentful, smarting from a tumult of suspicion and conjecture, and seeing menace in every shadow. He said: "Yes, he's so warm and affectionate he's hardly ever away from here . . ."

She gazed at him in angry amazement. "Oh! Are you—are you really trying to say—?"

"Put any name on it you want."

"Oh, that's despicable!"

"Is it?"

"Yes, it is—you're hopeless! He's a good friend," she repeated, and began to cry. "He's come by, stood by us all through this horrible, endless time . . . He hasn't written us off, he isn't standing there judging me, like some other people I could mention—"

"What do you mean by that?" he demanded, though he knew what she was going to say.

"I mean your sacred mother, that's what I mean," she answered hotly through her tears. "Sitting there. Acting as though I don't even exist—"

"She hasn't done that."

"Then what do you call it?" she whirled on him. "Hasn't even come by once, hasn't even *phoned* except that one time—and then she talked to me as though I were a corpse laid out for burial. Mercy call or something. Oh no, of course not, off to the shores of sunny Cape Cod without a care in the world—took Boo off with her too, without a thought . . ."

"Keep your voice down," he said sharply. "Look, Jan, you know it was bad for him here . . ."

"I don't care if it was bad for him here, it was his home! . . . Yes, I know, that's all got a so much finer atmosphere, full of background and ancestors—"

"At least it's based on *something* . . ."

"Don't tell me what it's based on—I know what it's based on and I detest it!"

"Keep your voice down!"

"Genealogy and all the things nobody's supposed to do because they might feel alive and human, for a change . . ."

"Jan, you said you didn't want to see her, you didn't—"

"No, of course I didn't want to see her!"

"All right then, what are you upset for?"

"That's not the point, not the point at all! The point is she hasn't even offered to come out here—she can't get far enough away from this filthy, despicable episode that's sullying her God-given reputation—"

"That's not true," he said tightly.

"Isn't it? Isn't it? Don't you think I feel it, too?—the shame, the rotten nastiness of it? How much more for her, then—how can she even *admit* that her own daughter-in-law could have this dirty, disgusting thing happen to her ...?"

She was weeping now, a low, steady sobbing, and he watched her helplessly, swayed to and fro by anger, exhaustion, resentment, his love for her. She looked so fragile standing in the middle of the big room in her slip, her hands clenched at her sides like a little girl in a classroom declamation who has forgotten her lines. He'd been hurt by her words about his mother but he overrode it, went up to her and put his arms around her gently, stroked and patted her bare shoulders.

"Honey, you're all wrought up," he murmured, "you're imagining things. You really are ... It's going to be all right, honey. Don't worry, now. They're going to pick up the fellow soon, you'll see, and we'll put it all behind us."

It was the wrong thing to say. Her head came up, she jerked away from him. "No," she protested, "no—oh, can't you see?—it isn't like that, any of it, it isn't what you think! The good guys don't always win in the end! ... My father saved a man's life and he ran off and took all the money and left him with debts to pay ... Oh, you don't understand anything!"

She was staring at him wildly, glaring into his eyes as if to catch there the cause of all this wretchedness and anguish, and it shook him.

"Maybe you're right," he muttered. "Maybe I don't."

"... They're not going to find him," she said after a moment in a dull, spent voice. "They aren't ever going to find him, it's going to go on like this for the rest of our lives ..."

"No," he said.

"And I don't think I stand it if it does. I just can't ..."

Once more she broke down and he sought to comfort her, standing in the master bedroom he'd designed with such loving care and which was now the seat of all their unhappiness, while on the television screen a portly man with a waxed mustache drew weather symbols with chalk on a blackboard map of the United States.

"I'm sorry," he said softly. "Really and truly sorry, Jan ... Don't torture yourself, now. Nobody's judging you. I think you're wrong about Mother. Honest I do. She—she just doesn't think about these things the way a lot of other people do ..."

Again it was the wrong thing to say. She stiffened and said: "No, of course not—anything unpleasant, anything that might cause *talk*..."

"No, it's not that. She was the same way during the war. The whole world was up in smoke and flame, blowing all to hell-and-gone, and all she'd write were, you know, little things—the garden down at Brewster or the roof at Mount Vernon Street, the furnace being out of kilter... You know, the even run of things. It didn't mean she didn't care. That's how she's always lived—it's, well, the way she was brought up, I guess..."

"Well, it's a terrible way to be brought up, then."

"Maybe it is. But that's the way I was brought up, too."

"Yes, and you're just as bad, you pick a fight with Franz over nothing, nothing at all, and drive him out of the house, turn everything all silent and mean..."

"I know," he said, and sighed. "I was tired from the day's drive—"

"All right, you're tired—my God, don't you think I'm a little tired, too? You hurt his feelings, you know that—calling him cynical and dumb and everything else..."

"I'm sorry, sweet," he said after a minute. "Really and truly. You're right: it was wrong of me. The wrong way to act." He didn't think it was, actually, he felt with every beat of his blood that he was right and Franz was wrong; but he was sorry for having created the rupture and he wanted to mend it. "I was tired and wound up and I let go at him. I'll call him up tomorrow and apologize. Solemn promise. All right?"

"... You didn't really mean that, did you?" she asked. "About the—the reason for his coming over here?"

"No. No, I didn't."

"You mustn't think that, Gard. You mustn't. Ever. We'll turn into creeps if we start thinking that way, it's terrible..." She ground her forehead back and forth against his shirt front. "If they could only find out who it *is,*" she moaned. "Find him, get it over with. How long is it going to go on?—this crazy, stupid, *hunted* kind of life...?"

"Not long," he said. "Not much longer, I'm sure. Reardon told me today he's confident they'll pick him up soon, they've got one or two new leads—"

"Oh, have they? Have they?"

"Yes. There's been another incident, in Milton; a case very much like ours. They'll find him, I'm sure of it. Just hang on now, sweet. Just a little longer..."

He gently chafed her neck and shoulder—a slow, firm rhythm he knew she loved. He had always taken the lead in their relationship and he did so now, steadying her by his voice, his presence, murmuring assurances he himself didn't begin to feel... until finally, with these and the aid of a blue pill she became drowsy and he put her to bed and then went downstairs to his study and worked on the drawings for the Siegersen house, driving himself into a dry-eyed frenzy of concentration, roughing in sketch after sketch, shutting out by a ruthless act of will everything that pressed against his equanimity—the quarrel with Franz, Brown's false, genial tones, the disagreement with McGrath and Henchey over the Pan-American Airlines building, Danny Shea pacing quietly through the rooms behind him...

At three o'clock, light-headed with sleeplessness, he crept up to the big guest bedroom and moved to the edge of the bed where Janet was asleep. He stood there watching the shell-like fragility of her face, the dark swirl of hair low over her forehead; then bent over and put his lips softly to her cheek. She did not waken.

Chapter Seven

The wind stirred and flowers of shadow swayed across the damp earth; in the euonymus thicket a song sparrow was singing, his little round head bobbing with the three staccato opening notes. Janet Lawring knelt in the garden, feeling the sun on her neck, the spongy brown soil under her hands, and thought about the dream she'd had that morning early. There had been a man—a dark, slender man in windbreaker and jeans who was sitting with her on a terrace, a high place full of sunlight and clear, pungent air; he was laughing, joking, telling her all about himself, his hopes and dreams and all the places he had been—a vagabond journey under brooding volcanoes, past palm-laced isles where huge Moroccans slapped intricate rhythms on tall ivory drums, through alabaster cities in whose narrow streets turbaned figures gesticulated and prayed, keening in the violent copper air. Somehow she made this voyage with him, marveling at the vibrant, multifarious glories of this world and the man in the windbreaker showed it all to her, pointing out its landmarks—minarets and mountains and machicolated towers where sentinels paraded like flamboyant toys. This, then, is the world, she thought in simple rapture; all the riotous splendor I've been missing...and she felt no fear at all, only this unbounded curiosity tinged with wonder. But the man was cleaning his fingernails with a knife—short, expert strokes which disturbed her subtly; she wanted to ask him to stop and decided not to—but he stopped anyway then, fell silent and merely looked at her and smiled a slow, unhappy smile: the smile of a man about to die. Why? she wondered—and then she had said it aloud: "Why? Why are you doing all this for me?" And his face became solemn, almost angry. "You know why," he muttered. "You know why." Now she felt the first twinges of fear, like escaping gas. "But—I don't owe you anything," she protested, stammering, "—I—I don't owe you anything at all . . ." And now the fear was too much for her, she could not stand it, she had leaped to her feet and was running along a stony parapet, a high windy place where there was no water and no shade and she was afraid of falling now, really afraid, sick with terror, but she was more afraid of the man in the windbreaker who was still there beside her and she fled dry-mouthed and panting along the endless high parapet while far, far below she heard the shrill cries of birds of prey—

She set down the trowel and rubbed a gloved hand across her forehead. She had never paid much attention to dreams but this was an important one. There was something powerful about it, something adamant and incontrovertible that rang in her consciousness like hollow iron, and she struggled to trace her way back through it, recall its early parts; but she could not. She couldn't even remember the windbreaker man, what he looked like: a bronzed, proud face like an Indian's, hawk-like, faintly handsome, and high loose hair like an Indian's scalplock that fluttered in the clear, dry air of the parapet. Like no one she'd known . . .

She sighed, picked up the trowel again and dug around the roots of one of the andromeda, loosening the soil, pulling up weeds and grass stalks and laying them on a piece of burlap beside her. Every now and then she would stop and gaze around her at rock pool and maples and shadowed lawn and somnolent summer sky with an uncertain, musing expression. Working in the garden was a kind of solace; but she could not look at it as she had. Her world had changed more deeply than she could have guessed. The great curved beak had caught her up and shaken her like a rag for one mad instant before it had let her drop again—and everything was altered. A born romantic who had everywhere seen beauty and cause for wonder, she now saw only the anarchic ferocity of brute existence. Two days before, working in the garden, she had come upon the dead field mouse. It was lying on its side, its eyes like black glass. She had turned away from it when out of the corner of her eye she saw it stir—a slithering, flowing motion that made her start. No: it was certainly dead; its body had the wasted look of a partly decomposed corpse. Then while she watched it moved again, and a large beetle with lurid yellow and orange markings flowed

over its carcass and down the other side; then another, painted in
the same overbright trappings of death and decay. The mouse
slithered along another half inch. They were moving it on their
backs, bearing it off to their hole with a fierce, single-minded
industry that nothing could withstand...She had dug a hole
and buried the mouse with a tremendous sense of despondency.
This was her world of form and beauty: plants grew in
purposeless profusion, insects of untold rapacity prowled
through the jungle of their stems and butchered and dismem-
bered. Everything was really chaos, then, chaos and savagery,
and the powerful alone survived, the weak were slaughtered...

Behind her in the kitchen amid the vigorous crash and batter
of pots and pans, Mrs. Pruitt was saying:

"—slouching around all day long with those nasty guns and
manacles. If you had one simple ounce of get-up-and-go you'd
find yourself a decent job, the lot of you. Live like decent,
God-fearing folks..."

And then Danny Shea's voice, soft and amused and
placating: "Ah now, don't be too hard on us, Mrs. P. It's a
living."

"Call it a living, do you. Blame sight more like lounging, if
you ask me. Well. Today's feast, tomorrow's famine."

"I get a pension at forty-five..."

"And you won't know what to do with yourself, you'll turn
into one of those JD's you're always complaining about.
Hanging around drugstores and bookie joints hour after hour,
all sorts of nastiness."

"Not me..."

"They're not all of them young boys, either. I've seen them.
Grown men old enough to know better and then some."

"Why Mrs. P, what were you doing around bookie joints?"

"Don't think you're going to trap me into some kind of
criminal admission because you're not. I know where those
places are and you people put up with them, too. Payoffs and
protection. Grifters. You think old arthritic ladies don't know
anything..."

"Why, I never said any such thing—"

"But you thought it. I could tell. Pension at forty-five!" she
sneered. "Suppose we all wanted a pension, where'd the world
be?"

"Well, I'm not going to fall down dead, you know. I'm going

to start that boat rental shop I was telling you about."

"Motor boats. As if that was a man's occupation..." There was a pause and Janet, still weeding, could imagine Mrs. Pruitt turning from the sink, the flash of her iron spectacles, the admonitory finger: "Charlie Albiston's been constable in this town for thirty-seven years, the best law-enforcement officer Holcomb Hill ever had, and he never asked for a pension. You young men are turning shiftless, that's what you are. Got a Democrat back in the White House again and you think the world owes you a living."

"Boston man, Mrs. P. More of a Bostonian than Calvin Coolidge."

"Don't confuse the issue. Always wanting something you can't have. Traipsing all over the globe, fly now and pay for it later, installment purchasing. Divorced and married twenty times—"

"Ah, not me!"

"No, of course not, you Catholics don't believe in divorce, I know that. Only thing stops you, though, popish decree or some such. You'd like to but you don't dare."

Danny laughed then, a burst of delighted Irish laughter. "Ah, Mrs. P, you give me such a hard time and I'm only trying to do my duty..."

"Duty!" Mrs. Pruitt gave her explosive cackle of disdain and bore down inexorably again, laying down the law. "Duty! Lounging around on Mr. Lawring's modernistic sofas all day, doing crossword puzzles, guzzling coffee at all hours. Some duty, all right. Pity you have to get out of bed mornings and go to work at all."

"Well: it isn't all fun and games, you know. See this?" There was a brief pause, during which Danny apparently turned up a shirtsleeve or trouser cuff. "Know how I got that? In the back of a liquor store on Salem Street at three o'clock in the morning. Fellow hit me with a World War Two Biretta. Those old war weapons—my God, they're still kicking around, you know? There were two of them. I got one with my second round and after a while the other one gave himself up. And some of the merchandise got shot up in the fracas and next day the proprietor wanted to sue me. How do you like that?"

"Oh well, if it's *scars* you want I could show you one that'd turn your hair gray. But I won't so don't ask me."

There was another pause. Mrs. Pruitt had obviously been impressed by the bullet wound. A newspaper rustled softly, dishes clacked, then a buzzer went off and Mrs. Pruitt called from the kitchen window:

"Mrs. Lawring, it's a quarter past. If you're going to get over to that function of yours you'd better look lively..."

"Be right in," Janet answered. She got up and went into the garage and dumped trowel, fork and weeder on the workbench, then remembered and hung them on the hooks Gardner had put up for them on the wall. They didn't look right and she wondered vaguely if she had got the correct nails. If he hadn't done that for her she'd have lost them all by now, probably. She was always losing things, misplacing tools or cooking utensils or clothing. When she heard some bottle or jar crash to the floor of the bathroom and Gardner curse under his breath she would instinctively cry out, *"I'm sorry!"* and could hear him chuckle in spite of himself. She just couldn't remember, though intermittently she tried. *An infinite capacity for taking pains.* Alexander Hamilton. Gardner was fond of quoting it, Hamilton was one of his heroes. Janet had heard her father's brother, who was a teacher in Somerville, refer to Hamilton once as that lousy fascist son of a bitch, and she didn't know herself what to think. He had been Jefferson's bitter opponent in Washington's cabinet, he had founded our monetary system and he'd been killed in a duel with Aaron Burr—whom she remembered, still more dimly, as a demagogue and a traitor...

Gardner's tools, on the other hand, were in fine order: the axes sharp and bright (he put edges on all his cutting tools himself), saws hanging in rows, hammers facing one way, hatchets the other. A place for everything and everything in its place. She'd laughed at him when she'd first heard him say that and he'd seen the humor of it and laughed, too; but later he'd remonstrated with her. "Don't you see, honey—if you have everything in an orderly way where you can put your hand on it at once, you save time and energy..."

"But I know where everything *is,*" she'd defended herself. "It just doesn't *look* neat, the way your things do." A half-truth at best. She didn't know: she never had, really—periodically she would waste an hour or more trying to find her wristwatch or sewing kit. Sometimes it seemed to her that she'd gone through life like a somnambulist, drifting from sensation to sensation, object to object, never really grappling with the grim realities, the arduous mechanics of existence that men live by and that make the world go round. Why was that? Her home, her upbringing, the chaotic conviviality of her family, certainly— but why hadn't she tried harder to order the pattern of her own living so that she would be able to put her hand on something whenever she wanted to?

"It's because you *want* to be vague about things," Gardner had said to her once. "You don't want to have things clear and orderly." This had made her surly and she'd demanded to know why *that* was, if he knew so blasted much about her. But he had only shrugged at her and smiled: that slow, rueful smile of his that always charmed her so, and she had gone up to him and kissed him passionately...

Probably he was right: he usually was. His buoyant, practical cast of mind, the product of generations of Yankee merchants and sea captains, was a perfect antidote for her French-Irish high spirits. Lying in bed with him in the early years she would indulge in fanciful speculations over what paragons of manhood and girlhood their offspring would be, combining as they were sure to do the best of two vigorous traditions. But after Brian the children hadn't come; she had grown apprehensive, then desperate, snatching at medical explorations and clinical expedients; then resigned. During the past two years she had broached the idea of adoption, but to her surprise Gardner had refused to even entertain the idea. No Lawring had ever adopted a child; no Alcock ever had; it simply wasn't done. She had argued with him for a while, then dropped it. Now she felt a pang of resentment. If she had children around her now, she wouldn't feel the way she did—depressed, fearful, at the mercy of things; she knew it intuitively...

As she came into the kitchen Danny was saying: "Well, I'm sure going to miss your cooking when this case is over, Mrs. P. When are you planning to serve some of that wonderful corned beef and cabbage again?"

"It's New England boiled dinner," Mrs. Pruitt retorted with icy implacability, "and I'll serve it when I'm good and ready. It won't come round for five days, possible longer, so you keep your shirt on."

"Yes, ma'am," Danny said meekly; he winked at Janet. "Get 'em all weeded out?"

"No—it's as bad as when I started, I'm afraid." She poured herself a glass of tomato juice from the plastic container in the refrigerator and drank it reflectively, chatting with him. He looked almost lethargic with his cherubic, fair face and heavy body; but one night when Lou Enright had decided, for God knew what reason, to come around to the back of the house to return a set of wrenches to Gardner, she had seen Danny come off the couch and move to the curtains beside the glass door at the end of the living room with astonishing speed. He's the kind of man I might have married, she thought suddenly, if I hadn't happened to fall in love with Gard and Gard hadn't been the maverick kind of blueblood he is ... Then in the next instant she wondered why she had thought that.

Upstairs she showered and powdered herself quickly, chose a light sheath dress of blue linen and matching heels. It was her first appearance since the episode, this remedial reading committee Polly had got together, and she had promised to attend; she was conscious of a rising tension, like the opening of a school play in which she knew she hadn't memorized her lines adequately. She shouldn't have shut herself up for so long, she knew—it would only make it more difficult when she did decide to venture forth; but she had felt a very real constraint, and the incident at Polly's two weeks before had shaken her badly.

She simply didn't want to see people, that was all. It was not so much the stigma of the assault (she would never use the actual term, even to herself) which stopped her, the fear of the prurient avidity of acquaintances; she didn't suffer under that so much (though she knew Gardner did, that it worked on him like a Chinese torture, turning him steadily more gaunt and tense); it was more that she wanted the culprit to be found and the whole tormenting affair to be cleared up and put aside if it could be, divested at least of this unreal quality of no proof, no valid clues, no fingerprints—as though a ghost had stood there in that doorway. But it had been no ghost. She wanted to confront this man, look fully and slowly on his face, gaze deep into his eyes and read there—whatever there was to read ... and until that moment she wanted to keep herself aloof from hospital ward visits and garden club gatherings and cocktail parties, much the way an athlete eschews liquor and late hours while he trains for an approaching meet. Only there was apparently no fixed date for this contest...

She combed her hair carefully, set down the comb and brush and looked at herself in the mirror. To herself she looked the same as before. A little thinner, rather tired, the shadows under her eyes more pronounced; but her face had the same eager, expectant expression it had worn ever since she could remember—the sense of life as a glorious vista she recalled on a camping trip with her family through northern New England twenty years ago: the turn of the road and the sudden prospect of a valley beautiful beyond belief, of farms and trim white houses and the pure white shaft of a church steeple darting through the feathery green verdure; all of it fresh and vivid and indelible in the washed morning light, disposed in a harmony that made her cry out in joyful astonishment. The world at rebirth, sparkling with promise and affection.

It was curious: our faces didn't reflect our internal transformations the way they should, then; for various reasons we no longer believed what we had, but our faces remained obedient to the old impulses, the old visions, like some grizzled man-at-arms still obstinately loyal to a master turned cynical or craven or even cruel...

She put on a pair of pearl earrings, took them off and chose instead a silver necklace in the form of interlaced stars Gardner had given her for her twenty-fifth birthday. They would all be wearing hats, all the others except perhaps Polly, but she was darned if she would. It was summer, and hats always made her feel vaguely nervous, ceremonial—as though she were attending a lecture or a funeral. When she was thirty-nine—the date she saw as the beginning of middle age—she would wear a hat, and not until then.

She got out her blue suede purse, set it down and began to empty her tan leather everyday bag. Rapidly she transferred wallet, house keys, car keys, pen, compact, two wads of Sperry and Hutchinson green stamps (which much to Gardner's amusement she saved avidly and then forgot where they were when she wanted to paste them into the book), a New Haven train schedule, lipstick in two shades, a theater stub from God knew what or when, a battered half roll of Stik-O-Pep lifesavers and two sticks of Wrigley's Juicy Fruit gum which she was fond of chewing when she drove the car—a habit Garnder loudly deplored but put up with when she told him it made her more alert at the wheel. There were also hairpins and several pennies and dimes and she fished these out with a fingernail, along with what looked like another ticket stub, folded twice on itself. She was about to throw it into the wastebasket when a little green wad of paper fell out on the floor. She bent over and picked it up. Money, folded tightly and with great care. She unwrapped it, fold by fold: three tens. Thirty dollars. She peered at the bills, set them down and began to unfold the stub, saw it was a card with a little antique lantern in the upper left hand corner. Holding it closer she read:

PAUL REVERE CAB CORP.
Promptness and Courtesy Our Watchword
HAncock 9-3535

She held it suspended in the air before her, frowning, reading it over again— a long dim cavern of bewilderment through which a sharp shaft of recollection burned. She felt her cheeks and forehead turn hot and heavy with the rush of blood. Revere Cab Corp. Her heart had begun to pound thickly. Her purse. He had rummaged in her purse. He had gone back to it and felt around in it again, before he'd left.

Revere Cab Corp.

"Oh," she said. A tiny, aspirate sound, lost and hollow in the bright midafternoon.

She felt as if she were suspended, swung free, were falling an immeasurable distance through scalding air. She had gripped the edge of the dressing table with all her might. Her image in the glass was blurred and remote, as though seen through a frosted window. She was standing in the center of the room; she was sitting in Gardner's chair, with no knowledge of how she had got there at all. Then she was conscious of sounds around her, a murmur of voices and kitchen utensils like faraway surf or household noises remembered from early childhood. Putting her hands to her head she held it rigid, as one might hold open a door—and in a rush of awareness all the images came tumbling in upon her, bright with time. Revere Cab. She sat motionless as a graven image of herself, swept with memory, and knew beyond a shadow of a doubt who it had to be.

• • •

She had recognized him at once, moving toward her along
the beach with his quick, lithe stride, looking somber and
strangely out of place in the short gabardine jacket and dark
trousers. The sand didn't seem to impede him at all. He
approached with a combination of boldness and deference, and
when he was within twenty feet or so of her she called:

"Well—hello there..."

"Hello." He came up and stood above her, looking down. He
had a thin, expressive face; a fine aquiline nose and lively,
restless eyes. His hair was long and curly and very black. The
breeze whipped his trouser legs hard against his shins, revealing
the edge of bone. He looked romantic and wild standing there,
with his black hair ruffling at his temples and his eyes flashing
against the pale blue of the sky. Yet there was a certain shyness
about him, too—an almost gauche gentleness she found
appealing: he had driven down here and found her, and now he
didn't know what to do.

There was a silence for a moment, and then she said: "Well,
this *is* a surprise! Sit down, won't you?" Her tone sounded arch
to her and she added, "I get dizzy if I look up too long. I don't
know why."

He sat on the sand, hands locked over his knees. "How'd you
make out?"

"With who?—the Robishaws? Oh, all right. It's all settled... Well, it was ridiculous," she declared. "That little boy
wasn't hurt at all, you know that."

"Of course he wasn't."

"But thanks anyway. For going to all that trouble. Testifying
and everything."

"It wasn't anything." He turned his head then and looked at
her gravely; when he was serious his face seemed delicate and
sad, like the face of a Medici prince. "I was worried, though.
About you, I mean."

"Me?"

"Sure. You were so—I don't know—so *confused,* there. I
could see you didn't know what had happened to you. And then
when I saw that character climb out from behind the wheel I
knew you were in for trouble." He paused, watching her steadily.
"But you know, that was bad driving. You were the vehicle
entering from the *left,* remember?"

"I know. My mind was on something else, I guess."

"How long have you been driving?"

"Oh, about three years."

"Three years!" he exclaimed. "I thought you'd just got your license or something."

She laughed. "I know it seems impossible. I never really learned how to drive. Pop tried twice, he took me to this place where an old factory used to be—you know, where I couldn't smash up anything—and he tried to teach me to start and stop and turn around. And he gave up. He said his nerves wouldn't stand it. Then my brother Fred tried for a while. Thank heaven the examiner had the flu the day I took my test. He just made me drive around the block and park and that was it. My lucky star working overtime again."

"You count on that lucky star a lot, don't you?"

"I've *got* to—if I hadn't been lucky I never would have got a license at all! I'm just a terrible driver."

"Yes, I can see that."

They laughed together in the warm sunlight, gazed out at the deep blue of the water and talked of the accident, which had taken place a month before at one of those unmarked intersections in Brookline. Janet had been on her way to pick up her sister Edna and do some errands. She had been running along, humming to some tune on the car radio, her mind wandering aimlessly over a dozen things—Gardner, his mother, Fred's little boy Tommy and his speech impediment, the sale at Filene's—when all at once there was the car on her right, a royal blue sedan, coming very fast. She stamped on the brake and wrenched the wheel, the blue car glided closer as if on tracks of glass, slid impossibly close—and there was a long, rending crash that sounded as though all the scrap iron in the world were being dumped down a mile-long concrete chute into the Atlantic Ocean.

Then they were stopped, the silence somehow louder than the collision. A woman was glaring at her through the glass, somewhere a child had begun squalling, and a block-like man in a checkered shirt was getting out of the blue car and coming toward her threateningly. He had raised a fist at her, was shouting:

"—you stupid, *stupid* bitch, what are you trying to do, didn't you *see* me—?"

She got out and stood there weakly with her hand on the

door, appalled at the tangle of torn metal and shattered glass, the curiously iridescent glint in the water streaming from under her radiator. It had all happened so fast. A few seconds ago these two machines had been all shiny and immaculate, humming along; now everything was broken.

"I'm sorry," she stammered. "I'm terribly sorry, I didn't see you—"

The man wasn't listening to her. He had struck the fender of his own car, was shouting to the woman in the rear seat, who held clutched to her breast a little boy of five or six. The child was crying, his face beet-red with pain or anger or fear, it was impossible to tell which it was. Janet put her hand to her throat; her legs were trembling, perspiration had broken out on her back and face. She felt very close to tears. How could all this have happened? without any preparation at all?

"I'm sorry," she began again. "Please believe me, I feel terrible about all this—"

"You!" the man in the plaid shirt roared, swinging back to her again. Florid-faced, choleric he rose above her, raised one great red hand as though to strike her down on the asphalt; checked the movement and contented himself with waving it back and forth in her face. "What you think you were doing, you shouldn't even be *driving,* you stupid God damn dumb bitch!—they shouldn't let you out of a—"

"Just a minute, Mac."

The voice was flat and very hard, so alien to this moment of calamity and imprecations that they both turned in amazement. A slim, rather handsome man was staring at Janet's tormentor, his eyes narrowed. He was wearing a visored cap, like a chauffeur's, set rakishly over one ear, and behind him an orange-and-black cab was parked at the far curb. There was no one else in sight.

"—What do *you* want!" the red-faced man shouted at him.

"You watch your language, you hear? Just watch it." The words came one after another like pieces of cut metal. "I saw the whole thing. Now you watch your mouth."

The heavy man stiffened, then cried: "All right, you saw it, you saw her—"

"You were doing fifty, fifty-five coming into this. You know what the speed limit is around here."

"Fifty!" the big man roared. "Fifty!" He launched himself on a sluice of obscenities, bit them off, wheeled around to the woman in the back seat of the blue car who was still glaring out at Janet, her teeth bared like a weasel's. "Mildred—you hear that? You hear him, he says I was doing fifty—!"

"Look at your rubber." The cab driver pointed. They looked back dutifully at the swerving serpent scales of skid marks. "You think they'd be that long if you were doing thirty-five?"

The blocklike man glowered at him, his mouth working— whirled on Janet again. "It's her fault," he declared as though she were some disinterested fourth party, "I'm telling you, her fault—she never saw me, she wasn't even looking where she was *going!*..." He shot the cabby a look of unutterable hatred, raced around to his own car and reached in and grabbed up the little boy in his great hams and squeezed him against his checkered shirt, crying, "You all right, Donny? You going to be all right now, are you, Donny boy?" The child roared still louder, wagging its big head in a frenzy of grief. "Don't move now, Donny boy, just relax, don't move..."

Janet watched them with agonized wonder, and felt the sweat sliding down her back like cold fingers.

"Take it easy." She glanced at the cab driver, who was watching her with an intent, sympathetic expression. "Don't worry," he went on in his steady, quiet voice, strangely audible under the uproar from the blue car. "They think they're going to take you."

"Take me?" she faltered.

"Sure. Clean you out."

"But I haven't any money..."

"You think they care about that? They'll attach your pay, your car, any property you might own... But they're not going to, so don't worry." His eyes shot away from hers, fastened on something behind her. "Oh-oh. Here comes the law. Better get out your license and registration." He looked at her again: a mournful, lugubrious gaze. "You *have* got a license, haven't you?"

"Oh yes!" She laughed—a sudden spasm of relief, watching the policeman move toward them with the ponderous tread of any patrolman approaching the scene of any accident. "Actually the car isn't mine..."

"It isn't? Whose is it?"

"It's my brother's—but I've got a license all right..."

The hearing was brief, as Brookline hearings go. The cab driver furnished what turned out to be the decisive evidence. The child was judged not to be hurt at all; and the insurance companies handled the car damages. When the case broke up Janet talked for a while with the cabby, whose name was Joe Castaldo, and thanked him for taking her part in the affair. He demurred, said he would do it again if he had to; and he asked her if he could see her soon. She saw then that he was attracted to her. Thinking to treat the situation casually she said Sure, she'd like to; she told him where she lived, and said she was going down to Brewster on Cape Cod in a few weeks, she mentioned Gardner whom she had only just recently met, and his family's place there; and thought no more about it.

Now, surprised and a little flattered at seeing him here in the flesh, on the bay beach below the Lawring house where she had been idly sunning herself while Gardner and Chuck Allerton were getting something on the sailboat repaired, she pushed her feet back and forth in the coarse warm sand and said blithely: "Well, it's all over and done with now. I hope that old Robishaw falls down a flight of stairs and breaks his hip and is laid up for two solid years."

Castaldo laughed. "I'll sign that. It never happens, though. Only the good die young. Don't you know that?" He paused, narrowed his fine sparkling eyes and said softly: *"The good die first: and they whose hearts are dry as summer dust burn to the socket..."*

That surprised her. She snapped her head around and asked, "Who said that?"

"I don't know." She couldn't tell whether he did or not. "Good, isn't it? Dry as summer dust," he repeated. "That's terrific."

She was conscious of a faintly pleasurable series of confusions, and tried to dispel them. "But tell me, what brings you down on Cape Cod?"

He shrugged. "I had a fare to Plymouth. We specialize in long fares. And then I kept on going. I decided I needed a change."

"A change—but you're driving all day long!"

"Busman's holiday. I like to do things suddenly," he announced. "Without thinking about them. Last fall I made up my mind one afternoon I wanted to see Quebec. You know, the Château Frontenac, all that. So I drove it in four days, round trip."

"Did you like it?"

"Yes. It's got a—a solid sense about it. The kind of place you'd like to take your family, raise your kids, even. All open and—full of sunlight, lots of space. Like this place here. You feel you can reach out and touch things. Touch beauty." He said this shyly, as though afraid she might make fun of him. When she nodded without smiling he gave her a firm, level look from under his dark brows and asked: "Don't you want to do things—you know, on the spur of the moment?"

"Oh yes!" she laughed. "That's the way I do everything..."

They sat on the sand and talked of one thing and another. The sea glittered under the offshore haze, a dense chill blue, and at the horizon the sky was the palest azure: two blues as unlike as heaven and earth. He unbuttoned his jacket and lay back on his elbows and she spread suntan oil on her shins and shoulders, and together they watched the terns fishing: the dipping beat-beat-beat of wings, the second of hesitation—then the wings folded and the sharp plunge into the water, *schloop* and up again, flapping hard, white pencil body and swallowtail, beating upwind ... It was quite obvious that he had driven all the way down here to see her; he had got directions from the local post office.

In the three weeks since the hearing her own relationship with Gardner had changed hugely: they had fallen in love, they had slept together, they were to be married in August. She knew she ought to inform Joe of this, send him away before his hopes rose any higher; but her instinctive warmth and geniality forbade her. It was such a beautiful day, it was so delightful sitting here chatting idly while the puffy white clouds marched overhead like browsing animals and the witch grass bobbed its silver sickles in the sun. She didn't have the heart to tell him: You're wrong—things have changed since we last saw each other, changed more than even I in all my romantic dreams could have foreseen...

She said nothing. She lacked the virtue of ruthlessness.

And so they sat on and talked of cabbages and kings. He had been brought up in Boston, in the North End. His father had been killed in a construction accident on the Jamaica Underpass when he was eight, and he was supporting his mother and two younger sisters. He had gone partners in a taxi with a high-school friend. "I don't make much—when you get through paying for your license and the hack and everything else. But I'm my own master, anyway. No construction boss to take orders from. None of that." He wanted to go back and finish high school, though he doubted if he ever would. "Once you break away it's hard to go back. What for? You're on your way, anyhow, for better or worse. And all the education is out there . . ." He gestured toward the bay, toward Boston, with his chin.

He had been in Korea, with the artillery, and hated it. "Only one good thing happened in all that time. There was this belt of land between the line and the reserve area and they wired it off as a kind of no man's land, and no Korean was supposed to enter it at any time. But they did, they sneaked in there and planted crops, rice and barley, it was good farm land, and then when the stuff came up in the summer they wanted to go in and harvest it. They were starving, you know." His eyes darted at her; they had little gold flecks in them. "I don't mean just hungry and broke, like us; I mean starving to death, slowly. You could see it in their faces, in the kids' bodies. So I took about all I could of that for a while, and then I got a bunch of us together and we went to see the sergeant and I asked him if we couldn't do something for these people. The sergeant, he was a real guy, solid and straight, no chicken, he was from Montana, he heard me out and looked at me for a minute and then said: 'All right. Fix them up Down Back of the Yards.' There was this little hollow behind the battery motor pool where an old Korean railway went, it was all smashed up now, and we used to call it Down Back of the Yards. I said, 'But where will we get the stuff?' And he gave me that long, slow look of his and said, 'Now Castaldo, does a bright young kid like you have to ask me a big dumb question like that? Just don't get caught, that's all,' he said. So we went midnight requisitioning, we cleaned out half the rear-area outfits around us. We scrounged tents and rations and clothing, we even lifted benches and tables and mess gear. Two of the guys made stuff. Then we set up a mess hall and a medical dispensary, we even put up a school and got it going—those little kids hadn't ever had a book in their hands, you know that? They didn't even know how to eat rations. I remember I found two of them eating dehydrated potatoes, just gulping it down dry—I got scared they'd drink water afterward and their stomachs would burst. It can happen, you know ... We had all that going, Down Back of the Yards." He laughed softly, and shook his head. "It was great. And afterwards the Koreans gave us a testimonial of thanks. In Korean. I put it up on the wall of my room..."

Then his face turned morose. "But the rest of it was stupid. I mean disgusting. We were supposed to take this hill, it didn't even have a name. Hill Four Ninety-six, something like that. We used to call it the Anvil, it went out to two points like horns, on the map." He looked at her again, his eyes snapping with anger. "We fired two thousand rounds in fifteen minutes, we kept firing until the barrels were so hot they'd take the flesh off your arms. And all for nothing. They couldn't take it anyway. Two infantry companies in the assault had a hundred and sixty casualties between them. It was an Anvil, all right. All this time the peace talks were going on, the word was it was going to be over in two weeks, a month at the most. It wasn't, of course, but why shoot up a hundred and sixty men trying to take one lousy hill? Disgusting..." And his lip curled.

But in a few minutes he was full of enthusiasm again, his mind dancing with plans and possibilities. He loved the theater, acting, he had worked with a group up on Joy Street for a while; he wanted to go into medicine, he wanted to try scientific research. "I don't have any training, I know that, I'd be willing to—you know, just help out here and there, there must be guys they need just to do the mechanical stuff. Imagine if you helped to come up with the cure for cancer! My Aunt Agnes died of cancer, it took her over a year; it was terrible. You know, if you found the serum or whatever it is, even if it half killed you tracking it down. Those guys work for days on end without any sleep, I read about them once, they go on and on and won't give up until they get what they're after ... To be able to accomplish something really tremendous, no matter what it costs you! ..."

He told her all these things in a warm, rather musical voice, speaking rapidly, half swallowing his words; and she felt the presence of exploding horizons, whole worlds unfurling like her own sparkling little Vermont valley. He'd thought of becoming a surveyor or perhaps a ranger, working out of doors in all weather, mapping unknown territory. He couldn't for the life of him understand how guys could become bookkeepers or shipping clerks or worse yet stay on in the army, that cold dead place, when there was so much to do all around you that was exciting, that called on every ounce of energy and determination you had, or gave you such simple pleasure: like walking along one of those trails up in Maine, he'd been up there year before last, with the rocks all covered with bright hairy green moss and the ferns bobbing like battle plumes; or sitting on a beach like this one and watching the gulls glide overhead like the ghosts of long-dead ancestors, craning their necks at you, looking down...

She found she liked him—this warm, intense way he had, the almost shy deference mixed with vestiges of North End Italian gang toughness, the flights of imagination his mind snatched at all of a sudden, without warning. Their lives had been much alike, she saw: the close, effusive family life, the chill edge of poverty, the spindly shoots of exuberance and hope sprouting in harsh soil; the fear of power. She recognized these things, sensed the depth of his vulnerability and desire, and something else, too—something fiery and hooded she couldn't place. She felt drawn to him with a chaste, almost personal affection—as though he were a very charming brother or cousin she hadn't seen in years.

"I've been thinking of getting into summer stock somewhere," he was saying. "Getting started with a summer group, acting. There's one down here, isn't there? Right around here somewhere?"

"Yes, there's a company in Dennis, and another one I think over in Chatham." She wondered vaguely if he could act. Did he have any real talent, or was he one of those people who faltered into head-waggling, hand-signaling, grammar-school elocutionary apology the minute they walked out on a stage? "But I don't know how you'd go about getting roles with them," she went on. "It's pretty late and I imagine they've got their personnel all set for this season..."

A horn sounded from the bluff behind them: three short blasts. She got to her feet and picked up her beach towel and cigarettes and said: "My goodness, it must be late! I've got to get a move on."

He got up too and began absently buttoning his jacket. He said nothing. His eyes met hers—that shy, furtive glance—and dropped away again. He's been hurt, she thought with an odd little flash of pleasure and sadness, he's been hurt by a lot of people and fought back, and he's afraid of being hurt again, and yet he can't help himself: the way I was with Jimmy. She thought of Jimmy for a shadowed moment. Jimmy sitting cross-legged on piled Tabriz carpets conferring with Arab potentates, Jimmy entering a Roman sala full of long-gowned women and glass chandeliers, walking very erectly, weight on his toes, lips curving in that beautiful smile, his eyes alight . . . It was terrible to think you loved someone who felt nothing for you at all—even if you were mistaken about yourself; it was the most terrible thing in life, the end of the world: as simple and terrible as that.

"Come on up," she said impulsively, "have a drink with us. We're going sailing. I think. If the queen truckle cotter bolt is delayed or something. I'm not much of a sailor."

She watched him look up and measure the house above them—the flash of fear and defiance she had noted before. Turning she tried to see the place through his eyes: that weatherbeaten old structure, fount and origin of the Lawrings, bristling with towers and wings and verandahs and capped by the widow's walk with its fine wooden railing; the old mulberry trees gnarled and corky and European-looking, their branches bent low to the ground as if by sheer venerable weight, the arbors burdened with their tangle of ancient rose bushes. The whole mélange meticulously put together by Captain Jared Lawring in 1685 and remodeled and expanded and renovated by a hundred thousand generations of sailing captains and statesmen and merchants. Every First Family was supposed to have at least one sailing captain in its history, Gardner had told her once; the Lawrings had five. As far as they were concerned the Cabots and Lowells and Forbeses were mere upstarts, North Shore interlopers and Johnny-Come-Latelys; the Lawrings had been one of the original Old Purchasers families at Plymouth Plantations, and had gravitated to Boston from Cape Cod. He had grinned as he told her this—but there was that tiny metallic glint in his eyes that meant he wasn't entirely kidding about it, either...

She glanced at Joe Castaldo again. It scares him too, she said to herself with the smart of self-detection, he too has to fight down that clutch-in-the-guts in the face of wealth and tradition. For the first time the idea of being Gardner Lawring's wife gave her a ripple of apprehension. She could tell herself with all the fervor of her romantic heart that it was one world, there was only one family of man and we were all of us brothers under our skins; she could tell herself objectively—and it was true—that today's aristocrat was yesterday's freebooter, that First Families would never have become what they were without their money (and money made often enough in not very commendable ways either, transporting rum or slaves or even—incredibly—opium; she knew what the phrase "West Indies Goods" meant, and she'd heard about the astronomical fortunes amassed in the China and India trade in the space of a few years a century ago); she could even slip away from that thought and dwell ardently on the fact that she and Gard loved each other and that there were no barriers of blood or background where love had entered— she could tell herself all that and more besides but she was only fooling herself royally, wasn't she? And this boy standing here beside her couldn't even do that.

"Come on," she said again, and smiled at him.

"All right."

She saw him set himself, the sloping shoulders stiffen ever so slightly. They began climbing the path from the beach. She was conscious of him moving close behind her—his dark, clothed presence following her bright near-nakedness. This excited her strangely, made her nervous; she began chattering again to conceal it. Locusts soared away from their footsteps in black fluttering lurches, and the early summer heat rose from the beach grass and wild pea and bayberry like a warm breath. The path met the drive just outside the gateway with its two stone pillars; from one of them a chain hung in a pile of red-rusty links, a dungeon image that depressed her. Why didn't they either put up a wooden gate that swung shut or take down that raw, scaly old chain? She had made a joking reference to it several days before to Gardner's mother, who had looked at her for a moment with raised brows and then replied that there was no need to incur the expense of a new gate, that chain had served perfectly well for years; besides, it kept strangers and sightseers from swinging casually into the circle and out again.

As they crossed the drive Gardner came out on the verandah carrying two canvas duffel bags. He leaned back in the house and shouted something, then came to the edge of the steps. The screen door banged. He was dressed in a pair of old, faded khaki trousers and a blue jersey; he looked huge and active and very handsome.

"Hi, sweety," he called, in the voice that she already knew meant his mind was occupied with something else. "Who took the cab down from Boston? Talk about extravagance . . ." Then she saw him notice her companion and his eyes widened a little: a look of surprise, and faint displeasure.

"Gard, this is Joe Castaldo." She introduced them with a quick brightness.

"Hello."

"How are you."

Joe came up the steps and they shook hands with crisp formality and remained looking at each other.

'You took a cab all the way down here?"

"No. It's mine. I drive a hack."

"I see. You just—drove down . . .?"

"That's right."

They're so unlike each other! Janet thought with dismay; and they don't like each other at all. Gardner's brows were knitted, his eyes very cool and gray and steady, like a northern sea. Joe looked dark and somber, his black eyes snapping and the little gold flecks in their centers; he had his hands on his hips. Why did people get on so well with some people, and so badly with others? A born romantic, her heart yearned for everyone to be friends, a universal congeniality that would lap out and out like some vast, benevolent tide and embrace all mankind. If a person had good qualitites—was, say, honest or generous or witty, why couldn't everyone see those qualities? why were some people blind to them? But there it was. Some kind of mystic chemistry probably, atoms colliding or repelling each other, whatever atoms did . . .

To break up this moment of confrontation she said: "Joe testified in my behalf at that hideous hearing with the

Robishaws. You know, the automobile accident I had in Brookline."

"Oh, sure," Gardner said carelessly and picked up the duffel bags again. Chuck Allerton came out on the porch at that moment carrying an ice container and another duffel and Gardner turned to him. "You got the pump with that?"

"Right."

She was about to introduce Chuck to Joe when Gardner said: "You ready, Jan? Better bring a sweater or a sweatshirt or something. It'll be blowing out there."

"... We don't have to hurry right off, do we?" she asked.

"What? Sure we do. Why not? We've been working on that damned stay for two hours."

"Yes, but I mean there's no—"

"Ted and Anne Henderson are out there already. We're racing them to Billingsgate."

He was looking at her inquiringly. *He doesn't even see Joe,* she said to herself, and the thought sent a taut tremor of fear along her spine; *he doesn't see him at all* ... If she could only seize the moment, bend it *her* way, just this once, get them all to go inside and have a drink, sit around a little while and come to know each other; but she couldn't. She felt silenced, overborne by Gardner—his size, his energy, the solid force of his personality. Surely there was something she could say to stop this foolish, unequal struggle—if it was a struggle. But what was it?

"Well, I better be running along," Joe was saying now in a very flat, metallic tone, the tone she remembered from the accident. "I was just down this way and thought I'd say hello."

But Gardner and Chuck had already gone down the steps, were carrying the equipment over to the car. Janet felt a surge of helpless anger and glanced at Joe, who was staring after them, his face like scorched stone. Gardner raised his head from under the trunk then and called:

"Come *on,* Jan, the tide's going..."

"All right." She'd said it before she'd even thought. She bit her lip and turned to Joe Castaldo. "Thanks for coming by," she said almost desperately. "I mean it..."

"Sure."

"If only we'd known we could have—planned something."

She stopped, angry at herself now, and offered her hand. He shook it perfunctorily but his face was working.

A car door banged, and Gardner called: "Janet, for pete's sake, shake a leg!..."

"All right!" she snapped back. Castaldo had turned away; she saw him move down the steps toward his cab, which was parked on the far edge of the drive near the gate—then all at once swerve toward the other two, who were stowing things in the back seat of the coupe.

"Pleased to meet you," she heard him say.

"Yeah, sure..." Gardner, his face red with exertion, glanced out at him and ducked back in again. He either had not seen or had chosen to ignore the proffered hand. Castaldo's body gave a swift little lurch, as if he were going to leap into the back seat of the car; the fist at his side opened and clenched twice. Then he straightened, stiff as a poker and as dark, and gazed back at Janet—a glance savage and importunate and wild beyond belief—whirled around before she could say or do anything, and walked quickly, his head lowered, over to his cab and swung in behind the wheel.

She wanted to call out to him—she wanted to cry, "Joe, it's all right, come sailing with us, Gard's not like that, really he isn't, he just gets things on his mind and acts this way, I understand him and I love him, don't be angry"—a tangle of entreaty, contradictory and absurd... She did nothing, said nothing at all; merely watched him start the engine and gun it twice—harsh, dry bursts. Then stung with shame and resentment she ran into the house and up the steep hollow staircase to her room, and from a window caught a last, extraordinarily clear glimpse of the black-and-orange cab tearing down the road, billowing tendrils of hot dust.

Constrained by Chuck Allerton's presence she held herself in; but when finally Chuck was in his own boat and she and Gardner were under sail, spanking through the westerly toward the low white shoal of Billingsgate, she said:

"That wasn't very nice, Gard."

"What wasn't, honey?" His face, wet with spray, was clear and joyful. He had forgotten about it entirely.

She looked at him a moment and went on: "It was rude. You weren't even civil to him. Joe Castaldo."

He frowned at her. "He's hardly what you'd call a close friend of yours, is he?"

"No. But that's not the point. You could have been nicer to him."

"And done what?"

"You could have invited him in for a drink. Or go sailing with us."

"Sailing with us—are you crazy?"

"He drove all the way down from Boston just to say hello."

"Did he? Well, bully for him."

This made her angry and she said: "You talk so much about good breeding and manners and everything—you don't use them much yourself . . ."

"What? Sure, I do. What's that got to do—"

"You didn't even have the common human decency to shake hands with him when he left. You could at least have asked him in for a drink or a Coke or something . . ."

"Why? Why should I? What do we have in common?"

He bulked beside her on the gunwale, superbly balanced, his feet braced, maneuvering tiller and mainsheet almost effortlessly though the wind was brisk and rising; and his size, his competence, his attitude of calm assurance—that he was unquestionably right in these matters and she was not—made her angrier still.

"That isn't everything," she protested. "Having things in common—if that were the case no one would ever get to know anybody else with a different background, a different point of view. I know he's just a poor, simple guy, he probably doesn't know what a Florence flask even looks like, but he has all these pathetic dreams—acting and exploring and things . . . Why hurt him for no reason at all?"

He peered at her curiously. "Look, you don't really *know* this character, do you?"

"He's not a character, he's a nice boy—he hasn't had all the advantages you've had, St. Mark's and Harvard and European trips and everything—"

"Of course he hasn't," he broke in on her, and for the first time there was a trace of heat in his voice. "Of course not, he lives one kind of life, I live another. Why should I give up my way of living, try to find some mythical *common ground* with him—there probably isn't one, anyway—just because he's taken it into his head to wheel down here and invite himself on the premises—"

"He didn't invite himself—he was doing a friendly thing, a friendly thing!"

"How'd he know about the house, by the way?"

"He knew about it because I told him after the—the hearing, and he did it to be friendly—an action you apparently can't even understand ..." She was so angry now she didn't care what she said, was sick with that instant of mortification and impotence when Joe had looked at her from the driveway. "For God's sake," she shouted into the driving wind, "don't be such a blueblood bluenose snob!"

He said nothing. He looked down between his knees as though he were listening for some dangerous sound, and she knew she had hurt him. She felt vengefully joyful, and then depressed. First quarrel, she thought with a tremor. Our first quarrel. And it wasn't true anyway, was it? Else he wouldn't be here with her, a French-Irish girl from Somerville whose father was a plasterer ... He was scowling down at the toes of his frayed, ratty-looking sneakers, his lower lip thrust out. She had hurt him and it wasn't fair. Contrite all at once—she did love him, this was silly, he was dearer to her than anyone she'd ever known, even Jimmy, she knew this was true beyond all doubt—she put her hand under his arm and said:

"I'm sorry, darling. I shouldn't have said that ..."

He raised his big tousled head and smiled at her soberly. "Maybe you're right," he answered.

"I lost my temper. I say things before I've thought them through, I know I do. It's a vice of mine."

"Maybe you're right at that. I forget things." He puffed out his lips, musing. "I ought not to forget certain facts ... I had no right to be suspicious of his motive. Or of you either. That's wrong."

She didn't know what to say. She felt a tremendous surge of love for him. This sense of monolithic fairness in him—his fine, implacable Yankee rectitude hung like a bright silver gyroscope in the murky, heaving world she'd known; it overwhelmed her.

She put her arms around him and hugged him hard, ducked her head behind his shoulder, away from the spank and lash of spray.

"Oh, you're wonderful," she cried. "You're so wonderful I hope the sun doesn't ever go down! . . ."

A puff of breeze lifted the curtains, made the Venetian blind tick-tack against the window casing. There were no voices now from the kitchen. She wondered how long she had been sitting here at her dressing table, feet together, hands clasped in her lap. Her neck hurt and her mouth was dry as old bone. An oriole trilled in the elm outside, a plaintive, lonely call, and the curtains billowed and sucked back against the screen. As if she had been asleep she reached up and slowly chafed her neck with one hand.

Joe Castaldo.

She was as certain of it as she was of the broken nail on her ring finger. But after *ten years* . . . Ten years almost to the day. Why had he done such a thing—and then left this completely revelatory card? Did he think he could trust her, for some reason? Was he trying to involve her in some deeper way?

She started to her feet and almost ran over to the telephone stand in the hall; pulled out the Boston directory and flipped the fat slabs of pages. Yes. It was there. Castaldo, Joseph A. 132 Endicott. She ran a fingernail under the name and address as if to impress it on her mind, clapped the book shut and walked over to the television set and back to the center of the room and stood there, her hand to her mouth.

"Why? . . ." she said aloud, a murmur. Why should he have singled her out for this? after ten years, and out of the blue? He must have wanted her to know who he was, then. But in that case why the disguise, the Negro accent, the clothes? If he had *wanted* her to know—

"Mrs. Lawring!"

She started as though she had been caught doing something shameful. Pruitt's voice, at the foot of the stairs.

"Yes?" she answered.

"It's twenty past. You're good and late already . . ."

"Thanks. I'm not going."

"You're not."

"No. I—don't feel well. I've decided not to go. I'll phone Mrs. Enright and tell her."

"Just as you like . . ."

She went over to the window seat and looked out. The lilacs were past blooming now: shrunken russet candles against the dense green of the leaves; she ought to clip them. The lilies nodded and swung their heads in the light breeze; they bloomed for a day and then they were through. One day, and never bloomed again . . .

She must go downstairs and tell Danny, and then Gardner and Inspector Reardon, she must tell them right away. The tight, hot wire had started its funny little dance through the center of her body, quick as fire. It was impossible to think.

. . . He was mad, then. Insane. A pathological case, a rapist, a sex pervert, Peeping Tom, night prowler—all the phrases she had heard Reardon and the detectives use and which she had accepted so completely, now applied to Joe Castaldo. She saw the waves curling in like charming little silver-and-blue scrolls, the gulls wheeling and diving through the golden light, the curving sickle-plumes of the beach grass, and a slender, handsome boy leaning on his elbow in the smooth white sand who was telling her of his dreams, his glorious plans for conquering the world . . .

"You're not discriminating enough," Gardner had said to her one evening a year or so ago. She had got them involved in a dinner date with the Flannerys, a young couple who ran the filling station and store at Hart's Corners, she'd decided to invite them along with the Wellivers and the Enrights, and he was cross with her about it. "You can't take the whole world to your bosom, Jan. There simply aren't enough hours in the day . . ."

"I know, but they seemed like such a nice young couple—"

"I'm sure they are, I'm sure there are ten thousand nice young couples within a fifty-mile radius of this house—but that's no excuse for having them all in to dinner. What have we got in common with these people?" He was sitting on the edge of the bed with his hands on his thighs and his chin thrust out. "Where do you stop? What do you want—a horde of hod-carriers and Buddhist monks and shipping clerks parading through the living room day and night? It's purposeless, it's goofy . . ."

"I know," she said, rueful and yet remonstrative, "I know you're right, only I can't help it, darling. I always think of what Ma used to tell us when we were kids: 'There but for the grace of God go I'..."

"Then pay attention to the grace of God! You *are* different—you're not a shanty Irish truck driver's wife in a three-family tenement in Dorchester, you're not a Negro cleaning woman in an attic room on Columbus Avenue, either."

"But I might have been."

"Sure we all might have been *anything*... But we're not. Are we? You're one thing—you're the wife of a reasonably successful architect, with a son in private school and a beautiful home and all the rest of it. Why should you want to pretend it doesn't exist?"

"Oh, I don't want to do *that*..."

"Well, you act as though you do. You're too sentimental, you won't face facts as they are..."

A car pulled into the drive and she darted to the window; her heart was beating rapidly and her hands were moist. Red Crowley stepped out of the Detlef's Bakery truck and swung up the walk to the kitchen, carrying two loaves of bread and a cake box by its twine.

"Afternoon," he sang out, his voice ringing in the warm air. "Isn't this a dandy?"

There were some exchanges Janet couldn't hear, then Red again, outside the kitchen door, his voice lowered: "Yeah. They ought to take people like that and burn 'em alive. Shooting's too good for 'em." He waved one hand toward the kitchen; his hair caught the sun and blazed orange. "Well, see you Thursday..." The wagon eased down the drive, its brakes whining like scraped gut.

After ten years. He had assaulted her and then, insanely, put his fate in her hands. *After Brookline, after what I did for you in Brookline that afternoon, are you going to turn me in?* Was that what the card was saying? But that too was insane... Yet he certainly had not acted on impulse, he'd known about her, the way they lived, he'd said as much; he could be watching her now, standing over there on the edge of the woods...

She raised her eyes and stared at the woods bordering the stone wall with a feeling of real fright. It was impossible to think clearly about this. The woods looked cool and somnolent, a place to wander languidly, lie down and sleep through the bright, hot hours...And what about her? Standing there motionless, dazed with discovery and wonder, the memory of that Thursday night almost a month ago enfolded her and again she felt the sticky pressure of the blanket, the shock of contact, and then once more her derelict body dissolving in acquiescence—and beyond that, caught aloft in a furious surf-surge of rapture—

She put her head down and gripped her neck in her fingers, hard. What in God's name had happened to her? Could she have known, in some subterranean way, it was Joe? Did that account for her response? No, that was impossible...But it had been after lying with her that he'd gone back to her purse: it was then that he'd wanted her to know who he was—maybe he even wanted her to get in touch with him, expected her to get in touch with him. He'd known: possibly her traduced ardor had led him to think she wanted to see him again. Would he return every so often, materialize in that doorway any evening she might be left alone?

She had better tell Danny and Reardon. What was the penalty for rape? Two years? ten years? In some states it was death, wasn't it? What if he already had a criminal record—it might be the end of him. Could he get off on psychological grounds, or at least have the sentence commuted to commitment to a sanitarium, something like that? He had to be sick to do what he had done. He had to be. But you couldn't just clear people of all kinds of crimes on psychological grounds—and the police would never agree to it, anyway: this was no impulsive act, it smacked of long and careful premeditation. If she showed the police this card it could put him in jail for the rest of his life...

"You're too sentimental, you don't face facts as they are." Was that true? Yes, it was probably true. But Gard wouldn't understand something like this. He was strongminded, he was impartial, he was honest as the day was long—but for a question like this he would have only one answer; he wouldn't recognize the conflicting shades of intention and misconstrual. He simply wouldn't understand. She drew her head up, shocked at the mutinous nature of the thought. But it was true: there was something here that she had to ferret out for herself, face calmly and honestly and quite alone...

She must sit down for a moment and organize her thoughts, make a few notes on what she was going to say to Joe Castaldo. Write them down one by one. If she possibly could she ought to draw him out, find out why he had done some of the things he had—why he'd used the Negro disguise, for instance; why he'd called her Roxane. She picked up an envelope lying on her dresser, a letter from her sister Alice out in Decatur. Above all she must not let him think she was frightened of him: if he sensed that, she was lost.

Nervously she jotted down a few phrases, stared at them in growing agitation, struck them out with a swift, looping stroke of her pen. This wasn't getting anywhere. What was his phone number? Endicott Street, she'd forgotten the street number already, she could never remember them. She looked it up again in the telephone directory and wrote it down—J A C and the number. But she couldn't phone from here: what was the matter with her? She picked up her purse and thrust the envelope in it—then looked up at her reflection in the mirror, her eyes bright with secretiveness. No: she must hide it more carefully than that. Until she'd decided what she was going to do. Where did you hide things? All her life had been an open, sun-dazzled room; she had never needed to hide anything, and certainly not from Gardner. She glanced around her in dismay, rejected drawers and shelves and bookcases, finally folded it twice and popped it in the bottom of her jewelry case, under the little velvet-covered tray. The Revere Cab card she put back in her purse. My first wifely deception, she murmured to herself, and the thought pricked her like a nettle. Well, it couldn't be helped. She could hardly tell her husband that her assailant, misled by her response to his sexual advances, had decided to leave his name with her for future reference. And Reardon—! No, no one on this earth would believe her. How could they? Fumblingly, maladroitly, she would have to handle this on her own.

"Mrs. Lawring!" Pruitt again, at the foot of the stairs.

"Yes?"

"Mrs. Lawring, how'd you like a cup of hot tea and a slice of cake?"

The dear old soul. Aid to the stricken. "Fine," she answered, "thanks—I'll come down for it. In a couple of minutes."

"All right..."

She went into the bathroom and pressed a cold wash cloth against the back of her neck until pink-and-indigo blotches bloomed against her eyelids. She would have to plan it out very carefully. Phone him from a pay phone and confront him, ask him why he had done what he had—burst in upon her and shattered her life so irrecoverably. Perhaps she could get some kind of assurance out of him—a promise that he would never molest her again if she didn't report him...

Slowly she dried her face and neck, changed back into shirt and slacks. But first she needed time to think, work out some kind of plan. It was all so foreign to her: she needed time to think about it for a while.

Chapter Eight

"I like it," Maltisiak said. He stroked his broad nose with thumb and forefinger, a curiously sensual gesture; his skin was leathery and dark, as though it had been cured many years ago. "I like it a lot. It's got what we want. Class. Distinctiveness. Those little piazzas there, whatever you call them. Those baby terraces." He scowled and took his hand away from his nose. "Won't the kids fall off of them, though?"

Henchey, his glasses riding high on his pink balding head, grinned at Maltisiak and then at Lawring. "Not a chance, Arnie. There's a two-inch mesh below those railings. Oh, maybe a couple of the little monsters'll chop a hole through them and fall out, now and then. Keep the population down."

He and Maltisiak laughed together, easily. Maltisiak's eyes roved slowly around the office, passed over drawings and photographs and maps, returned to the board again. "How many units?"

"Twelve hundred and sixty-eight. In the eight structures, that is."

"Nice," Maltisiak answered. "Very nice."

They were grouped, the three of them, around one of the boards in Henchey's office, looking at the artist's renderings for the North End Urban Renewal project, which Maltisiak's people had decided to call North Church Towers: tall concrete boxes of buildings with pale splotches of grass, young trees washed in with the deft, suggestive strokes of the artist, families strolling happily on the broad sidewalks. Unreal. Lawring looked at them bleakly. They were ugly, and that was the best thing you could say about them: needlessly and unforgivably ugly. Everyone had spent a lot of time on them and they liked to tell each other that these structures were better designed, with more fenestration and better utilization of existing space, than other high-rise projects like it; but they were the same building-block monstrosities that had been put up everywhere since the war—raw red or dull gray piles with all the warmth and individuality of an iceberg. Their apartments were cramped, noisy boxes whose ceilings pressed down against your forehead, where cracks shot across the walls within weeks after occupancy, and whose farcical cribs of balconies looked down on stunted saplings and the usual meandering blacktop driveways choked with parked cars. Why had he spent so much time and energy on them? This had nothing to do with Boston—this could be a multistory development in the Bronx or the South Side of Chicago or Los Angeles, and the most carefully trained eye couldn't begin to tell the difference.

He bit the pencil he held between his teeth, felt the wood give way reluctantly. Under the aspect of eternity, not a particularly captivating image. When the first visitors from the red dwarf of Lalande alighted on the deserted mud flats of the Charles River Basin and gazed at these gaunt ruins, what reports would they send home? *Any of numerous pale-colored, soft-bodied social insects who build nests of brick or poured concrete several hundred feet or more in height, where they store their food and raise their young. Each colony consists of distinct castes. In addition to the sexual forms (king and queen) there are workers, often more than one kind, and often soldiers, all of which are forms of undeveloped females. Many of them have remarkable habits, such as capturing and enslaving the members of other species. The perfect organization of their communities, which is exceeded only by that of the family Formicidae and equaled only by that of the order Isoptera, is maintained by instinctual behavior . . .*

What was the matter with them? Why were they perpetrating this absurdity? Why hadn't they set their towers on platforms created by roofing over each block for ground-level parking, and then built on the platforms, let the cars run down below the pedestrian level and connected the roofs with footbridges, the way Wurster and Bernardi were doing out in San Francisco? or gone up really high, sixty-odd stories in a circular central-core construction with projecting balconies, like the Marina City project on the Chicago River? Maybe they were failures, as some

said, but if they were they were at least imaginative ones—they
weren't simply pounding another nail in the dull old coffin of
high-rise urban housing. Why had they succumbed to the whole
dreary mess? Why hadn't they had the courage to break up the
whole waterfront with running patterns of bridge structures and
man-made islands, the way that magician Tange was doing in
Tokyo, or opened it up with central and flanking malls as
Womersley had done at Park Hill in Sheffield? What a sorry
comedown. Why hadn't they found and fought for a way to let in
the country, maples and oaks and pines and sloping expanses of
lawn—that vibrant prevalence of *green* for which the stone-
oppressed heart hungered?

He took the pencil out of his mouth and set it on the desk;
glancing at Maltisiak he bit at a fingernail. They couldn't
because this man was important. Among other things. Because
he represented very powerful real-estate and construction
interests who had the ear—and a good deal more than the
ear—of City Hall. Among other things...And he, Gardner
Lawring, had once lain on the bank of the Charles River above
Larz Anderson Bridge and beheld his future creations rising in
glory from the Chelsea and East Boston slums, a linear city
spanning Belle Isle Inlet and the Chelsea River—lordly,
sweeping worlds of spaciousness and light; the air-built castle
and the golden dream...

Henchey and Maltisiak were talking about modular
coordinates and construction costs and time schedules, and only
half listening Lawring looked out of the window, along
Congress Street toward Haymarket Square, where trucks and
bulldozers groaned and clattered in a wasteland of rubble and
dust. It was a sound like war, the assault on an enemy town,
house to house, and he thought for a brief moment of
Hexenbach and Lippstadt and then, inevitably, of Diersdorff
and the SS captain in the iron doorway and Sonking lying in the
street with his eyelids fluttering and the blood running from his
nose and mouth. "Lawry, I never—I never—" Sonking's pale
round eyes gazing up at him with tremendous urgency. What
had he never done, that he wanted to tell them so badly? So long
ago...Staring north he felt his eyes sting, and thought of
Sonking with a sharp thrust of grief. He was dead, he had died
three minutes later and they'd left him behind and there had

been no one to mourn for him, no one at home to remember him, pass on the memory of his courage and goodness from generation to generation. That was terrible, the most terrible thing of all, not to be remembered with respect or affection. Most terrible—

He ran his lips back from his teeth, and closed them again firmly. For a single yawning instant he had the sensation he had lost his mind, that he was awakening into madness as complete as any committed idiot. What was he doing standing here, listening to Henchey and this grubby character Maltisiak, watching those old walls collapse in a slam and puff of yellow dust and bulldozers crawl over the masonry? What was he doing? All of that was going, over there—Cornhill and the bookstores and the Italian spaghetti places where he and Chuck and the others used to eat on Friday nights; all the crooked, damp little streets where Paul Revere and Ben Franklin had been reared, where the city had begun. It was all going—all the old city, his city; and he was helping to destroy it. Worse: he was not helping to put up anything of grace or dignity in its place ...

"—ought to work out very pretty," Maltisiak was saying, stroking his nose again . "Start at a hundred and forty, then go to a hundred and eighty on the corner apartments ..."

Lawring turned around. "Hundred and forty a month? Monthly rental?"

Maltisiak's heavy-lidded eyes came up to his. "That's right."

"But—it was to be a comparable rental. They can't afford that ..."

"Who can't?"

"Those people over there ..." Lawring swung his arm toward the plumes of yellow dust. "That's double what they're paying, most of them. More than that."

Maltisiak's lips slid forward in a smile. "So?"

Lawring said in a level voice: "You told them a rental comparable to the current one. Not in excess of fifteen per cent."

"Told who?"

"The North End Citizens' Committee."

Maltisiak looked away and shrugged. "I can't help that. With building costs what they are, we can't do it for less than that. Anyway, that's the basic rent the Corporation has decided on."

"But you promised them—at the hearing. Before the City

Council. That's what they voted on. It's not square."

"Gardner," Henchey said, "I fail to see what this has to do with the topics at hand..."

Maltisiak took his fingers away from his nose and smiled at Lawring again, blandly. "Suppose you let us worry about that, okay?"

"Maybe a lot of people ought to worry about it."

Maltisiak frowned then, for the first time—an expression of mild concern; his little round black eyes rolled around to Henchey. "He isn't going to be difficult about this, is he?" he asked the older man as though Lawring were not in the room.

"Look," Lawring said tightly, "you can talk to me, buster, I'm standing right here in front of you..."

Henchey interposed: "Gardner, we're off the subject entirely—"

"Maybe I am," Lawring went on, watching Maltisiak. "Maybe I'm going to be real difficult. More difficult than anybody you've ever seen."

The contractor stared at him out of his hard, seamed face. "You're one of these Beacon Hill types, aren't you? A blueblood Harvard boy. Aren't you?"

"That's right. That's exactly what I am."

"Then what do you know about rents, comparable or otherwise? What do you know about what North Enders can or can't pay? You never had to meet a rent in your life. I bet you don't even *know* a North Ender—"

"I know when somebody's sitting in a chair at City Hall and lying through his teeth..."

Maltisiak's face turned smooth and somber all at once; the cured-leather skin darkened until it was a thick purple except for his lips, which were almost bloodless. A look full of hatred, hard and savage; the look of a killer. Lawring could see him setting his body, sizing him up. Good, he thought. Just swing on me and I'll give you all you want, buster. I'll break every bone you possess, I don't care how many construction gangs you've bossed. With the greatest of pleasure. He was filled with raging revulsion and held it with great care, like a fragile brazier, let it beat into his veins and heat his face and hands, stiffen his shoulders; he could feel his nerves almost crying for the release of violence. Come on, he said silently; come on, you filthy rotten thug, take a shot at me. Come on, now!

"Gentlemen," Henchey was saying in a high, nervous voice, "gentlemen, this is absurd, over a technicality—there's no need for this, is there? Let's get back to the points at issue..."

"You want to mix with the Corporation, blueblood?" Maltisiak queried softly. "You better be careful how you walk. You've got a little problem of your own right now, haven't you?"

"Never mind my problem! We're talking about *you* now..."

"Gardner—" Henchey said.

"You just watch yourself, sonny," Maltisiak went on.

"Is that some kind of threat?"

"It's anything you want it to be. But you mix with the Corporation you've got your work cut out for you."

"If you think for one minute I'm afraid of your kind, you've got one hell of a lot to learn..."

"A piece of advice." The contractor held up one fat forefinger solemnly. "Stay out of this if you know what's good for you."

"...Don't you *dare* tell me what to do!" Lawring heard himself say through the blood-beat of rage. "Who are you to tell me anything at all? What sewer did you just crawl out of?" And he brought his hands up. Despicable scum! But the moment had passed: Maltisiak had turned away, his leathery face sullen and vengeful; Henchey was hovering around him, saying, "Arnie, I'm sorry about this, believe me I am, can't we forget it and move on to something—"

"And I've got a piece of advice for *you*," Lawring said, his voice crackling with tension, "...you can take that dirty little Corporation of yours and shove it!"

Maltisiak turned at the door and smiled: a smile that made him look like another man entirely; a smaller, fatter man, quite innocuous. "Such language, from a blueblood."

He was gone. The door had slammed shut. Henchey was glaring at him, his face mottled with red patches. "What's got into you, Gardner? You looked ready to hit him. You looked—"

"Scum," Lawring muttered. Now that Maltisiak had left he felt nervous and unsure. "Scum. Hundred and forty a month. You heard him, you were up there..."

"Of course I heard him. That doesn't concern us, Gardner."

"It doesn't."

"Of course it doesn't. We're an architectural firm, we're not a rent control office—"

"It's rotten...Who are these people?" he burst out again.

"Where do they come from—out of some swamp near Taunton?..."

Henchey walked around behind his desk and cleared his throat once—a dry, harsh bark: the sign that he was very angry. "Are you trying to tell me this comes as a surprise to you? Is that your drift?" Lawring said nothing. "You realize what you've done, don't you? You've alienated the head of the Landsdowne Corporation—"

"I know all about the Landsdowne Corporation, they're a pack of small-time chiselers and hoodlums who decided in their infinite wisdom to get into real estate and public housing... I've gone along with a lot of things, Horace. But to sit there and lie in cold blood to the City Council—"

"Gardner, they've got the whole deal in their pockets. It's Landsdowne or nobody. And they play very, very rough."

"Does the Old Man know about this?" Lawring asked suddenly. "This rentals business?"

"Of course he knows all about it—do you think just because he isn't prowling up and down in there all the time"—Henchey tossed his head toward the east wall—"he doesn't know everything that's going on? Jack and I went over the whole operation with him not two weeks ago... Look, everybody's doing it. You can't set up some private standard of morality and refuse to have any dealings with anyone who won't conform to it. Those days are gone, boy. That's simply how it is, that's where the contracts all are going. Either work with them or cut yourself out entirely: that's the deal."

Someone knocked on the door: a timid tapping. "Not just now," Henchey answered sharply. "In a moment." The two men looked at each other for several seconds without a word. Far off, the sounds of demolition bumped and clattered, and somewhere a pile-driver was beating out its double rhythm: *dom*-chut; *dom*-chut; *dom*-chut—

"Gardner," Henchey said with a trace of entreaty. "Give him a ring."

"Who?"

"Maltisiak."

"Maltisiak!"

"Tell him you're sorry you blew up, it was a misunderstanding—"

"Are you serious?"

"Gardner, I know you've been under a terrific strain this past month, and you've been trying to work through it heroically. We're all proud of you. We really are. But you must realize you can't go along like this—blowing off at everyone and anyone who happens to differ with you . . ."

"—But this is wrong, it's rotten!"

Henchey whipped his glasses off his head. "And so we're supposed to turn our well-bred little noses up at the whole deal, is that it? Don't be an ass. Where have you been all this time? You know what Dougherty's done out in Jamaica, you know all about the Baer Brothers down in Quincy—you've been working in this city for fifteen years . . ."

"But this is different, Horace . . . to make a deliberate misrepresentation—"

"What's *different* about it is that it is Arnie Maltisiak and the Landsdowne Corporation, and we are on the verge of nailing down the biggest contract this firm ever saw. You're acting like both kinds of fool, plain and damn. I didn't know you were born last Tuesday afternoon." He replaced the glasses on top of his head and dried his hands with a handkerchief. "You get on with them, Gardner. You work with them. That's all—nobody's asking you to live with them, invite them home to dinner . . ."

There was a little pause. Lawring said: "I've got to see McGrath about the airport building at three," and looked at his watch.

"Will you phone Arnie?"

"I'll think about it."

"I'm counting on you. This is a very, very important moment for the firm."

Lawring rolled down his sleeves and took his jacket off the clothes tree in the corner. "I'll have to think it over, Horace."

Henchey said, not angrily, "God, you're a stubborn one."

"I know."

"Jack isn't going to be any happier about this than I am, and neither is the Old Man. I can tell you that."

"I know. I'm sorry."

After he'd seen McGrath he drove straight home, although it wasn't four-thirty. His anger had ebbed, leaving him perplexed and heavy-hearted. Now it was his domestic trouble, everything was put on that: he was under a strain, he wasn't himself, wasn't behaving rationally. And so on and so on. Henchey would never in this world believe he'd objected to Maltisiak on principle ... And yet of course he shouldn't have got as angry as he had: it was a serious loss of control. And what if he'd hit Maltisiak, hurt him badly? Like many powerful men he knew his strength. Rumors of private individuals who had crossed the Corporation drifted through his mind—threats and beatings and damaged cars and even, it was hinted, an unsolved murder, written off as suicide. God knew he had troubles enough as it was without taking on any more ... Drawn up at a light he slapped the wheel in vexation, glanced across at a man very much like himself at the wheel of the next car, sweating stolidly in the heat, engine idling. The man cocked his head in that ancient gesture of commiseration and grinned and Lawring grinned back at him as the light changed and they drew apart.

Of course he knew it went on all the time. Did they think he was an infant? Sure—chiseling, under-the-counter deals, preferment, inside-trackism—everywhere you looked it went on. Look at the Queen Emma development out in Honolulu. Commissions accepted prearranged bids whenever they pleased, half the juries awarded contracts to the firms that made the loudest splash, not the best designs. Contractors cut corners on materials, and pulled the steel rods out of the floor slabs the minute the inspectors walked away from the job. He'd heard of it and he'd seen it with his own eyes. But not this—out-and-out lying to the tenants themselves. What it amounted to was cold-blooded eviction: you got the tenants to sign off and move out with rosy promises of light, modern flats, and then you neatly crossed them up and went after luxury rentals. Slick as a skate. Sure, costs were high—but they weren't that high, and everyone knew it. Wait until they'd mastered slip-form construction, and they'd be able to work straight down the core from a tower without even having to reassemble the floor forms as they went; they'd knock twenty to thirty per cent off the overall costs—and they'd bounce the rents anyway. If it weren't so rotten it would be funny ...

Janet and Danny Shea were sitting in the living room playing double solitaire with a vengeance. There had been no anonymous calls for some weeks now and Reardon had withdrawn the policewoman. Lawring found himself wishing that Franz were there. Relations between them had been rather cool since the night of the argument. Lawring had called up and apologized the day after, and Franz had dismissed it all graciously enough and come over for a brief visit a few evenings later; but the quarrel had nonetheless created a breach which even Janet's extravagant affection hadn't been able to efface. Lawring felt badly about it but there seemed to be nothing to be done.

He watched the double solitaire game silently for a while; but he didn't want to infect Janet with his mood. Upstairs he changed into khaki trousers and a T-shirt and hunted up a job around the house. The hole in the big maple at the edge of the pool had begun to fill with damp rot. He got out the extension ladder and climbed up there, scooped out the muck with chisel and gouge, then drilled into the cavity from underneath at a sharp angle with the brace and bit. He found a piece of quarter-inch copper pipe, cut it to the proper length with a hacksaw and tapped it in with a maul until its inside end was flush with the cavity; that would hold it until it got good and dried out in the fall, when he could cement it. One of the limbs near the crown had split in the last wind storm and he decided to fix that, too. He climbed up in the crown with a pruning saw, made the short undercut, then the top cut a few inches farther along. The branch split back neatly. He tied it with a light line and lowered it to the lawn. While he was trimming the cut flush to the trunk he heard a car door and peering down through the limp green leaves he saw Inspector Reardon coming toward him across the grass.

"Say, you're pretty good," Reardon said. "Where'd you learn to do that?"

"I worked for a landscape outfit one summer, during college. Tree surgeon's assistant." Lawring came down the ladder and wiped the sweat from his face and neck. "Now you paint it with Cabot's tree paint and that's that."

"Got to be Cabot's, eh?"

Lawring glanced at him, smiled back. "Nothing but the best."

"Sure." Reardon watched him a moment, then took the cigar out of his mouth. "Come on over to the house. I've got some news for you."

"Really? What is it?"

"We've got your boy."

Lawring was conscious of a tremendous sense of relief: he felt faintly dizzy and ten pounds lighter. "God, Janet will be glad to hear that."

"I'd certainly think so."

They went in through the big glass door. Danny and Janet were still playing solitaire; Janet was beating him badly this time, slapping the cards on the ace piles one after another and laughing.

"Hello, Chief," Danny said.

"All quiet along the Potomac?" Reardon inquired.

"All quiet."

"Inspector Reardon's got some great news, honey," Lawring said. "They've got him."

Her eyes went very wide and a strange expression swept across her face—that look of eagerness and fear and terrible regret he remembered from the night at Franz's house. She closed her hands on the playing cards.

"You found the man?" she asked Reardon.

"Yep." The Inspector sat down on the couch facing Janet, popped his hat over one knee and bit into his cigar. "Not two hours ago. You can relax, Mrs. Lawring."

"Who is it?" Lawring said.

"Fellow from Roxbury. Works for a dry-cleaning outfit in Coolidge Corner, runs a delivery truck. Did duty with the army in Germany. Got a taste for white girls while he was there, apparently."

"A Negro?" Lawring asked him.

"That's right. Squad car from the Ninth caught him trying to enter an apartment building out on Commonwealth. He was the one in the Morrill case, and the older woman, the nurse, in Roxbury. She identified him right away." He sat back and looked at them genially.

"What's his name?" Janet said.

"Roche. Harrison Roche. Here's his mug shots." Reardon drew some photographs out of a manila folder and put them on the card table. Lawring saw a slender face, thin cheeks and rather defiant, glassy eyes.

Janet was shaking her head. "That's not the man."

"You're quite sure of that?"

"Yes. I'm sure."

"But—he's confessed, Mrs. Lawring."

She kept staring at Reardon, as though she couldn't free her eyes from his; her hair whipped around her face as she shook her head agitatedly. "I can't help it—it's not the man, I know it's not. I told you that afternoon in Boston he wasn't colored."

"But you *first* thought he was, remember?"

"That's true—but I was mistaken, I know now I was mistaken..."

There was an uncomfortable little silence. Reardon had the look of a veteran physician confronted by a refractory patient. Danny was separating the decks of cards into two piles; his expression was still cherubic, but when his eyes met Lawring's they dropped to the cards again. Lawring didn't know what to say.

"I'm sure when you see him," Reardon pursued easily after a moment, "you'll realize it's your assailant. He had a delivery over in Wellesley only two days before. We checked it out." He was watching Janet carefully; now his amber eyes seemed to hold the faintest trace of jubilance, and Lawring felt all at once a twinge of disquietude. Why was everyone acting so damned queer about this?

"Well, it's easy enough to resolve," he said aloud. "All Mrs. Lawring has to do is look at him and see."

"That's right.—You remember," Reardon turned again to Janet, "you weren't really able to give us anything very definite in the way of physical description."

"I did—I told you he was thin, and dark—and he moved very gracefully," she stammered. The Inspector raised his eyebrows as though to say, "Well?" and gestured toward the photos. "But that's not the man," Janet repeated.

"How do you know?" Reardon asked suddenly.

"—I don't know, I can't tell you." She was twirling her engagement ring round and round on her finger. "I just know it isn't, that's all..."

"How about driving over with us and taking a look at him?"

"No—there's no need to!" she burst out.

Lawring said: "But Jan—surely you haven't any objection to going in and looking at the man..."

She recovered herself with an effort, and looked down. "No, of course not. Of course not. I just meant it wasn't any use, I'm so sure about it . . . I'll go in. In a day or so. I don't want to go in right now."

"All right. Whatever you say. He won't be going anywhere, I can promise you that." Reardon paused, glanced at Shea and then at Lawring; but now it was impossible to tell what he felt. He got to his feet and slapped his hat against his thigh. "Well, that's it," he observed. "I hate to take you off a plush detail like this, Danny."

Shea smiled. "That's all right, Chief. Luck of the draw."

"I want everybody I can use on this Burroughs case, anyway." He looked at Lawring. "Someone rang a doorbell and threw acid on a nineteen-year-old girl the other afternoon." He shook his head, his face sullen with contempt. "They've got her over at Mass. General now. They're trying to save one eye."

"My God," Lawring muttered. He saw the girl at the open door, the other figure darkly clothed, indistinct, the sheet of acid brilliant in the summer air, splashing against her face . . . He shut out the rest of the image.

"Wonderful, isn't it? The things people find time to do to each other . . . Well," Reardon turned deferentially, "good-bye, Mrs. Lawring. Thanks for being so cooperative about everything. We really appreciate it. A lot of folks don't even try to be helpful at all, times like this. It's amazing, but they don't."

"Wait . . ." Janet got to her feet and came toward the three men. "Wait—you're not going to leave us, are you? Leave us here like this?"

"Mrs. Lawring—"

"It's not the man, not him at all—I'm sure of it! I'll be here alone—" She gazed at each of them, her lower lip trembling. Lawring knew she was trying hard not to cry.

Reardon said: "Believe me, Mrs. Lawring, you're not in any danger. Never in all my experience has a suspect returned to the scene of a crime after twenty-nine days—even if we *didn't* have him. And we do. There hasn't been a phone call in two weeks, you know."

Janet started to say something, bit her lip; her eyes filled all at once with tears. She stood in front of them a second longer, her lovely little face vacant with bewilderment and reproach—then turned and ran upstairs. The three men watched her go.

"Well—" Reardon said indecisively, and began to crease the crown of his hat with his blunt fingers. "I guess we better be getting along."

"What about the press?" Lawring asked him.

"The press?"

"You'll keep this out of the papers, won't you? I mean, on the chance that Mrs. Lawring *is* right and the man is still at large, I don't think he ought to know that you've withdrawn surveillance."

Reardon smiled his easy smile. "Really, Mr. Lawring, you haven't got a solitary thing to worry about on that score."

"Perhaps not. But would you keep it out of the papers anyway, as a favor to me?"

"All right. If I can I certainly will."

"Thanks. I'd appreciate it."

They shook hands, and Reardon started off down the hall.

"Why don't you take her on a trip, Mr. Lawring?" Danny Shea said. "Maine, the Sebago Lake area. Or Moosehead. It's beautiful, this time of year."

"I know. I've suggested that we drive up into the Whites, get away for a few days. She wanted to stay here—you know, till the man was apprehended. She wouldn't leave."

"It might do her a lot of good. Get her away, some restful place. Just sit around, lie on a beach and talk." Shea's eyes rested on his, perfectly serene and blue. "Just talk with her a while."

"Maybe I should."

"You coming, Danny?" Reardon was standing impatiently by the front door.

"Right with you, Chief." He said goodbye to Lawring and the two policemen went down the walk, putting on their hats. Lawring watched them get into their cars, the doors slam. They swung around the circle past the rhododendrons and pulled away, the engines fading. There was the spilled barrel rumble as they crossed the wooden bridge, and then silence. It was over. They were alone again. Back to where they'd been that Thursday evening four weeks ago. Four weeks and a day. He felt like a man who has wakened in the middle of a particularly harrowing dream; but the elation he had expected would not come.

He found Janet sitting on the window seat in their old bedroom; she had put on a light sweater and her hands were gripped between her knees. He went up to her and put his hands on her shoulders.

"What is it, honey?" he asked.

"Nothing."

"Are you cold?"

"No." She was trembling slightly although the afternoon was very warm.

"But—aren't you relieved, at least?"

"Relieved?" She twisted around and looked up at him, her face drawn and unhappy. "Why should I be relieved?"

"That it's over..."

She was silent, and looked away again. "No," she said after a moment, "it's not over. They're wrong, they're wrong!" she cried with vehemence and got to her feet. "That isn't the man and I know it. And they know it, too..."

He threw open his arms. "Honey, do you honestly believe they invented this person out of thin air—"

"I don't know what they've done but they're wrong! They've just washed their hands of the whole thing and gone off, left me here alone, all night long—"

"Janet, I'm here," he protested.

"Not all the time... How can I be calm, knowing he's still around, maybe watching me right now—"

"Jan, look—"

"—how can I *sleep?*..."

"Sweet," he said, "the guy has confessed, Reardon says he's *admitted* he did it, what more do you want? You never even got a good look at him, you've said that yourself, it was dark, you were understandably scared and—and emotionally upset and everything... He never took off his dark glasses, there was only the light from the TV, he didn't say two dozen words to you—and you say they haven't got the right man..."

"No, they haven't!"

"Then how in God's name do you *know?*"

"Because he wasn't a Negro, he wasn't—he didn't look anything like that man! I—just know, don't you see, Gard—I *know*, that's all, I know!..." And she began to weep, her shoulders hunched, one hand over her face. Troubled he went up and put his arms around her, which released a fresh flood of tears; but it seemed to relax her a little. Holding her he felt chagrined with himself. He shouldn't have let go at her like that, raised his voice: it was selfish, selfish and absurd, she was worn down from the strain—fear of the man's returning, the tension of the police living in the house; and the reaction now that it was over . . . But she didn't seem to feel it was over at all. And why was she so absolutely sure this Roche wasn't her attacker, without even seeing him? Standing there holding her in the warm, dim room, murmuring softly, handing her in his handkerchief—she never had one with her—absently watching the shadows sift like dust over the lawn, the dense green of the lilacs, he thought of the expression on her face when Reardon had told her about Roche—that startled, covert glance, almost as though she'd been caught doing something wrong . . .

"What is it, sweet?" he murmured. "Is there something you didn't tell them?"

She made a sudden little movement at this, a convulsive shiver, and said, "I don't know, I don't know, it's not that—please don't hound me, Gard, I can't stand it if you hound me about it, please leave me alone!" She thrust him away, went off across the room and sat on the edge of the bed, sobbing sharply now, her voice hoarse and wild. "Oh, I'm so unhappy!" she moaned, and put her face into the crook of her arm. "I'm so unhappy! What is going to happen to me?—you can't *be* this unhappy and not have something happen to you . . ."

He remained rooted to the center of the room; he felt as though the blood were being drained out of him from a dozen places. What had happened? They had never had anything between them before—their life had been like a high glass pillar gleaming in the sun . . . Like most vigorous, unreflective natures he was slow to react to a sudden shift in relationships; he felt simply depressed and full of confusion.

"I'm sorry," he said very quietly, after a few minutes had passed. "I'm sorry, Jan. God knows I didn't mean to hound you about anything . . ."

Still she said nothing; went on weeping hopelessly, her face averted. The moment grew into silence. It seemed to swell to terrible proportions, the bed was a ship easing out from a pier, slipping away from him, they were sliding inexorably away from each other while each second passed. Why didn't she say something? any damned thing at all? Did she by any chance think this had been a joyful little period for *him,* these past four weeks? But she didn't need him, apparently; she didn't want his strength, his comfort, his support. It was the first time in their marriage that she had rejected him, and the realization was like a blow deep in his vitals. He thought of theater evenings, sailing parties, post-game gatherings in Cambridge and how Janet had sparkled, delighting some of his old classmates; of spring trips hunting for wildflowers in the swamps and streams around Sherborn or fall evenings raking leaves together and burning them—the still clarity of the fall air and the sea rustle of leaves and the beeswax-and-iodine odor of leaf smoke all around them...

He shut his eyes. It can't last, he told himself doggedly, it's too preposterous. This recalled an afternoon long ago, when he was nine, playing croquet with his older sister Emily on the lawn at Nount's Head, the day of the thunderstorm. He had been playing along, his usual steady game, keeping his two balls live on each other as much as possible, approaching the wickets cautiously—the kind of sober, steady game that drove his sister crazy and usually beat her in the end (she let her balls get split and overshot wickets outrageously, a gambler's attack), when the storm hit. A sudden quick chill in the air, the flat cannon salvo of thunder and two buffeting swells of wind; and then all around them raindrops as big as quarters splashing on their bare feet, followed by sheets of water in hissing waves, a tropical monsoon right out of the movies, and they had dropped their mallets and raced for the barn, yelping like Indians; and standing just inside the big weathered door, panting, Emily had wiped her face with the palm of her hand and said seriously: "It can't last, it's too preposterous." For some reason he never forgot that moment, nor what she'd said. It became the most important phrase in his life: he adopted it as his personal amulet, spoken at times of crisis to avert disaster or dispel his fear. In the worst moments of the war, in the open field near Havelange or in the black ruins of Diersdorff he would repeat it, like an invocation: It can't last, it's too preposterous...

Only sometimes, perhaps, it could... Remembering the croquet game made him think of Emily and something she'd said when she'd thought her own marriage had gone all to pieces. "It's funny—the one quality in a person you think at first is the most appealing is the very one you find you can't stand later on." He had come in from a skating party one winter vacation afternoon to find her sitting at the kitchen table, her hat still on, her chin in her hands. He had wanted to ask her what quality it was in Cameron, then decided he'd better not, and asked instead: "Is that true?"

"Oh yes," she'd said with that quick, quiet intensity of hers that always reminded him of Grandma Endicott; she'd wagged her head at him, half smiling, and suddenly tears were hanging in her eyes like great glass drops. "Oh yes. The very thing."

Was that true? Did it happen, then, to everyone, sooner or later? It was the very quality he'd first loved in Janet that was now baffling and exasperating him—her delightful, wanton generosity of spirit, her mercurial extravagance. What a fresh breeze this had been in the somber room of his upbringing, where all experience must mean something, accrue to some stern truth concerning human aspiration!...Janet was such a miraculous spendthrift in her emotions; she gave people absurd gifts, did elaborate errands for them, she squandered an entire day reading some twenty-years-dead best seller like *Anthony Adverse* or she lay for hours on the living-room couch, inundated in the thunderous, bellowing finale of the *Symphonie Fantastique* turned up to a hundred and twenty decibels...Life for her was a parade of vivid little adventures, gestures, ceremonies which might be mistakes or wastes of time but which bore their own dancing importance and reality; and who was to say they weren't as meaningful, ultimately, as the rock-ribbed tables of the law?

He went over to her and put his hand under her chin and slowly raised her face to his, and smiled down at her: a smile full of all the sympathy and love he possessed. It didn't matter; she could turn from him in her fear and consternation, she could even reject his solace and it didn't matter at all. He had enough trust and resolve for both of them, he could carry their little world on his shoulders from now till doomsday, if he had to. He was a Lawring, and the Lawrings were indomitable, the Lawrings were resolute. It was a family hallmark. Just as Cabots were plain-spoken, Lowells were haughty, Forbeses were unruly

and Lothrops were frugal, so Lawrings for three hundred years
had been famed for being undismayed. His great-grandfather
Joshua had brought his ship back from a harrowing voyage to
the Orient in a week of financial panic and disaster; his father
and his brothers had run out to meet him on the front stoop
under the graceful white Ionic portal and his father had said:
"Joshua, you have returned to a ruined family." Joshua had
looked at his father's gaunt, gray face, the ring of stricken
countenances; the muscle in his cheek had flexed once. "Perhaps
so," he said. And he had turned then and gone back down to
India Wharf, unloaded the virtually worthless merchandise that
same night and set sail in three days—to return six months later
through a Hatteras hurricane with the cargo of cocoa that
recouped the family's fortunes . . . That was what Lawrings were
like. His love didn't know about any of this—or if she did she
had forgotten—but it was true. He smiled down at her until she
smiled back, rather tremulously, and then he said:

"Do you know what we're going to do? We're going to sleep
late tomorrow morning and then you're going to get all dressed
up in your Sunday best and I'm going to take you to lunch at
Joseph's."

Her hand went to her cheek. "Oh, no . . ."

"Oh, yes. I have decreed it. Anything your little heart desires,
price no object. And after that you can go to Elizabeth Arden's
emporium and get a haircut and a facial and all those womanish
things you've been so busily procrastinating about. And then I'll
pick you up after this meeting I've got at the office, and we'll
have dinner at Locke's and take in a play."

"Oh, Gard . . ."

"How about it?"

"I can't, Gard. Really. I don't think I could do it."

"Of course you can. Look, you've got to start going out
sooner or later, you know."

"But walking around Boston, alone—"

"Big bad Boston. I'll be there, with you. I'll take you to lunch,
and I'll drop you off at Elizabeth Arden's. All you'll have to do is
make it on your own steam over to the Vendôme or the Ritz or
somewhere until I pick you up again. I'll get you a bodyguard
and an armored car from Brink's."

She looked rueful. "I know it sounds silly, Gard; but I *am*
afraid."

"Sweet, you've got to get it out of your system. What are you afraid of?"

"I don't know." She paused. "I'm afraid I'll see him, run into him."

He sat down beside her and took her hands in his. "All right, suppose you're right and Reardon and the whole Boston police force are wrong: suppose the character is still at large. Let's look at this calmly. People who—do the things he did don't hang around in the Ritz or the Vendôme or go shopping along Newbury Street...Suppose you did see him on the street? a nice, light, crowded city street? What could he do?"

"...I don't know." Her eyes grew large, and turned the deepest violet. "If I saw him again I think I'd die of fright, Gard. It was bad enough that night—but now I think I'd go crazy."

"But honey, you're not even sure what he looks like."

"I know—but I know I'd recognize him. In an instant. You just aren't wrong about a thing like that."

"My poor, sweet, over-imaginative darling." He smoothed back the lock of hair that had fallen over her forehead. "Trust me," he said gently. "Trust me that I'm right, honey. You'll have a nice, easy, relaxed time in town and you won't run into him, and you'll begin to build up your confidence again, and the next time it'll be even easier, you'll see. And before you know it it'll be really behind you, for good. You'll see..."

He believed it implicitly: with a love like theirs they could defeat anything, obliterate any shadows or demons real or imagined. All it took was the will to obliterate them. Despite his weariness and the residue of the quarrel with Maltisiak he felt for the first time in weeks the stirrings of passion, virile and alive; but holding Janet he sensed in her a shell of constraint he knew it would be wrong to press. Everything in its season. They sat side by side, talking now and then; the trees roared softly in the evening wind, the door at the end of the hall bumped against its latch, and far away a jet plane traced its shearing course through time.

Later they had dinner, and he persuaded her to go in to Boston with him the next day. She went upstairs and got into bed with a magazine and he went into his study, flung the green paisley shawl off the plans for the Siegersen house and studied them hard. They looked exaggerated, all out of scale: too much pitch to the roof, too much overhang on the south side—the glass panels flanking the blue stone chimney, the pattern of circulation spaces, the whole modular concept was all wrong. It looked like a Los Angeles oilman's idea of modern architecture. Rotten, rotten: he'd done better work than this in graduate school. Why was it coming so hard?

He resisted the temptation to tear the big sheets to pieces, shoved them out of the way and turned to the new plans for the Pan-Am building he'd been discussing with McGrath. Here was something he could take hold of right away. The entrance was alien to the convention of the building itself, he saw it now: the tetrahedron framing looked tacked on, disproportionate. He sat down and began to work up some sketches. Work. Work and a cold shower, his father used to say. Cold water, inside and out. His father had only drunk liquor at family celebrations. He recalled the lean, bony face with its heavy brows and the buccinator muscles which bulged like chestnuts when he was very determined or very angry—which might often be on the same occasion. When Lawring was eight his father had given him Theodore Roosevelt's "Message For Young Boys" in a neat black frame; it was the code he had been brought up by and it was good enough for his son. *He works hard and plays hard; he is not a bully, a shirk, or a prig.* Lawring had known it all by heart once. His father had been very explicit and firm on the subject of masturbation, he remembered. It had nothing to do with insanity or dizzy spells or all the rest of the rot you could hear from misinformed or superstitious souls; it was simply a matter of conservation—you spent your capital and eventually you went into bankruptcy. There was just so much energy—this was energy's fluid—and if you were too prodigal with it in your youth and young manhood you would wake up one fine morning and find yourself destitute.

Lawring had listened to all this very attentively at fourteen, and his subsequent indulgences were governed by a speculative caution. He wanted to be a good athlete and a fine all-around boy in the Teddy Roosevelt image, and fine all-around American boys didn't masturbate—or at least they didn't very often. This concept had received a severe setback during the war, when he had seen men turn from horrific bouts of debauchery to Homeric feats of physical strength and fortitude; and Kinsey's reports had torn down the last bricks in this crumbling wall.

People simply differed, apparently: some could indulge themselves prodigally, others could not. That was all there was to it. There was no magic barrel deep in one's innards.

His father nevertheless had continued to believe in the barrel thesis (they had never discussed the problem in detail since that evening long ago, but the success of the Kinsey books had given rise to much argument and reminiscence at odd moments) and affected to scoff at the "findings" of effete sociologists, so-called. He had no truck with this newest branch of the sciences; he went his own way. He walked five miles every day (he had been a superb athlete at Harvard, and his record for the mile set in his junior year had stood for two decades), took two cold showers, one in the morning and one just before bed, and played a very creditable game of squash until the day of his death. But he had nonetheless died at fifty-nine. Had he come to the bottom of the magic barrel? The Lawrings were not famed for longevity, as were the Adamses and Sohiers and Lowells; but his father's death had been premature, there was no denying it. He had died at fifty-nine—and this Maltisiak, for instance, who cared about as much about physical fitness as he did about honesty, who obviously drank and helled around whenever and wherever he felt like it, was still going strong...

Staring down at the glazed white paper, watching his hand guide the pencil in bold, black strokes, Lawring thought again of the dark, veined, purple face, the lidded eyes and the big flabby nose; and felt again the feathery tingle in his hands. Alive, living, swollen with life—and his father, who was worth twenty of such scum, fifty, a hundred, was dead ... Don't look for justice there, that's a fool's game—but he was unable to divert the course of his thoughts. Filthy, degenerate swine ... If Henchey hadn't been there in the room he would have hit him. And then what? Then he would be on the Corporation's list—if the Corporation had a list. They probably did. Maybe he was on it right now.

And Henchey wanted him to call up Maltisiak and apologize. For the good of the cause. For the sake of a contract greater than any the firm had ever secured. Was he really going to do that—was he, Gardner Alcock Lawring, really going to beg the pardon of this chiseling little hoodlum of an Alsatian or Croatian or Dalmatian or whatever the hell he was? bend the knee to this pack of gangsters who had decided the big money was in buying land and building houses now instead of bookie joints and numbers pools? He knew what his father would have said—he knew what he'd have done, for that matter, in scant seconds; and no bones about it. But Thomas Endicott Lawring had been his own master, and his son was not. This contract was very important to the firm; very important. Henchey had been extremely serious about this. If he refused to make overtures to Maltisiak he might find himself out in the cold: eased out one way or another, for all the fact that he was old Glover's fair-haired boy. Henchey and McGovern and Whitlaw were the powers there now, the ones with the contacts and connections, who knew instinctively how to temper the wind, trim sail, say the right few words at the auspicious moment, get the unexplicated message—they were the ones; not he. His kind of man was going, along with the buffalo and the whooping crane. Right wasn't right, wrong wrong, any longer: it had all been bewitched somehow, transformed into some nebulous, crepuscular no man's land where expediency slapped the back of ambition, compromise got drunk with opportunity, and all four blatted out four-part harmony in some South End tavern run by the Corporation...

There was a sound in the dining room, something ticking on glass; barely audible. He thought of Danny Shea—suddenly remembered he wasn't here now, and went rigid with attention. The ticking sound came again. He was on his feet before he'd thought about it, stepped noiselessly over to the closet and lifted the driver out of the golf bag and stood there with it in his hands. The first night the law had been withdrawn. The first night! Did this monster know *everything?* But they'd caught him, his name was Roche, he'd confessed to the deed ... But Janet said it wasn't the man—and he knew now, standing here gripping the driver, that he believed Janet, that it was some other man entirely.

He heard the sound again, more distinctly this time, and stepping back to his drawing board snapped out the big light, blinking in the sudden rush of darkness, watching round, luminous balls flare and dissolve against his lids. Of course the Holmes Agency alarm would go off if any door or window were forced now; but this was unquestionably glass. It was the fixed pane adjacent to the glass door at the end of the dining room. He knew that too, then: he knew everything. How? Shapes were becoming defined in the gloom now. What he needed was a flashlight. Soundlessly he moved into the hall; he could tell by the absolute black at the end of the dining room that the heavy linen curtains had been drawn. He passed on into the kitchen, turned off the manual control on the alarm system, eased open the drawer at the end of the counter and lifted the three-cell flashlight out of it and closed it again, all with his left hand. At the kitchen door he leaned forward until he could see out of the big glass pane. Nothing was visible. He slipped the driver under his left arm, put his hand on the knob and set himself. All right. He was home this time. That was one thing the son of a bitch didn't know, or else didn't care about. All right: let him be there. Oh Jesus, let him be there!

His legs were quivering, the muscles at the base of his neck were tight as a fist. Good. It would be out in the open now, wound up and solved, one way or another. That was all he wanted—he wanted that more than anything in this world. There was the tick at the glass again; he could hear it from the dining room. Carefully he released the catch, turned the knob until it was disengaged—swung open the door and switched on the flashlight, snatched the driver from under his arm and plunged out into the back terrace, all in one motion. Trees, rocks, the little silent pool leaped into being like a world created— and at the base of the glass pane a little animal gazed up at him with shiny round eyes. Red squirrel. It stood there a second longer, dazzled by the beam, one forefoot tapping against the metal edge of the fixed pane in an incredibly rapid rhythm—then shot away across the lawn, its tail rat-like and meager.

Lawring switched off the flashlight and reentered the house. Back in his study he turned on the lamp, replaced the driver in the golf bag, and sat down at the board again. He mopped his face and neck, squinting at the drawings, not seeing them. His hands were trembling and he clasped them together. He didn't know whether he might laugh or utter a roar of rage or burst into tears. He did none of these things, however; merely sat there motionless, his hands clamped together and his mouth firm. It was catching, apparently—suspicion was as catching as the flu: Janet's lurid imaginings were infecting him, sweeping him off into puerile cops-and-robbers theatricals in the dead of night . . .

Well: Brian would be delighted, at least.

He sharpened his pencils and bent his scrutiny to the board again but his mind, cut adrift by the silly little episode, wandered about among half a dozen problems. The North End Citizens' Committee had been given another hearing Tuesday with the City Council; another appeal. Foredoomed. He thought of the brooding, impassioned Italian faces and sighed. Townsend had changed his mind about the plans for the art museum for the Civic Center. It was obvious that he was just as much under Helena Pinchon's thumb as the rest of them: he wanted Lawring to meet with her and see if they couldn't "arrive at a meeting of minds"—which meant, put plainly, that Lawring was supposed to spend several hours with that frosty, perverse, grandest of grandes dames and more or less agree to her outrageous dream of a multi-turreted Kraut gun emplacement, complete with flying buttresses and a Japanese garden where elegant ladies could sip iced tea amid the gas-pipe-and-sheet-metal sculpture of the New York School. God. Crotchety old Mrs. Jack herself would have been easier to work with...

How had he got into all this mess? He was an architect, a designer of buildings; wasn't he?—*whatever* he was, he wasn't a committeeman, an operator, an oily public relations character out of Madison Avenue with a slap on the back and a bland and easy answer for everybody concerned...

What was he going to do, then? Call Maltisiak and smooth it all over, say the words Henchey wanted him to say? or cause an unholy row—and incidentally row himself right out of a job—forsake all chance of making his mark, of attaining any real prominence in his field? And there was Brian. How would something like this affect the boy's future, the proud, majestic things he had planned for him? The future. He had always thought of the future as something that would take care of itself, with the clear saffron flush of the sun's rising; now it lay before him like a marsh in November—tricky, impenetrable, wreathed in fog...

Then he thrust that thought, too, out of his mind and worked on while the night breeze hissed in the maples, and from the swamp behind Franz Hoelder's house the whippoorwill shouted its lunatic love call.

Chapter Nine

Emerging from the Elizabeth Arden Salon Janet Lawring walked briskly along Newbury Street toward the Public Garden. She felt blithe and alert from the haircut and facial, her skin all atingle in the warm, windless afternoon, alive with scents. Dolores had shown a solicitude that had touched her: she'd made no mention of the episode, and had given her one of the separate rooms at the end of the hall. It was good to have her hair the proper length again. She never left a beauty parlor without feeling she must be more attractive—and this sensation, after the long confinement, was stronger than ever. As she walked she began to look around her—at first a series of furtive glances, then more boldly as she gathered confidence. A young girl passed her, wheeling her baby away from the Garden, a pale, pink baby who was squalling with astonishing volume; his mother was trying ineffectually to hush him, not caring really, her lips curved in an indulgent smile. Farther on two little old ladies in faded print dresses and wearing hats that looked like crushed wicker baskets of fruit were standing in animated conversation, and the imitation cherries and apricots bounced gently above their noses. The world. The world had begun to readjust itself again—trees and stone and human beings were slipping out of their purposeless, uncaring savagery into an ambiance clothed again in beauty and order and amiability. It reminded her of the first day she'd been allowed outdoors after a six-weeks' childhood illness—that same scrubbed *strangeness* lay over everything: the sunlight was far too bright, the low-hanging leaves were too palpably green, too painfully vivid to be real. Life was like an unhoped-for Christmas present, out of season, hung from a mantel above her head . . .

At Arlington Street a girl came out of the Ritz, a girl dressed very high-style—too high-style for Boston—crossed the neat beige squares of sidewalk and got into a fire-red Fiat sports car with practiced ease: sitting in backward, then folding her knees and swinging her fine long legs in after her and drawing the door to her with a bump. She started the engine with a thrust of one hand and glanced at Janet—a bold glance, almost severe, out of eyes brilliant under the purple-and-green eye shadow. And Janet, watching her unsmiling, thought for the first time in almost an hour of Joe Castaldo, and thought of him with a heavy urgency.

She had done nothing since she'd found the money and the card in her purse three days before. The next morning, after Gardner had left for the office, she had lain on the window seat with her arms over her eyes and tried and tried to think it out. She ought to tell the police about the money. Then she realized that the money by itself would mean little or nothing without the accompanying card; but every time she thought of telling the police about him something inside her froze. She did not abandon the idea—but she kept putting it aside temporarily. When her assailant had been a nameless marauder, a capricious emanation that had loomed out of the night, she had been frightened enough; now that she knew it was Joe Castaldo she had to bear the added burden of indecision. She could not act. Perhaps they would catch him, perhaps he'd left other leads they could follow—in which case she would go in and identify him and that would be all right: she would be merely confirming an arrest already made. She wouldn't have betrayed him in all his insane vulnerability—if that was what it was...

Frowning she entered the Public Garden, moving indolently along the fine-swept asphalt paths, skirting the edge of the pond where couples sat on the green-slatted benches and children crouching on the gray stone curbing shoved little sailboats bravely out into the still water. It was the part of the Garden she liked: the other end, the Beacon Street end, was filled with wealthy, hawk-faced homosexuals or crusty grandes dames with silver-headed canes or retired counselors-at-law now in the process of writing their memoirs every afternoon at the Athenaeum. Over there, beyond the Garden and the Common, stood the brick bastion of the Hill, looking smoky and remote through the trees. *Enemy territory,* she had always thought of it as a child: the world of entrenched wealth and social position, the citadel of the frosty Brahmins who ran the city in a grip of iron—without ever appearing to do so; the world into which, amazingly, she had married.

She paused, a finger to her lips. The home of her mother-in-law was over there, right over there; it seemed impossible, but it was true. Gardner Alcock Lawring had fallen in love with her and married her, in the face of the traditions of ten generations—not to speak of his mother's wishes (Janet had not been party to any of that, but she could imagine that duel of two indomitable wills in the long, shadowed living room; terse exchanges, the set lips, the long, hostile pauses). But she could never think of herself as a Lawring, or a member—even a second-class one—of a First Family, no matter how hard she tried. Gardner hadn't seemed to care: he had his club in town and his final club from college, which he said he no longer had much interest in, since the war. There were various Harvard functions he attended religiously, and the periodic family gatherings at Thanksgiving and Christmas and, more importantly, Labor Day weekend down at Brewster; but aside from these there were no others involving pressures. Lawrings had always been mavericks, more or less, he'd once told her, coming as they did from Cape Cod rather than Cape Ann: they had refused to take part in the mass exodus out to Chestnut Hill and Milton, they had occasionally married outside the Boston pattern (though not, she'd thought wryly, the daughters of Somerville plasterers), and they had persisted in the China and India trade long after most of the other Boston families had gone into railroads and mines and other pursuits...

She looked at her watch, and moved along again. She had two hours until Gardner picked her up at the Statler. That in itself was a trivial instance of the problem: she knew Gard would have preferred the Ritz-Carlton or the Vendôme or even the Somerset, but those hotels made her feel uncomfortable; there was too much of Old Boston surrounding them—they were too redolent of the Junior League and the Horticultural Society and charity balls, all the stately sodalities and assemblages of the rich she had sensed from afar. Now, vaguely troubled, thinking of Gardner, she wondered if she'd been the unwitting cause of a kind of ostracism he was too sweet ever to mention. She probably had been. She'd tried, rather ineffectually, during the first years of their marriage, when they'd lived in Cambridge. The bleak fact was that she had nothing to say to these women. There they sat in front of her, so neatly, so *contained;* they were involved in a thousand and one social and fraternal plans and functions she'd never even heard of, and worse than any of that they laughed at different times than she did, and looked at her strangely out of their cool round gray eyes...

She couldn't for the life of her understand the Hill; it amused and baffled and enraged her. It was a strange, cranky little world, full of unpredictable quirks and measuring sticks. It was bad to go around in rags, of course—but it was worse to be overdressed: if that was the only choice, threadbare garments were preferable. You never polished your car, as her brothers had done, endlessly—but you kept it like some kind of antique timepiece, with meticulous scrupulosity, for decades; Mrs. Vassall, she discovered, still owned and operated a 1916 electric brougham, and had been arrested for speeding on the Worcester Turnpike. You never mentioned money—but you made sure you had plenty of it. True gentility—Boston gentility—apparently lay in an instinctual recognition of the subtlest nuances in a maze of authenticity and value open only to this tight little clan of initiates.

"If the Mount Vernon Street house is so old, darling, why doesn't it have some of those lovely purple panes of glass in the front windows, like the houses over on Beacon Street?" she'd asked Gardner once.

"Because, love," he'd replied, "those lovely purple panes you're rhapsodizing about don't stand for antiquity at all. They happen to be from a batch of imperfect glass some unscrupulous British merchant fobbed off on people in Boston, and at a comparatively recent date. Sometime about 1820 or so."

Then there was the matter of taxis: she loved to take them—jumping into a cab was for her a little adventure in extravagance. A good Bostonian never took a cab unless he were aged or deathly ill, or it was a matter of life and death. This held true even if you were wearing your best pair of heels and it was raining cats and dogs and the gutters were roaring. She'd been desperately glad when they'd moved out of town.

She'd done her best, too, at the family conclaves, especially the Labor Day affairs, which always lasted three days and were masterpieces of rigor and repetition. Gardner's sister Emily was married to a man named Cameron Bournham, a State Street securities broker, whose two interests seemed to be professional football and the stock market reports. Emily wasn't in love with him—Janet knew that from several allusions of Gardner's and five minutes' observation on her own hook—but like a good Boston Yankee housewife she had determined to stick it out; and what little spirit and imagination she possessed had been bled away in the process. Prill hadn't done much better; her husband was an Episcopal minister, a New York man named John Askew with a soft, chinless face and a faintly popeyed expression. He looked perpetually clean-shaven no matter what he did, and was one of those clergymen who pride themselves on being up-to-date and sophisticated—regular fellows despite the cloth; he continually affected a tone of slangy banter, and his conversation usually consisted of not very witty tales about his congregation in a small town in western New York State.

There was also Gardner's Aunt Eliza, his father's sister, a tall gaunt spinster with a lantern jaw and flashing, worried eyes who busied herself in dozens of philanthropic causes in and around Boston. She and Marcia Lawring formed the center around which the others grouped themselves, on the wide verandah at Nount's Head. It was their dialogue that dominated the conversation—an unhurried recitative of an illustrious and cantankerous ancestry: there had been a grizzled old sea-dog named Asa who had become so incensed at the contentious miserliness of an India Wharf merchant that he had halved a penny with a hatchet and nailed it to the stempost of his vessel as a warning to that merchant and all his kindred to give him a wide berth in the future; there had been another intrepid forebear, also a sea captain, who had been captured by pirates in the Malacca Straits, and who had sat on a palm log deep in the pirates' lair for two days and nights and successfully beaten down their ransom demand until it reached a sum he considered more consonant with his means—whereupon he had arranged to have them paid off, and had gone his way; there had been a woman named Sarah who had taken a broom to a detail of Hessian soldiers who had entered her home during the British occupation of Boston, and had sent them flying... The two women talked and the family listened, while the wind sang in the screens and the children played fitfully among the rose arbors, where yellowjackets stung them and their mothers went out and tried to offer comfort.

And there was also—praise God—Uncle Archie, who sometimes came and sometimes didn't; and for whose presence Janet fervently prayed. He was slight and courtly and handsome, with curly black hair and a charming smile. They had been allies from the very first. She remembered at the wedding reception—he'd arrived too late for the ceremony—the way his eyes had sparkled at her with delighted astonishment.

"Gardner, congratulations," he'd cried, "—for taking complete leave of your senses!" He had kissed her demurely on the cheek and taken both her hands in his. "Think you can cope with this family, do you?"

She'd laughed. "I'll try my best..."

"Oh, you'll have to do better than that! Lawrings and Alcocks have always been sans pareil—particularly in their own awareness of it. Won't it be grand when we all go to heaven and are equals before God?... You're a very courageous girl," he went on, and nodded toward Gardner, who was greeting two militant old ladies with Queen-of-Austria hats. "I don't know that he's worth all the effort, but I've an idea you'll make him very happy..."

Things bubbled and danced around Uncle Archie. He made flimsy kites for the children, he made powerful drinks for the adults. He would break in on one of Gardner's mother's ancestral recitations:

"Oh come now, Marcy—aren't you going to tell 'em about Great-granduncle Timothy, that soul of generosity, and how he gave his clerk Andrew Archer ten dimes as a bonus—one for each and every year of faithful service? Or how about Aunt Leona and the family silver? You know about that, don't you?" he would inquire of the circle with disingenuous charm. "I'm sure Marcy couldn't have meant to leave her out. She'd been feuding for years with her brother Nat's wife Amy, and when their father died—that would be Joshua, wouldn't it, Marcy?— she wouldn't agree to a division of the spoils. Nat finally got it across to her that an equal distribution of the crockery was specified in the will—whereupon Aunt Leona reared back and said, 'Well, it's all right for *you* to use 'em—but I won't have Amy eating off 'em!' Don't you know that saga?" he would ask into the laughter, his eyes raised, and then turn again to his sister, who looked martyred and vexed. "Marcy, I do believe you're bowdlerizing the family history!"

"Archie, there's no sense in picking over all that rubbish..."

"Perhaps not, perhaps not. Still, it's nice to give the rising generation a rounded view, don't you think?"

"I can see nothing *rounded* in dredging up a pack of unseemly stories—"

"All right, Marcy. Have it your way. You go ahead and I'll just sit here and put in an occasional aside... Can it be that after all these years I'm actually in danger of becoming your conscience?"

And there he would sit, drink in one hand and onyx cigarette holder in the other, ebullient and urbane; waiting for another chance to disconcert his sister and set them all off again. He refused to let her faze him.

"Well, and what have you been doing with yourself this past winter?" she would demand.

"I've been reading," he would reply with easy equanimity.

"Reading? Reading what?"

"Oh—Catullus, Ortega, Thucydides... It's extraordinary, the timeliness of that man's work: you'd think you were reading about some town in Algiers. When have you last read Thucydides, Marcy?" And Janet could see her retire into the narrow cave of her disapproval, fuming and resentful.

Sometimes Cameron would try to get him to invest in the market.

"Oh, dear boy, no no." Archie would shake his head with a soft, engaging smile. "Something'll get stuck in the middle of the Suez Canal or De Gaulle will have a sneezing fit or some senator will go off to Atlantic City with someone he shouldn't, and the stock market'll go into a nosedive—and then where would I be? No, I better stick to the things I know about."

And then there had been the croquet game. It had started decorously enough: Janet and Archie against Cameron and Prill. The Lawrings played according to the strictest rules she'd ever seen: there were crossed wickets at the center of the court—an aperture barely wide enough for a tennis ball—and a fiendish array of rules governing out-of-bounds, mallet's head proximity to another ball, offensive and defensive shots and penalties... A grim, interminable kind of game: she was wrung with boredom almost before it had begun. Prill and Cameron were huddled over a wicket, going over their next shot like a legal brief, and across the court Archie caught her eye—a swift, roguish complicity in the middle of all this ponderous, arduous decorum. When his turn came Archie belted his ball all the way down to the far end of the court, missing everyone else wildly.

Cameron gaped at him. "What's the sense in that?"

"I felt like it," Archie answered. "Just an idea. It was fun."

On her turn Janet shot diagonally the length of the court and passed through a distant wicket, illegally.

"Bravo!" Archie called. "Two points!"

"For heaven's sake," Cameron spluttered, and Prill looked concerned.

"That's the spirit, gal," Archie said. "Now we've got 'em!"

And the conspiracy was on. They went through wickets backward, hit the back court stake three times in succession, they wandered around in the weeds. They reduced the game to a shambles; even Prill got to laughing. Cameron finally quit in disgust.

"If you're not even going to *try* to win," he said, shaking his head scornfully.

"We're playing our heads off."

"That game's never been played that way on *this* court."

"Well, I'd say it's high time," Archie whooped, and hugged Janet to him with one arm. "High time!"

Of course he was lonely; she knew he must be. She'd heard Cameron say Archie had lost his head over an Italian woman, some years ago. She rather doubted it—she imagined he'd lost his heart, and that he would do it again if the occasion offered...I want Boo to live that way, she thought, with the quick emotional tug she felt now whenever she thought of the boy. Gard thinks I spoil him, but I don't—I just want him to *live,* I want him to risk things, risk his heart; *everything* doesn't always have to be for some sober, solid, concrete purpose...

A breeze fanned over the pond, quick little fingers of cats'-paw, and the women's hats and dresses in the swan boat passing near her fluttered and swirled. Nevertheless she was a Lawring: if being Gardner's wife meant being a Lawring that was what she'd be till doomsday. That was what she wanted to be—Gard's wife. She felt vaguely ashamed of her outburst the previous evening, a regret compounded by Gardner's amazing forbearance. He was a darling, a sweet, undaunted man and she had acted like a hysterical idiot. All at once she was filled with a rush of affection for him, an awareness that completely enveloped her—she could almost feel him moving beside her with his sturdy self-possession, steadying her, calmly restating her topsy-turvy universe merely by his presence. She couldn't imagine her life going on without him: the idea was like some unspeakable void she couldn't pierce—as though the earth were flat and she would drop off its edge and fall endlessly through time...

I don't know how to *act,* she thought; I don't know what I am as a social being, that's the trouble... She had come to terms with herself as a person: she knew who she was and she had accepted it, the sweet and the bitter; but her marriage—she saw that now, suddenly—had made it impossible for her to behave as she used to. She was too sincere (and too transparent) to try to ape Gardner's First Family Bostonians, and she was too sensitive to ignore the difference, as Polly could. She wanted with all her heart to live up to Gardner's standards—and yet she felt obscurely that they were not really her own: it was just that which left her dangling.

She went out of the Garden and started along the Boylston Mall. She must do something about Joe Castaldo, she must use this time she was here alone in the city to think out some meaningful course of action, free herself of the whole problem. She must let him know her silence did not mean assent, that she felt he had acted horribly, irrevocably... but that she would not actually turn him in to the police. Gardner wouldn't agree to that, of course: Gard would say justice and the state must be upheld, that to knowingly leave a man like that running around unapprehended was in itself a crime against society and one's fellowmen—that was what he would say, wasn't it? But there was something in her that sided instinctively with the underdog, whoever it might be; and apart from all contentions about justice it seemed beyond her to cruelly shut off a man's life—even a stranger's, even Joe Castaldo's...

But of course he was not a stranger: he was a man she had known, even if only briefly. A man she had surrendered to—or

at least her body had. This was where her mind inevitably
bogged down. At one end of the emotional teeter-totter was the
fact that Roche's confession had set her assailant scot free; at the
other end lay her sense of shame, and the oppressive fear that if
Gardner knew the story—the whole story in its shocking,
incredible entirety—it would hurt him terribly, and he might
hurry to some irreparable decisions. She feared that more than
anything else on earth. So attuned was she to all his thoughts
and moods, so wedded to the very chemistry of his being that she
could see with perfect clarity the pain invade his clear gray eyes,
his face harden like beaten metal—and that she could not bear.
She would chance anything before that. Perhaps Castaldo
would never approach her again—or possibly she would never
be free of him if she didn't act now. Who could tell what he might
be thinking? In ten years anything at all could have
happened—he could have become the most dangerous kind of
psychopath ... Simply to have remembered her all those years
and planned that evening as he had, made him loom as some sort
of madman. And now he was free ... Why had this man Roche
told them he'd done it when it hadn't been he at all?

Rather guiltily she hurried into the Statler lobby, and
abandoned herself to the sense of anticipation this hotel always
gave her. When she'd been in high school, in town with girl
friends for Saturday afternoon shopping and a movie, she would
resort to all kinds of ruses to lure them into the Statler lobby,
where all the romance of the world was suspended, she knew,
under those great square marble columns. World travelers,
celebrities and financiers swept up to the desk, bellhops rushed
to pick up handsome leather grips, old friends greeted each other
among the potted plants with expansive ardor, gesticulating and
chattering incoherently. Every time a man and woman
embraced she had felt a sudden catch at her heart—a moment of
delight that was both shameful and pure. Once she and Milly
Devereux had seen Joseph Cotten step out of one of the
elevators looking romantic and tired with his long hair and soft
tweed jacket. Gardner didn't like the Statler lobby. He called it
the Hostelry for Visiting Elks, and gave her his slow, mournful
grin of disapproval whenever she alluded to it. But she knew.

Perhaps she'd go to a movie, if there were one she wanted to
see nearby. She bought a paper at the magazine stand, found
herself a large, over-upholstered chair and began to watch the

comings and goings. An imperious, bird-like woman carrying a small Italian leather folder—a visiting lecturer, probably— strode into the elevator, and a very tall man with a weatherbeaten face and a milk-white ten-gallon hat purchased a cigar at the magazine counter and began joking with the girl in a rich, easy drawl, then snipped off the end of the cigar with a silver cigar cutter hanging from his watch chain. Texas cattleman, or maybe an oilman from Oklahoma, here on a big deal—perhaps he was after financial backing from Cameron's firm. Seated near her a sallow-faced, worried looking little man was bent toward a heavy woman in a black silk dress, talking to her earnestly, stressing each point by tapping a spidery forefinger on his knee: a lawyer advising a client—or no, the relationship was too intimate for that, he was the woman's brother, giving her pointers on how to handle a willful son, an alcoholic husband...

Her eyes roved around the pleasantly cooled, gently lighted room, watching its occupants, inventing tales about them. Basking in the stately pace of the Boston summer's day, her returning confidence, she wanted to prolong this blessed state of anonymity that had enfolded her after all the weeks of being a mark, target and captive both. None of these people knew anything had happened to her, she was just like any one of them now, resting in the pattern of light and shadow, face to open, smiling face. It was good to be close to people again, responsive to them; even if they all knew just how to act, and she did not... I should have come in to town weeks before this, she thought; what was the matter with me?

After a while she tired of the game and opened the paper she'd bought. There was no film she wanted to see badly enough to make the effort and besides, she wasn't sure there would be time—above everything else she hated to leave a picture, even a bad one, in the middle. She had once been forty-five minutes late to meet Gardner because she hadn't been able to leave a Cary Grant–Ingrid Bergman movie, she'd forgotten its name. Gard had been cross with her—then actually furious when she'd told him the reason. When you said four o'clock you should *mean* four o'clock; punctuality was one of the true marks of breeding, a sign of respect and consideration for the other person—and to keep someone waiting on account of a stupid, ridiculous, worthless moving picture... He had sputtered and scowled, all hot under the collar; and she'd felt contrite. "But darling," she pleaded, "wouldn't you rather I told you the truth?"

Smiling faintly, remembering the episode, she turned the pages, ran her eyes dreamily over the columns: a new polio vaccine which could be taken orally, Tshombe angry over something, the Sheikh of Kuwait worried about something else, a shake-up in Korea's military junta—checked all at once on the headline: SEX OFFENDER SEIZED. *Metropolitan police disclosed today they have taken in custody the man responsible for the wave of Greater Boston burglaries and assaults. Harrison Roche, 27, was apprehended yesterday by Patrolmen Hugh Downs and Patrick J. Milligan as he was entering the home of Mr. and Mrs. Richard G. Weeks at 47 West Cleveland Way in Brookline. Roche has already confessed to at least three of the most baffling of the criminal assault cases, those involving Miss Margaret Hannegan in West Roxbury, Mrs. James Morrill in Needham, and Mrs. Gardner Lawring of Holcomb Hill. Chief Inspector John J. Reardon, in reply to questions, said, "We are convinced that Roche's arrest and confession clears up the majority of these cases in the Greater Boston area." Miss Hannegan, a nurse at City Hospital, identified the suspect instantly. "There is not the slightest doubt in my mind," she told police. "It's the same man." Mrs. Morrill and Mrs. Lawring had not as yet appeared to confirm the identification, police told reporters. Miss Hannegan—*

Janet Lawring put the paper down in her lap, conscious of the fact that her face was lightly burning. She had never seen her name in the newspaper before this affair: it was as though there were two Janet Lawrings, the one sitting here in the Statler lobby and another one who served as subject for police reports and newspaper pieces. But for everyone else there was only one Janet Lawring of course, the one they read about; and anyone reading this—

She had drawn in her breath tightly. Her eyes fastened on the base of a huge stainless steel ashtray, scratched and scarred from the shoes that had scuffed it.

That meant he knew. Joe Castaldo. He knew that the police had been withdrawn, that the case was closed. He knew she was without protection. Everybody who read this paper knew that.

Her eyes moved around the room warily, dropped to the

newspaper again. She would have to call him at once. Take it into her own hands—phone him and get him to promise he would never bother her again. It was the only way. What was his number? She couldn't remember it, she'd left the slip of paper back at the house. She got out of the chair and went over to the row of phone booths and looked up the number again, saying it over several times under her breath to memorize it, and stepped into a booth, which seemed unendurably hot and airless. For a moment she sat there, listening to the thin insect-whine of the toy fan above her head, trying to plan it out. She must be steady—very steady and firm. No trace of emotion: treat it like a—like any kind of transaction. Jordan Marsh or the Shawmut Bank. Perfectly impersonal. If he became abusive she would simply hang up. If he seemed penitent, genuinely sorry about it, she would agree not to take any action herself.

Her fingers were tingling and her mouth was dry. She swallowed and dialed, listening tensely to the clicks. There was a funny treble ring, curiously loud, and the operator's voice sang:

"What number are you calling?" Janet started, gave it before she'd thought. "I'm sorry, but that number has been discontinued."

"What?" Janet said. "What do you mean?"

There was a brief pause, and the voice said with a faint trace of impatience, "It has been discontinued, madam. It is no longer in use."

"But it can't be... Are you sure?"

"Yes, madam. I am sure."

"Well, can't you tell if he has another one? what the new number is?"

"There is no new listing for that name."

"Well, when—can you tell me *when* it was discontinued?"

"No, madam, I couldn't tell you when." Then, relenting a little: "It's quite recent, though—I'd say within the past few days."

"Thanks, operator..."

She hung up disconsolately, nudged the folding door open with her knee but remained sitting there, her hand to her forehead. This was bad. Very bad. She couldn't say exactly why but she was sure of it. He had disconnected the phone so she couldn't contact him, then. Perhaps he had moved away from that address on Endicott Street. He could be anywhere, anywhere at all—he could be tracking her down in the city at this very moment—

She was being silly about this. Completely silly. She left the booth and went back to the center of the lobby. Her seat had been taken by an elderly gentleman with a full mustache and a carnation in his buttonhole, but she found another and sat there very erectly, her hands gripping the newspaper. The world of careless menace had moved forward again: a giant step. She knew she ought to do something, take some bold, creative action: she tried to think what Gardner would do in a situation like this, but that was no help at all; he wouldn't have got into a mess like this in the first place. She could write Castaldo, of course—but what good would that do? He had probably moved somewhere else by this time, and left no forwarding address. And suppose the letter were returned, and Gard saw it and opened it? What could she say to him?

She felt deeply disoriented again, harassed and vulnerable, and to escape her dilemma sought to lose herself once more in the surge of travelers: this man wearing a black homburg, that woman flicking a pair of yellow gloves against her thigh. But after a time the game defeated itself; one face became all faces, one greeting all greetings and departures, and she watched them all with a dazed expression while around her time flowed forward and backward like a tide—to Beacon Hill and her marriage to Gardner; to Jimmy, the man she might have married and didn't, to whom she'd given herself with such joyous abandon, and Ray Thomas, the boy who wanted to marry her; and beyond that to the first boy who had put his hand on her breast, a shy, handsome, rather awkward boy named Victor DiLeo—she could tell from the way he had cupped his hand over her breast that it was the first time he had ever done it, too—one evening at Revere Beach, fast fading twilight, her shoulders smarting faintly from sunburn, behind them the reedy tinkle of the carnival and down near the water a group sitting around a fire singing, "Shine on, shine on, harvest moon . . ."

And again at the beach at the age of fourteen with a neighbor, Tommy Pieroni, who had taught her how to kiss under water: his round face swelling near, black hair hovering above his brows, and then the quick, anesthetic pressure of his lips and the burst of silvery bubbles as they both had laughed and risen to the surface... Back and back, to a long, square touring car with its top down and grown-up people piling out of it, dozens and dozens of them, white flannels and scarlet and lemon dresses against the rich emerald green of the lawn, her arch-image of extravagant frivolity; a hand-wind phonograph that played moaning, thumping music and the couples danced on the grass, calling to each other and laughing, and a girl with short red hair and slanted brown eyes that were so light they were almost yellow blew a great golden bubble out of her mouth—and then it popped and she winked down at the little girl watching; and beyond that to a face—a worn, gentle, smiling face, it had been her grandfather—leaning down to her out of an aureole of light, and then she'd been lifted swinging high into the light and feeling the warm, gentle arms had nuzzled the scorch-and-lemon smell of shirt and laughed and kicked in joy... A going out and out, that heedless offering of her self to the adventure of life, which had been the source of all her strength and all her weakness—had it all led to nothing more or less than that night of June sixth? Was it only Somerville catching up with her? Was that why Joe Castaldo had reached her so fatally—was it because she really ran on his level of responses, and not Gard's? She shivered. When she'd played in the back yard with Tommy and Edna and the other kids, what had she thought would happen to her? Life was the unfurling pennant of a thousand thousand lives, and then as you grew up it became hundreds, and then dozens, and finally only one—which was the life you were destined to have all along... Was that what it was all about? But why was it that—

She started violently. A man was looking at her from across the lobby: a slender young man in a print shirt and khaki trousers, staring at her with a faint, mocking smile. Before she'd blinked and her eyes had focused on him he had swung away and was walking off down the hall. It was him. Joe Castaldo. Was it? Amazement, indecision swept her, held her rigid—then she had come to her feet and was hurrying after him through the grouped chairs and potted plants. A woman looked at her in astonishment, a child flung against her knees and recoiled, its small face puckered, ready to cry; but the woman and the child were mere impediments, solid forms in the way of her catching up with Castaldo and confronting him. She reached the edge of the lobby. He was at the end of the corridor now, had passed through a glass door and turned right. He was whistling "La Paloma." She hurried along, half running, her heels hitting like shots on the marble. At the corner she caught one last glimpse of the flowered shirt, turning left this time. She ran the distance of the corridor and again rounded the corner. Nothing. A little foyer, opening on the street, and opposite that a closed door. She stepped out into the street, saw no one, stepped back inside. The door facing her said NO ADMITTANCE. She walked up to it and knocked. There was no answer. She tried the door: the handle turned but the door would not open. NO ADMITTANCE.

She knocked again, pounded with the heel of her fist on the metal; then gazed at it, wordless. Turning she hurried back to the lobby, which now seemed a blur of alien faces and forms and garish lights; not like the Statler lobby at all. She went up to the desk clerk and said, "Did you see that man standing here?"

The desk clerk and two men who were registering turned toward her. The clerk was a thin man with a bony face which was wider at the cheeks than at the top of his head. He squinted at her and said, "What man, madam?"

"The man standing right there. In a yellow sport shirt. He went down that hall and through a door..."

"I don't understand, madam. You mean he was here at the desk?"

"No, he was right there, right over there by that pillar."

The clerk looked at her narrowly and frowned. "Just a moment, if you will." He stepped back into the office, a discreet limping gait, as though he were walking on glass, and said: "Mr. Prence. There's a lady here—"

A short man in a double-breasted suit, with the creamy jowls and small flicking eyes of a bank manager, came up to her and placed his neat white hands on the counter. "Yes, madam?"

"There was a man standing right here a few moments ago," she repeated. "In a yellow sport shirt. You must have seen him! He went down that hall and through a door marked 'No Admittance.' Do you know who he is?"

"'No Admittance.' You mean the door at the other end of the—"

"The door down there—at the end of the corridor. Who is he? I have to find him."

The manager's eyes widened slightly. "No one is authorized to enter that door."

"I tell you I saw him!" she said, raising her voice. "I *saw* him go through that door marked 'No Admittance'..."

The manager shook his head forbiddingly. The clerk and the two men registering were watching her now, with the somber, wary astonishment of people present at an unpleasant scene, in which anything might ensue. God help me, she thought, I'm going crazy. But he was here, right here!

"I tell you I saw him," she insisted, "—can't you find *out* about him?"

The manager's eyes became shuttered and flat. "Has he been annoying you, madam?"

"Annoying me—! I tell you I have to *see* him..."

"If he was annoying you, I can call the house detective and you may speak with him. Do you wish me to do that?"

She stared at him mutely, her mouth working. They were looking at her, all four men, with annoyance and displeasure and something else—which she soon realized was an amused mépris. They didn't believe her. They thought she was a tart, or crazy, or both. My God. They thought she—!

"Never mind," she said stiffly. "That's not—that won't be necessary. I will wait for my husband." She wheeled around and walked back to the center of the lobby again, knowing they were still watching her, that the manager or whoever he was had probably already signaled to the house detective to keep an eye on her. She looked about for a vacant chair. She felt numb and faintly giddy. She'd made a perfect fool of herself. Ridiculous! I can't stay here, she thought, I'll go down to Gard's office and wait for him there, till he gets through, I'll take a cab—

The word froze her again. Of course. With his cab he could be everywhere. Anywhere he chose. He could be waiting outside right now in the line of taxis that was continuously edging up to the main entrance and roaring away. This was terrible.

She realized now she was afraid to leave the room under any circumstances whatever. She recalled her pursuit of Castaldo of a few minutes ago with terrified astonishment. Then for the first time it occurred to her that it probably wasn't Castaldo at all, and she felt still more depressed and shaken. She darted a quick glance toward the desk. The manager was gone but she saw the clerk avert his eyes awkwardly and study the register before him. I can't stay here any longer, she told herself, I'll go out of my mind.

She crossed to the booths again and dialed Gardner's private number. There was a pause and then she heard Marjorie Kane's voice: "Gardner Lawring's office," and her heart sank. She never knew how to address Gard's secretary. Marjorie Kane had the bright, arch assertiveness of the Katherine Gibbs secretary; her voice held intimations of participation in enormously esoteric and earthshaking events, far beyond the layman's ken; and there was something else—a kind of arm's-length reserve you could never cross no matter how hard you tried. Janet disliked her immensely. She knew she ought to assume a haughty tone, force an edge of superiority into her voice that would put the girl in her place—after all, she *was* only a secretary; but she never could. Consequently she wavered between ingratiating pleasantries and a terse matter-of-factness, and hated herself for both attitudes. Now, impelled by urgency, she said:

"This is Mrs. Lawring. I'd like to speak to Mr. Lawring, please."

"Oh, Mrs. Lawring," Marjorie Kane's voice took on shades of condolence. "I'm awfully sorry—there's a meeting about the art museum for the Civic Center."

"I know, he spoke to me about it this morning. Do you know when it'll be over?"

"No, I'm afraid I don't, Mrs. Lawring. I imagine it'll be on for at least another hour. Can I give him a message when he comes out?"

"No, I guess not. It's all right."

"Would you like me to ring you back when it breaks up?"

"No—I'm out now. I'll call back, thanks."

She hung up unhappily, mortified at herself, her lack of assertiveness, the fear that had hold of her. Very probably she was wrong, it was merely someone who looked like him. Boston was full of slender, rather good-looking young Italians. But once outside the booth again panic assailed her. She was here in the Statler lobby, helpless and alone, and suspected by the hotel management of being a nut or a nymphomaniac or God knew what—and he could be anywhere, anywhere at all . . .

She ducked back into the phone booth without any more cogitation and dialed again. This time the line clicked open to the muted bedlam of television voices and the sounds of children, and her sister's voice said matter-of-factly: "Hello."

"Eddie? Janet," she breathed.

"Oh hi, Jan. How's everything?" And with the warm, familiar voice, the echoes of home and childhood and the turbulent domestic background she knew, she felt herself go weak with relief.

"Eddie," she asked, "would you do something for me? A real favor? Right away quick?"

"Sure—I guess so. If I can. What's up?"

"I'm in Boston, at the Statler. Would you come get me?... Eddie, I can't stay," she hurried on, "I was supposed to wait here for Gard to get through at the office and I can't. And I can't get up the nerve to leave on my own. I—I think I just saw the man."

"You *saw* him? There—at the Statler?"

"I think so. I'm scared, Eddie. I got here and now I can't stay and I can't leave, either..."

"You poor kid. I'll be right in."

"I'm terribly sorry, but I don't know when Gard will be through with this meeting, it may be for hours and—I've just *got* to have somebody around. Can you come get me?"

"Of course. Of course I can, Jan. Be in there in twenty, twenty-five minutes. You just hold on tight, now. All right?"

"Thanks, Eddie. God bless you."

"Don't mention it. Bye bye."

"Goodbye..."

She called Gardner's office again, and said to Marjorie Kane: "Would you tell Mr. Lawring when the meeting's over that I've gone to spend the evening with my sister?"

"With your sister."

"Yes, that's right. Tell him I'm—tell him it was rather unexpected. And urgent..." She would have liked to say more, but the girl's manner checked her. "Tell him I'll call him later this evening."

"All right, Mrs. Lawring."

Out in the lobby again she resolutely ignored the registration desk, and picking a seat that faced directly toward the main entrance on Providence Street she pressed the newspaper hard against her lap and fixed her eyes on the doors. Edna would come through them in fifteen minutes or so; she had only to hold on tight. It wouldn't be very long; not long at all.

Chapter Ten

————She had her hand raised for me. Then she saw the OFF DUTY card on the sun shield and instead of dropping her arm and turning away in disgust, the way most of them do, she motioned to me again, her fat little wrist cocked, one finger pointing to herself. An order. Simply refused to believe I wouldn't pick her up. Marvelous. Light gray suit, medium heels, little round hat with a veil softening its edges; around fifty-five, well-preserved, nice full body, not too heavy. The rich, the groomed, the enemy. Why in hell not? I swung in and reached back and flipped open the door and she ducked her head and got in, making that confused, fussy effort to get seated. Building her plush-lined nest. Her skirt hiked up; her knees were soft and dimpled. Then she plumped back and tugged it down and I took off.

"I saw your sign and I didn't know whether you were going to pick me up or not!" A light breathy laugh, easy and assured. The kind of laugh that knows the world will laugh right along with you, all right all right. "That's okay," I said. "Where away, ma'am?" "Twenty-four Pinckney." Nice and crisp and assertive. Familiar voice. The voice that has given the orders for a thousand years. Send him to the tower under guard. Lay below, you scum. Give me a draft on ten thousand pounds sterling. "Right you are, ma'am," I said pleasantly. "On our way." My old theory: stay on Newbury, Boylston, Marlboro and Beacon as much as possible when cruising. That's where the big fares are, the solid tips. The hell with South Station, Huntington Avenue. Bare bones.

"No, actually I just decided to pick you up," I said. I saw her eyes dart at me in the mirror and added: "You see, you're my last fare." "Really?" Not knowing how to take this. And how would she? "Yes, this is just a kind of sentimental journey. Like the

song, remember?" "I'm not much of a hand for popular tunes,"
she said. I whistled the melody through my teeth for a few
seconds. "Yessir," I said, "I'm selling my share in the old hack.
My last day behind the wheel. After eleven years, off and on."
Rolling down Commonwealth now, the lights dropping as if you
wished them green, the green wall of the Gardens looming up
like a pocket vacation: cool and green and sleepy, the trees
bending toward the water sadly. Summertime. And the living is
crazy. "Yeah, I up and decided to break out. Going up into
Canada, Manitoba. Uranium mines." "That's fine," she said
vaguely. Her pale unlined brow knitted. "Are you sure it's
a—sound investment?" Looking unsure now. Unsure for me,
not for herself. "Some of these uranium mines, my husband says
they're not all they're supposed to be . . ."

"No, I'm kidding actually," I said. "Just spinning. Actually
I'm going out West, going partners in a mink ranch. Fellow I was
with in the army. Lots of money in that, you know: hundreds of
thousands if you hit it lucky." "I suppose so." She was smoking,
glancing out at the Gardens drifting by, her eyes now and then
flicking back to mine in the mirror. "You *are* Joseph A.
Castaldo," she said with that wonderful clear assertion of hers.
"Oh absolutely," I answered. "It's a good likeness, I'm told. All
things considered. It was taken a while ago, though, I'll admit
that." She was looking at my cabby's license, I could almost feel
her eyes memorizing the numbers. 53416: a busted inside
straight. The story of my life, more or less. She was still studying
my card, a long hard glance, and I had a quick little flash of
excitement—was she going to report me or something?—then it
faded and I felt numb again. "I'm looking for something utterly
different," I said. "Something adventuresome, unique. You
know?"

Her eyes shot up to mine sharply now, gimletlike, inquisitive,
a little puzzled. How I always loved to do that: snap a fifty-dollar
word at some pompous uppercrust fare. Incontrovertible,
chicanery. Words. That evening I picked up old MacCausland
and some sidekick outside the Harvard Club, both of them half
seas over, some big academic pow-wow just breaking up.
Maundering on about the Holmes-Cardozo concept of law.
Kerosene funnel of a nose and beady black eyes, a fox in a
thicket. The law as pure, immutable absolute, the bulwark of

our civilization, last defense against a sea of shoddy relativism and the preposterous doctrine of extenuating circumstances. The sidekick's head wobbling around, hair down over his glasses. "Yes, sir. That's certainly true, sir. Wasn't it Justice Holmes who once said . . .?" On Soldiers Field Road in the blued light I handed MacCausland his change and said: *"Robes and furr'd gowns hide all. Plate sin with gold, and the strong lance of justice hurtless breaks; arm it in rags, a pigmy's straw doth pierce it.* Right Professor?" His mouth open, a small and perfect black O, his eyes snapping. Affronted. Outraged. How dare the barbarous hordes quote the bard! Astonished too, sure—but I could see the hate in his little fox eyes. Clear as crystal. Oh, the son of a bitch! I handed him back the quarter. "Good night, Professor." "Wait. Your tip—" "I wouldn't dream of it," I said, and I grinned my most vicious grin. "Good night, professor. Pure, immutable dreams."

We were stopped at the new light between the Common and Gardens. When I was a kid you took your chances and shot across here—or if you were a blueblood banker you just put up your hand and walked calmly across, looking neither to left nor right, trusting in the all-powerful God of the Brahmins, who would never let you down. "Going to miss the old town," I said conversationally. "All the crabbed, cockeyed things. Cross Washington on Winter Street and suddenly it's Summer. Did you know West Cedar was one-way north when I was a kid? Now it's one-way south . . ." She was smiling now, nodding. "Reassured. That's all they need: just a little reassurance, old home week, down memory lane, the feeling that their tight little right little snug little world is going to run on forever, gilded and inviolate, world without end, amen. Oh sure. Well, now and then it doesn't. Now and then. Across Beacon in the roar of trucks, up Mount Vernon. The house was there, on the right; the nameplate worn with age. All you could see were the loops of the *L* and the way the *g* curled back under the name like a cat's tail. Shutters all closed now. Mama gone down to Brewster for the summer, to escape the dreadful heat. Curious, going by their house on my last fare. Life full of signs and ironies, boiling with them. Maybe there *was* somebody up there, pulling the levers and switches, somebody with a streak of corn a mile wide; it was possible.

Left on Joy, around onto Pinckney. I slowed, hunting for the numbers. "Right there, by the gaslight," she said. Not a gaslight at all, of course—a streetlight like all the rest of them, but they'd kept the old iron fixture and if she wanted to pretend it was gas-fired that was her business. I pulled up and said: "Home, ma'am. Safe and sound." Her gloved hand extended a dollar bill. I made change, not all nickels and dimes, either, like the tip-spongers, the sucks. "Good luck on your new venture," she said. Pleasant blue eyes, pleasant smile. Nice woman, probably. In spite of everything. In spite of just about everything this universe can offer. "Thanks," I said, "I'll need it." She tipped me fifteen cents, just right. I watched her walk up the steps. The outside door closed behind her and I could see her profile, blurred by the sky reflection on the glass as she pawed in her purse for her key. I would never see her again. And why should I? Why see anyone again, ever? *Remember,* I said to her: *remember.* She'd remembered that, all right. Forever and a day. Her face all aglow in the light from the TV, her eyes huge, her lips moving but no sound coming out of them. What did she want to say to me?

The woman turned and saw me idling there, was peering out. I slid away before she started getting ideas. I drove fast now, shot down the backside of the Hill and along Cambridge, weaving in and out around the semi's and carry-alls. Pleasant day for July, not too hot, faint whisper of east wind. I found a parking place on Prince, cleaned out the hack and went over to Lou's, climbed the dark stairs and gave the old club knock: three-four-two-bump. Three dits, four dits, two dits, dah: Harvard, Harvard, siss boom blah. Connie opened the door: big flat face, dreamy eyes, hair brushed low over her forehead. "Hello, Joe." "Greetings," I said. Lou was sitting at the table reading the sports page. Red oilcloth, grease stains, yellow curtains sucking like death against the screens, woodwork thick with paint and soot, refrigerator clattering away like a coffee percolator gone goofy. Domestic scene 3A, with percussion. No more of that, dad. "She's all yours," I said. I put the keys and trip record and sack of money on the table. "Lock, stock and barrel." "Is that right," he murmured. "I wouldn't snow you, dad. Right as rain." He turned and looked at me steadily. Sunlight from a window high across the court caught on the edge of his jaw where he'd broken it in the jeep accident when he'd been in service: a curving pouch of wax. "He isn't kidding," he said to Connie. "Nope," I answered, "this time it's for real..."

I turned it into the song and sang it, slumped a little, hands gripping a purely imaginary mike, one leg pumping, the way old Sinatra used to ride it in his salad days: lots of dreamy nasal, sliding around. "You dizzy bastard," Lou said. "Lou," Connie said. "Well, he is," Lou said, looking at me again and scrubbing his bristly black hair with his big knuckles. "No, what are you going to do? no kidding?" "I told you," I said. "Tell me again." "Take me a little trip. See America. Maybe I'll take off for Europe, Paris, the Riviera, the works." He kept staring at me, puffing out his lips like inner tubes. "I can't figure you out," he said. "Well, that's all right, lots of people can't." "Yes," Connie said, "and I knew several of them." She nodded at me meaningfully as if she'd scored a big point and I laughed at her, my eyes almost closed. "When are you coming back?" Lou demanded. "I don't know," I said. "You don't know!" "That's right. I'm going to leave it in the lap of the gods." "Jesus," Lou said, and began to rub his scalp with his knuckles again. "I can't tell when you're serious or kidding any more." "Neither can I, dad. That's what keeps it all capistrano."

Neither of them said anything for a moment. Connie took a cup and saucer down from the shelf and I said, "No thanks, Con. I've got some errands to do. Got to go over to London Harness and select my flight luggage, drop in on Brooks Brothers and have a final fitting on my wardrobe, hit Shreve, Crump and Low and pick up my twenty-one-jewel watch. Minor details before embarkation. You know how it is." "You know something, pal?" Lou said, and he began to stir his coffee with a spoon as though it were paint. "If I didn't know you as well as I do I'd think you were off your trolley, you know that?" "I am," I said, "I'm a scrapping schizoid. All *you* see is good old Joe Castaldo, cabby, raconteur extraordinaire, tipping his forelock to the rich and famous. You don't know about my night life." "I know you're going around with that disgusting Paula Ricciardi," Connie said flatly, "I know that much."

I ignored that last, I knew she'd been waiting with bated breath to slip that in. And it was only part true, anyway. "You don't know that in my night life I'm really living," I said. "In my night life I creep into the bedrooms of the wives of the rich and famous and glut my lust on them. I wallow in sex and blood." "For heaven's sake, Joe," Connie complained. "So you're the Back Bay rape artist, are you?" Lou asked me, grinning. "You bet." "How do you manage to escape detection?" "Planning," I said. "Planning and discipline. I case a mansion for—oh, say two, three years at a crack, until I know every last thing about them. I know when hubby's out on a long poker evening, when the kids are off on vacation visits, when it's the maid's night out, I know every last little thing about them—I even know when they go to the can." "Joe, that's enough!" Connie protested. "Honestly, you don't care what you say..." "And then discipline," I went on. It was funny, I couldn't seem to stop. I genuinely wondered what I was going to say next. "Rule One: never return to the scene of a crime. Rule Two: never do a thing the same way twice. Rule Three: never act on impulse." I wagged my finger at Lou impressively. "That's the most important rule of all. At the moment of deepest immersion in the deed, stay outside of it, right up in the old cerebral cortex, and you'll never get picked off." "Is that right." "Absolutely. Hold yourself in a state of perpetual tension, balanced like an acrobat on the real high wire, slip from one role into another, dance right along the precipice of disaster, let your senses quake with the vivid, clutching intoxication of danger—danger *in and of itself*—and you'll never be the same again..."

I stopped myself. Finally. They were both staring at me as if I'd fallen from the back side of the moon, like that old dazzler Mr. C. "Jesus H. Christ," Lou said. Then he grinned. "Well, you can relax, Casanova," he said. "You're off the hook because they've thrown the book at somebody else." "What do you mean?" I said. "They just got him. Jigaboo from Brookline. Man, I don't envy that boy at all." He started to turn the pages of the paper and I snatched it out of his hands. "Hey, what are you doing?" It was there, the whole thing. NAB HUB RAPIST. *Harrison Roche, Reign of terror appeared ended with arrest of.* Lou whipped it out of my hand, laughing. "What's the matter with you, ain't you got any manners?" "Let me take it," I said. "The hell I will. Go buy your own." He stopped laughing at me then, his eyes very funny; a slow, measuring look I couldn't read. Connie was watching me, too. I shrugged and got a grin on my face: it felt like tearing parchment. Too close. Much too close. "Right," I said. "Buy my own. Why not? I'm loaded. Got to light a shuck for the tall timber, pardner. Ta-ta, kids. "Give it up, Joe," Lou said. I stopped clowning for a moment. "Give what up?" "Whatever far-out scheme you've got cooking. Stick around. You want me to tell you about France, about Paris?" He'd been there with the army. "Oh, no," I said. "One pic worth a grand of prose. Confucius say." I sidled off toward the door then, lazy soft-shoe routine, old trouper, Ray Bolger maybe, going offstage softly, rag-doll arms and legs, bug eyes, big homely grin. Hyuck hyuck. "Bye bye, all. Bye bye..." They didn't say anything, just stood there watching me, Connie standing motionless behind Lou's chair, a goofy family tintype; frozen there, silent and troubled. Last exit. So be it.

I swung the door behind me gently, took the stairs three at a time, swinging around the iron corner posts. Out in the street I spotted a cigar store and bought a *Traveler,* a *Globe* and a *Record-American.* There it was, all right. *And the case involving Mrs. Gardner Lawring of Holcomb Hill. "As far as we are concerned this clears up a very distressing situation,"* Chief Inspector Reardon told reporters. *"We are all very relieved."* My heart was pounding. I felt as though I couldn't get any air into my lungs. Why was that? Crazy. I walked along holding the papers wadded against my hip. Why in hell should I care? If it was closed it was closed. A flock of pigeons swept down toward me, beating their wings in a frenzy, almost collided with me. So this was how it was going to end. Jesus! I thought I was about to burst with rage, suffocation, something or other.

Then that too faded and the numb dry coolness came back again. No matter what happened that feeling would come back in a matter of minutes and lie like ice over my heart. I turned around and walked back along Salem and went into Tomaldo's without looking at anybody and took the third booth. Dino was behind the bar, polishing it with a rag and a bottle of polish. It smelled like burnt pitch pine, a very old smell. He nodded and I nodded back, just barely. We never liked each other very much, we'd had a fistfight in grade school, he'd been picking on little Joey Araujo, a Portuguese kid half his size. A long fight, full of gasping and murder, neither of us won really, and since then we'd walked around each other. I watched him out of the corner of my eye. It seemed impossible I could ever have fought him to a stand-off: moonface, big belly, rolls of fat all over, forearms as big as my leg. Why was it so many Italians let themselves run to fat, went all buttery and shapeless? I wasn't going to, ever: no matter what. I'd do setting-up exercises twice a day in my room, make a barbell out of two lard cans filled with concrete and a length of pipe.

"Angie!" Dino shouted. And Angela came out, looking sullen and half asleep and said, "What do you want?" So friendly. "Coffee," I said. She nodded and went away without a word. God, what a sourball. I watched her go and then I spread the papers out on the table and read them all through again. I tore each item out as I finished reading it. So she didn't know. It was impossible. Could she really think it was this Negro Roche? Christ, what a laugh. My accent was so good it had snowed her completely, then. No. I wouldn't believe it. I would never believe it. She knew. That moment when I threw the blanket over her head. The struggle. Why didn't she know I didn't want to hurt her? The hard, fiery *solidity* of everything, like one drink—but only one—too many, like the instant of falling out of a swing, like playing skid late at night down on Commercial on the ice, slam on the brakes and spin the wheel, and warehouses and ships and lights all wheeling round and round like a spinning barrel, and then the jolt when the tires hit the curb. And the girls squealing. Elena loved to do that, she could never get enough. "Again!" she'd cry, her eyes shining like washed coals. "Again, again!" Driving all night to New York City, laughing and joking, telling each other the plots from old movies to stay awake, the rain coming in sea waves against the windshield and the lights of oncoming cars like phantom fish nine miles down. The two of us huddled inside the car, safe and dry, the whole wet lashing world outside; and then the traffic and in the gray felt light the high, hard fingers of the city and Times Square looking lonely and whipped, with the old newspapers blowing and the bums under the marquees.

And then old D'Ambrosio yelling at me over the phone, she had to call them up, I begged her not to but she wouldn't listen. "You think you're going to get away with this you're crazy, I ever see you again I'll kill you, I swear your blood will run in the gutter—" "Now, listen—" "—no daughter of *mine* is running off with a no-good hack driver!" "Now listen, it just so happens we're married—" "Not in the eyes of God you aren't!" The eyes of God. And Elena crying most of that night and all of the next day, more rain and the lousy hotel room crummy and faded and bare, like a one-night-stand. Her tiny face all crumpled up with confusion. "My God—that's all there is to it? Oh my God . . ." Sitting there on the edge of the beatup hotel bed trying to console her but she wouldn't be consoled, I could see it in her face: Oh my God, I went through all this, broke with my family and turned them against me and this is all there is. I couldn't explain anything to her, she wouldn't listen. The rain spattering on the window ledge and down below the horns braying and bleating and moaning like a menagerie in a nightmare. And then later: "Oh, they'll never forgive me, I know they won't—why did I ever do it! . . ." And I realized how young she was, eighteen, she hadn't seemed like such a little girl back in Boston, going dancing at Iandoli's or the Grove. I took her to see a play, we went to Radio City and two places on 52nd Street where the music was good, and Café Society Downtown and some other place in Greenwich Village where a fellow I'd heard of did take-offs on our way of life and a Negro pianist played blues tunes in between sets, the chords ringing like old bells tolling at the bottom of the sea . . . But none of it made any difference. She cried every night, she insisted on sleeping with the bedside light on, her face pale and white with purple hollows under her eyes, and whenever she spoke you didn't know whether she was going to break down or not. "What are we doing to do, Joe? What are we going to *do?*" And then finally: "No—no! You don't love me, you never loved me, oh God I can't stand it—!" And I tried to deny it but it was true, I knew it then, I didn't love her, but I thought we could be happy, I was willing to do everything I could to make her happy and that's God's truth.

Angela brought me the coffee then and I smiled at her and said, "Thank you." She turned away without a word. It was sort of a game—I had decided to see how long it would be before Angela would reply. So far no luck. And possibly this was my last chance. I looked down at the papers spread out all over the table like a patchwork quilt of disaster, blasting black and white, and thought again of Elena. Annulled. They had it annulled. Not in the eyes of God, you see. After nine days together. I kept running my eyes over the columns of print, the dense black splotches of headlines. As though it hadn't happened. Just like everything else. Those poor bastards from the Bay of Pigs invasion laying around in some stinking excuse for a prison waiting to get exchanged for some tractors. What part of a tractor do you suppose you're worth, dad: the distributor, the gearbox, couple of rocker arms? Hit the beach—and then no support: trapped like flies against a wall, and old Mr. Castro with the fly swatter. All as though it happened. That's what we like. My house gone as though it had never been there. A man was walking down a street in Algiers shooting Arabs with an automatic pistol. Just knocking them off, biff baff, in broad daylight. Nobody saying a thing. Open season on Algerians, Cubans, Italians. Why not? Nobody needs them.

I took the ticket out of my pocket and slid it out of its half-envelope. Long dull orange ticket like a paper-thin checkbook: down to your last nineteen million. MEXICO, D.F. What did D.F. stand for? I would have to learn Spanish: was it anything like Italian? Hombre, sombre, puerta del sol. All I knew. And hasta luego. Hard hot sun and red dust drifting and old pocked ruins deep in the jungles where the Aztecs sacrificed hundreds of thousands of victims in a single day. Well: we did it, too—but now we called it Urban Renewal or Algérie Française. *Ra*-da-da boom *boom*. I rapped it out on the table edge with my knuckles and sat there staring at the plane ticket, wondering what Mexico would be like, what I would be like in Mexico. Everybody is different in a new place. In Quebec I felt smaller, younger, all quivering and full of hopes—as if I were starting life over again. I tried to get up some enthusiasm for Mexico, new sights and sounds and smells, the warmer winters and the jungle, but nothing came: no bright, dancing excitement at all.

In the corner booth Tony Fricano was laughing at something one of the others with him had said. What? What did he have to laugh himself sick over? His eye caught mine, he winked his crafty hoodlum's wink. Reporting every Saturday morning to the parole board, and then sitting around planning some two-bit job, a liquor store on Blue Hill Avenue or a gas station out in Brighton, every Saturday night. You could tell how he'd wind up: he'd get sent up twice more, and then he'd try something really ambitious on the strength of his record of failure, and this time he wouldn't be able to get rid of the weapon before they grabbed him, and that would be it. Or maybe not. Maybe he'd get in with one of the big organizations and show up in a two-hundred-dollar suit and a thirty-dollar hat, making the rounds of the stores, shaking down the bookies and little operators. Or maybe some girl would marry him and make him go back to swinging a pick for Scalzo Brothers. I doubted it: but it was possible. How could you know what would happen to you in ten years; how you'd wind up? If Julien had known how he'd wind up, would he have left Verriéres and gone to the seminary and then to Paris? Yes. He would have gone anyway. And so would I. They tell you the only worthwhile things are the ones that last, that you can hold in your hand, the things that endure: but that's not true. Nothing lasts, neither a man's health nor the mightiest nation they ever put together, your only grandson may become a drunken wastrel and your best friend betray you to your face—and the only things you can count on are the isolate moments of triumph or thrill or defiance. *That* is the truth: why in the name of Christ won't they admit it! An actor plays a great role for one night, Al Gionffrido makes that miracle catch off Big Dimag in Yankee Stadium, a Frenchman in the Resistance utters one quiet word of contempt for the Germans who cut him down—those moments, brief as fire, are as real as anything on this rotten globe, more important than the Roman Empire or Manhattan Island or the H-bomb...

Tony Fricano was telling a story now, screwing his face up into weird shapes and sizes, doing imitations. I watched him absently, knowing he knew I was watching him. If I were rich, a wealthy heir like one of the Boston blueblood Harvard boys, I would take ten men of our time and follow them through life: ten prominent men who have done great evil, like the head of the chemical outfit in New Jersey that put that untested drug on the market that crippled all those elderly people, or the wheeler-dealer who took all the stockholders' money and skipped out to Rio and is living like an emperor down there now, or the Alabama police chief that fired on those Negro school kids—there'd be even better examples than that, you'd only have to keep your eyes open, keep a file on it—and then travel around, follow them through life, chronicle their successes, watch them move from position to position, while every honor is heaped on them. People like McCarthy or that swine Thayer, who boasted about burning Sacco and Vanzetti. Then compare those ten with ten other men, such as the Korean vet from Brooklyn who went off his rocker and stabbed his wife and baby to death and got the chair, or the Fuselli kid who stole the bottle of milk for his little sister and got two years. I would call it *An Immoral History of Our Time,* it would all be documented, just the evidence as it unfolded from year to year. Maybe I'd do it anyway. Down in Mexico. Maybe I'd do a lot of things down there: money enough, and all the time in the world.

Paula Ricciardi, going by outside. I started to duck behind my hand, thought better of it and froze. She spotted me anyway and stopped, her eyes wide, her mouth open, and tossed her head in that dumb-ox greeting everyone seems to feel he has to give everyone else. Jesus, what baboons we are. When you come right down to it. Baboons. And just about as appetizing, from either end. She was coming in. Of course. Well, let her come. The last supper. Hoc est corpus meus and all that dominocus. Another fakeshow. She came up to the booth as if she knew I'd been waiting for her six hours with slavering chops; her teeth were bared in a tremendous smile. "Hi, Joe." God, the self-assurance of the simple-minded. Like asbestos, couldn't even burn it away. "Greetings and salutations in the highest," I said. That always puts them off. They think it's faggy or foreign or something, something queer. She frowned at me and slid into the booth. "Do sit down," I said. "Oh, you . . ." She made a face, then blinked. "What you got there?" I still had the ticket in my hand. "A plane ticket," I said. "TWA Flight Seven-seventy-two to Paris." "Go on. When are you coming back?" "I'm not coming back. It's a one-way ticket." "Ah, come on . . ." Her face always looked lopsided when she was puzzled, as though she had a toothache. "Where've you been? I've been looking all over for you, for two days." "I've been winding up my affairs," I answered. "Last will and testament. Wardrobe suitable for travel. Should I buy a Burberry? or had I ought to get one of those private-eye trench coats with all the hooks and buckles and belts and a detachable lining?" She grinned at me, disbelieving. "What about the cab?" "Got rid of it." "You *what?*" "I sold out my share. Converting all my assets into cash: more mobile." "What a joker you are." "Ask Lou, then." She blinked at this. "Joe, are you up to something?"

All at once she made a grab for the ticket. I jerked it back out of reach and stuck it into a jacket pocket. "Let me see it," she pleaded. "No," I said, "I think not." "Pretty please? Show me and I'll believe you." "If I've got to show you in order for you to believe me," I said, "it's all pretty silly, isn't it? Why won't you believe me sight unseen?" "I'm from Missouri," she said and laughed, but her eyes had the same uneasy look I'd seen with Lou and Connie. I looked back at her without any expression at all, thinking of that night again, the tree toads peeping and the jittering square of the TV set, the crazy blue light; the stealthy, trembling culmination of things. That instant in the doorway. And she didn't know. She had no idea. Impossible. I thought of going back, the cops had pulled out for sure by now. Tackling the problem again of finding out what *he* was doing now, what his schedule was, avoiding him at the station at 128 and all the rest of it. Then I dropped it. You can't go back. You can't: you go back and it's something else entirely. It isn't the moment any more. Of course it could be a trap: maybe she knew and had told the law and this was all an elaborate ruse to draw me in and nail me. It was possible. For some reason, thinking this, I felt a sharp twinge of fear, pure as a diamond. Why was that? So I *was* afraid, then, after all . . .

"Penny for your thoughts, Mr. C." Paula was hunched forward, little round mirror up in front of her: putting on lipstick with a firm hand. I hate girls that do that, in public especially. Jesus, what vulgarity. *She* would never do it in a public place, I knew it. "Julien said he was a coward but no one would ever know it," I said aloud. "What?" She gazed at me, stupefied. "What did you say?" "I said, Julien was a coward but no one would ever know it." She shook her head at me; her hair, done in some kind of pouff, shook like a shaggy dog. "Who's Julien?" she demanded. "Honestly, sometimes you don't make any kind of sense at all." "You asked me what I was thinking and I told you."

She looked away, perplexed and cross; her profile was nice, with the long sweep of cheek, the full lips echoed in the chin, her eyes narrowed. She looked exciting when she was cross: more intelligent, sensitive, really alluring, and for a second I wanted her. Then she turned back and her eyes were all wide and bovine and mawkish again. "Will you take me dancing tonight? Iandoli's?" I shook my head. "Why not?" "I have to commune with my thoughts," I answered. "Oh—sometimes you're hopeless, you know that?" She felt angry again but she beat it down and flicked some of the hair back from her forehead. She was trying not to feel anger, I was trying not to feel fear: like Julien. Everybody has something he has to try to put down. "Next week then, maybe?" "I told you, I'm flying down to Rio." "You said Paris." "Oh yes, that's right, I did. Paris." "You know, sometimes you're not very funny, Joe." "That's true," I agreed. She clicked her nails on the Formica, a fast mambo rhythm. "Franky Parella's just started his own trucking company. Did you know that?" she demanded. "No, I didn't." "Well he has, a fleet of six trucks, they're all painted bright red with canary yellow fenders. I just saw one a little while ago. He told me he's going to open a big new office on Atlantic Avenue." She paused, watching me, her tongue hovering below her teeth. "He's going to be a big success, you know that?" "I'm sure he is," I said. "Why don't you go to bed with him, Paula?" She looked at me as if I'd slapped her hard. For the first time it dawned on her that I knew she'd slept with Frank, not once but several times. She was raging, ready to hit me, and for a second I thought she would, I hoped she would, I was half praying she would. Why was that? Why did I want that so badly? Then the look of bafflement and rage and vengeance drained out of her face like heat out of iron and it became plain and rock hard, like her mother's.

"I don't like you, Joe," she said quietly. "I don't know what's got into you lately, but whatever it is, it's not good: I can tell you that. You're another person. You know that?" She tapped one finger on her crossed forearm—a slow, even tapping that upset me to watch it. "Another person." "What makes you think that?" I asked. "I can see it. It's in your face. You don't care who you hurt or what you say. You're in a bad way." She was going to say more and stopped, pressed her teeth on her lower lip and swung her head slowly from side to side. All at once there were tears in her eyes, heavy silver tears that built and built and then broke over her eyelids and began to run down her smooth cheeks, glistening against the powder. "You're mean," she said in a low voice. "Cold and mean and no-good, Joe. You are. You think people will take it off you for ever and a day, but you're wrong. They won't." "I don't think any such thing," I said. "Yes, you do," she answered, "and you're wrong."

Inane. Yes you do no I don't yes you do. I looked down at my hands and picked at the callus on the heel of my left hand, from the wheel. It was like a movie, a bad Grade B movie, or a Sunday morning hangover daydream: no reality to it, no force. I was sitting across the table from a girl I'd lived with off and on, gone to bed with, taken to Revere Beach and dancing at Blinstrub's and the Grove and once even to the Colonial Theater to see *A View From the Bridge* (she didn't like it, she said it was too depressing)—I'd done all these things with her and she didn't exist, it was as though she were on a screen or inside a fish tank, gaping at me, mouthing sounds. Or maybe I was inside the fish tank, it didn't matter which. Watching her biting her lips, the tears like two mercury streaks on her face, all I could think of was that night, the drive from the station at 128 with the storm coming up, parking in that wood road the other side of the bridge I'd picked out earlier, and walking through the woods along the old tumble-down stone wall, moving slowly around the house with the tree toads in the little pond going silent and the thunder groaning... and then inside the house, standing in the hallway, my skin on fire, really on fire and the blood beating at my fingertips, I thought I would cry out for the sheer fierce aching *glory* of it—and then the doorway, and she was there on the bed watching TV: leaning forward a little, her face pure and glowing like ivory, as I knew she would be. So beautiful. And then her awareness, and the fear flowing up over her face like water, as though she were sinking in some awful water, I hadn't expected that, I wonder why: why hadn't I?—and the Negro routine, the knife and the money, the stupid farce of it, all a prelude to that instant when I stripped off my clothes and was with her, one with her—ah, the burning sweet agony of that moment! and we were one, really one body as I'd dreamed, and then she opened up, came all alive, pulsing and thrusting rhythm, swooping and diving, and lying there in chaos throbbing I rejoiced, *I knew it, I knew it!* And later I had to stay, prolong it a little, I couldn't bear to end it on that note, so brusquely. But there was nothing then to say. How sad it was. That we should have been so close, and then so far apart, with fear quivering in the room like black wire coils. *Remember,* I said, and I went down the stairs and through the living room and hall and out the kitchen door and down the driveway and along the road, walking through the still, electric air without a care in the world, if a car came by, if a cruiser came by, let it; along the road and past the ghostly gray glint of the stone wall to the cab. Over. Over and done. I had lived for that moment, had lain awake till all hours sweating and scheming and praying for it—and now it had come and gone and there simply wasn't another thing in this world to care about. Not a bloody thing. Numb. My whole body and soul were like a hand you've slept on for hours and hours: thick, furry slab of nothing at all. And now they're wrapped it all up to their satisfaction and she hadn't found the card, or she'd forgotten—it wasn't possible: it wasn't possible that she didn't know!...

"Joe," Paula was saying, "what's the matter?" Her face looked old and worried, as if she were afraid of me. Yes, exactly. Afraid of me. I felt as though I were strangling, I was afraid I was going to break down and cry like a twelve-year-old. What in Christ's name was the matter with me? "Joe," she was saying in a funny little voice, "are you in trouble? Joe?" I got up with a lurch, bumping the table, and began to gather up the newspapers. "What are you doing, Joe? with all the papers?" "Reading them," I said tightly. "Getting educated. Getting—" But I couldn't finish the sentence, I was afraid I'd break down. I had never felt so awful. "Joe," Paula said softly, "Joe, I could go home with you. If you want." I shook my head rapidly, scrunched the papers into a wad, I couldn't fold them somehow or other. For the record. Last entry. Oh Jesus, it would be good to get out of this town! Never see it, never even hear of it again! "No, I've got to go," I said. "Go do some errands. I'll see you around." "All right," she said. "All right, Joe."

I couldn't look at her. I walked out of the place quickly. Tony Fricano winked his slow, evil wink and I rocked my head once, just barely. Tough Tony, going down to hell. Outside it was cooler and the sky was overcast, a pale gauze web, and you could smell the coffee houses over on Atlantic Avenue. Southeast wind. At Hanover I turned right and walked toward the Expressway. The streets were crowded, kids playing hopscotch and pat-ball and tag, and souped-up jobs cruising around hunting up a place to park. Someone said, "What you say, Joe,"

but I didn't recognize who it was. At Cross Street I stopped at
the corner and looked up at the Expressway, with its cars
roaring along like bugs in a high trench. My home was there.
Right there, where a fellow and his girl were running, their arms
around each other, skipping through the feed-in traffic from
Washington and Federal. I had painted a cross there once at
four o'clock in the morning, where my house had been. Bright
red paint. It had lasted for nearly three months, in spite of the
cars. Our building, and then the niche behind the iron grating
where Gramma used to sit in the warm weather, and then two
more and then the blank wall of Scalzo Brothers warehouse
where we played stoop ball. If you caught if off the wall it was
out. Lou said that wasn't right, it ought to be hit the way it was in
the majors, but we voted him down. Beyond the curve of
concrete I could see the new Court House, the backside of the
Hill, looking rusty and ragged against the gray film of sky. A
beautiful city, I used to think: compact and beautiful, like an
Italian hill town, with its golden dome and the sweep of river
under the trees, crabbed streets with narrow brick buildings and
the S-irons below the shutters, in Korea. I used to brag of it to
the guys from Chicago and L.A. But I was wrong, there are no
men to go with it. Wherever I look I see men like swine, monsters
in Caddies and two-hundred-dollar suits, grinding down their
neighbors: men who lived up there, on that filthy castle of a Hill,
and cut down everyone else, so pleasantly, so easily! You
bastards, I said, I'm carrying around enough dynamite inside me
to blow you and all your kind to hell and gone, set the whole
scrimey earth afire if I wanted, spinning flaming ball sinking
through darkness to eternal night—and I'm not through yet, do
you hear—I've just *begun* to pour it on—!

But that wasn't true, I knew it wasn't true any more. If it ever
had been. They'd shut me out again, closed the case slick as a
skate, just as though nothing had happened, and she didn't
know, it was impossible but she didn't know—they'd won,
they'd won the way they always do—oh, it was unendurable that
they should always win!...

An old woman with a shopping bag was looking at me
strangely, then a man in a felt hat with the brim turned down all
around. The old woman started to speak to me, then thought
better of it. I muttered, "Take your eyes off me, old hag," and

turned away and wiped my eyes. Traffic kept pouring along the Expressway overhead, making a great tearing sound like the ripping of some endless expensive fabric. The case was closed. Insufferable! I struck the iron lamp post near me with my hand, a high hollow ringing, and my palm stung. So this was how it was going to end. Like this, by the Jesus. Like this!

I started walking up toward Scollay Square, past the bookshops, what was left of them. I decided I'd go sit in a movie for a while, I knew if I went on thinking about it now I'd break into a roar or smash something, do something stupid and get myself in trouble. More trouble. The golden kettle on Court Street was still spouting its steam, even in the summer air, and below it a drunk was trying to work a sobersides businessman for some change: trying and not making it.

The rage was gone, my eyes were dry and grating; the heavy stunned numbness had come back. If I hadn't kept on walking I would have sat down on the curb like a rummy. My life was over. Was that it? Over. I didn't care any more about anything. I didn't half care if I lived or died. My life was a solitary mountain peak, with everything in it leading up to June sixth, hanging on that dizzy, glorious crest for half an hour—and now back down again, sloping off to what? Mexico City, D.F. Only I, in the privacy of my heart, know what I might have done. Like Julien.

What was I going to do? Was I really going to fly to Mexico, live out the rest of my life there? Drink tequila, and wheel the goggle-eyed tourists around? Busman's holiday.

No. I would never believe it, I would never, *never* believe she did not know it was me! No matter what...

Jesus God, what is going to happen to me?———

Chapter Eleven

DEAR BOO:

It was great to get your fine, long letter and hear you're doing so well at swimming. Glad you got Mummy's letter and the cookies. Remember to share them with the rest of your hut if it's allowed; if they get all gobbled up we'll send you some more. Mommy stayed with Aunt Edna and Uncle Jim last night and Mrs. Pruitt is down with her sciatica (isn't that a terrific word? Looks as painful as the ailment) so I'm keeping bachelor's hall, as Grandpa used to say. The place seems very big and lonely without anyone around, but I've been so busy I haven't had time to think about it.

Don't feel too bad about not being picked to play third base. I played the outfield a lot myself, you know, and it's just as important out there, too. I wish we'd practiced more with fly balls but you'll get the hang of it fast enough. Remember: don't run backward or you'll catch your heel and fall down. *Turn and run* to wherever the ball is headed, and keep watching it over your shoulder. Maybe you could ask Ray Lynes or Tom what's-his-name to hit some fly balls to you and practice it until it becomes automatic.

You must not be upset or angry over losing. It is no disgrace to lose if you've played as well as you can. One side must always lose, that's what sports mean. The main thing is to lose well, congratulate your opponent, then forget about it and go on and try all the harder to defeat him next time out.

Sorry your tent lost the week's inspection. Try and keep your bunk well made, you remember Mummy showed you about that hospital fold and turning down the top sheet twice over the blanket, etc. And your trunk in good order. Just between us, you have a tendency to get careless about things like keeping your room neat and your clothes put away, we've talked about that, and this will give you a chance to show what you can do. There's nothing sissified about keeping your clothing neat and making a bed well, no matter what Jerry says. We all had to make our own beds in the army, and occasionally even do our own sewing, and most men can make beds better than most women these days. When you're grown up and doing your stint in the army you'll find that's just as important as many other things.

Don't worry about the other boys, Boo. They will accept you in time. I have the feeling that maybe you get to talking a little too much, and this upsets them. Am I right? Like the canoe business—everyone tips over a canoe sooner or later, but maybe seeing that osprey got you all excited and you forgot where you were for a moment. Try to school yourself to talk a little less and let your actions—in swimming, on the ball field, on hikes— speak for you, and they will respect you more.

I sent the fielder's glove off to you yesterday afternoon, you ought to get it almost as soon as this letter. Remember to choke up on your bat. Fine .300 hitters like Pesky and Fox (you remember we saw Nellie Fox last summer at Fenway Park?) choke up on the bat handle themselves.

Boo, I know you'll do well. Just relax and take it a day at a time. I know it's hard, but one of the most important things in life is sticking out a situation even if it isn't all that you might want it to be. There's a great satisfaction in that, and one day you'll look back on it with real pride in the accomplishment. I know you never liked tennis much, don't worry about it. If anything comes up, any problems or anything, remember Ray Lynes. He's a fine man and I know he'll be very understanding. We'll definitely be up to see you on the first weekend in August, which isn't far away at all. Mummy is still very tired but wants to see you and particularly watch you swim, and so do I. If there's anything else you need let me know and I'll send it along soon as I can.

> Much love,
> MUMMY AND DAD

Lawring folded the letter and inserted it carefully in the envelope, smiling faintly, wondering if his father's letters to him had been pretty much like this one, full of assurances and platitudes and poorly concealed concern. Well, they weren't platitudes really, they were some of the truths men lived by, and

if they sounded platitudinous that was the fault of the times.
Addressing the envelope he thought of Brian; so little and so
sensitive, with the battery of alien boys' faces, the roar and
babble of the dining hall, the gloomy mountain trails and teetery
canoes, the fear of newness like a raw varnish over everything.
He felt a sudden pang of worry. Maybe he *was* too young, maybe
Janet had been right and they should have waited another year
or so. Brian's last two letters had been short and rather
petulant...

No: the boy was eight—good Lord, he himself had gone to
camp at six and had loved it. So he wasn't entirely happy. That
was all right, too. It would do him a world of good to meet the
problem and overcome it. That was how you grew, and there
weren't any short cuts. He needed to be away from his mother
for a time, stand on his own two feet. Janet coddled him terribly,
and she knew it: there was too much sheltering, too many
theatricals. If there was anything he feared it was that Brian
would turn into one of those timorous, languid esthetes sipping
sherry and reading Baudelaire all afternoon in someone else's
room at college. Awful... For a few moments he indulged in a
fantasy of Brian as a man grown, attired in jacket and slacks, his
chestnut hair short, coming out of the doorway of the Mount
Vernon Street house with a quick, lithe stride, going downtown
to the office.

He sealed the envelope and thought, Well: as long as he
learns to stand on his own two feet.

And the boy's mother—what about her? Was she going to
learn to stand on her own two feet?

He had called her that evening after he'd come out of the
meeting and Marjorie had given him her message. A confused,
erratic conversation. Janet had sounded both troubled and
elated.

"I'm immensely sorry, Gard, I couldn't help it, I—I panicked,
I guess. I was all right until I got in the Statler lobby and I
thought I saw him there, I swear..."

"In the middle of the *lobby?*" It had been a long, purposeless
meeting, dominated by Helena Pinchon and her whims of iron,
and his voice sounded exasperated in spite of himself.

"I know it probably sounds loony to you, darling, silly or
hysterical or something and maybe it was; but it certainly looked

like him. I'd just been reading the papers—did you see the papers?"

"No. What's in them?"

"It's all there—about Roche and the other two women and me. And Inspector Reardon calling the case closed."

"God damn," Lawring said. "He promised me, too."

"He did?"

"Yes, he did. Yesterday afternoon. I specifically asked him to keep it out of the papers and he promised me."

"Well, maybe he couldn't help it."

"The hell he couldn't." He clenched the speaker in his fist; he felt beleaguered and crossed. Nobody's word meant anything any more. Not a soul...

"And I couldn't reach you," Janet was saying, "so I rang up Eddie and she ran right in and got me, like the lamb she is."

"I see."

"Don't be mad at me, please, darling."

"I'm not mad at you..."

"—Yes, sweety, you come up. On my lap. That's right," Janet said, her voice muted. There was a pause and then a soprano voice gurgled incoherently into the phone.

"Hello there, whichever you are," Lawring said.

"That's Suzy," Janet chided him. "Can't you tell them apart? We've been playing circus. And pattycake. And 'Here's the church and here's the steeple'... Oh Gard, I'm having such fun here, with the kids. Can I stay on for a little while? Jim's had to go out to Rochester on business and Edna's asked me to stay with her overnight. Is it all right with you?"

"Sure, honey."

"It's so free and lazy! After all the dungeon routine at the house. I feel as if school's just let out..." There was a loud blast of military band music, confused singing and some shouted commands, then it faded and Janet said: "You don't really mind, do you, darling?"

"No, of course I don't."

"You *sound* as though you do..." Her voice had a mock-mournful ring of exaggerated reproach, and Lawring decided she and Edna had been having a few drinks together while supper was being got ready.

"Eddie made me a powerful drink," she said then, and he

started and laughed. "I know—what you were thinking. I always do. And you're right. But Gard, I needed it: I really did . . . What are you going to do about dinner?"

"I'll get a bite here in town."

"All right. There's the end of that roast beef in the refrigerator, you know."

"Fine."

"Do you know what I'm doing right now?" she asked him. "I'm lying on the couch with my shoes off and the phone on my stomach and Suzy's climbing all over me and Gard, I feel so wonderfully relaxed I'm practically dissolving . . ."

It was their old ritual from the days before they were married: the nightly phone call, when each would describe to the other what he was doing at that moment. He loved Janet's voice over the phone: it was soft and musical, with great range—and there was a vibrant quality in it, as though it were promising all kinds of flamboyant and delectable things . . . Once long ago during an altercation Janet had demanded, "What on earth did you ever marry me for, anyway?" and he had answered, "For your telephone voice," and had watched her face glow with surprise. Remembering he smiled.

"What are you thinking?" she asked.

"I was thinking how tremendously overpoweringly I love you," he said.

She whispered, "Oh, Gard . . . I love you too, so much. I wish you were here right now. Gard . . ."

"Yes?"

There was such a long pause he thought she must have left the phone or the connection had been broken. But he could hear her breathing. Then there was a little sigh and she said: "No, I'm not going to spoil this delicious, lazy-dazy moment: I can't.—I'll be with you soon," she said.

"Do you want me to come and get you tomorrow?"

"No. I'll—I'll call you. We're going to take the kids to the beach, but I don't know when . . . I'll give you a ring tomorrow afternoon or evening," she repeated. "I've got some things I want to think out for a little while." Her voice dropped into that rich, exciting contralto again. "Good night, darling."

"Good night." He heard her mouth a kiss once, then again, and he smiled as he responded, in spite of a twinge of disappointment. She was his wife, she was staying with her sister's family, she was a little high, and she loved him: if that wasn't good enough for him, what was?...

Now, this following Sunday morning, he tossed the letter to his son on the dining-room table and went outside, squinting at the weather. It was completely windless, the sky veneered with a hard pewter surface and not a trace of sunlight or shadow; a still, mean-spirited day, the kind of day when small nasty things happen—when you might find a young catbird with a broken wing or the left rear tire on the car is flat for no reason at all, or you cut your finger opening a can of soup. A day without depth or contrition. Lawring walked around the corner of the house and looked at the leaky sillcock: a steady running drip on the peat moss. He knelt and examined it, found the thread of crack in the pipe, and went down to his workshop in the cellar. Selecting the tools for the job he found himself wondering what Janet was doing now. Playing volleyball or jackstones or Chinese checkers with Edna's kids, or gossiping with Edna; or maybe they'd already gone to the beach in spite of the weather, and she was sitting in some suit she'd borrowed from her sister, her legs slim and straight, one hand shading her eyes against this depthless pewter glare, gazing dreamily out to sea...

Was she thinking of him, standing in the cool dim cavern of the cellar in khakis and T-shirt, scratching his wishbone with a thumbnail? If she wasn't she would be soon—her mind danced and darted like a barn swallow in flight, snatching out of the blue incidents he himself had forgotten, recalling them to him at odd moments: the herd of antelope in the early morning driving west from Laramie, their coats burnt orange in the dawn sunlight, rising and falling in great dreamy bounds; or the truck driver in the diner outside of Davenport with the lean, sad face watching the line storm coming toward them—and then they had passed the overturned cab and trailer in the bottom of the ravine early next morning... Had the driver had a premonition of disaster, some tremor in the depths of his being that had led him to go on talking idly with them and the waitress, smoking still another cigarette? Janet thought he had; she believed in foreknowl-edge—messages, she called them—though he himself always suspected it was a way of indulging her whims. For instance, had she had any kind of message about his row with Maltisiak? Doubtful. He himself certainly hadn't. He took the hack saw down from its place on the wall and got the big Stillson wrenches out of the chest of plumber's tools. The Maltisiak problem had been left in abeyance for the past several days: Lawring had done nothing the day after the quarrel, Maltisiak had left Chicago the day after that, and wouldn't be back until Monday. A brief respite, of sorts. Henchey was extremely nervous about it though, and angry with Lawring; he'd been very cold at the art museum conference, and earlier he'd implied that if Lawring didn't apologize, and handsomely, there would certainly be a general trial of strength in the firm...

Upstairs in the bedroom the radio, which he'd forgotten to turn off after hearing the news and weather, was playing "Moonglow," an Artie Shaw recording that brought back memories of the war years, camps in the Carolinas and Iowa, the raffish bonhomie of dance halls and recreation rooms. I was happier then, he caught himself thinking; life was simple, simplicity is happiness. Was it? When he and Janet were first married life had been simpler: they played tennis Sunday mornings with Chuck and Mary Allerton, or if it was raining they lay around on the eight-foot-long custom couch he'd had in his room at college and read the papers and listened to *Don Giovanni* or *Rigoletto* and planned the arresting, beautifully proportioned house he was going to build out in Holcomb Hill. Now he had built the house, and he was looked upon as one of the two or three most prominent young architects in New England, and they didn't have the indolent Sunday mornings in bed any more at all...

He shook the feeling off brusquely. Morbid maunderings, his father would have called them. Thomas Lawring hated self-pity, or anything that even smacked of self-pity, more than anything else. "Surest way to go into a decline," he used to say. "Keep busy enough, your mind won't have time to magnify its troubles." Busy. Lawring thought of Janet's voice during the phone call last night, with a slow surge of desire. He should have gone out there anyway, whether she wanted him to or not, and brought her back home here with him. Had she wanted him to, in that languid, unaware way women often longed for things? Sometimes he wished he were more impetuous, did things on the spur of the moment: it might have been the propitious, the restorative time... Fiddling around in the cellar, he was filled with a sense of Janet and their love, their life together; the fine, free ardor she had brought to their lovemaking before this trouble, the sweet inventiveness that had been able to take his breath away. He hadn't thought about any of this while he'd been talking to her over the telephone; but now his failure to interpret that low, vibrant receptivity in her voice seemed to him suddenly of enormous gravity, a dereliction whose consequences would be nothing short of disastrous. He spun the iron lever of the vise at the end of the workbench with a snap of his wrist. He was used to dealing with tangible substances, things with edges, with corners—and essences and intimations baffled him...

Perhaps she was shaken in some deeply feminine way—perhaps she associated all men now with the assault, invasion: the brutal sex. Maybe that was what it was. His grip on sexual psychology was elemental and unsure, and his mind half-recalled things he'd heard about sexual traumas, catatonic states, displaced affects, withdrawal symptoms; groping about like an old man in a cluttered room. Troubled, he wondered about the possibility of psychological counseling, but his protestant nature rebelled against the idea: you didn't need intercessors, lay confessors who would pass their hands over your soul like housewives prodding broiler chickens in a supermarket; the problem in life was to straighten up your own attic, throw off the trauma or whatever the devil it was and keep on going. Time was needed, probably: simple time. Maybe a few days with her sister and the kids would relax her a little, give her back herself; and slowly, gently they could draw near each other again, and heal the breach...

He shut off the water line running out to the sillcock, picked up his tools and went outdoors again. It was his somber boast that he could fix anything around the place that didn't require two men or a licensed electrician. He removed the faucet, sawed off the pipe end just above the fissure; and locking one of the Stillsons with his knee and the other against the siding he began to rethread the pipe end with the die. As he was making the last few turns the upper Stillson slipped and caught him across the back of the left wrist: a sharp crack. He looked down at his watch. The unbreakable crystal was all right, but the stem came loose in his fingers and the minute hand fell off, tangled with the sweep second hand and stopped it. He swore under his breath, put the watch in his pocket and finished rethreading, smeared the pipe with joint cement and drew the faucet up tight on the threads.

There were two other chores he'd had his eye on for a while and he did those, glanced at his wrist to see what time it was, pulled the watch out of his pocket and was astonished all over again at the sight of the minute hand lying blackly across the six numeral. There was something profoundly disturbing about it—as though the time had decided to have fun with him, slip away and leave him tethered to some past hour, caught on dead center. He couldn't repair *this,* it had been his own carelessness into the bargain, and irritated and sweaty he thought of his old service chronometer and went back into the house, and up in the bedroom rummaged about among cufflinks and abandoned keys—all at once remembered Janet had put it in her jewelry box a long time ago, for safekeeping, after it had been cleaned. He went over to the pale blue case on her vanity and opened it, lifted the tray and pawed through a tangle of necklaces, earrings of silver and shell and pearl, a cameo pin, a dozen silver charms, more necklaces—and at the very bottom under a ring box found the chronometer. He lifted it out and slipped it on his wrist; it still had the old olive-drab fabric strap that fitted under the back. The hands said eleven-fifty-one. He set it to the clock on the vanity and wound it thirty turns, gazing absently into the jewelry case, and saw the pebble Janet had picked up on the beach at Nount's Head the afternoon he'd told her he wanted to marry her: a smooth plain little jet-black stone. Holding it in the palm of his hand he smiled fondly, remembering her face flushed with wind and sun and newly found love. They had kissed, then she had turned away and looked down at her feet, and then she had bent down and picked up something almost surreptitiously.

"What you got there?" he'd asked.

"A pebble."

"A pebble?"

She nodded; her eyes sparkled mischievously. She showed it to him. "I'm going to keep it all the rest of my life. From this moment on!"

It became a personal talisman; she carried it around with her for years, and once when she lost her purse she was plunged into an agony of remorse.

"It's all right, honey," he consoled her, thinking of the usual farrago of keys and money and driver's license and credit cards, "it's all replaceable."

"No it's not, it's not—that *pebble* isn't replaceable!"

He started to laugh, then saw the look on her face. He'd found the purse, too. After a battery of questions, tracing her movements, and a meticulous search he'd found it under the bushes at the edge of the drive—she'd parked the car poorly, in a hurry, and it had apparently fallen off the front seat when she'd climbed out with her arms full of packages—and after that he'd told her to put the pebble in the house where she wouldn't lose it. Now, with that special power of evocation tiny objects have to release the broadest floods of memory, he saw her face glowing with love against the drifting silver clouds, the fine blue mantle of sea.

"I'll make a rotten wife," she'd said, and brushed her hair out of her eyes. "I haven't got any sense of organization or anything, I get all enthusiastic about something and then get off on something else, I can't cook and I can't sew very well, either—*all* I can do is love you, really! . . ."

That was all he wanted, he'd told her, he'd settle for that, and he'd held her exultantly in his arms and watched the gulls slide away downwind, uttering their hoarse, wild cries. A magic moment: a moment when his life had turned . . . Still smiling faintly he put the pebble back in the box. The cameo pin, a huge caramel oval with the head of a goddess his mother had once given Janet, was disturbed. Beneath it was a piece of paper folded twice. He took it out and looked at it.

J A C L Y 3-6049

He stood there frowning, holding the paper, conscious of a slow, deepening concern like cloud shadows over sand, an uneasiness that pressed at his vitals. *J A C.* And a phone number. Placed in the bottom of her jewelry case. He peered in again, brushing the pins and necklaces about with his forefinger, but there were no other notes or bits of paper. She did strange things, she did unpredictable, unthinking things often enough, God knew—

He turned the envelope over. A letter from her sister Alice. Above the address there were some words, bits of phrases in Janet's handwriting, set down hastily and arranged like a list, and crossed out. *Refuse all,* it said, and then there was an uncompleted word, indecipherable, and under it *Roxane—why?* and below that in capital letters: *SHOW NO FEAR.* A long, looping line had been drawn through them all.

"Roxane," he said, half aloud; and now realization moved in on him in a slow, ponderous wave that made him grunt and blink his eyes. She knew, then. This was why she knew Roche wasn't her assailant, wasn't a Negro at all—this was why she'd been so afraid when Reardon and Shea had left. Was that it? His thoughts skittered and danced around—Danny quietly sorting the two decks of cards, Reardon staring up at him through the maple's limp green leaves, Janet weeping on the edge of the bed, her head in the crook of her arm. What had she said? *I don't know, don't ask me, don't badger me, why are you badgering me . . . ?*

He crossed to the telephone stand and dialed Edna's house in Swampscott, listened to the dead sizzle of the ringing; put down the receiver. Gone to the beach. And anyway, if she'd wanted him to know about this she would have told him. Wouldn't she? J A C. He sat down and pulled the city directory out of its stall. There were just so many C's. He ran his finger down the columns, checking for the exchange only. Maybe it was unlisted: it probably was. He had covered almost twenty pages and was about to close the book when he saw the fingernail mark, quite fresh, a few columns ahead; and then the name and the matching number. Castaldo. He shut the director on his thumb, saying the name to himself over and over, thinking he'd heard it somewhere, imagining episodes, social functions, chance meetings, straining to remember; while the blood began to beat in his temples and his skin turned hot and chafing.

Castaldo.

He got to his feet and went over and picked up the envelope again. *Refuse all.* Refuse all what? It was impossible to tell what she could have intended to write there. *SHOW NO FEAR.* The poor kid, he thought with a sudden rush of pity; the poor kid. Awful. Awful.

But that she knew the man and hadn't told him. That she knew who it was—

He sat down again and put his hand over his mouth. His calves were shaking and his back felt cold where sweat had quickly broken out on it, and as quickly dried. On the radio a cultured, authoritative voice had succeeded the nostalgic dance band music, was saying with astonishing rapidity:

"—because science never fails. The doctors of this land are working every day for *you*, to solve *your* problems. Science has an answer for *every* problem. And this *one thin* wafer can spell the answer to those hours of gnawing, bitter hunger pangs, the ceaseless, numbing fear of that *master killer*, overeating. Science never sleeps. We *want* you to find this one thin wafer lacking, we *want* you to ask for a refund because we *know* Kope can cure you. Kope is the protein-laden, satisfying wafer you've been waiting for. *One, thin* wafer of Kope and we *guarantee* you'll feel as if you've eaten a dozen steaks, chops, mountains of mashed potatoes, all the pastry and candies you can possibly desire—"

He went out on the sun deck and gripped the smooth teakwood railing. The sky had a hard, steely quality now, and the sun hung in it like a dissolving lozenge. He remained there for several minutes taking deep, even breaths, watching the tree tops and the sky; and slowly the steady logicality and indomitable self-possession that were his heritage and his mainstay returned. She was his wife. She was his wife and she loved him, he knew that beyond question: it had to be. So if she hadn't told him about this Castaldo it was because she couldn't tell him. And she couldn't because he had some hold over her she could not break. That was why she had been so fearful when Reardon removed the surveillance, and why she'd been so shaken when she saw the papers yesterday afternoon: her assailant—her blackmailer—was free to return and make further demands. *Refuse all.* Yes. Refuse all demands. For a hot, panicky instant he thought of Janet's personal account at the Shawmut, their joint account, the vault at the State Street Trust, the Dalai-Nor emerald his great-grandfather Joshua had brought back from the Orient in a black lacquered box over a century ago. *SHOW NO FEAR.* Maybe she'd met Castaldo at the Statler, had tried to dissuade him and got into an argument—and then had called Edna to come and pick her up in order to get free of him.

No. She wouldn't lie to him like that, she wouldn't do that ... But if she hadn't told him about Castaldo—

He closed his mind on the thought; went into the bathroom, undressed and showered quickly and began to shave. His first thought was to go to the man, confront him, if necessary beat the truth out of him. Then he remembered the shuttered, wary look on Reardon's face the day before yesterday—that sharp glance of displeasure and suspicion. He knew too, then, did he? No, he couldn't—of course he couldn't: Reardon had only seen that Janet was constrained, fearful, withholding something—and had probably jumped to the conclusion that she was having an affair with this man, something like that; he couldn't have known it was blackmail—

This new thought led to such a multiplicity of conjecture that he closed his eyes. It actually hurt to look into the bathroom mirror, follow the course of the razor along his jaw. Mistrust and jealousy were so foreign to him that the train of his suspicions was like a physical burden, making his shoulders sag. Back in the bedroom he caught sight of the jewelry box with its lid open and the tray set to one side. He went over to it. She thought I would never look there, he said to himself, staring down into the case which now seemed animate, rings and necklaces like exotic insects in some crystal-clear tank, stirring their glittering bodies, slowly writhing . . .

He put the tray back and closed the lid. A hard black knot of pain had formed in the center of his body and sat there implacably. Blackmail or no, whatever it might be, why couldn't she have told him? They'd had ten good years together in which he'd met every problem, every crisis—if not perfectly, at least as well as or better than the next man—why hadn't she let him resolve this crisis as he had the others? . . . The sense of sundering he'd had after the police had left—of a chasm widening inexorably between them despite anything they might do—came back on him again, looming like some awesome tidal wave, churning up sea bottoms, menacing whole cities in their coastal plains . . .

But he would meet it. There was nothing you could not come to grips with, given the proper intelligence and fortitude; it could be met. Above all she needed protection: she needed all the protection she could get and she needed it at once—before she was back here in this house. He went on dressing rapidly and methodically, shirt and tie and green Dacron suit; and gradually his face began to compose itself in spite of the solid black knot of pain, became hard and firm again. A news broadcast was coming from the radio but he didn't hear a single word of it.

● ● ●

There was a vacant lot littered with beer cans, bedsteads, old bottles that winked like coins when the sun intermittently caught them, rags of newspapers sliding and flapping in the rising wind. Two squad cars and another unmarked sedan were parked there and several policemen were in a far corner of the lot, bent over what looked for a distance like a gray gunny sack. Inspector Reardon was standing by the sedan, talking to two other men in plainclothes. When he caught sight of Lawring his eyebrows rose, and then the smooth, genial smile broke over his seamed face.

"Mr. Lawring," he called, and the two detectives turned. "How are you?"

Lawring came up to him. "Could I talk to you for a minute, Inspector?"

"Why not?—I'll be right with you," he said to the others, and moved off across the lot with Lawring, toward a two-family tenement in faded yellow clapboarding. "What seems to be the problem?"

"I'd like you to reopen the case."

Reardon shoved his hands deep in his pockets, spreading his trousers like a Dutchman's breeches, and looked at Lawring carefully. "Why would you want to do that?"

"I think I know who the real assailant is."

"Oh." Reardon moved his lips extravagantly, a distended pout, and stared down at his shoe tops. "And what leads you to that conclusion?"

"Some evidence I found."

"I see. And what evidence may that be?"

Lawring paused. He had driven swiftly into town obsessed by the idea of finding Reardon, no matter where he was or what he was doing. The desk sergeant had sent him out here to this vacant lot in Dorchester where he'd found him immediately— and now he realized he didn't want to say anything about the envelope at all. Reardon's taciturn, cagy attitude filled him with resentment, and he fought it down. Over the Inspector's shoulder he could see the two detectives waiting impatiently by the open car doors.

"A slip of paper. With a man's name and phone number on it." Reardon made no reply and Lawring handed him the envelope. "And these notations on the other side. Remember when Mrs. Lawring said the man called her Roxane?" The

Inspector still said nothing, merely twisted the piece of paper back and forth between his fingers, studying it. "It's obvious he'd approached her, with some kind of threat."

Reardon frowned. "These initials—"

"I checked the name in the city directory. The name is Castaldo. Joseph A. Castaldo."

"Castaldo." Reardon seemed to be trying out the name, a policeman's reflex, instinctive; shook his head. "What did Mrs. Lawring say when you showed it to her?"

"I haven't spoken to her about it yet."

"You haven't?"

"No—I haven't been able to get in touch with her. She's staying with her sister in Swampscott."

"I see." There was another little pause, Reardon glanced at him and looked away. A patrolman standing by one of the squad cars called: "Chief! Captain Crowley says can you get over to Coolidge Corner right away on that two-eleven...?" and Reardon turned and shouted back, "All right, in a minute..." When he turned back to Lawring again his face was as bland and expressionless as an Oriental idol's.

"We're satisfied that Roche is our man," he said.

"But Mrs. Lawring wasn't—you remember she said she was sure it was someone else..."

"He's confessed to all three assaults. Written depositions. It's open and shut. The Hannegan girl identified him right off the bat. So did Mrs. Morrill. Your wife hasn't even come in, Mr. Lawring."

"I know. I'm sorry about that. I'm sure she intends to..."

He said more sharply: "In point of fact, she was pretty upset yesterday. Seeing it in the papers that way—that you considered the case closed. She was in the city alone at the time and she became very frightened, that's why she went out to her sister's..." Reardon was staring off toward the far corner of the lot, whistling almost soundlessly through his teeth, and Lawring's resentment broke through the impersonal tone he'd striven to maintain. "You promised me two days ago you wouldn't give it to the papers..."

Reardon turned to face him again. "I did not promise you, Mr. Lawring."

"Yes, you did. You said—"

"I said I'd *try* to keep it out if I could. It was out of my hands."
The Inspector made a sudden little movement as though to walk
away, and Lawring regretted the trace of heat in his voice.

"Look, I'll be frank with you, Inspector," he said quickly. "I
can understand your—reluctance about the case, your irritation
the other day. But I think you'll see now that it's a very different
situation from what we thought it was. I'm convinced from this
that Mrs. Lawring can't talk—this Castaldo has some kind of
hold over her. It's obvious now that she's got to have
protection—even if it's only to protect her from herself..."
Reardon's expression underwent a subtle change at this: an
expression half-skeptical, half-sardonic, that Lawring couldn't
read. "It's clearly blackmail of some sort," he pursued, "there's
no doubt in my mind. Let's pick this fellow up right away and
check him out."

Reardon started to say something, stopped himself; then,
"I'm afraid it's not a police matter, Mr. Lawring. The fact is we
can't mix in personal affairs."

"Personal affairs—"

"That's right. Your wife could be involved with twenty men,
and that simply isn't our province. I'm satisfied that the case is
closed, and so is the entire department. If you have some
personal score to settle, that's your affair. I'd be glad to give you
the name of a private firm, some reputable investigators you
could call on if you want to follow up on your own. But we
can't."

Lawring was stunned; he hadn't begun to realize how hard
Reardon was—he listened to this steady marshaling of
arguments, underlain by an implication he only dimly sensed.
The tight little knot of pain in his belly doubled and redoubled
on itself.

"Why not?" he demanded. "You're our law enforcement
agency, you're what we rely on—"

"All right, what evidence do you have?" Reardon handed the
slip back to Lawring. "This is no evidence—some initials and a
phone number. What can we do with that? Do you have any
eyewitnesses, any threatening letters? If you've got evidence,
bring it to us—if we have evidence we will certainly act. But
believe me, the Boston Police Department has more important
things to do than go running around tracking down every

husband's domestic problems."

Lawring said very quietly: "You seem to have the wrong idea about Mrs. Lawring."

Reardon's eyes opened very wide. "I'm sorry if I do. All I meant to make clear is our own official position in an affair of this nature." Some children playing a variation of stoop-ball on the other corner of the lot had begun to stray over near the police, and Reardon called: "Keep those kids out of there!" One of the cops began shooing them away.

"Then you won't even pick him up," Lawring said. He found he was trembling with agitation and it made his voice still sharper. "You won't question him about it..."

Reardon shrugged. "I'm sorry, Mr. Lawring. I know how you must feel. All I can say is, we are satisfied that Roche is the offender. We simply can't go around picking up people on no evidence at all."

The unmarked sedan had pulled up near him. He said goodbye and walked quickly over to the car and got in. The other cars followed. Lawring stood at the edge of the lot and watched them all drive away. The beer cans winked and flashed as the sun rolled out from the film of cloud, the newspapers flopped and trundled against the wire mesh. The children had gone back to their game. The boy in the batter's position flung his arm down and the ball soared up and out, a bright red dot against the streaky plate of the sky, and a thin boy in a royal blue polo shirt ran back and back through the weeds, leaped up at the last second and caught the ball with one hand; and someone called: "*One* gone, *one* gone..."

Then, standing there watching the kids playing ball, with the knot in his belly swelling and tightening, Lawring thought of Brian in the camp at Ossipee, of the Maine lakes lying like cobalt scarves under the feathery green gloom of the pines, and Danny Shea standing by the door that afternoon talking of Sebago and Moosehead, his eyes perfectly friendly and serene.

He found Shea all by himself at a booth in a diner out in Jamaica, eating a large piece of blueberry pie à la mode. The detective glanced at him in surprise, then smiled his bright, boyish smile.

"Mr. Lawring. Sit down and have a cup of coffee."

"Thanks." Lawring eased his weight into the booth opposite

Shea, ran his eyes over the plaid pink Formica and over-shellacked woodwork. "It's just for a minute."

"What's on your mind?"

Lawring took a deep breath and said: "I'm convinced Roche is not the man who assaulted my wife. I believe I know who it was."

"Really? Who is it?"

"A man named Joseph Castaldo."

Shea frowned, holding his fork just above his plate. "What makes you think that?"

"I found a note with his name on it. Just this morning." He leaned forward on his elbows. "I'm certain my wife's in danger and needs protection. I'd like you to come with me and pick him up."

Shea was still watching him attentively with that soft, cherubic face. "You'll have to see the Chief about something like that," he said after a moment.

"I already have."

"And?"

"He—brushed me off. He didn't believe me. But I'm sure of it, I really am. Will you go with me and find this guy, ask him some questions?"

Shea finished his pie and took a long, deliberate sip of coffee. Then he shook his head once. "No. I won't."

Lawring cried, "What is this, a conspiracy?"

"It's no conspiracy, Mr. Lawring."

"Then why not?"

"You say you've found a slip of paper with this man's name on it."

"That's right."

"How do you know it has anything to do with the assault? How do you know it isn't the name of a dry cleaner or something?"

"Because of what she wrote here . . ." He pulled the envelope out of his pocket and thrust it at Shea. "Do you write yourself personal memoranda like that about a dry cleaner—?"

Shea studied the paper for a moment, put it down. "I don't see that there's anything conclusive there."

"But the reference to Roxane—to refusing something . . ."

"That's no evidence. You must know that."

Lawring said in exasperation: "My wife's the victim of some

kind of extortion, there's no doubt in my mind...Won't you even go look up this man and question him?" Shea shook his head again. "Why in Christ's name won't you?"

Shea wiped his mouth with a paper napkin and crumpled it into a neat white round ball. "All right, Mr. Lawring. You asked for it. I think that if this Castaldo were the real offender your wife wouldn't prefer charges against him."

Lawring stared at the detective. Anger began to rise in him, fused with the knot of pain of the morning, beating in his blood like surf. "You—" he started, could not finish. "Do you—are you trying to tell me my wife was not assaulted?"

"I didn't say that."

"You implied it. You implied—"

"I'm only telling you what I think." Shea paused; his eyes were blue and clear and very mild. "The attitude of the department has been for some time that this was not a matter for the police at all. If it weren't for—your name, we'd have been called off the case a long time ago."

"...You know," Lawring muttered, after a moment. "You *know,* and you won't act."

"I don't know anything. I said *if* this Castaldo *were* to turn out to be the man."

"You admit Roche wasn't the man, then!"

Shea's eyes widened. "Roche confessed to it."

"—That's immaterial!" Lawring burst out. "Who do you think you're kidding with that routine?—I know how you people like to clear the book..."

The detective said in a quiet voice, "Roche confessed to the assault, and of his own volition. *Why* he did it I have no idea—but he wasn't persuaded, if that's what you're trying to say..."

"What do you call it, then? You people make me sick..." Lawring felt half nauseated with frustration and disgust. "Haven't any of you got the strength of your convictions?"

"Look, Mr. Lawring. I'm paid to do a job and I try to do it to the best of my ability.... Yes," Shea repeated, nodding soberly as though to himself, "the best of my ability." His mild blue eyes held a saddened expression now, vaguely commiserating, and it stung Lawring to a fury.

"—You *know* and yet you won't do anything about it!" he

cried. "What kind of peace officer are you?—you're a lousy fraud..."

Shea became very still. "I'll overlook that," he said after a moment.

"You'll overlook nothing! You know what I think? I think you're afraid—of Reardon and the whole cheap, rotten system. You're just plain afraid of them..."

"Careful, now," Shea said softly. "Don't push me too far."

Lawring put his hands flat on the table. The rage and grief that had swollen inside him seemed to have burst like some vile sac and spread through his whole system; his guts churned on themselves, and his sight was blurred. "You want to make something of that?" he demanded hoarsely. "Come on, then. Come on..."

Shea watched him for several seconds. Then with two fingers he slowly pushed his cup and saucer out into the exact center of the table. "Mr. Lawring," he said in the same quiet voice, "you're very upset. You're not yourself, and I don't blame you."

"*Blame* me!"

But Shea had already risen and was moving quickly toward the cash register at the end of the counter. Lawring jumped to his feet. Shea left some silver with his check and went on to the door without a pause. On the step outside Lawring overtook him and caught him by the shoulder, pulling him around. "Now just a minute—"

"I don't want to talk to you any more," Shea said.

"What?" Lawring glared at him. "I want—I want you to know what I think of you," he stammered. "Yes! A law enforcement officer who won't go where his conscience leads him who doesn't even *want* to find out the truth!..."

"Do you?" Shea said, just as softly as before.

"What?"

"Do you want the truth?"

"—God damn it, I'm begging you to help me find it!"

"Then go talk to your wife."

Lawring reared back. For an instant it was in his mind to hit Shea, and the detective must have guessed it, for Lawring saw that barely perceptible dropping of the shoulders as Shea set himself. Then the moment passed, and Lawring relaxed and put his hand to the back of his neck. It came away slick with sweat.

"I'll talk to my wife when I'm good and ready," he said in a dull voice. "If it's any of your business."

"It isn't any of my business," Shea answered him evenly. "You're trying to make it mine, remember? So long, Mr. Lawring."

He went away down the street. Lawring gazed at the faces through the windows of the diner, two unshaven men who looked like lumberjacks and a waitress watching him with an angry, distraught expression. He mopped his face with his handkerchief. He felt one last tempestuous surge of rage—and then in its place a still, glacial calm.

"All right," he said aloud. Shea was half a block away now, but Lawring had the illusion that the detective could still hear him. "All right, then. If you haven't got the guts for it, I have."

He crossed the street and got into his car.

He walked upstairs and down to the far end of the hall—an even, unhurried tread; opened the door to the storage closet that occupied the entire northeast end of the house, and snapped on the light. Trunks, cartons, old suitcases with broken straps, their leather raw as rust. A stand lamp minus its shade, looking like a sick wading bird. A rocker with a split rung, two of Grandma Lawring's Hitchcock chairs with bad legs (why did chairs always go first?), a rolled rug, a mirror with an oval rosewood frame, his old val-pac: G A LAWRING 1ST LT AUS stenciled on the slick green fabric. His surf-casting rod with its black cork handle from days at Nauset Beach before the war; Brian's old toys—the rocking horse with its dappled skin and real buckskin mane and western saddle, the baby carriage with its ribbed hood and shiny little silver wheels. His own skis and skates and hockey sticks, the old toboggan he and his father used to slide with down the hill in Boston Common. The Harvard escutcheon his great-great-grandfather Jared had hung in his room at Stoughton, and which he'd meant to put up in his study and hadn't ever got around to. All the gear up here was his, his family's: Janet had brought nothing with her, no heirlooms, no possessions. Just herself.

And now she had taken herself away, just as lightly.

He moved carefully past the bumps and angles, found in the far corner the old brass-bound trunk that said *T. E. Lawring* in hand-painted letters, beautifully Spencerian, and bore the hotel stickers of a dozen foreign cities. *Brown's Hotel, London; Hotel Boston, Roma; Hotel La Trémoille, Paris; Pensione Berchielli, Firenze.* Not the best hotels in these cities, the de luxe ones, but the quieter, more austere ones where you often ran the lift yourself and the dining room at breakfast was like a faintly shabby tea room on Joy Street; the ones where most good Boston families invariably chose to stay. *Kurfurst, Wien; Egmont, Köbenhavn; Acropole, Athinai.* Why in God's name did they take trunks with them? Because that was the way it was done then, obviously. You sent your trunk on ahead and then caught up with it. He'd been too young to remember much of the later trip, the trip that had included him. There had been a garden with little trees like balls and cones and cubes, and two children who called to him in voices he couldn't understand. He had spoken slowly and carefully, but still their faces became distrustful; finally he had got angry and wanted to fight them, but his sister Emily had come up and intervened. Somewhere there had been a parrot with a bright yellow crest and blood-red eyes that barked at him and then laughed, ruffling its feathers; and somewhere there were red and yellow candy-striped triangles slipped magically over an expanse of blue, and his mother was saying, "Those are sails, dear; *sails*"—the word ringing in his consciousness like pealing bells...

He unsnapped the cast-iron acanthus-leaf catches, lifted the heavy lid. The stuff was all there, where he'd stored it so long ago: barracks and overseas caps, web belt, canteen, medical pouch, sleeping roll. Olive drab. They gave off a funny odor now, mildew and cinnamon and oil combined. Packets of letters—from his parents, from his sisters, from Chuck who had been sent halfway around the world to New Guinea, from girls he'd known and thought he loved—

In the bottom left corner of the trunk he found the heavy, crooked bundle, unwound the old skivvy shirts, two of them, and hefted the weapon in his hand. A long-barreled .38 his father had given him before he'd shipped out. He'd had it in his trousers pocket that terrible night near Havelange, and later he'd made a holster for it from a .45 holster and had carried it with him through Belgium and Germany; though he'd used it only once... Crouching by the old trunk he saw, clearer than the maple trees outside the window, clearer by far, the street in Diersdorff, the smoking black scaffoldings and the rubble heaps—heard behind him the flat tearing rip of the Schmeisser and Sonking's cry, felt his own carbine slapped out of his hands as though by the paw of a great bear and turned toward the etched-in-acid image of the SS captain standing in the black iron doorway, bareheaded, grinning, steam coming from his mouth in little bursts. In a dream of nervous haste he had stepped behind the shattered column of wall, pulled the revolver out of its holster with numbed fingers, leaned out into the open and fired—watched in a slow agony of trance the flash from the Schmeisser barrel and then the captain, his features contorted in a still broader grin, bending, bending—then spilling out into the street like a slender tackling-dummy scarecrow, one arm pointing to where Sonking lay...

Allen & Thurber, it said on the barrel; *Worcester, Mass. 1879.* It gave off the thin, grassy odor of gum oil. The cylinder turned like a snake stirring as the hammer rode back. He checked the barrel against the light bulb: smooth gray-white whorls. The holster he had turned in when he was discharged: it was government property and you didn't keep what wasn't yours. A lot of them did, but he would not.

He rummaged around in the bottom of the trunk and found the little cloth sack of bullets, loaded the weapon carefully, slammed the trunk lid and got up, clenching and realizing his grip on the smooth wooden butt of the revolver, and snapped out the light. His hands and feet felt stiff and strange, as though it were someone else, some brother or friend he himself was watching move along the shadowed wall of the house with a gun in his hand. His mind slowed and started fitfully, lighted on some plan (the car: should he drive the car in to town? where would he park it? should he wear gloves?) and darted off again, careening through a tangle of sensation and conjecture. I'm hungry, he thought abruptly—aware for the first time of lightheadedness and a slow, persistent griping in his belly, apart from the black knot. I'm half-starved, that's what the trouble is. I'll get a bite to eat first, that leftover roast beef, make a couple of sandwiches and a cup of coffee to hold me, then I'll take off.

He nodded, as if to approve this decision, came down the stairs still carrying the revolver—and walked right into Franz Hoelder standing just inside the front door.

He stopped. For several seconds the two men stared at each

other. Franz's eyes went to the weapon, back to Lawring's face again.

"Gardner—" he began, but Lawring broke in on him harshly:

"Is it your habit to walk into other people's houses unannounced?" He felt foolish standing there on the stairs holding the gun and this made him even angrier. He jammed it into the waistband of his trousers, and buttoning his jacket over it came on down the rest of the flight.

"I'm sorry," Franz said in a quiet voice. "If I offended you. You yourself gave me the key. Four years ago." Lawring made no reply. "Janet phoned me a short time ago. She said she'd been trying to reach you most of the day."

"Did she?"

"Yes. She wanted me to leave a message for you to call her when you got in. I knocked but you didn't hear me. She would like very much to talk to you..." Lawring still said nothing and came toward Franz, who had closed the door and remained standing with his back against it. "I—I would like to talk to you, too."

Lawring was now directly in front of him, and made a brusque gesture as though to reach by him for the door handle. "I'm afraid you'll have to excuse me. I'm in a bit of a hurry just now."

"No—stay. Only a minute." Franz's tone was importunate, but there was a note in it—of insistence, almost authority—that made Lawring pause. "Just—" he gestured "—for a cigarette..."

"I don't smoke."

"Gardner, you—" Hoelder stopped, said: "I have something to tell you."

"Another time, Franz. Really." Lawring felt as though he would split in two if he had to utter one more civil word to anybody on this earth; he was conscious all at once of an intense dislike for the older man.

"... You know who it is," Franz was saying softly.

"Yes. I know." Lawring's eyes narrowed. "Do you?"

"I? No." Franz Hoelder shook his head. "I wondered, when—" He broke off. "What are you going to do?"

Lawring burst out: "—Never mind what I'm going to do!"

"I see.—Have you talked to Chief Inspector Reardon?"

"Yes, I've talked to Chief Inspector Reardon. That sterling soul of honor. And Shea. They wouldn't listen to me, they told me the case was closed."

"And so you're going to reopen it yourself." Lawring said nothing. "But Janet—have you told her about this discovery of yours?"

Lawring opened and closed his hand. "You ask too many questions, Franz. Questions that are none of your business. Do you know that?"

Hoelder frowned, cocked his head—a curiously antiquated movement. "Perhaps I do. Yes. I suppose I do . . . Gardner," he said sharply, "it could be the end of your life!"

Lawring grinned at him mirthlessly. "Maybe so, maybe not. You know what they say: If you want a thing done right, do it yourself."

"You must not do it."

"Do what?"

"What—you are planning to do." There was a new ring in Hoelder's voice, a forceful edge Lawring had never heard before. He said crisply: "Gardner, I forbid you to leave this house with that gun."

Lawring stirred. He became aware of what the professor's presence in the room might mean. He extended one finger slowly. "I'm warning you, Franz . . ."

The phone rang; both men started. Lawring did not go to answer it. At the third ring Franz Hoelder said: "That is your telephone, Gardner."

"Let it go. I'm not interested."

"I could phone the police," Franz said after a few seconds. "They would pick you up before you got to Brookline."

Lawring regarded him silently. The phone stopped ringing and the air seemed heavier and more fraught with menace than before.

"Franz," Lawring said slowly, "you've been a good friend and we've had a lot of good times together. But I'm telling you right now I'm not going to let you or anybody else prevent me from doing what I've made up my mind to do. Now I want you to give me your word that you won't try to stop me tonight."

The professor glanced at him with bleak humor. "My word. How do you know I won't give you my word and then go back on it five minutes later?"

"You won't. I know you won't. Not to me. I want your word."

There was a short silence. Outside, at the edge of the woods a thrush called softly—four notes, then four notes again, inverted: distant, silvery pipes of Pan.

"Franz," Lawring said in a low, hoarse voice, "I haven't got a lot of time. *Give me your word!*"

"All right." Franz relaxed all at once and put his hands in his pockets. "I'll give you my word on one condition. That you stay here long enough for me to tell you something. A story."

"You're full of stories."

"But this is a true one. And short. A very short one, really. It is in two parts. I was in the camp at Les Milles. Near Nîmes. In the spring of 1940. The French had interned us there, all of us aliens, and they had taken away our papers. France was collapsing, hour by hour, the Germans were coming down the Rhône, and the camp authorities wouldn't release us. Finally I got permission to go with two other internees as a committee of three to plead with the camp commandant. After a quarter of an hour he received us in his quarters: a captain, dressed in an immaculate uniform, and he was playing Mozart. You know that sonata that runs so lightly and gaily, like a fountain in the morning sun? The F major, that one. I waited for him to finish but he nodded for me to speak anyway. I said we requested permission to have our papers returned to us and leave the camp—that the Germans, as he must know, would certainly execute nearly every one of us when they got there. I thought of the men I was speaking for, I spoke as eloquently and forcefully as I knew how. I would have moved a field of stones! And he smiled at me. Still playing the Mozart. 'Oh,' he said, 'you are too apprehensive, my children, you are agitating yourselves unduly.' 'But the Germans are only eight hours away, my commandant—for many of us it is a matter of life and death . . .' 'No, no, no,' and he shook his head at me like a wealthy, indulgent parent. 'You are worrying yourselves about nothing, there is no danger, the Germans will not harm you.' No danger. There he sat, smiling at us, his little mustache quivering, playing so beautifully, so impeccably! 'No, no, no. There is nothing in this matter to concern yourselves about, my friends, nothing at all. You may go now,' he said, and he dismissed us with a graceful little flourish of his hand that became part of his playing of the passage. And the next day when the Germans came he had skipped off in his Peugeot, and the Germans deported and executed every single man they found in the camp at Les Milles. But by then my two friends and I had escaped, without out papers..."

Lawring stood scowling at him, his hands hanging at his sides. Franz nodded, as though to punctuate the episode. "Part One. And then later, three years later, in a little town called Chargeron, I lay frozen and exhausted and half dead with fever in this attic and heard them debate whether or not to kill me. The man and his wife. An interminable conversation. The husband said they could be executed if I were found there by the Germans or the Milice—which was true—that if I were a spy I would probably betray them—which was also true—that they could not afford to jeopardize the lives of his old parents, their children would also be involved... and what did they know about me? Only that I had been lying on their back stoop in the snow, scratching at their door like an animal in the night. And all that was true, too. What was I to them, why had I chosen *them,* crashed in on *their* lives with my beard and my fever and filthy clothes and false identity papers—why in the name of God had I had to menace his life in this way? He was frightened and burdened with my presence, he wanted to do away with me—why not? What was the life of one man more or less in the blood-soaked winter of 1943, one homeless wanderer without any real identity? It would be simple enough, it would solve their problems in one stroke, he could dispose of the body at his leisure and they would be rid of this worry, this fear. It was possible that I might die anyway, in which case one couldn't really say it was murder at all... And I lay there, helpless and weak as water, and listened and listened. And he almost won. Almost. But his wife said no. She had no proof of what I was or was not, she had no sound reasons such as his, she didn't even have a plan. She drove him half crazy! He brought out all his arguments again and embellished them, and she still said no. All she had was the blind conviction that I was a good man, and that it would be wrong to kill me—that if they put me to death as he wanted to do, their own life together would never be the same. And after three hours and a half she prevailed. They hid me and fed me until I was well, and could leave them..."

He reached out and put his hand on Lawring's arm; his face

looked white and worn, as though some of its substance had been eaten away by the abrasive force of memory. "Don't you see?—it is not the man, the person who is at fault—it is the attitudes, the things we believe and do not believe that make us what we are. Why shouldn't I have killed the commandant of the camp at Les Milles? Why shouldn't the farmer at Chargeron have killed me? You cannot change the shape of mankind—you can only accept it for what it is and go along as best you can. That is life—that is what life is, no more and no less: moving through this world with dignity and honor, no matter what has happened to you..."

Lawring gazed back at him. "I don't understand you," he said thickly.

"Listen to me, Gardner. I have always been an agnostic, an agnostic and a humanist, but I am beginning to think there is something very great in the Biblical exhortation, something very durable and profound. *Love your enemies, bless them that curse you, do good to them that hate you, and pray for them which despitefully use you, and persecute you* ... Why not? That is all that distinguishes us from the beasts, that one solitary thing—forgiveness in the face of evil. All our cunning, our logic and cold reason, all our wheels and fire-making and electricity and all the rest of the complicated things we love to make long speeches about during college commencements and patriotic holidays in the heat—all that is so much dust and ashes..."

He stopped, and his arm dropped to his side. For a moment the two men gazed at each other—the defenseless, painful look of old friends who know they cannot be friends any longer. The thrush called again, a short note touched with grief, like a lament for innocence, then was silent; and the scissor-hum of insects returned.

"...I'm sorry," Lawring said in a hard, hollow voice. "My—charity doesn't extend that far." He started toward the door.

Franz Hoelder struck his thigh with one hand. "Don't you understand?—what I've been saying? ... Where are you going?" he demanded, as though upbraiding a disobedient pupil. "What do you *want?*"

Lawring spun around at this: all at once he felt tears sting his eyelids. "Justice!" he cried. "That's what I want!"

"By hunting down one poor, pitiful fool?"

"If need be—yes! Justice, is that so despicable? My forefathers died for it—am I too good for that?"

"Justice, that's just it—there *is* no justice—not the kind you're looking for, anyway..." He caught Lawring by the arm again. "Don't you see—there is only confusion and fear and cruelty, a terrible, endless iron road of it, and here and there a few moments of truth and love. Yes, love! Here and there. You think I don't know what I'm talking about..."

"—I don't *care* what you're talking about!"

Lawring wrenched away from the older man, threw open the door and half ran to the car and flung himself inside. Groping in his pocket for the ignition key, he watched Franz standing on the front stoop, his silvered hair awry, waving one hand at him wildly.

"All right," Franz was shouting, "go on—with your black metal toy you think will solve things for you... Go on, hunt the poor fool, track him down—only watch out for what you will find there. Watch out!" Lawring started the engine and swept out of the drive; and Franz Hoelder suddenly darted toward the car, still waving his arm. "Watch out!" he cried. "You may find out more than you want—!"

Chapter Twelve

The street was very narrow. The old brick buildings gave the impression of leaning toward each other at the top, as though for moral support. Transistors blared in a jungle-yowl babel from a hundred windows, heavy-breasted women leaned on pink pillows at the sills, children danced on the fire escapes, raced in and around the parked cars in shrill pandemonium, playing stoop-ball, pat-ball, kick-a-bar, some variation of hopscotch he'd never seen before. Doddering old men, stupefied by beer and heat, watched him apathetically from worn steps, babies squalled in carriages, clutching at the light, Lawring moved through it rapidly, his head lowered a little, observing with equal unconcern a young couple embracing in a doorway, a man surreptitiously lifting a bottle of wine out of a baby carriage, a melon lying shattered in a gutter: apple-green rind and pale bloody chunks of meat. There was a park paved in brick where leathery men in straw hats were clustered—a card game, some kind of card game—slapping the cards down with vehement gestures; and Paul Revere, in queue and tricorne and looking astonishingly handsome and virile, glanced down at him from his powerful stallion. *And I on the opposite shore will be.* The sky was heavily overcast now, and the wind came in quick, swirling gusts through the square. He passed the Old North Church, turned left, turned right again.

Endicott Street. The one he wanted. Named for his ancestor, possibly: Governor John of Naumkeag. His mother would know: his mother would be able to tell him who it had been named for, and why, and where they had all lived and what they'd done, and even whether they had been buried in the Old Granary Burying Ground or in the Copp's Hill Cemetery that looked off toward Chelsea and the Navy Yard. A girl passed him with straw blond hair like spun-sugar candy and saucy eyes rimmed with blue eye shadow that flicked at him like a tongue; and farther on three heavy-bodied young men in white shirts were pushing each other around, laughing. One of them called something in Italian and the tallest, a handsome fellow with thick black hair, made a face at the speaker and mouthed the words: "You—kiss—my—ass!"

Stillman, Cooper, Thatcher Streets. All the old names, the people who had come here and made this city; now they were gone, and most of their descendants were gone. His breed was menaced from this quarter too, it wasn't only the Hencheys and McGoverns and Maltisiaks, his kind was being swarmed over by these hordes of swarthy, broad-nosed, flat-upper-lip people who spat on the sidewalk and called *kiss my ass* to each other. But he felt no hatred for this clamor and fury and squalor. He felt very little of anything. He was barely conscious of the dig of the revolver barrel against his left thigh, or the heat, or the burning knot of pain deep in his vitals. He had walked a long way, quite a long way really since he had, for no quite discernible reason, parked his car back on Cambridge Street, near Bowdoin Square. But he wasn't tired at all; his legs seemed to float out ahead of him like dream legs, effortless and tireless and perfunctory, they would carry him for a thousand miles if need be, past taverns and funeral parlors and pastry shops where kids clustered around the glass counter and housewives argued and flashed their hands like flags...

132. Without pausing he turned and went up the cracked stone steps and into the hall. A woman with white hair and a dark, lugubrious expression had watched him from the stoop, impassively. Eight, ten names. The outside door was open. Yes, there it was: *Castaldo*. Just the single name. That meant he was probably living alone. 3 B. A good six or seven people had seen him enter. Well, it didn't matter. So much the worse for them. He climbed the stairs through odors of fish and cabbage and garlic and a sour, full smell like vomit and rancid wine; on around the first landing and up again, past the doors standing ajar, the sententious clamor of radio announcers over half a dozen stations with the six o'clock news, telling of the arrest of seventeen more Negroes in Jackson, Mississippi, a full-scale attack by the Vietcong in the Mekong Delta area, the search for

the killer-abductor of a fifteen-year-old girl in the desert
badlands near Fallon, Nevada, which was still going on without
success. Lawring smiled grimly, reached the third floor landing
and walked to the end of the hall. 3 B. He knocked, a sharp,
peremptory rap. Earlier, driving in through the summer Sunday
traffic, he had decided he would play it completely by ear. If
someone came to the door he would force his way in. If anyone
called, "Who is it?" he would sing out: "*West*ern Union!" and
then force his way inside. If there were just a girl in the
apartment, or parents, he would hold them there until his man
came back.

No answer. Better. Best of all. He looked around him. Only
one door was open on the floor, and whoever lived there was
either down in the street or in the far end of the apartment. He
pulled the string of keys from his coat pocket. Ancient Corbin
mortise lock, lever tumbler: simple enough. As an architect and
member of the Metropolitan Planning Board he had masters for
a hundred like it. Someone on the landing below yelled: "*Gloria!*
I'm going over to Angelo's!" There was an answering shout, then
the bounding thump of rubber soles taking the stairs three at a
time. Lawring ran through the keys, easily, without haste. The
radio inside the open door was saying rapidly:

"... the sixty-one-year-old insurance executive apparently
left no note in explanation for his wife and family, but Mrs.
Enderson said that her husband had been depressed ever since
his return from the Harschman Clinic in Danvers, the week
before..."

On the fourth try the lock turned. He stepped inside quickly,
eased the door shut behind him. A shabby little room, cramped
as a foyer, gray with the shades drawn against the heat. A worn
wine-red sofa with sagging springs and rumpled pillows jammed
in the corners, green casual chair with a torn arm; cheap pine
end-table, its shellac surface flaking away from a dozen glass
rings like some cryptic design. A lamp in the shape of a ship's
wheel, a calendar with the print of a clipper ship on the wall
between the window and the doorway to the bedroom. He could
be asleep in there, or a girl could be, or a relative. Lawring
crossed the living room in three soundless strides and glanced
into the bedroom, then the toilet. No one. The little closet of a
kitchen had a single coffee cup, one plate with a slice of toast

scalloped by three bites. He lived alone, then. Lone wolf. Of course.

Back in the living room he stood uncertainly, listening. Everything had a burnished quality that seemed to reach out and seize hold of him. That absurd ship's-wheel lamp, that ripped and dirty casual chair were the quaking, luminous essence of chair and lamp and there were no others anywhere. It was as though for years he had been semi-conscious or on drugs, and had only begun to sense things around him sharply for the first time. On the end table lay a souvenir ashtray from Quebec and a pack of cigarettes. Lucky Strikes. He stared down at them—on an impulse drew one out and put it between his lips, lighted it from a book of matches adorned with a yellow inverted triangle inscribed with a huge black question mark. *Want to be the life of the party?* the folder said. *Learn the secrets of the great actors, the art of make-up as practiced by famous stars. Thrill guests with impromptu performances and imitations, fool your own family, friends, job associates with these amazing disguises. Earn up to $500 a week in night clubs. Write for our kit and free instruction booklet: Box 3997, Chicago Ill. . . .*

He tossed the matchbook on the table. He had stopped smoking six years ago, alarmed at his shortness of wind after a game of squash with Chuck Allerton. The first inhalation produced a sharp giddiness, like the initial instant of loss of balance. He remembered he hadn't eaten anything since breakfast; but now his hunger had left him, supplanted by this hard, indelible *tangibleness* which cloaked everything around him. He peered at the cigarette in his hand, then at the pack on the table . . . He had never smoked a Lucky Strike before in his life. Why was he smoking one now? His mouth was bone dry, his eyes filled, the peripheral vertigo increased; he started to cough, suppressed it and sneezed instead, wiping his eyes with the back of his hand.

He went back into the cubicle of a bedroom again. The closet door was open. Hanging from the rod were a blue serge suit and a windbreaker and two short jackets and a hip-length mackinaw. Why were they all short coats? There was no raincoat. A pair of black loafers, nicely shined, were on the floor, and beside them a ragged old pair of sheepskin-lined slippers. At the back stood a brand new Samsonite suitcase in saddle tan, still with its sales ticket tied to the handle. That surprised him; he straightened slowly and let his eyes roam over the bureau top, which was cluttered with old ties, still knotted, more books of matches, a pearl-handled jackknife, and several letters. Lawring picked one of them up, tossed it away in sudden irritation. No: he was damned if he was going to pry into the bastard's personal affairs. He had come here to do one thing and he could do it; and that was that. You could hate a man's guts for trying to destroy your life, you might even have come to the conclusion that the world would be well rid of his particular kind of monster—but you didn't go rummaging through his personal effects. He had always had very strong feelings about that kind of thing. In the replacement depot at Soissons a huge Indiana farm boy named Harden, a good-natured simpleton and a bully, had once picked up a letter from Lawring's cot and started to read it aloud to the hut. He remembered a roaring in his head like the prelude to fainting, and the next thing he knew he was on top of Harden in one corner of the hut and five of the others were trying to pry his fingers from Harden's throat. Several of the replacements had regarded him as a dangerous crackpot after that episode, but neither Harden nor anyone else had ever considered fooling around with his mail again...

He snorted, pressed the back of his hand against his cheek and nose. Scruples. Scruples and principles. He had entered this man's domain—such as it was—by stealth, he was guilty of breaking and entering, of illegal entry anyway, he was going to threaten him with a deadly (and concealed) weapon—why in God's name should he harbor any compunctions about reading his mail? This Castaldo had illegally entered *his* home, had assaulted his wife and played lord of the manor there for over an hour—it was an eye for an eye and a tooth for a tooth, dog eat dog and all the rest, wasn't it? Why shouldn't he go through the bureau, see if he had a gun—or at least check for that knife of his? Maybe he was insane, dangerously so, maybe he always carried a gun or knife on him, lots of these types did, it gave them a sense of security, their paranoia was lulled or fed or whatever paranoia needed, by the presence of cold iron in one's pocket. Perhaps he would go crazy when confronted—possibly there was something in those bureau drawers that would tell him something he very much needed to know about Castaldo. Who did he think he was fooling, standing in another man's house and prating about moral scruples at a time like this?

"... It's going to be the death of you." Janet, bending over him in the quilted blue dressing gown he'd given her, her hair beautifully disheveled.

"What's that?" he'd asked her, amused.

"Your New England conscience. It's going to drive you to an early grave." The first year in the house at Holcomb Hill, a sparkling October morning with the maples like bronze and golden towers and the air bathed in crystal; a Saturday morning and he had said he really ought to go in to the office, and she had wanted to go on a picnic.

"You know what's going to happen to you?" she'd said in the light, teasing voice he loved. "You're going to be healthy and wealthy and dead from overwork and no play, and you're going to be at the River Styx, standing on the shore with all the other poor devils, wanting to be ferried over into Paradise. And Creon or Criton or whoever it is—you know, the leathery old gaffer that paddles the boat back and forth—is going to say: 'All right, son, you can come aboard if you can remember *one day* you threw away completely. Just plumb wasted, without a tap of work or chores or anything else.' And you know what?—you're not going to be able to think of one." He was slumped on the enormous living room couch in a welter of newspapers and coffee cups, feet stretched out like old logs, and she was standing in front of him, her hands on her hips, head on one side; her hair was full of silvery glints and hollows. "And each time the boat lands and all the others are clambering on board to be taken over to Paradise he'll chaw down on his quid of tobacco and spit on his hands and holler, 'Well? You remembered one yet?' and you'll have to shake your head at him sorrowfully, over and over. How'll you like that?"

"Not very much, I guess."

"You're such a *vexing* man," she said judiciously, as though he were one of several pairs of gloves before her on a counter at Sterns. "You're big and strong and good-looking and intelligent—well, *fairly* intelligent as big-and-strong-and-good-looking men go. You dress reasonably well—for a crusty, parsimonious old Yankee, that is—you read the necessary papers and magazines and you mix drinks well and at times you can almost be charming..." Her eyes roamed over his face, sparkling with glee, and she put her teeth on her lower lip. "But you have absolutely no capacity for dolce far niente."

"What's that?"

"You see? You don't even know what it means. It's the most important foreign phrase in your life and you don't know it at all... Come on," she said softly. "Waste this day with me. All of it. Who would you rather spend it with?"

"Nobody," he answered in all sober truth. "Nobody at all." And reclining there looking up at her, her lovely animate face with its rich chestnut hair and her fine lithe body, it came over him like a thunderclap that nothing in his whole life would ever be so important as this day with her, wrapped up in her presence, loving her... He reached out and drew her down to him.

"All right," he said gently. "We start right now."

"Sweet—" Her mouth curved in that slow, tantalizing smile and he kissed it, and it stopped smiling. And then neither of them said anything more and the sunlight, filtered through the big sugar maple outside, washed the room in waves of deepening gold...

There was a burst of laughter from down in the street, a chorus of male voices in crashing laughter; and Lawring put his fist to his cheek. Standing in this mean little bedroom remembering that dancing October day with all its indolence and ecstasy, its sheer careless exuberance, the knot of pain in his belly swelled in a rush, clenched and contorted with an intensity that made him clamp his hands to his sides and gasp, his eyes squeezed shut. Then after a moment it passed, and he took a puff on the cigarette and wiped his forehead with the heel of his hand, and looked around him.

There was a picture on the end wall, or rather a frame with its picture covered by a sheet of brown paper and held at the edges with Scotch tape. Stepping up to it he peeled back one of the pieces of tape and lifted the paper—started as his own image leaped at him. A mirror. A perfectly good, uncracked, unbroken mirror. His brows drew down, he lowered the sheet of paper as though he'd seen something unspeakably shameful, and again looked around him warily. But still he did not open the bureau drawers. He wanted to; but he could not. Down in the courtyard someone shouted: "I'm telling you it's going to *rain!*" and someone else answered scornfully, "You think so..." their voices sinking into the wash of other noises like figures submerged in quicksand.

He glanced around for an ashtray to put his cigarette and his eye caught on the glass in the corner of the windowsill; a jelly glass, with what looked like several chestnuts lying at the bottom—but staring at them he knew they were not chestnuts, and before he'd picked up the glass he knew what they were. He poured several of the leather buttons into the palm of his hand, studying them as though they were the very rarest of jewels. Proof. If proof were needed. He saw that the strap of one was cut; recalling the cut segment of leather on the jacket he slipped it along with two others into his trouser pocket, then replaced the remainder and set the glass back in the corner of the windowsill. This time he went up to the bureau and put his hand on the top right drawer; but still he could not open it.

He went back into the living room and looked about aimlessly. A stack of newspapers in the corner by the couch, and on the windowsill two books. *The Red and the Black,* which seemed to be filled with a wad of newspaper clippings, and *Cyrano de Bergerac.* "An educated one," he said between his teeth, "an *educated* creep," and was filled with boundless rage. He picked up the Stendhal, which was worn with use, flipped open the cover and glanced idly at the clippings, and saw immediately that they were about the case; all neatly trimmed and kept in strict chronological order. Lawring turned them one by one, reliving the whole hideous episode—the first lurid disclosures, the police surmises, the discovery of the jacket, the dreary procession of suspects, and the final apprehension of Roche in yesterday's editions.

He put them back neatly inside the cover and leafed through the novel. Many passages were underlined, some with a double bar. Four pages from the end of the book the sentence was heavily marked: *"What will I have left if I despise myself?"* and inside the back cover was a flight ticket to Mexico City. The date was for July 8—and Lawring realized with a shock that it meant the next day. One-way ticket. To Mexico City. He was skipping out—the miserable creep had decided to fold his tents and silently steal away! Slick enough. Lawring found he was trembling with anger again, quivering with a desire for vengeance. The filthy rotten swine! It was all he could do to restrain himself from slamming the book against the opposite wall. I am being rewarded, he told himself wryly, for not going through his bureau drawers. He put the novel down and picked up the *Cyrano*. This was even more worn with re-reading. Dozens of places were underscored, and with marginal comments; a passage in Act Two was bracketed with red crayon, and he read it slowly.

> in a word,
> I am too proud to be a parasite,
> And if my nature wants the germs that grows
> Towering to heaven like the mountain pine,
> Or like the oak, sheltering multitudes—
> I stand, not high it may be—but alone!

He closed the book on his thumb. He had seen the play at the Colonial long ago; his mother had taken him. One of those perennial farewell performances of Walter Hampden's. All he could remember now was a pastiche of flamboyant costumes and bombast, the flicker of rapiers, and an old man sitting in the dying light with the red-stained bandage around his head. *My white plume.* And then through the falling leaves the curtain. How long ago that seemed! Third form at St. Mark's, he was best athlete in his form and fifth in studies, the whole world opening up before him, his life charted on a golden highway gleaming like the State House dome, all their lives were—and now Perk Houghton was head of Canberra Corporation and Dink Ryder had a Pulitzer Prize in journalism and Jumbo Fralingham was a surgeon at Peter Bent Brigham and Chuck was Consul General at Bonn... and his life was on the edge of ruin, home and wife and reputation trembling in the balance because of the whim of a vicious piece of scum who ought to be wiped off the face of the earth—

He felt himself swaying, and pressed thumb and finger to his closed eyes. *Not high it may be—but alone.* Another world. Boston had been another world then, a different city invested with gentility and grace, and on vacations he could mount the stairs to the tinkle of cups and saucers, where in the long living room the Parnassians would be sitting in a large, vague circle.

His mother or Mrs. Purcell would be reading, the single voice in soft, unhurried cadences (they would be reading Hawthorne or Emerson or Henry James, or possibly Santayana or Van Wyck Brooks) and there they would all sit—erect, intent, in perfect silence, with the shadowed indelibility of a Dutch portrait, and almost as still: Mrs. Haddon, who had gout; Miss Pipersham, who was very rich and who darned her own stockings over a blue spunglass egg; Mrs. Vassall, whose breast was like a great bass drum and who had once been head of the Watch and Ward Society, and little Miss Barrows, who was ninety-one and loved the Boston Red Sox with a holy passion (she could quote the batting averages at you like any fourteen-year-old boy); now and then she took a pinch of snuff from a tortoise-shell snuff box her great-great-grandfather had used when he had been governor of Massachusetts Bay Colony. And there was Miss Whittier, whom the older women called Tinker, and who was a militant pacifist. She was eighty-three now and wore faded silk dresses that smelled of crushed lavender, but in her day she had led protest marches against Admiral Horthy and picketed the Japanese delegation at Geneva. She and the Queen of Greece had been old school friends; and once through the Queen's good offices she had obtained an audience with the King, and after two hours of unflagging and utterly irresistible argument had persuaded him to abandon his plans for a war of revenge against Turkey. She liked to wear rouge and on festive occasions drank a little sherry in a small stem glass...

And there were the younger women, Mrs. Shippard and Miss Burcliffe and Chuck's mother, who refused to sew or knit during the reading and sat with her hands folded and the trace of a smile on her face, placid and at rest, as well she might after bearing nine children and running three households each year...There they sat in the gentle, faintly green light, hearing about the Boston of a hundred years ago, the years of Boston's primacy and glory, when a citizen was known to his fellows, when a man's word was his bond and the New England conscience had been the standard of conduct for a restless continent; there they sat, listening, occasionally exchanging a glance or a nod while in the westering light the motes drifted down, turning softly, delicately, like flecks of the most carefully burnished gold—

There was a step in the hall, the hard clack of a key. No. Not

in the living room—let him come in and close the door behind
him. Quick as thought Lawring darted into the bedroom and
stood just inside the doorway. The *Cyrano* was still in his hand;
he tossed it soundlessly on to the bed and put his hand on his
belt. The key rattled and clacked again. Round, voluminous
minutes seemed to pass as he waited, erect, his back flat against
the woodwork. His head was throbbing but he felt surprisingly
calm and sure. Everything lay in a pool of perfect clarity: the
ribbing of a sweater draped over the foot of the bed was a manila
cable, a pair of loafers under the dresser gleamed like the soul
and body of all leather ever tanned and cured.

The door opened; there was a little pause, then it clicked shut.
The person cleared his nose with a quick, guttural sound and
there was the fibrous whack of a newspaper dropped or thrown
on a hard flat surface.

Now.

He drew the revolver from his belt and swung into the
doorway. A thin face, dark. Large dark eyes now white with
surprise, mouth open. The man, in the act of reaching for the
package of Lucky Strikes on the end table, froze, his whole body
contorted oddly. Then it began slowly to straighten. Lawring's
amazement knew no bounds.

"So it's you," he said with a sigh of air; remembering the face
with many others at the North End Citizens' Committee
hearings. Once he had even got up and spoken; only then the
eyes had been narrowed, the features tight with hostility.

"I get it," he said, and nodded. "I see."

Castaldo made no reply. His glance had frozen on the gun.
When Lawring spoke it had darted to his face; but it was back on
the gun again.

"All right," Lawring said. "Sit down." Castaldo still made no
move, remained in the partial crouch, half-turned, as though to
dodge the menace of the weapon. "I said *sit down,*" Lawring
repeated. "No—over there. On the couch." Castaldo relaxed a
bit then and shrugged, sat down on the sofa, whose springs
moaned softly like struck wires. His eyes kept whipping around
the room, as if he were trying to will his body out of there,
somehow, anywhere—into one of the cracks high on the wall or
the pipe-like ventilator that wound its way along the ceiling like
a fat white boa constrictor to the recess above the open window,

through which cries and calls and snatches of song were rising in tumultuous medley.

"All right," Lawring repeated, and half sat on the arm of the chair. "Now I might as well tell you right off you've got a choice. A very simple choice." He paused; he was amazed at how flat and factural his voice sounded. "You're either going to write out and sign a confession about what you did to my wife on June sixth. Or I'm going to kill you. Right here in this room. Do you understand?"

In a dead, sullen tone Castaldo said: "I don't know what you're talking about."

"Oh, yes you do. We won't have any of that nonsense. The buttons are right there in the bedroom. And I've been reading your collection of clippings. If we needed a clincher. That was real careless of you, wasn't it?" With his free hand he reached into the breast pocket of his jacket, drew out several folded sheets of paper and a pen and tossed them on to the sofa. "Go ahead, buster. Write it out."

"Came all prepared, didn't you?"

"Don't be tough, buster. You've picked the wrong moment. Believe me. Don't play tough with me. I mean every word I say." Castaldo was staring at the floor. "Or if you want I'll dictate it and you can just write it down. You *can* write, can't you?"

Castaldo's eyes shot back to him, bright with hatred. "Yes. I can write."

"That's good. Go ahead, then. Write."

There was a short silence. Castaldo drew a slow, deep breath and then reached over and took a cigarette out of the pack on the table and lighted it. In a very calm voice he said: "You don't really think I'm going to write anything, do you?"

"Yes. Oh yes. I do." Lawring could feel the blood quaking in his chest and throat and it angered him. "I'll have to make you do it, then."

"You've got your work cut out for you."

"All right," Lawring answered tightly. "You've got your choice." He glanced at the black face and greenish-white numerals of the combat chronometer, which made him think of the jewelry case and the Stillson wrench slipping and the early morning with its sticky, metallic light. That morning. Jesus, he thought with a throb of pure anguish, following the spidery, darting course of the sweep second hand. That stupid leak in the sillcock. Oh Jesus.

"Three minutes," he said aloud. "Three minutes from now. Seven twenty-six. If you haven't picked up that pen and started writing by then I'm going to shoot you dead."

The word rang in the little room. Castaldo sat picking dirt out from under his nails with a match stub. His face looked sullen and bored, but a muscle high in his cheek flickered. Lawring was flooded with rage. To be toyed with like this! It was unendurable. His hand tightened on the gun butt.

"You don't seem to think I'm in earnest about this, Castaldo," he murmured, trying to hold his voice low. "You seem to think I'm bluffing, I haven't the guts to go through with it. Is that the idea? Is it?"

Castaldo still sat studiously cleaning his nails; all at once he raised his eyes to Lawring's—a brief gaze in which the architect could read contempt, amusement, and the most savage defiance. Then he looked down again at his hands.

"All right," Lawring said. "If that's how it is... Just as a token."

He raised the revolver until it pointed just outside Castaldo's left shoulder, and squeezed the trigger.

The roar was tremendous: a reverberation like an apotheosis of all destruction, a thunderous instant vast as time itself when everything—radios, cars, the cries of children—seemed to stop, to hang arrested, as though the film of our time had broken in its even flow. Then some omniscient hand had apparently mended the break: a feather of smoke swirled away from the barrel, and the sounds of life began again. Castaldo had jumped with the explosion, an absurd lurch, and cried out, *"Jesus!"* then had fallen back, and for the shadow of an instant Lawring thought he had hit him. Then he realized he hadn't, it had been only a reflex spasm, and he felt a thick surge in his bowels, half nausea, half release. An hour seemed to have gone by since the gunshot. Castaldo was looking around wildly now, his face screwed tight with fear, his hands gripping the sofa, his knees flexed. He's afraid, Lawring told himself, at last he's afraid of me... and the thought almost made him weep.

"That's just to let you know," he said levelly, but his voice cracked and betrayed him. "Don't look at that door. Nobody heard a thing. As if they could *hear* a shot in this filthy bedlam . . . I'm not bluffing, Castaldo. Before God I'm not. *Don't look at that door!* I could cut you down before you got halfway over there. Before anyone came to save you, either. As though you're worth saving, you despicable son of a bitch . . . Why did you *do* it?" he heard himself saying hoarsely, as though the solitary shot had destroyed all his calm, his inflexible resolve. "Sneak into a man's home when he's gone and take advantage of a woman alone—?"

"—Homes!" Castaldo's face broke apart all at once, a violent grimace; he seemed to have completely forgotten the gun. "*Homes*—don't talk to me about homes! What are you tearing the whole North End apart for?—why did you smash it to pieces with an iron ball, the house I was born in? It gives you a big thrill, doesn't it—you get your rocks off smashing up the houses of the dirty Italians . . . You think nobody can figure you out, is that it? No, of course not—nobody's going to blast *your* home, not on Beacon Hill, out in Holcomb—no, it's always our homes that have got to go—ours, ours!" He struck the couch beside him in a spasm of grief. "You frigging monster!—you haven't got the feelings of a lizard . . ."

He stopped, panting, his mouth open. It was as if he had only just realized what he had said.

"Go on," Lawring answered. He could feel the palm of his hand tighten on the butt of the revolver, an involuntary pressure; the thin face in front of him blurred, narrowed in fluttering, wobbling strips of face. "Go on. Have your say."

"—Always an easy solution for you people, isn't it? Something bothers you, offends your lovely polite tastes—just tear it down, that's all, blow it to hell and gone, kick the shit out of it! More bang for a buck. The scum will move somewhere else, anywhere you want them to—some barracks or a rathole farther away, so you won't have to know about them, you just push them and they'll go, they always go . . . Well, there are some who won't be pushed, you understand?—some of us who won't be pushed forever—"

"Then why didn't you come to me, have it out with me!" Lawring demanded bitterly. "Why didn't you have the courage to face me on it—why did you have to rape my wife, tear my home apart—?"

"You!" Castaldo laughed—a burst of laughter, full of hate. "You! You wouldn't even see me, you wouldn't even know I was

there . . . No—you'd have got your lawyers and senators to wipe me out without a trace, you'd go right along without seeing me at all. It's what you always do, your kind—hide away behind your money and your influence, do what you want to do all the time . . ." His eyes glowed like raked embers. "Sure—but *she* saw me, all right—*she* knew I was there . . ."

"It gave you satisfaction, it gave you a big boot, didn't it, to take on a defenseless woman you'd never laid eyes on before and—"

"What? You tell me that! . . ." Castaldo's lip curled in disgust. "Never laid eyes on her—I sat on the beach there with her for three hours while you were fooling around with your lousy yacht—"

"You what?" Lawring said.

"I met you that day, you were going sailing. You going to deny it? Yes, she invited me down, I saved her bacon in that car accident in Brookline, they could have taken her for every cent she had. I drove down to see her. Your folks' place in Brewster . . ."

Lawring blinked. He had no recollection of this . . . then all at once he did remember—a dim memory of some meeting, a fellow in dark clothes: a cab driver. But his face—

"No—you don't remember, do you," Castaldo was saying savagely, "of course not, you're so frigging important you can't even *see* anyone else. We don't piss champagne all day long . . ."

"And you . . ." Lawring felt shaken, weak as a reed in the wind. He didn't think he could get the words out. "And—you have been seeing my wife?" He had said it.

"No, not for ten years, not since that afternoon . . . but I *remembered!*" Castaldo cried, and his face was tight with triumph. "And *she* remembered, too . . ."

"She knew it was you—?"

"No. Not with her head. But in here—" he jabbed his chest with his thumb "—in here she knew . . ."

". . . You knew I was gone."

"Of course I knew. What do you think? I've sat at 128 and watched you for years, off and on. I drive a hack. I even took you home once. That sleet storm last winter, you didn't have a hat, remember? I know everything there is to know about you; and Janet, too . . ."

"—Don't mention my wife's name," Lawring said thickly.

"Sure, your wife—you're so busy racking up other people's lives you've forgotten all about her, too—you don't even love her, you haven't time for that, Christ no, why should you?—all the rest of it gives you so damned much charge . . ." His voice was suddenly feverish and shrill. "You can't even satisfy her—but I did, I reached her in a rush and took her with me!—I thought about her and watched over her for ten years through thick and thin, and never stopped—and you don't even know she's there half the time, that jewel! Don't talk to me about your wife . . ."

". . . How—" The word stuck, dryly, emptily. Lawring felt as though a knife had been thrust deep in his guts and was calmly resting there. All that hard bright steel. His lips were like drying leather. "How—do you know that?" he asked in a whisper.

"How?—I felt it, I saw it!" Castaldo's face was alight, almost ecstatic. "It was there, to feel! She loves a thrill, it's there in her face. She's alive, a young tree—what do you give her? . . . You think I'm stupid, I don't know something like that?—just a dumb clod, no sensibility, no understanding at all?"

Lawring licked his lips. A wave of despair black as a mountain went over him. "You're mad," he breathed.

"You're totally mad . . ."

"You think so—!"

"I don't believe you."

"Ask her, then. Go ahead! I knew she was mine the moment I saw her. On that street in Brookline, ready to cry. Where were you? Out in your yacht, I suppose—with your clients . . ."

"Ten years," Lawring said numbly. "You saw her ten years ago . . . You monster. You wretched monster."

"Oh no—not this time! *I'm* not the monster this time . . ."

Lawring pulled himself to his feet. All the blood had been siphoned out of him in some subtle, deadly way while he sat there. He swayed over Castaldo, gripping the gun desperately; it seemed to be anchored in space, something to cling to, something to give him purpose in the midst of this maelstrom of madness and terrible revelations. Around them the dirty little room slid toward dusk.

". . . I'm going to kill you, Castaldo," he heard himself saying. "Can you get that through your head? I know: you think I'm afraid to do it, afraid of what they'll do to me. But you're wrong. I don't care *what* they do to me." He shook his head slowly from side to side. "I'm not going to try to beat it, I'm not going to sneak out on it... I'm going to wipe you off the face of the earth," he declared, his voice shaking, "and then I'm going to turn myself in."

"All right." Castaldo stared up at him. His face was slick with perspiration and his eyes were dilated, but they were steady and very clear. "Good, then, go ahead—it doesn't matter... I've won!" he cried softly. "Shoot me, go ahead. You've recognized me then, you've made us equals..."

Lawring's head went back. "What do you care?—you'll be dead, you God damned crazy fool—dead and buried and done with..."

"—Not everything, Lawring! That's not all of it. You think you people are the only ones with a code? I've got one, too. Sure—" his voice broke now, he swallowed and hurried on; great gouts of sweat were standing on his face, "—you can finish me and nobody knows at all. But *I*—" he jabbed his breast again, "—*I* know, and you know, even if you get off light, and—" his eyes blazed terribly in the gloom "—and *she* will know most of all! ... I'll trade," he cried savagely, "I'd trade five lifetimes for this moment, don't you think I won't—I'd even trade a life like yours..."

There was a little silence. Down in the courtyard, probably at the back windows of the tavern he'd passed, several boys were singing along with a jukebox, a ragged chorus under the band singer's shrill soprano, and from the wall behind the ship's-wheel lamp a television voice, some commentator probably, turned up very loud, pounded on. Castaldo ran his sleeve across his eyes and then gripped his hands together between his thighs.

"All right," he muttered. "All right. Only let's get it over with. Come on... *Come on*," he shouted, looking up.

Lawring felt sick. Physically ill, on the verge of nausea so great he didn't think he could contain it. Sharp pains drove across his eyes and down the back of his skull; the room turned dark, lightened, dipped into deeper darkness and the floor heaved... It was horrible: he was nailed to this spot, chained and manacled to this room forever, all his thoughts in a turmoil, torn in pieces with discoveries too painful to absorb; rooted here pointing an ancient over-size revolver at this handsome, sweating Italian face. Condemned to an eternity of nausea and confusion and despair while he gulped in slow, deep lungfuls of air and watched distantly Castaldo, who was gazing up at him now with the look of a miler nearing the tape, a look desperate and glowing in the dusk, a terrible, agonized eagerness—

He turned and walked to the door, yanked it open and slammed it behind him. On the top step he stumbled and nearly fell, and only saved himself by clutching at the iron railing at the last instant—a wrench that sent forks of pain dancing up his arm and shoulder. Halfway down the stairs he remembered the gun dangling from his nerveless fingers and he jammed it back in his belt and buttoned his jacket, all three buttons, with great care. A couple passed him on the next flight, coming up, the girl with her arm around the boy, giggling and talking to him in a high rapid voice, but Lawring couldn't hear a word she said.

Outside it was nearly dark. He put his hand to his mouth, swerved toward the gutter and bent over, but nothing came up. His stomach turned on itself and he retched once, again; then walked on weakly. White shirts, yellow and orange summer blouses of the girls bobbed and floated in the dusk like flowers, and the street cries were muted now—as though sound itself was like a flower closing, its petals wearied by the long hot day, seeking rest and quiet. Seeking sleep. His head was aching so fiercely he could hardly see. He walked on through the narrow streets, past abandoned pushcarts and empty stalls, past shattered walls and mountainous heaps of rubble, gray in the sinking twilight. Urban Renewal.

The look on his face! The sheer hatred . . . Lawring cut across the razed area, stumbling over the chunks and hillocks of battered concrete and brick. No, it wasn't hatred, exactly. It was more like—it was more like contempt. He was looking at me with contempt, Lawring thought with raging wonder. And why not?—why in Christ's sweet name not? What did he say? He said he would trade five lifetimes for that moment, he'd even trade a life like mine. Powder rose gritty and acrid around him, making his eyes sting. He sat there and looked at me and beat me. He faced me down.

Lawring turned his ankle and almost went sprawling; sat down on a piece of cornice and chafed the foot with both hands. The physical pain was an actual relief. And I thought it was blackmail, he told himself with a groan. More fool me. But if you loved someone, if you lived with a person for ten years and loved him—

On his right the girders of the Expressway rose like pillars of night, crowned with the diadem lights of cars. Watching this slow parade of home-comers returning from Revere Beach and Marblehead and Cohasset and Cape Cod he smiled to see each one of them—dazed from the sun now and weary, squinting into the tail-lights ahead, gripping the wheel a little too hard, the kids sunk deep in sleep in the back seat, sprawled in a welter of sweat-shirts and soggy bathing suits and deflated rubber rafts and plastic ice containers and dented tin pails; speeding and slowing with the thickening traffic, half-listening to the Sunday evening news, conscious of the rasp of sand in the scalp and between the toes, already summoning up energy for tomorrow morning... What were they doing? Why in God's name were they doing it, over and over? And with the slow wash of despair he realized he didn't know anything at all about the occupants of those cars; the appurtenances, yes, the frills and trappings, but he knew nothing of what they were really like—their shadowed fears and hopes, the way they looked at the world in all its menacing complexity, what it was that kept them pacing their iron treadmill year on dreary year...

He had never in all his life felt so desolate and wretched and alone. Sitting there under the black, webbed shadow of the Expressway he thought: It's impossible, completely impossible—why should I believe him—a raving madman who tapes up mirrors and pores over *Cyrano de Bergerac*; a madman and a fool?

He got to his feet thinking, I've got to see her, I've got to get in touch with her right now, right away, I must go out to Swampscott and get her—and then: No. I don't want to see her. Not now. Not for a while... And what in God's name would he say to her when he did see her? What was there to say?

He walked past the site where the old Williams Book Store had been, with its absurdly overcrowded shelves, its prints in splotched and yellowed paper and its faded maps and the neatly lettered signs tacked here and there which said, among other things: *What we inherit from our fathers we must earn in order to possess*... Uphill now and to the left, moving with the insentient sureness of familiarity, along the curve of Cornhill and into Scollay Square with its gin mills and arcades, a jiggle of lights where sailors fired rifles at sliding toys and newsboys waved their papers at him like the half-furled flags of disaster; and all at once he found himself walking, not down Cambridge toward his car but across the square and up Pemberton Place, toward the Hill—past the site of Daniel Maude's First Free School in the New World, the birthplace of Elihu Yale, the plaque commemorating the home of the Reverend John Cotton, who had said: "If the people be governors, who then shall be governed?" Past the law bookshops with their rows of grim black and brown tomes. Silent leges inter arma, lex talionis, a law for the lion and a law for the lamb. Was that true? Who had said it? He had been brought up to believe there was only one law.

But perhaps he had been brought up to believe in a fallacy . . .

The façades at Ashburton Place were tiny and withdrawn. This would all be torn down too, to make room for something else, something big and glassy and impersonal. There was Ford Hall where as a schoolboy he had gone and listened to Stefan Zweig and Thomas Mann and Anton de Haas and Chancellor Gruening, those weary, noble spirits warning them of a nation gone mad, a people that had lost its sense of right and wrong, its respect for the dignity of the individual citizen. Did a whole nation go mad, or did only a few guiding spirits—and then the rest, through apathy, fear, insecurity, ambition, fall meekly into line? Or did everyone go mad, briefly, and the accretion of derangement decide their actions? He wasn't sure: he'd used to believe Fascism and the war had been the work of a few madmen, psychopaths and paranoids—but now that didn't seem true, somehow. He himself had gone mad briefly this evening, Castaldo—oh Jesus, Castaldo!—had been mad for ten demonic, tigerish years, Janet had been mad for a few moments that night . . . Had she? We were all mad, all sane, all certain and unsure and perceptive and blind as bats, it seemed. Franz would have the answer to something like this.

Yes. Franz.

He turned on to Mount Vernon Street, passed under the State House, plodding wearily on the slick, undulant brick, conscious of the ache in his thighs and calves. He hadn't walked this far in almost twenty years, not since the war. Now again, moving down the street on which he'd been born, toward the ancestral homes of Cabots and Adamses and Searses and Hemenways, he slowed his pace, examining every gate and doorway as though invading enemy soil. When he reached his mother's house he stopped across the street and leaning against the trunk of one of the elms studied it impassively. The curtains were drawn, there were no lights. His mother was down at Brewster. His home. But tonight nothing was what it seemed to be, nothing was familiar. His sickness, the fire in his belly and the stabbing, persistent pains in his head had changed all that. Even if you were to disregard the curtains the house certainly did look withdrawn, aloof, almost hostile. If he were, say, a Hungarian refugee newly arrived, without money or friends or knowledge of the language, he could not take much comfort from that remote brick façade...

"The place gives me the royal skooks." Janet had said that once, long ago, and rolled up her eyes with that expression of extravagant foreboding that delighted him. Why? he'd wanted to know. "I don't know why—it just does. It's as though there wasn't any other world anywhere else. No San Francisco or Paris or Cairo or Tasmania or anything. It says: *I am all there is. Get lost.* In letters of ice." And then, both dead serious and droll: "I couldn't ever live there, Gard. Will you still love me if I can't?"

"I think so," he'd answered, grinning. "I certainly don't plan to chain you up in it. God knows it's a holy terror to keep up." Thinking, Maybe she'll change her mind after a few years have rolled by and she's grown more familiar with the place, and things are less strange to her. But she never had...

A figure approaching, quite near—a bulky figure, dark gleam of light on the cap bill. Cop. Callahan, coming toward him with that incredibly soundless, unhurried patrolman's tread. The briefest of hesitations, suspicious, quickly calculating—then the start of recognition.

"Mr. Lawring!"

"Hello, Callahan."

"What are you doing mooning under the trees in the dark of night? I almost took you for a nocturnal prowler."

Lawring started at the kindly red face. "I don't know," he said after a moment. "I honestly don't know what I was doing."

Callahan nodded, worked his mouth. "Mr. Lawring, I was

sorry to hear of your trouble. It's a terrible thing. A terrible thing, to happen to so fine a girl as that. Your mother told me all about it one day. If there's anything I can do, now, I want you to call on me."

"Thanks, Callahan."

"Ah, they've all gone to the devil, these young hoodlums." Callahan clicked his tongue once sharply, like a cocked rifle; his fine melodic tenor carried the faintest trace of brogue. "All the bloody murder and destruction on TV and of course they want to emulate it. Fighting like Kilkenny cats, pitched battles in the South End, I could tell you stories that'd make your hair curl... And there's no place to send them, either—the farms are full to bursting, judge can only give them suspended sentences and the punks know it, every last one of them. I've seen them come up down there and defy the bench. They put a premium on being booked, you know: it gives them gang status. Yes. Some status, all right."

He clapped his big hands together, and the knuckles popped like snapping twigs. "Well, what do you want? They see some of those tinhorn hooligans in the unions get away with it, and certain eminent politicians whose names I won't mention, they see that big operator down in New York City make all that money and then skip off to Rio with his boodle when the jig is up, they figure: 'I'm going to get mine, take the system myself.' So they try." He swung away, swung back again with gusto, warming to his theme. "Ah, there's no morality around these days. I remember your father tipped me off to my first pinch. I was a rookie then, just learning the ropes and your father called me over, it was right by that parked Oldsmobile, and he said, 'Officer Callahan, I want you to question that man over there,' and he pointed him to me. 'Why's that, sir?' I said. 'Because,' he said, 'he doesn't belong here on the Hill. He goes out of doors and drives his car around in his shirtsleeves. You look into him.' And do you know, I did—and your father was right. It was the man they wanted."

"That so," Lawring said, vaguely, frowning. He didn't want to stand there passing the time of night with Callahan. Some of the nausea was wearing off now, replaced by an overpowering weariness. What he wanted to do was sit down on the curb and lean back against this tree and go to sleep, for days and days; but he knew he would not fall asleep.

"Ah, your father was a born gentleman. Always knew what was right, and he did it. I remembered seeing him come over the Hill one evening, tearing along—you know, the way he used to walk, as if he was going to a fire—with a scowl on his face black as thunder. 'Why Mr. Lawring, what's the matter?' I asked him. 'I've just made the worst enemy in Greater Boston,' he said, 'I've just got into an unholy row with Jack Brennan.' And he glared at me from under those beetling eyebrows of his and said, 'And I'd do it again—and you can tell him I said so!' You remember that Old Harbor business, all the shenanigans Brennan's crowd were trying to pull over the old government bulkhead lines? That's what it was all about. And he wouldn't give an inch, either. They took it all the way up to the circuit court and he won on it, too. You remember that?"

"No, I'm afraid I don't..."

"No, you wouldn't. That would have been before you were out of school. 'There are two sides to every question,' he used to say, '—but one of them is demonstrably wrong!' Ah, he was a born gentleman." Callahan sighed audibly and shifted his weight. "Well, row the galley."

"What?" Lawring said.

"That's why my wife's old lady used to say. She was French Canuck. That terrible winter of '36 my father and my brother Jack out of work, no money coming in and fourteen mouths to feed, I was wearing newspapers under my blouse that winter, and Hitler and Mussolini screaming for war every night, and then you'd read about some larruping Valhalla of a blowout down in Palm Beach with Russian dukes and dancing girls and feeding caviar to the guests' canines at twenty dollars a throw. And we'd roar at each other with rage, and when we ran out of wind my wife's old lady would turn from the stove and say: 'Well, row the galley.' And she was right, you know? It's all a man can do at times..."

Lawring murmured something inaudible. He felt an overwhelming need to get away from this tiresome old cop with his interminable reminiscences and cunnythumb philosophizing. He had to get away.

"Well, take care," he said, and started to move off up the hill again. "I've got to be going."

"You're not going to stop in, see your mother?"

Lawring turned. "She's on the Cape..."

"No, she isn't. She went out not more than an hour and a half ago. Said she was going to hunt up the worst movie she could find. I told her she'd have a fine job of it."

"I see." It was just like his mother to take it into her head to drive back from Cape Cod in the hottest week of the summer and stay on for a few days; without a word of warning to anyone.

"Well, so long, Mr. Lawring." Now it was Callahan who was moving away up the street, toward Joy. "Don't do anything I wouldn't do."

"I won't."

"One thing," Callahan swung his dark bulk close to him again. "Mr. Lawring, I know how you feel, and I don't blame you a bit after the ordeal you and young Mrs. Lawring have been through. Living out there in the woods and everything. But," he paused and lowered his voice, though there was nobody anywhere near them, "don't be too obvious about it, will you? Some rookie'll spot that hand-cannon and want to run you in and there'll be the devil to pay all around. You know?"

Lawring stared at him. Callahan's eyes under the visor were twinkling. "You could tell," he murmured.

"Plain as the nose on your face. Good evening, Mr. Lawring."

"Good evening, Callahan. Thanks."

He crossed the street and ran up the steps, reaching for his key ring. At the inside door he dropped the ring on the black rubber mat, picked it up and dropped it again; and all at once the reaction hit him full force and he put his fist to his mouth. The knot in his belly redoubled and burned at him like lime. He thought of his mother's fine, firm face and Sonking lying in the street at Diersdorff and the taped mirror in Castaldo's room, and muttered soundlessly, I don't know anything about life. I'm nearly forty years old on this earth and I've just been going through the motions, walking behind a screen—I can't put any of it together, I've made a stupid bloody hash of everything I've touched and that's the sober truth of it...He saw Janet laughing, dreaming, coming toward him with that rueful, little-girl entreaty glowing in her face, tried to thrust it from his mind and couldn't. Swaying in the dark little vestibule smelling of new paint and old rubber he gave vent to a sob of rage and struck his hand against the oak door.

"—I want to do what's right," he said with a groan, and pressed his cheek against the worn wood. "The right thing. I want that—and I swear to God I don't know what is right. I simply don't know..." He had the sensation of joists giving way beneath him, venerable girts and headers snapping like straws, leaving him to plummet a thousand thousand fathoms down. What in Christ's name was right? This Castaldo had violated his wife—and yet he hadn't exactly, it was worse than that, different and worse, and Janet hadn't known who he was but had found out later somehow and then kept it to herself—and then *he* had found out and nearly killed Castaldo; and yet he hadn't...

Oh Jan, Jan, he murmured silently and felt tears burn his eyelids, I've loved you more than anything else on this earth and in a moment you betrayed me, why?—didn't these past ten years mean more than that? We held between us the sense of indissoluble trust, nothing more valuable in earth or high heaven either—why did you do it, why did you betray me?... And now, leaning like a clumsy drunk against the door of his mother's house, choking back his weeping, all he could think of was Janet, her lovely face shining in sunlight, her hair blown sidewise by the wind, shrieking into the driving spray, or picking blueberries in the dove-gray evening air on Nount's Head, her expression placid and intent; or vivid with some hilarious impersonation in the middle of the living room.

"Do you know what I love about you?" she had said once. "The crow's-feet at the corners of your eyes." Her finger had touched them lightly. "They're like no other crow's-feet anywhere else in the world. And the wonderfully aristocratic bump at the bridge of your nose."

"It's been broken three times," he'd answered.

"I know. That only makes it more aristocratic, somehow."

They had wondered if a blood and urine test was required for a marriage license, and she'd exclaimed: "I don't know about you, but I'd rather give 'em urine than blood any day!" and he'd laughed, amused and wildly shocked, stirred by that swift little prickling sensation of delight she could arouse in him by a random word or gesture. There had been the summer his mother had been in Scotland when they had the house in Brewster all to themselves, and waking early they could hear the birds in the garden singing in a clamorous June frenzy. Neither of them knew then the different species and they had hit on the names of famous violinists; the little red-eyed bird with dun and yellow wings was Szigeti, the fat one with the rusty belly and black-and-white tail was Menuhin, the song sparrow was Heifetz, the catbird they named Bumpus after a neighbor in Cambridge who played execrably and was the bane of all amateur groups in the area. "That's enough, Bumpus!" Janet would call, and beat on a pan to frighten the bird away for a little while. That was the summer she found she was pregnant and she had put her head in the hollow of his neck and said, "Do you think I'm going to be an oedipal mother?"

"Of course not," he'd murmured, "no Lawrings have ever been oedipal."

"I know; isn't it comforting?" and she had pinched his navel. "The oedipus complex is a malignant, ubiquitous, lingering disease which has infected everybody in the world except the tribe of Lawrings..."

He thrust himself away from the door with a groan, turned and went out again into the gusty heat; and saw his mother getting out of a taxi. She was talking with the driver—what his father had used to call, somewhat tartly, "Marcia's perennial travel piece"—leaning forward, her hand out for the expected change. She caught sight of Lawring and waved her hand once, a brief, peremptory gesture; got her change and climbed out of the cab and came up to him and kissed him firmly on the cheek.

"What a lovely surprise, dear! How did you know I'd come back to town?"

"I didn't. Callahan just told me."

"Oh yes. Callahan."

"He said you'd gone to the worst movie you could find."

"I did." She laughed once. "I outsmarted myself. It was so bad I couldn't stay through to the end." She preceded him up the steps and opened the door. She seemed to expect him to go in with her, without preamble or inquiry, and this struck him as very singular. "It was all about this dreadful fat-faced man who goes around strangling different young girls because they remind him of his dead sister. Preposterous." She flicked on the hall light. "Gardy, what's the matter? Why, you look simply awful..."

"Yes. I imagine I do."

"Are you coming down with a cold?"

"Bubonic plague, more likely."

She chose to ignore this, as she usually did his efforts at facetiousness. "Do you want something to eat?"

"No, thanks."

"You've got that gaunt, broody look you usually have when you're hungry. Let me get you something."

The thought of food was like an overturned garbage pail in a bath tub. He said: "No. I ate."

"When was that?"

"I don't know when. Let's forget it."

She glanced at him sharply at this. "All right, then, we'll go up." They climbed the long, carpeted flight of stairs to the living room. "I just had to get away," Marcia Lawring said. "I decided it was high time to have the roof shingled, it's beginning to look like a chicken with its feathers blown all the wrong way. And you have to take Walter Atwood when you can get him, you know." She sat down on the Sheraton couch, very erectly, and picked at invisible flecks on the front of her blouse. "Well, they made such an infernal racket yesterday I thought I'd get away for a bit. Do they really need to make that much noise, tacking on a few shingles?"

"They have to drive the nails into the sheating..." He sank into a chair and put his hand over his eyes. He felt so depleted, so frankly and absolutely despairing that to lift both arms above his head seemed beyond him. Flaring against the wall of his mind he saw again the bedlam of the North End, the parade of lights along the Expressway, and then, unrolling as if on some lurid, relentless diorama, the dead gray scaffolding of the North End Towers development he had helped design, rising on a grassless plain like totems to some mocking deity, against a background of smoke and burning; and after them all the towers he had not built—white cruciform shafts standing simple and dramatic against the dense sweep of great trees, reflected in gently meandering pools of water, along whose verdant banks children skipped and sang in heedless delight... He had done nothing. Nothing at all. He had been full of dreams, on fire with energy and high resolve, he had the discipline and fortitude of any twenty men—and it had all gone wrong. What in Christ's name had happened to him?... All at once, with a gripe of panic, he thought of Brian—that bright round vulnerable face, flushed with excitement, rushing toward life. Janet's boy. Yes, but he was his boy, too, with a future he wanted with all his heart to guide. And how could he guide him? What right did he have to think he could guide anybody at all?

His mother was talking about the garden down at Brewster, something about the effect of the salt air on the daphne cneorum and he let her go on, thankful for the comforting timbre of her voice, and let the tumultuous rush of his thoughts, the dead grinding weight of his desolation slide off in darkness. If I had a boat, he thought with the fervent desire of an eight-year-old boy, a beautiful blue-hulled sloop, I'd sail it down the Inland Waterway to the Caribbean and knock around the islands, wear nothing but a pair of raggedy chinos and let my hair grow halfway down my shoulders, lie sprawled on the deck in the shadow of the main and slip past ivory sleeves of sand ringed with palms and the morning sky all purple and rose and coral . . .

He looked up. His mother had stopped talking, was staring at him. "Gardy. That's your father's chair."

"So it is." He looked at his hands on the carved, worn arms. He was surprised himself; but he felt disinclined to move. "So it is," he repeated.

"It's the first time anyone has sat in that chair since your father died." She said this wonderingly, with a trace of reproach, and he looked back at her steadily.

"I seem to be doing things today that haven't been done before," he observed. "At least not very often . . . Maybe it's time somebody sat in it. Have you ever thought of that? Though I may not be the one, of course."

"You're worn to a frazzle," his mother said. "You haven't been taking care of yourself properly." When he made no reply to this she asked: "Are things better with you now?"

"Better?"

"Now that they've caught the person."

He gave a mirthless chuckle and clapped his hands on the chair arms. "No. You couldn't exactly say things are better right now."

"I'm sorry to hear that. What is it, Gardy?"

He studied his mother's face for a moment. That brilliant, expectant gaze before which he'd always quailed—he saw that now, suddenly—had offered up everything on the altar of his filial devotion: his hopes, his little triumphs, his fears and dreams and high ambitions. Everything. Not the war, because she hadn't wanted to hear about that, she knew it had all been boring and unnecessary and dangerous and that was that—so he'd never told her about Brokaw and his fear of rats or when Hendrick's platoon got bombed by mistake at Kronenhalle, the planes diving in and the cries, and how he had raised his fists and screamed his hatred of all planes with whatever markings, friend or foe, and later cried when they found the bodies, bits and pieces; or Sonking lying on the icy cobbles, begging them not to go on and leave him there alone . . .

None of those. But the other things he had brought her with the shy gladness of some eager acolyte—the copy of *Mont-Saint-Michel and Chartres* awarded him for his essay on the Acropolis in fifth form, his football and hockey letters, the Dean's List announcements his sophomore year and later his thesis on Romanesque architecture in Burgundy—had come to her and placed them at her feet, a votive ritual, and then stepped back and waited for the radiant smile of approbation he knew would come . . . Only it never had. Her expression had remained pleasant, gratified, assured—serene with a prospection which seemed to say: Yes, this is fine, of course, this is to be expected; but you are capable of far, far more than this—I know it and so do you. And so each time he had turned away, his heart sore from the withheld balm, and had strode forth to collect still another trophy . . .

He let his hands fall loose over the chair arms, felt the angular pressure of the gun against his thigh bone and belly. Now he had nothing to offer her but frustration and rupture and disaster, the wreckage of his marriage and probably his job. And she would not want to hear that. For her life was erected on an adamantine conviction that mankind progressed steadily, as though on some kind of celestial express elevator, toward better things; that truth and goodness would benevolently, eternally prevail. He had believed that too, hadn't he?

"I wish you'd tell me what you're thinking, Gardy. Won't you?"

He looked at his mother again. He was reminded for no accountable reason of a long-ago afternoon at Symphony when the woman sitting next to them, on his mother's right—a friend of Mrs. Pinchon's presumably, since she was occupying her seat—had begun to cough repeatedly in the middle of a delicate passage. Lawring, more interested in the woman's predicament than the Brahms, had seen the expression of censure settle on his mother's face. Marcia Lawring had stirred, her lips had pursed, she'd glanced at her neighbor twice, severely; then as the compulsive coughing had erupted again had rummaged in her handbag where she invariably carried cough drops, throat lozenges, peppermints and a dozen other miscellaneous winter remedies, and with her eyes still fastened on the restrained, imposing figure of Serge Koussevitsky, drew one out and plumped it into the hand of her neighbor, who gratefully popped it into her mouth. There was silence for several seconds—and then a violent commotion as the lady sprang to her feet with a series of muffled exclamations and fled the hall in the rumble and creaking of chairs. At intermission, when the woman hadn't returned and was nowhere to be found, Marcia Lawring was assailed by uneasiness and began to paw around in her purse. Lawring, standing in the foyer beside Emily, remembered his mother's eyes going quite blank, and then fastening on his with the strangest expression he'd ever seen.

"Gardy," she said. "I didn't give that woman a cough drop. I gave her a plant-tab."

"A what?"

"*A plant-tab,*" she repeated with such sharpness that he winced. "What do you suppose—?" For a moment she looked around the gray, draughty vestibule, chafing her fingers against her palm; then her fine, etched lips drew together again and her eyes narrowed with decision. "You children go back inside," she ordered. "I'll have to miss the Beethoven. I've got to locate that woman."

But this was a crisis, and Lawring and his sister had no desire to sit through the Beethoven if they could avoid it; protesting that they wouldn't desert her under any circumstances, they accompanied their mother to a drugstore on Massachusetts Avenue where they clustered around the last of a series of phone booths. Marcia Lawring called Helena Pinchon; her maid said she was away visiting family out in Lincoln. She then dialed Hough and Gentry, their pharmacist on Charles Street, and was answered by a high-pitched adenoidal voice Lawring and Emily instantly recognized as that of Larry Hraba, the soda-jerk.

"No, I want to speak to Mr. Gentry," Marcia Lawring said. "You tell him I must speak with him immediately. It is an emergency." Mr. Gentry came on. Lawring's mother explained the situation in clear, terse phrases. "What I want to know is, how dangerous is the reaction?"

There was a short pause, and then Mr. Gentry's voice, drier than ever before. "There's no danger, Mrs. Lawring."

"You're quite sure?"

"Yes. Quite sure."

Marcia Lawring stared grimly into the speaker. "After all, I *am* responsible, and if there's any reaction..."

"No, Mrs. Lawring. There's no danger whatsoever." And then, in a sudden crackle of exasperation: "After all, Mrs. Lawring, it's pure manure!"

"... I was thinking of that friend of Mrs. Pinchon and the plant-tab," he said aloud now. "At Symphony."

"Good heavens. Whatever made you think of that?"

"I'm sure I don't know. I've found myself thinking of a lot of curious things these days."

Marcia Lawring seemed to gather herself together, like a horsewoman getting ready to take her mount over a barrier. "You're at an impasse with Janet," she said quietly.

He looked at her. "What makes you say that?"

"Don't you think I've been aware of it? I've seen it coming for years."

"Have you?"

"Yes, of course. I foresaw it, you remember..."

"You did, didn't you?"

"Gardy, I'm your mother and I've known you a good deal longer than she has."

"That's true. You have." He got to his feet and walked over to the window and gazed out at the windy dark, the shiny black helmets of parked cars. "Well, you're wrong," he said. "It hasn't been coming for years. It's just happened. If that's any consolation to anybody."

"Oh Gardy, I am *so* sorry... What do you plan to do?"

Still staring out of the window he smiled; a slow, bitter smile. If he should take the old revolver out of his belt and lay it on the rosewood coffee table in front of them. If he should say, "Mother, I almost killed a man tonight: I came within a razor's edge of shooting a man to death, not three hours ago." "Mother, I sat in this squalid little room deep in the North End and heard a story too fantastic, too outrageous to be believed—and if believed, to be endured. Should I tell it to you? Will you listen?" ... He could see her clear gray-blue sea captain's eyes widen in disbelief, in mounting aversion, her handsome face set coldly. "We don't talk about such things, Gardy," she might say, as she had when he was a little boy. "Yes, they happen now and then but we don't acknowledge them, we don't talk about them. They certainly don't happen to us."

Peering down at the dull glint of the bricks at the base of an elm he thought of the Battle of the Sidewalks that bitter February afternoon—and realized all at once that it was not quite what he'd thought it was. Marcia Lawring could sit defiantly on those worn bricks and cross swords with the Irish foreman and his work gang because she knew they respected the power her name and her position bespoke—and beyond that, that they were prompted by the same antique idealism she herself honored, that the individual's person should not be violated. She knew they would obey the rules. It was not an act of sheer courage and tenacity, as he'd thought, but a game—a rather sophisticated game, perhaps like the game of the plant-tab (had she *really* been afraid it would kill the woman?), which ran on the immensely secure knowledge that come what may, she would be neither arrested nor physically harmed. But how would she fare against the man who recognized no such rules? who saw around him only force and hatred, who dealt exclusively in violence, violence given and violence taken—and above all who didn't care what happened to him on this earth...?

He saw again Castaldo's burning, tortured eyes, the great beads of sweat gathered on his face, felt the churning nausea in his own belly, and shuddered. That was how Castaldo had beaten him, he saw that now. Castaldo had refused to play the game according to the old rules—he had invented new ones, had chosen to step into a world invested with different values entirely: a grim abjurement because ultimately this *new* game could mean loss of life or at least loss of freedom—but the very

violence of its repudiation had given him power. He was
unassailable in the mad purity of his position. And when he,
Lawring, had taken the gun and gone into the North End he had
abandoned his own code and stepped into Castaldo's world—
and he had still lost. He had to lose. Given their relative
positions and the rigid old counters of a dissolving era, how
could his kind of man ever hope to win?

For the first time in his life he turned and looked at his
mother as though she were simply another human being on this
earth. "Has it ever occurred to you that maybe we're not the
center of the universe any more?" he asked softly.

Her glance was quick and inquiring. "What a terribly odd
thing to say, Gardy."

"Is it? I suppose it is." It was true, though. The world had
changed in far more fiery ways in they were willing to admit; and
there it was.

"Do you really feel that my views are that inflexible?" his
mother was saying. Her face looked pale and long now, a trifle
unsure.

Mother, he wanted to say, you have no understanding of this
world—*this* one right here close around us. Not an iota. You've
lived according to your lights—and that's all right, that's
good—but it just isn't good enough any more.

"... It's not what you think," he said aloud, suddenly. "You
can't conceive of all that's going on out there, you haven't got
any idea—" He gestured vaguely toward the backside of the Hill,
a futile thrust of his arm.

Her eyes were white with astonishment. "There's no need to
dwell on it all, if that's what you mean..."

"Maybe we'd better," he said, and nodded somberly. "Maybe
we'd damned well better dwell on it, with all our might and
main." She was upset now, upset and angry, and her face held a
flicker of doubt—yet even now she expected this situation to be
solved in some dignified, equitable way, like all the others. And
it wasn't going to be. It wasn't going to be solved in the old way.
That was what he had passed nearly forty years of his life
without ever finding out. The mirror was taped over and he
would never know why.

And now he'd better go home.

He passed his eyes along the molding at the edge of the

ceiling: cyma recta, with broken fillet. Nobody made molding like that any more. Nobody made fourteen-foot mahogany doors that slid apart with a touch of the fingers, either. Why couldn't they?

There is no home, he thought bleakly. No home to go to but yourself, no solace on earth but what you can dredge out of your own folly and despair . . . And if you can't? If you can't roll your own particular boulder up the mountain?

His mother had started to say something but he cut her off.

"—I don't know anything!" he cried all at once. "About the world or my life or my wife or anything else . . ." He thought he must fall under the sheer dead black weight of his anguish. "Don't you see?—I haven't been educated right—I don't know anything, anything at all—!"

He walked out of the room and started down the stairs.

"Gardy—" His mother was at the edge of the banister, leaning down. She was frightened: he could see it in her eyes now, reflected by the hall chandelier. He had never seen her frightened before. But there was nothing he could do about it. "Gardy, *what has happened?*"

"I'm sorry, Mother," he said. "I'm sorry. I'm acting badly."

"Don't drive all the way out there when you're so distraught . . ."

"I'll drive carefully."

"I want to help you, Gardy . . ." But the very plea was a confession of inadequacy: she could not help him, and he knew it.

"Good night, Mother," he said. "I'll be in touch with you in a few days."

He walked down the rest of the flight, passed his hand over the smooth whalebone disc embedded in the newel post which proclaimed that Jared Lawring owned this house free of all liens or encumbrances; drew the front door closed behind him and thrust himself away from it and lurched out into the dark. Oh, he'd drive carefully all right; very carefully. He would get in his car and roll carefully away west along the Turnpike through the hardscrabble farms with their gray stone walls like the heaped skulls from some interminable battle, through the Berkshires and on past the wet, rolling farmlands of the Mohawk Valley, the chill heave of the big lakes; on across the flat, barbaric

cornfields, the Sodom plain of Joliet, the raw red earth of Iowa
to the slow meander of the North Platte, with the willows like
low lemon clouds and the sky white with immensity; through the
high blue wall of the Rockies, and the pitiless ferocity of the
desert with its salt-rimed sea bottom, and then the pine-sheathed
gorges of the Sierra, all black and silver in the California sun;
and then at last the Pacific shouldering its long rollers over the
green rock, and far out the kelp gently tossing their Zulu
heads...

Yes—and every mile of that hot, dusty journey he would
think of Janet.

And where would he go then? What would he do? He could
not drop out of sight, the way Sanderson had done after that
South Shore waterways indictment. He was a Bostonian, a New
England Yankee—he could wash dishes in Fresno or drive a taxi
in Oaxaca or sleep under the towering palms on the chalk-white
beach at Recife and he might as well be painted in aluminum. He
could not change what he was.

He had to go home. That was all. Go home, for better or
worse; and—well, row the galley.

Far off, over on Arlington or perhaps Boylston, he heard a
siren, held low, a cat's hoarse growl—all at once much nearer,
and looking off down the Hill he saw the police car streak along
Charles Street, black and intent. The hunt was still on, the cat's
prowl through the jungle of cities where men feared and hated
and fought back with any weapon that came to hand.

Life was lonely: that was the bleak fact of the matter. Lonely
and brief. Maybe we were all of us Sonkings, lying in the
shattered street of an alien town with the steel deep in our guts;
lying unhonored and unremembered in the lonely grave of our
blindness and betrayals...

He had to go home. Home, and drag his life along with him
like a dirty, overloaded gunny sack. Where had he left his car?
Down on Cambridge, somewhere near Bowdoin Square.

He went down Charles Street to find a cab.

Chapter Thirteen

The house was dark. He stopped the car at the edge of the drive with the motor running, and studied it. It seemed hugely different to him, altered as radically as though he'd melted it down and recast it in bronze, or painted it a strident orange. It looked menacing: looming and indistinct, its clean outlines blurred. Yet it was the same house with the same good proportions, the same oversize wind tunnel between the kitchen and the garage. It was he who was different, then.

He drove into the garage slowly, made himself turn off the car lights and got out and entered through the kitchen, groped for the switch and felt himself relax with the quick flood of illumination. The electric clock Pruitt hated said 12:47. Where had all the time gone? Somewhere. Somewhere or other. He couldn't rid himself of the sense that there was someone in the house, and it vexed him. He was getting jumpy, after all the cops-and-robbers. He'd used to get that way in combat, he remembered: worried and exhausted and over-alert, with all kinds of threatful little objects slipping away from the corners of your eyes, and finally you began sensing and hearing dangers that weren't even there at all. But now he was only weary and spent, apathetic. If Castaldo were to appear now he didn't know what he would do. He supposed he would shake his hand and ask him to come in and sit down. Or maybe he would throw something at him.

The thing to do was to put something in his stomach, whether he felt like eating or not. That roast was still in the refrigerator; or should be. He started over to it when his eye caught sight of the cup and saucer in the sink, beside his breakfast dishes; and his heart gave a lurch. He turned and hurried through the dining room and flicking on the upstairs hall light started up the stairs.

"Gard?" Janet's voice called softly.

300

"Yes." He stopped in the doorway and looked at her. She was lying on the new bed in their old bedroom; a magazine was curled beside her on the floor. She looked wan and pale, so fragile lying there that she struck him as an invalid, the victim of some long and undiagnosable malady. Then she reached out and turned on the bedside lamp and the illusion vanished.

"Do you want something to eat?" she asked.

"Everyone seems to feel that'll do it, tonight."

"What?"

"Nothing. No, thanks. Not hungry."

He was home. Back home with his wife. He started to take off his jacket, remembered the revolver—that God damned revolver—and left it on. He wasn't ready yet, was all he knew: not ready for seeing Janet, talking to her. He needed time to get his thoughts together: they had scattered like birds at a gunshot. Seeing her now, silent and still and watchful in the big bed, the pain had come back, and the hard knot high in his belly. He was afraid, more afraid than he had been at any time at Castaldo's, and he didn't know what he thought about anything. Avoiding her eyes he sank into the deep sling chair and bending over began to unlace his shoes.

"I phoned you several times during the day," she said. It was not an angry tone: not recriminatory but searching, unsure. She was off-balance and fearful herself and this discovery, instead of relieving the knot in his belly, served only to make him sadder and more apprehensive.

"And then I called Franz," she went on.

"I know," he answered.

"I wanted to get in touch with you . . . and then Franz called me back."

"Did he?"

"Yes. He—said he'd been over here and seen you."

"What did he tell you?"

"He said you had gone in to town on an errand."

"That's right."

"Eddie drove me back in to Boston after supper. I took the old local out here, the 9:17." There was a little pause, during which he removed his shoes, which felt like cones of hot iron. Then in a very tiny voice she asked: "Where did you go?"

He raised his head and looked at her. "I went in town to see Joseph Castaldo."

She caught her breath as though he'd struck her.

"I found your slip of paper. The name and phone number. On the envelope."

Her eyes were very dark and steady; she nodded. "Yes," she said, as though to confirm this. "I thought I'd mislaid it. But I knew I hadn't."

"I didn't mean to," he went on tonelessly, feeling her stiffen. "I was looking for my old watch. My service watch. I broke the good one, the Girard-Perregaux. I was trying to fix the sillcock, the one that's been leaking." He felt he had to explain this in detail—why, he didn't know. "And I remembered it was in your jewelry box. I found it there. Just this morning." She looked down then, and he watched the soft yellow glow of the lamp on her cheek and neck.

"Why didn't you tell me?" he asked.

"... I don't know."

"I see." He got to his feet and had started to go into the bathroom when she said suddenly:

"It isn't what you think..."

He swung back, his hands hanging at his sides. "What do I think?"

"I—I don't know." She was watching him fearfully now. Almost inaudibly she said, "It was—I had to think about it. Think it out."

"Yes," he said. "Well, I didn't."

"You saw him? went to his house?"

"Yes." His lip curled bitterly. "An informal call, you might say." He was sick of it all at once—sick of this terse, wretched little question-and-answer business which had sprung into being between them. He wrenched out of his jacket, pulled the revolver out of his waistband and set it on his bureau top with a bump. He heard her gasp again; her face was white with fear and she was shaking her head slowly back and forth.

"Oh no," she breathed. "Oh no, Gard..." Removing his tie and peeling off his shirt, he continued to watch her without expression. She started to say something, stopped herself. Finally, "What did you do?" she whispered.

"Do? We had a long talk. A very long, very enlightening talk. What did you think—that I shot him through the heart and then phoned the *Herald?*" He felt an almost uncontrollable impulse to laugh hysterically—or perhaps it was to cry: he wasn't sure.

"He managed to convey the idea that he'd been infatuated with you. Castaldo. That he's been in love with you ever since a certain afternoon on the beach down at Brewster—" His voice had begun to get away from him, and he broke off. Janet made no reply, merely went on staring up at him with that expression of solemn, fearful entreaty, and it angered him. "Is that true?"

She said with soft gravity: "I—guess I thought he was sort of drawn to me, yes."

". . . And you," he began harshly, and cleared his throat. "Do you love him?"

She gazed at him as though he had just addressed her in Arabic and she were trying to divine the meaning of what he said by his intonation.

"Why, no. No—I don't love him . . . How could I love him?"

"It didn't mean anything to you, then?" he said. "That night?"

She became very still. "Why do you ask that?"

"Because I want to know. I have a right to know . . . You didn't feel anything, then?" he pursued.

"I—I—" She looked down.

"Nothing at all? You weren't at all moved?"

"Gard, it wasn't—"

"You weren't affected the least little bit? There in the bed?"

She gave a sharp little cry then, a cry of exasperation and despair, and struck the pillow with her hand. "You want too much!" she cried. "You push on after things, you press and press, you push too far . . . Yes, I'll admit it then," she said, and her eyes filled, "he moved me, I felt—oh, why do you ask these things of someone?—Yes, if that's what you want, all right then, I felt something, I don't know why, I was so frightened—I just did, that's all, in spite of everything—I couldn't help it, I was so ashamed and I couldn't help it, I couldn't help it . . ." She broke down then and began to weep, steadily and hopelessly, her voice muffled, the tears falling like silver drops on her clenched hands. "And so when I found out who it was later, when I found the money and the card he left in my purse, I couldn't understand it, can't you see?—I was all the more confused. I wanted to know why—I couldn't believe he did it out of meanness or savagery, just plain cruelty, he was too decent a boy for that. I knew he wasn't drunk or anything . . . I wanted to know why—but I was afraid, at the same time I was afraid . . . Can't you understand that?" she demanded, and she raised her hand before her face as though to ward him off, or perhaps dispel the veil of misunderstanding between them, he couldn't tell. "Can't you see how that could happen? And so I didn't do anything about it, I didn't try to look him up at all..."

He said in a low voice, "Couldn't you have told me, Jan?"

"Tell you?—how could I tell you when you wouldn't understand, you don't understand..."

"About what, Jan?"

"About life, about people—you see everything so *finally*... What would have been the good of telling you? You'd have said, 'I see, a slut, cheating on her husband, getting it on the side'—and I *did* act like a slut, I know, I know, I'm ashamed of it—but it's not that simple... Gard, I'm afraid of you!"

"... Afraid of me?" he whispered.

"Yes, yes, of you..." She nodded her head at him rapidly, an odd little half smile on her face, her cheeks still streaked with tears. "Everything is so obvious to you, so clear-cut and *certain*, there's no room for muddles or—or extenuating circumstances or anything... I was afraid you wouldn't even hear me, you'd just make up your mind and walk right out the door forever, just like that—go off without listening to another soul. That's the way you live and it's frightening, Gard—have you ever thought what it's like for the other person? It's like living on a revolving witness stand. Why did I open a charge account at Filene's, why didn't I remember to roll up the windows in the car, why didn't I think ahead about inviting the Wellivers to dinner on Friday night—at everything I'm inadequate, incompetent, hopeless..." She dropped her head again, her hair spilling forward over her arms. "I love you, Gard, and I'll always love you and no one else but you all the rest of my life—but you're wrong! Something can be black and white too, both at the same time, true and untrue—but you can't see it, I guess, you'll never see it, you're a Boston Yankee..."

He watched her sitting hunched over, her knees drawn up, hands over her face; went over to her and sat down on the edge of the bed. Her misery touched him to the bottom of his heart, fused with his own stunned desolation of spirit. He realized that he had underestimated her capabilities, the cast of her mind. He had always been the realist, the steady one with the firm grip on life and she the fanciful adolescent, the irresponsible and lovely child . . . Now he wondered if that had been true at all.

"I see," he said gently. "I'm sorry. You're probably right about that . . . But what about Reardon? What about the police?"

". . . I didn't know what to do," she said after a pause. "I couldn't make up my mind."

"Don't you think what he did was wrong?"

"Yes—of course I do. But it isn't as simple as that, Gard. You should have heard him that afternoon on the beach. He was so full of wonderful dreams and hopes—the theater and medical research and exploration . . . I know it sounds silly to talk about it this way but he believed in it, he wanted to give all of himself, do something fine and terribly difficult—and what chance did he have to realize any of it? Ten years, and he's still driving a taxi."

"So are several hundred thousand other guys, and they aren't going around breaking into people's houses and assaulting defenseless women."

"But he's different, Gard—he isn't like the others . . ."

"Yes, he's certainly different, all right." He thought of the copy of *Cyrano,* and the taped mirror, and the savage, anguished, triumphant ring in Castaldo's voice; the scene in the grubbly little room was still so vivid the memory of it drove out of his mind what he'd been going to say. "But he broke the *law,* Janet," he protested.

"But what is the law? Your ancestors ran the country and made the laws to suit *them*—can't you see it from his point of view? We never let him feel he existed, that he was anything at all, so he decided to force us to acknowledge him . . . I'm not excusing him," she went on agitatedly, "God knows I've been miserable and terrified enough because of it. Only if he's to blame we all are—we all ought to go to jail, too . . ."

She had raised her head and was gazing at him with earnest entreaty, wiping at her eyes. "The *world* is unjust, Gard," she cried softly, "—that's what you don't see . . ."

He sat there on the edge of the bed and looked down at his hands jammed together between his knees. "No," he said after a moment, "that's true. I didn't. But I see it now." He looked at her then and nodded. "The world is full of injustice, and the people with the money decide pretty much how the rug wrinkles." He felt like an idiot saying this out loud, but he was even more chagrined that it had taken him so long to learn what most of the world knew from infancy on. It made for a kind of penance, reciting it like a scout's creed...

"But what do you do, then?" He watched her soberly. "Throw it all over, because of the injustices? The laws are all we've got, Jan. They may be clumsy and unfair, but they're all we've got to separate us from those terrible ages when there was no law at all, or practically none anyway, and one man could destroy another without cause..."

He broke off. Oh yes. And he was a fine one to talk, going to a man's house with a gun, threatening him with death and then coming within an ace of murdering him... All at once this whole discussion seemed absurd, utterly insane, and he above all. What in God's name was he doing sitting her half undressed, prating of justice and the law? He was a rock-ribbed Boston Yankee who had lived, or tried to live, according to a rigorous enough code—and if he were to be perfectly honest with himself right this minute he would have to admit he didn't know what he believed about crime or punishment or justice or anything else. For thirty-eight years he had been perfectly sure of what he was: but now none of that seemed so very valuable. He looked at Janet, his belly stabbing him with pain, and he knew he loved her in spite of this thing he'd learned, that he would go on loving her, come what may. That was all that mattered: there was nothing else.

"I love you, Jan," he said. He reached out then and touched her arm. "Will you forgive me?"

"Forgive you..."

"Yes. I mean it. Will you?"

She gazed at him, her eyes very large, her lips trembling—then fell against his chest with a little moan. He took her in his arms then, as gently and lovingly as he knew how, felt her crying with release now, not anguish, and thought simply: She's mine, I'm hers, we have each other and the boy and this is the one solid, incontrovertible fact of our lives and the only one that really matters; everything else is a play of shadows.

"It was wrong," she was saying, her breath warm against his throat. "Not to tell you when I found out. I knew it was wrong but I couldn't, darling. I don't know why—I wanted to find out in my own way, if I could. Face it out, about myself. I felt as if I'd been put under some kind of spell or something, can you see?—and ashamed. I didn't know what to do. I didn't have enough trust in you, I was so afraid..."

"It's all right, honey," he answered. "It's all right, now."

My life could be over, he thought. Right now. I could be sitting right this minute in Suffolk County Jail behind the old Charles Street Station, slumped on a cot in one of those pale green cells. I almost destroyed us all, with one squeeze of the fingers... He shivered involuntarily and gripped Janet tighter. This warm, sweet flesh he was clasping to his own, the stark affirmation of this embrace filled him with such simple gratitude he felt the tears start in his eyes.

"We'll go away," he told her, "we'll find us a place on a lake somewhere up north for a couple of weeks. Where there's nobody at all. Would you like that, darling?" Holding her he could see it with the clarity of a childhood memory; there would be a still blue lake with the mountains rising behind it, a lake full of coves with lily pads in the shallows and here and there dragon flies resting on its surface like tiny green jewels; and high over the mountains the ashen silhouette of an osprey hunting...

"But your work," Janet was saying, "the Commission, and Urban Renewal—"

"The hell with Urban Renewal. I'm getting out of it."

She drew back and looked at him. "You are?"

"That's right. My mind's made up. No more conferences, no more deals. Going to do things my way for a while."

He'd had no idea he was going to say anything like this, but now that he had he knew it was right. He gave it no more thought. "A place on the edge of a lake," he went on, "for a couple of weeks. No one but the two of us. We'll go canoeing the way we used to, and read all the books we've wanted to read for five years, and swim and go for walks through the woods, and when it rains we'll go to the local picture palace and sit in the back row and hold hands. We could even run over and visit Boo every once in a while... Wouldn't you like that? Come away," he begged her gently, insistently, "come away with me..."

"*Yes,*" she said with a soft ferocity that surprised him, "yes, let's go away, I want to go away," and she put her arms under his and raised her face to his and kissed him. The corners of her mouth were salt from tears.

The moonlight, released by clouds, crept in the window and fell across the floor like silvered dust and they remained holding each other fast, swaying gently to and fro while the night insects hummed and from the woods behind the rock ledge an owl hooted mournfully. Embracing her, his lips buried in her hair, Lawring became conscious of a pressure that grew, strengthened, rose to an insistent ardor that beat in rhythm with his heart. He was himself again—and that this could come about at the end of a day burdened with such mounting fury and despair made him want to laugh aloud in wonder.

"Sweet..." he murmured.

She put her hand on him, as though for confirmation, although she already knew. "Oh, Gard," she said. Then with a little shuddering sigh she lay back and drew him to her. Yet, flooded with thoughts of this room, the past five weeks, he hesitated.

"Do you want it? Are you sure?"

"Yes, yes, yes," she breathed. "I've lain in there and longed for it, I've dreamed of it, can't you *know?*..."

And the moonlight faded, returned again in long rhomboid patterns across the bed where they lay together.

Later he watched Janet sleeping in the moonlight, one hand thrown back above her head, palm open, her face so lovely and serene it made his heart ache faintly just to look at her. One breast, exposed above the sheet, was white as alabaster; it rose and fell with her breathing. A miracle, he thought soberly, rejoicing: a kind of miraculous dispensation, the whole turbulent day...

Life was astonishing. What did Henchey call it? a journey through flypaper? Hell, Henchey didn't know—it was a lot more like a race through a museum in the pitch dark, a spunglass museum where we twisted and turned and barely missed toppling whole cases in an avalanche of glass. How near we could come to destroying everything within reach! How very near... What had Franz called it? An endless iron road, with here and there a little love. For Callahan it was a galley to keep on rowing, for Janet a series of enchanting adventures, he himself had always seen it as a broad highway climbing to the pinnacle of a venerable mountain; but none of them were right—it was all these things and a good deal more. And our salvation—if we were lucky enough to stumble upon it—was often enough not of our own making at all. We toiled and blundered along on our private night journeys, and in our fear and anger hit out at the shapes that loomed up near us, sinned against and sinning...and who could say—and often in our blackest deeps of tribulation—what glance, what word, what hand would redeem us?

One of the frogs in the pool emitted a sudden bass croak, another; relapsed into silence. Lawring passed his fingers over the lump at the bridge of his nose. He had behaved inadequately, it seemed. And not just today, either. Behaved badly. It was hard to admit. A Lawring never behaved badly, a Lawring couldn't behave badly.

But this Lawring had.

He stole out of bed without waking Janet, drew on his trousers and crept barefooted down the stairs in the dark, went to the telephone in the dining room and dialed the number by feel. The phone was picked up on the first ring and Franz Hoelder's voice said tensely: "Yes?"

"Franz?"

"Gardner—?"

"Yes. Did I wake you?"

"No. I was sitting here. Where are you?"

"Home. Over here. I just wanted to tell you I owe you an apology."

"Are you all right?"

"Yes. I'm fine. You were right, Franz. I got justice, all right."

"You did not—"

"Only it wasn't the kind of justice I was looking for. But that's all right, too."

"You did not use the—the toy..."

"No. Everything is fine. I can't begin to tell you how fine it is!"

"And Janet—have you..."

"She's home with me. I should say: I'm home with her. That's why it's fine."

"...Thank God," Franz said after a moment.

"Yes, I'll join with you on that."

There was a little pause. "Well. That's that." Franz's voice sounded rather dry and matter-of-fact. "Then..." and Lawring fancied now he could see the older man's eyes twinkle, "...I can go to bed now?"

"You mustn't complain. Remember:

Our days begin with trouble here, our life is but a span.
And cruel death is always near, so frail a thing is man."

"God in heaven," Franz moaned. "What is that?"

"Verses from an old New England primer. A very old one."

"It's so comforting. It makes you—what is it Brian always says?—it makes you kind of choke up, pardner. It makes you glad that you have two hundred and eight bones, any one of which might snap like a twig without any warning."

"Doesn't it?" Lawring realized that Franz too was consumed by the same great need to talk. "That's how we teach stoicism to our young. It's the only way they can stand the New England winters." He paused, said in another tone, "Many thanks, Franz. For the story. It was a very important story."

". . . It did not dissuade you, however."

"That's hardly your fault. You can lead a horse to water but you can't make him drink."

"Is that from an old New England primer, too?"

"No. The Manual of the Village Smithy . . . Franz?"

"Yes?"

"Forgive me if you can. Will you? I mean it."

"There is nothing to forgive." Franz Hoelder sighed—an old man's gutsy sigh. "As long as you both are all right."

"And come over and have dinner with us tomorrow night. Or the one after that. Can you? We're going away on a vacation and we want to be sure to see you."

"I will be delighted. My fond greetings to Janet."

". . . And her love to you. Good night."

"Good night . . ."

He put the phone softly in its cradle and went back upstairs and out on to the deck beyond the bedroom. Around him the moon shifted colophons of silver through the trees. Leaning on the teak railing he gazed down into the smooth black oval of the pool, which now and then gave up little oily glints and ripples. He felt so disoriented by all that had happened to him that day, so benignly dislocated by it, that he could have been at the rail of a ship bound for Mombasa or Haiphong. He was conscious of the odors of azalea and new mown grass and swamp water, the delicate fret of the night air on his back and shoulders, and a sweet, slow ache in his loins.

He would have to start over: in his thirty-ninth year. He would have to begin all over again. The world, people, truths were not what he had been taught they were, not at all what he had thought: we were not *one thing,* fixed and immutable, however many ministers and schoolmasters proclaimed it from a thousand New England desks and pulpits. He himself had been, in the scant space of fourteen hours, a betrayed husband, a vengeance seeker (like the Italians, the vendetta Italians of the North End he had despised), a burglar, a near-murderer—and at the end of all that a successful lover and a wiser man. What was he, then?

He thrust his hands into his trouser pockets—and felt, among his keys and nailclip, the hard little nutlike forms of the leather buttons; drew them out of his pocket and hefted them in his hand, trying to remember that day.

"... It's true, what he said," he murmured aloud. "I never saw him." I didn't even know he was there, I'd forgotten he ever existed ... And now he was flying to Mexico City and he would never come back. What would he do there? Drive hordes of chattering tourists over the red, dusty roads? become one of those bony men in threadbare suits one saw everywhere on street corners, watching with eager, fearful eyes? The poor devil. Why hound him? He was haunted and hounded enough as it was. Let him go. Poor devil. And yet, in a terrible, demonic way, he was—Lawring knew it—a better man than he himself was: coming from no venerable traditions of aspirations and standards, he had yet fought his way to something about which he cared so deeply that he would die for it without a moment's hesitation ...

One by one he thrust the buttons forward under his thumb and flipped them into the night air, heard them splash in the pool—and the little quicksilver rings ran out to the edges. Then it was still again.

... It doesn't matter what happens to you in your life, he thought with the abrupt force of discovery. Triumph or disaster, power or obscurity. It is what you are, whatever *does* happen: the man you become within yourself. No matter what the world says, it is more important for me to spend a few weeks at the edge of an isolated lake with my wife than anything else in the world ... And he would do it, too. He would give himself to Janet for these next weeks, help to restore the love and unanimity of vision that had suffused their first years. Their whole future—and Brian's, too—depended on it.

And then he would come back and go to work, and to hell with the Hencheys and Maltisiaks and McGoverns. If they wanted him out, if he was a roadblock in the path of their own peculiar brand of progress, he'd leave—and with bells on; and break out on his own. Maybe he could get backing from Cameron. He'd get it from somebody. He'd compete for the commissions and the contracts, and he'd find some honest builder he could work with; and if he won he would build houses full of simplicity and light and grace, houses he could walk past with a sober pride, that would stand for what Gardner Alcock Lawring believed a human habitation ought to be.

He gripped the smooth, oily teak in his fingers. And if he lost—well, then he would have lost. But he'd win some of the time—he knew it with every beat of his blood—and that was good enough, that was all he asked ... And he would remember. Those people creeping home from the beaches in the glare of lights, all the Sheas and Pruitts and Sonkings and Callahans— and yes, even the Roches and Castaldos—he would battle and build for them, too. He had found them tonight in the rubble below Cornhill and he wasn't going to let them go again; because—and there was no truth he'd learned today so well as this—unless their needs were met there would be no towers left anywhere ...

He would do it. All that stood in his way was the weight of a noble but no longer omniscient tradition, and his own deplorable blindness, his self-righteousness, his overweening self-esteem—

From the rock ledge behind him the whippoorwill began; he dropped his head back, halfway between sleep and waking, and listened to the inane, mesmeric call—and found that he was smiling. Maybe with time he could even enjoy the whippoorwill.